D0921113

What critics and reviewers are saying about
The Grigory Trilogy #1
Stalking Tender Prey

"Dark, sensual, and mysterious—Storm Constantine weaves sensual enigmas from familiar tapestries. Old Gods fantasy of the highest order."—Phil Brucato, developer of *Mage: The Ascension* and *Mage: The Sorcerers Crusade*

"Storm Constantine's love for her characters, their love and lust for one another, and her celebration of their beauty fairly drips from the pages of her work. She is a daring, romantic sensualist as well as a fine storyteller."—Poppy Z. Brite

"Storm Constantine is a powerful visionary, and her lush and haunting dark fantasies explore the secret nooks and crannies of our mythologies and religions, places most of us only *think* we know. A storyteller who has mastered the alchemy of the sacred and the profane and knows the heady revelations such mixtures release, she's the genuine article."—Caitlín R, Kiernan

"*Stalking Tender Prey*, is such a strange book that it all but defies description so imagine the following: Jackie Collins has spent a few months living in England reading up on Tom Stoppard and Alan Bennett. She begins to write a mystery thriller when she meets Aleister Crowley, Tanith Lee and Joseph Campbell in the local pub. The bizarre local beer fuses them together and they come up with this. The novel manages to balance the aforementioned combination, producing a work that reads with the energy and POV-shifting pace of a bestseller. It also contains well-observed characters and supernatural powers strong and dark enough to satisfy the discerning fantasy reader's desire for wild magic."—*Nova Express*

"To combine the natural and the uncanny on epic scale is a matter of novelistic skill, and Constantine succeeds well."—*Vector Magazine*

"This housebrick of a book is possibly the best novel I have ever read. Do yourself a favor, buy Storm's book. You won't be disappointed."—Ian Read in *Chaos International #20*

"It's atmospheric, the language is rich and the settings vivid. Constantine stays firmly in control or the intricate plot, conveying the necessary information deftly by shuffling the characters so that the experience of each forwards the story."—*Dark Side Magazine*

"The name Storm Constantine conjures up images of sexy heroes with long hair and leather trousers, enigmatic races with supernatural powers, and dark tales of science, sex, and magick."—*SFX Magazine*

"If you have read any of her work before, you will already know that she is a brilliant and imaginative writer. The style of the writing is beautiful and often shocking in the way it draws the reader in, and so vividly describes the events that take place. Stalking Tender Prey also has a dangerous amount of realism, leaving you thinking 'the Grigori could be among us.'"—*The Scone Magazine*

"Gothic, cruel, and sometimes startlingly funny, Storm Constantine's work takes on the subjects of beauty and power with a ferocious storytelling energy far beyond the usual genre formulas. She's worth reading even if you *aren't* a young person who wears lots of black."—Patrick Nielsen Hayden

"Storm Constantine defines Dark Fantasy. People who don't read fantasy (like me) are for whatever reason tempted to read her, and discover themselves lost in worlds of sinister glory, or tense beauty. Her language is rich and intense, drenched in metaphor but always following compelling storylines. Her wordsmithery doesn't drown her vision."—*Carpe Noctem Magazine*, July 1998

"*Stalking Tender Prey*—such a delightful premise. It conjures up images of tall, lean, and mysterious predators who walk the shadows around us, winnowing out the weak, making love to the strong and generally doing their part for the unnatural order. Nobody does this better than Storm Constantine who understands that sensuality without irony is meat without salt. Irony frees Constantine's other-worlds from the constraints of heroics and villainies. Every predator is prey to something and survival is a delicate dance of nuance and perception. There's no telegraphing on these pages, no way to know for a reader to know where sympathy may be safely bestowed. Every character has sufficient strengths and foibles to insure an interesting, unanticipated fate. Manners matter among the Grigori, as they always have among those who dwell in the English countryside. Once lost, innocence can never be recaptured. Indiscretion has dire– sometimes fatal and spectacular– consequences. In the end, few things are more revealing than what one of Constantine's chooses to drink in public or in private. *Stalking Tender Prey* reads as if Jane Austen had dyed her hair black. Buy this book."—Lynn Abbey

"With razor-keen prose, Constantine weaves a complex tale of passion and mystery. While possessing the flavor of her *Wraethu* novels, this is wonderfully different, new, and should win her the larger audience her work deserves."—Robin Wayne Bailey

"Constantine weaves all these late twentieth century concerns-the impending Millennium, the Nephilim, and love transcending death-into a tapestry of desire, faith, and power. Her darkly erotic prose is captivating; the breadth of her vision astonishing."—Helen Knibb, BSFA

SCENTING

HALLOWED

BLOOD

BY

STORM
CONSTANTINE

Scenting Hallowed Blood © 1996 by Storm Constantine.

SCENTING HALLOWED BLOOD

An MM Publishing Book
Published by Meisha Merlin Publishing, Inc.
PO Box 7
Decatur, GA   30031

Editing & interior layout by Stephen Pagel
Copyediting & proofreading by Teddi Stransky
Front cover art and design by Rick Berry
Back cover design by Neil Seltzer

ISBN: 0-9658345-5-7

http://www.angelfire.com/biz/MeishaMerlin

First MM Publishing edition: June 1999

Printed in the United States of America
0 9 8 7 6 5 4 3 2 1

A few words from Storm

The landscape of *Stalking Tender Prey*, the first book of this trilogy, was that of the Peak District of England; a place where tiny, mysterious villages nestle in ancient moorland and shadowy paranormal beasts are reputed to roam. Although the village of Little Moor, where most of that story takes place, was inspired by the quaint hamlets of Derbyshire, I had no particular one in mind when I wrote the book. But the locations in the novel you are about to read are more faithful to the places that inspired them in my imagination. As some readers have said to me they'd like to visit the places I write about, I thought this would be the perfect opportunity to give some directions. Turn left at the crossroads and walk up along the rays of the moon.

At the end of *Stalking Tender Prey*, the characters moved south, escaping everything that had happened in the no-longer sleepy village of Little Moor. Near the beginning of this second book, when you first meet Lily, Shem and the others again, you will find yourself in a place called the Moses Assembly Rooms. These are based on a real location in London, which is often used as a venue for conferences and conventions of an occult or earth mysteries nature.

Conway Hall, in Red Lion Square, is very different in appearance from the Moses Assembly Rooms, being clean, airy and spacious, rather than dark, Gothic and foreboding, and neither, to my knowledge, do Grigori live in its upper rooms! But the little square it's set in, with its central gardens, and the house across the way where some of the Pre-Raphaelite painters lived and worked, is a wonderfully evocative area. It seems cut off from the hubbub of the city, even though it's part of the busy West End. This just had to be the place where Shemyaza and his followers hid out for a while. I've attended Psychic Questing Conferences and a Fellowship of Isis conference in Conway Hall, and walking along the wide pavement to its front doors has always inspired my thoughts. I imagine the days when Jane Morris, the famed wife of William Morris, and model for many Pre-Raphaelite paintings, alighted from her carriage on this street and entered the tall, pale stone house, her gown rustling on the step outside.

In a small side alley off the square, just to the left as you come out of the Hall, is a cosy pub called The Dolphin that we always frequent when attending events. This also makes a brief appearance in the novel, when Lily and Daniel go out for an evening.

A large part of the story takes place in Cornwall, on The Lizard Peninsular, which will be the centre of attention in August this year (1999) as the location where the full eclipse of the sun will be most visible in England. (This eclipse actually features in *Stealing Sacred Fire*, the third part of the trilogy, but I very much doubt whether the bizarre paranormal events that occur in that story will actually take place, though it would be nice if they did!)

The coastline of The Lizard is a very magical place, its serpentine cliffs riddled with caves, while the wild landscape inland is dotted with ancient monuments and important historical sites. The atmosphere that oozes from the rocks themselves can affect you profoundly. Cornwall has a reputation for sending people *fey*. You can walk the cliff path from Pistil Meadow to the head of Azumi, the lion simulacrum in the rock that plays a significant part in this story. I should point out that Azumi is the name for this guardian feature that was picked up psychically by my friend and colleague, Debbie Benstead, when she was once working in Cornwall. Azumi stares out to sea, looking as much like a lion as if he's been carved by human hands, complete with eyes and whiskers. If, in ancient times, as legends suggest, the descendants of the Watchers did come to these shores and landed at The Lizard, the first thing they saw would have been the inscrutable leonine face gazing out at them from the red, green and gold cliffs. Cornwall abounds with legends of giants, and many of its features are named after them. Perhaps these are ancient memories of actual individuals, not of monstrous people, but simply members of a tall race, who came to these islands from far over the sea. Debbie picked up a rhyme psychically, which seems to be an ancient Cornish song, remembering the advent of the Watchers:

"Winter sun alight the sea, brings in a boat for all to see.
Red, gold and green in colours bold, bringing in giant men of old.
They spilled their blood upon this land, across these coves they drew their hand.

And every *killie* moved by thee, turned to colour red, gold and green."

(We presumed that the word 'killie' is an old term for a cove, bay or cliff.)

The Michael Line, which is a renowned path of natural earth energy that cuts up through England, begins at St Michael's Mount off The Lizard. This too has a part to play in the story. The ancient spiritual English town of Glastonbury is on the Michael Line, and it is said that the Glastonbury Zodiac, (otherwise known as the Table of Stars), was laid down by the ancient giants, magi from a far land. The Zodiac consists of natural and manmade features that relate to astrological and equinoctial symbolism. The giants supposedly bound the secret knowledge of the grail at the centre of the Zodiac, which would only come to light when the true king, who would be a descendent of their race, came to power.

I have already explained, in the introduction to the first book in this series, that the trilogy came about through my working with earth mysteries investigator, Andrew Collins, who was researching his non-fiction book on the fallen angels, called *From the Ashes of Angels*. Andy let me use his research notes to help me construct the background to the story. Some of his information was inspired, in that it derived from the visionary work of psychics, notably Debbie Benstead. This material had no place in an academic study of the subject, as the majority of people are very sceptical and scornful of psychic information. However, it was perfect for fiction, when the writer can say what she likes. Well, it's all made up, isn't it? Debbie and Andy had many adventures in Cornwall, and a lot of very strange and wonderful things happened to them, which would make an absorbing book in itself. I borrowed from a few of their experiences in constructing this novel. Most of the story, of course, is completely fiction, but not always the bits you might expect!

There is reputedly an order of witches in Cornwall called the Peller. While their name and existence inspired the creation of the Pelleth for this book, I do not wish to imply I know anything about the beliefs and practices of any real Cornish witches. The Pelleth sprang entirely from my imagination.

Stephe Pagel, my editor and publisher at Meisha Merlin, has told me he's had a lot of enquiries from readers, who after reading *Stalking Tender Prey* would like to get hold of *From the Ashes of*

Angels, in order to learn the background information for themselves. Unfortunately, its author Andy Collins is not yet published in the States, but his information service in England does sell UK copies mail order through their web site. The book, and its follow-up, *Gods of Eden,* are also available through a postal mail order service. The details for these are as follows:

Web site: http://members.aol.com/edenelder/index.html

Postal address: Andrew Collins, P.O. Box 189, Leigh-on-Sea, Essex, SS9 1NF, England.

I hope that you, via the pages of this book, will enjoy roaming through the enchanting landscape of ancient Cornwall as much as I enjoyed writing about it. If you get the chance, go visit. Sit upon the head of Azumi, explore the caves at Caerleon Cove, or creep into the camomile grove of Pistil Meadow, and see what dreams spring into your mind. I guarantee they will be strange.

Storm Constantine
February 1999

Chapter One
The Women of Cornwall

He was little more than a boy, gleaming in the candle-light like an icon, while the night wind cleared its throat in the long, narrow chimneys of stone that threaded down from the cliff-top to the cave. Candles were set at his feet in a ring; rough wax obelisks, ill-formed as if shaped by hasty hands. He sat upon a giant's throne that was as ancient as the land itself, his body dwarfed within the great stone chair, his toes just touching the worn rock beneath it. There was an oily smell to the air, slightly fishy, and the sound of the sea, the eerie lament of the rising storm, came faint and threatening down the tunnel of rock that led to the beach.

Outside, white waves would thrash upon the bleak Cornish shore and the rain come down in blades.

Symbols of his goddess littered the floor of the cave, like gnawed bones left by a predator; bleached and fragile shells; osseous tree branches, sculpted by wave and sand; the long, alien-looking skeletons of serpents, with their heads like fishes; the feathers of sea-birds, bedraggled in damp sand. The youth himself seemed made of shell; delicate and translucent. His eyes were black, yet his hair was pale, wet and clinging to his shoulders, snaky tendrils like tiny eels plastered across his face. He wore only a skirt of feathers and his head bore a crown of coral.

Beyond the light of the candles a group of seven women, the inner circle of the Pelleth, stood robed before the boy. They were breathing quickly, having just ended a stamping dance of invocation. Echoes of chanting still vibrated in the folds of the rock walls. Two of the women were old, their grey hair loose down their backs. Two were voluptuous and mature, with snakes fashioned from coloured folded paper in their hair. Two were teenagers, their eyes sly and watchful, while the other was a girl-child, clad in ragged grey-green lace, into which tiny shells had been threaded and the skulls of infant vipers.

The women were silent, patient, and the only sound was that of spitting wax against the dull, distant roar of sea and storm. For hundreds, if not thousands, of years the Pelleth had tended the sacred Cornish sites and waited for the return of the Shining One. Now, they sensed that change was imminent and consulted their oracle within their holy cave beside the crashing shore.

Presently, the boy sighed and shuddered upon the throne. His head jerked back and a word came out of his mouth in a bubble of foam.

The women glanced at one another. The word meant nothing, but they dared not ask questions for fear of breaking the trance.

For some minutes, the boy sat with his head slumped upon his breast, then he sucked in his breath sharply and looked up, his dark, colourless eyes focused ahead of him, on the black maw of the tunnel that led to the sea. The candle-flames shivered in the brine-soaked wind, which fretted the grey muslin robes of the women. The boy uttered a keening sound, and his lips were wet. His head rolled upon his neck, tearing his salt-sticky hair from his throat and shoulders. The thunder of the waves outside grew momentarily louder, then abated with a faint sound of shifting shingle.

The boy spoke, his voice clear yet strangely sibilant. "Who calls the serpent mother, Seference, She Who Gives Life to the Dead?"

One of the oldest women stepped forward. She held a long, carved staff, which seemed to denote authority. "It is I, Meggie Penhaligon, and my sisters. We call upon thee, Serpent Mother for the wisdom of thy quick tongue."

The boy's eyelids flickered. "She is the serpent goddess, and She is with us. I am here and everywhere. The moon lights a cruel path across the sea and She walks it. I am walking the path of light to the shore, along the old highway, the serpent path to the land."

"What is thy prophecy, Mother?" Meggie Penhaligon knew there was something to learn. She had felt it in her bones, and the younger women had felt it in their blood and bellies: a flexing, a quickening.

"He has awoken in the north." The boy's voice sounded hollow, as if echoing through empty corridors of stone.

Meggie leaned forward. "He?"

"The Hanged One..." The boy sighed, his whole body shuddering, but a smile came to his lips. "Yes. He is with us once again, but he covers his face. There are guardians around him, for many will seek him. They covet his power."

Meggie Penhaligon felt her body stiffen. This was what she and her sisters had been waiting for. Now that the words spilled from the lips of their oracle, it seemed almost too fabulous to be believed. Myths made flesh. *He walks...*

"Give me his name," Meggie murmured.

The boy answered without pausing. "Shemyaza, who was in Eden. Shemyaza, who lay with mortal women and cursed his race. Shemyaza, father of giants and monsters, who was condemned to hang for eternity in the constellation of Orion. Shemyaza, giver of forbidden knowledge to humanity. Shemyaza, whose name is also Azazel, remembered as the scapegoat. He was punished, and his soul was sundered."

The crashing of the waves became momentarily louder, amplified by the tunnel's length. Meggie's soft voice was barely audible because of it. "How has he returned?"

The boy's eyes fluttered in their sockets; only a sliver of white was revealed. "He was born into a body whose hands were death. With these hands, he craved to open the star-gate that leads to the source of all. He sought to paint the gate with blood that it might open to him, but he was ignorant of the truth..."

Meggie nodded. This was as she'd thought. Shemyaza would not come back to the world clad in light and visible to all. "Is he still ignorant of his origins?"

The boy's face creased into a frown, as if he struggled to discover the information, then his brow cleared. "He is aware but sleeping. I have a name: Daniel. The seer and vizier of old Babylon. Daniel lives in this time, and with the hybrid twins, who are Grigori, angel-born, brought Shemyaza to consciousness. But Shemyaza will not be the scapegoat again. He hides his face beneath his wings and they are black with fear and doubt. Now the world is full of him, and his potential is for great change or great destruction. Always there will be pain associated with his works, for even the most beneficial of changes will break hearts and nations."

Meggie's throat was dry. She could barely speak. "Where is he?"

"In hiding. There are guardians around him."

"Can you give me names?"

The boy was silent for a moment, then murmured. "Daniel, the seer. Lil...Lilian? Emilia...She is human but has tasted Grigori essence. Her life is extended. And there is a void, a youth whose soul is bound. I cannot see his name."

"How can we find Shemyaza? How can we bring him to us?"

The boy's face twisted into a mask of rage. "You ask me this? No! The gate is cracked, but still it holds. He creeps between it. He is the bringer of the new age through death and sacrifice. Around his head is a halo of dried tongues of fire!"

Meggie sensed the presence of Seference was disintegrating. She was aware it was her own fear, and that of her sisters, that prevented the information being delivered. Should she let the essence of the goddess go, or try to retain it? Did she really want the physical presence of Shemyaza near her? For centuries, her ancestors had worked with the *idea* of the Fallen Ones. They had invoked the influence of the lesser entities; Penemue, Kashday, Gadreel. As the wheel of time turned inexorably around them, they had sensed that, one day, the Fallen Ones would become a living reality and wake the serpent power that slept beneath the land. But this soon? Meggie acknowledged that she had hoped, in her secret heart, she would have left this world by the time this great responsibility fell upon them. Soon, she and her sisters would look into the scrying-pool, and attempt to divine more details concerning Shemyaza's whereabouts and companions. For now, Meggie had heard enough.

She raised her arms to thank Seference for her words, as a preliminary to bringing the boy out of trance, but the oracle suddenly lunged forward in the chair, his slender fingers gripping the long, stone arms. When he spoke, it was not in the hollow, distant voice of the goddess, but in a broad Cornish accent. His normal speaking voice was southern, but cultured, for he was the son of gentry. "He will find you anyway. Did you think otherwise? He is drawn by the serpent, the voice of the thunder, the slumbering one. He will come, for he has no choice. Feel the serpent power flexing in its great sleep, Mother. It will not be long before it wakes! Then out of your grip it will slither, to empower the great alignment and all the serpent paths within the land, and every king and giant who sleeps beneath the earth will rise to its scent!" Then, slowly, the oracle leaned back into the chair, his eyes fixed on the tunnel ahead of him. A light seemed to go out of his body. Presently, he began to shiver.

Meggie Penhaligon gestured at one of the teenage girls. "Jessie."

The girl, Jessie, stepped forward and held out her hands to the boy in the stone chair. Wincing, he lowered himself to the floor, and allowed her to lead him out of the circle of candles. Jessie wrapped him in a coat of feathers, while the women donned enveloping woollen cloaks.

As they gathered up their ritual paraphernalia, Jessie asked Meggie a question, one that was on the minds of all present. "Who spoke through Delmar at the end there, Megs? It was a woman, wasn't it?"

Meggie nodded. "I believe we heard the voice of another like us who, in her lifetime kept the vigil for the Shining One. She gave us advice, or a warning." Meggie fixed one of the other women, a voluptuous, fair-haired creature, with a dark, steady eye. "Wouldn't you agree, Tamara?"

The woman shrugged as she carefully placed a brass incense burner into a carrier bag. "I suppose so."

Meggie sensed a veil of smugness emanating from Tamara Trewlynn, which screened her true thoughts. The younger woman clearly had her own ideas about what they'd heard, and Meggie had no doubt that eventually Tamara would deign to reveal it to the others, probably at a moment when it could subtly undermine Meggie's authority. For over a year, Tamara had been challenging Meggie's words and actions, but now was not the time to deal with her tendency to rebellion. Meggie knew Tamara had a frustrated desire for power within the group, but Meggie was not too concerned about it. She did not expect, or want, her sisters to be passive slaves to her decrees. The moment she could not cope with outspoken Pelleth was the moment when someone like Tamara deserved to replace her.

The crash of the storm could be heard plainly now, and Meggie did not relish the thought of crossing the wind-harried beach, where the spiked fingers of the elements would stab at her old bones. Neither could she imagine the tortuous climb back up the cliff would be an easy task. Still, it was done. The omens had been heeded, and the ritual completed. Seference had spoken, and confirmed their hopes and fears. Lord Shemyaza, fallen angel, disgraced prince, was made flesh in the world.

The women extinguished the last of the candles and, by the light of hurricane lamps, made their way down the tunnel to the beach. Here, the weather was as bad as Meggie had feared. The waves crashed angrily against the rocks, throwing stinging spray across the narrow walkway of sand. They were like angry monsters, those waves, and Meggie knew that if they took a shine to the thought, they would thresh their way further onto the shore and devour the group of women. She made a few conciliatory gestures at the pounding sea, hoping the storm-beasts were too intoxicated by the madness of their own power to notice the fragile creatures of flesh feeling their way along the cliff to the place where the upward path began.

Lissie and Tamara, the two snake-crowned women, walked either side of the oracle, leading the way. The boy seemed not to notice the wind or the rain, his back erect, his head raised. Meggie, walking behind them, the hand of the girl-child clasped firmly in her own, noticed how tall the boy was getting. Soon, the time might come when he would be given to the elements, too much of a man to fulfil his function, as androgynous channel for the Shining Ones and their minions. She had seen many beautiful boys hold the office of oracle in her time. Already, a boy child of five years was being groomed to take over the role when the moment came. A boy, who had grown up with the thought that his life would be short, extinguished during his late teens or early twenties. One she had known had made it to twenty-five, but he had been an exception. All children, Meggie knew, were primarily female, as they had been at the moment of conception. In the womb, mysterious processes decided whether a child would be male or female, but even so, they were predominantly female in their hearts during their growing years. All children were psychic, hovering between the world of reality and that of the unseen. They were innocent, joyous, full of potential. Then the curse of puberty would begin to curl its cold, steel fingers around their bodies, and the veil between the worlds would thicken in their sight. Women, privileged because of their moon cycles, could sometimes keep on the way of the wyrd, but boys grew up to be men, changed into those creatures. If their blood coursed to the tides, it was often only to manifest as madness. Men had no place in the ranks of the Pelleth, the wielders of the secret ways. Men were providers, lovers and fathers, but magic was weak in their angry hearts. Neither must they ever discover the mysteries, which was why all the oracles were slain once their function was over. They could not be trusted, as men, with the knowledge they'd acquired during their office.

As the women slowly climbed the path from the private beach, the storm lashed them cruelly. Meggie could feel its mad passion. It was like an exuberant animal and its rough attentions were without malice. It was simply unaware of its own strength, playing mischievously with those who knew its heart. The child, Agatha, suddenly pulled on Meggie's hand. "Look, Gran!" She pointed into the air. Meggie nodded.

"Aye, love." No doubt the elemental spirits were clearer to the child. With her fading eyes, Meggie could make out the dim suggestion of impish faces, of long, attenuated limbs. When the wind gusted, the skeletal fingers would reach out and pinch the billowing cloaks of the women.

Agatha laughed and waved her free hand.

"Mind!" Meggie chided. The spirits were not beyond taking advantage and plucking the child from the cliff-face.

Eventually, the top of the cliff was within reach. As soon as Meggie stepped off the path, the wind caught hold of her, and if it hadn't been for Agatha, with the help of Jessie behind her, the old woman would have been tossed back down to the beach. It had been easier in the past to match the elements, to give herself to their arms without fear. This body was too feeble now, and sardonically the spirits teased her. It was the same for her sister, Betsy, Meggie knew. One day, when life became too onerous, she and Betsy would surrender themselves to the storm for the last time, and let it take them to the next world. But that time was not yet.

The lights of the Penhaligon house were visible from the cliff-top. In fact, the garden ran right to the edge. At one time it had been longer, but the weather and the sea had eaten away at the land. The beach below belonged to the Penhaligons and had done so for as long as anyone remembered, or was recorded. The giant's chair was a great relic, but no-one save the Pelleth knew of its existence. When the tide was high, water gushed into the cave, and whoever sat upon the chair was marooned until the waves receded. Over the centuries, the action of the sea had created a plinth for the chair. All initiates to the Pelleth were required to spend a tide's-time in the cave, sitting upon the throne of the Old Ones, pondering the power of the Fathers of Thunder.

Long ago, when the giants had come to the island, they had hewn the chair out of the rock for their own, mysterious rites. The content of those rituals were mostly lost and forgotten. All that remained was the knowledge of the serpent power that they had left below the earth, and how the dreams of its eternal slumber could be tapped, and shaped into forms of magic. Meggie's people were the inheritors of this knowledge. For many thousands of years, their ancestors had kept the legends of the giants alive. They knew that the giants themselves had been half-breeds of an ancient race, who were remembered in myth as angels and demons. They also knew the significance of all the sacred sites of the land that the giants had constructed, and worked with the latent energy that was enshrined in these places. In the distant past, the giants had been served by the people of the land, revered as gods, feared as warrior kings. The tall strangers from far across the sea had built themselves fortress eyries in the highest places, and with some of the women of the little people, they had bred, further diluting the blood of their forbears. The children of these unions drew away from their mothers' race to share the power of their fathers. Eventually, the giants and their children had melted into the wild land, leaving their places of power behind them, untended. Workers of magic, such as the Pelleth, were attracted to these sites, and learned to work with their energies. Over the centuries, memories had become folk-tales, and the giants had grown in both stature and potency in the memories of the local people. Now, they were almost feared, and seen as a force to appease.

The Pelleth always consisted of women, but for the oracle. The Conclave of Seven was led by the eldest members of the group, and various other offices were held by women of a prescribed age and appearance. The oracle, Delmar, was the son of the Tremaynes, who owned Enoch's Hall outside the village. Ellen Tremayne, his mother, was a member of the Pelleth, but as she was not a member of the Conclave, she never witnessed her son's trances. Delmar had been marked for the position of oracle even before his birth. The Pelleth had delivered him in a sacred pool that was hidden in a sea-cave and refreshed by the tides every day. Sea-born boy; on land, or out of trance, he seemed barely alive.

The group walked back through the rain to the grey-stone house. Smoke curled from the chimney to be dispersed by the wind, indicating that Meggie's youngest son, Tom, had arrived home to stoke up the fire, and hopefully greet the women with hot tea and toast. About thirty yards from the house, the rambling garden stopped at a wall, beyond which was the cultivated area that Meggie and her family had tended for generations. Here, she and Betsy grew their herbs and special plants. Locally, they were regarded as healers of the ancient kind.

Tamara pushed open the soaked wooden gate set into the wall, having to give it a good shove with her shoulder because the damp had warped it, and led the line of women up the path towards the back door of the house. Agatha hung back, gazing out through the gate at the slope of the wilderness.

"Come on, girl," Meggie said. She smiled, envying and admiring the fact that the child seemed oblivious of the bitter wind and slicing rain.

Agatha glanced round at the older woman. "Gran, will we see the giants one day?"

Meggie laughed, and stroked the girl's wet hair back from her forehead. Not too much had been explained to Agatha, yet she'd made her own connection between mention of Shemyaza and his half-breed descendants, who had come to England so many thousands of years ago. "Child, the giants are dead and gone. All that remains is the memory of their power, and..." Here the old woman grimaced. "...those that came from them. But they are not the same." She shook her head. "Come now, shut the gate, will you. My old bones are calling for the hearth."

Agatha obediently pushed her small body against the old wooden slats and fastened the latch. She skipped beside Meggie as they went towards the house. "Shemyaza is a giant, though, isn't he, and the goddess said he's here again?"

"Hush now!" Meggie chided. "We don't talk that way in the open, now do we?"

"Sorry," Agatha said, covering her smile with her hands. "But will you answer me, Gran, just this once?"

Meggie put her arm around Agatha's shoulder and pulled her close. "Yes, he is a giant. Tall and strong and fearsome, with a shining face. He is an angel, darling, fallen from grace. You could not look upon him, you know, for it would burn out your eyes."

Agatha giggled. "Oh, Gran!"

"No laughing matter," Meggie said, though without harshness. "It is all true, which is why it's a frightening thing to hear he's abroad in the world."

"Then it would be dangerous for him to come to us?" Agatha's smile had faded a little.

Meggie nodded. "No doubt of it! This is our heritage, child, our curse and our blessing. We shall have to be careful and cunning, won't we?"

Agatha nodded gravely. "Yes, but you and Aunt Betsy will keep us safe."

They had reached the back door, which stood open, as everyone else had already gone into the house. Meggie was warmed by the child's confidence in her, but found it difficult to share. What form would Shemyaza wear in the world? She did not think he would be clothed in light or visibly inhuman. They already knew that the body he wore, and the mind that contained his essence, were not yet aware of what and who he was. He would have been born to one of the descendants of the giants, of this she was sure. Although the Pelleth had no direct contact with these people, it was known that they called themselves Grigori. Long ago, the Pelleth had attuned to the faint power that the giants had left in the area. They respected the great serpent that had been left slumbering beneath the earth. But Meggie and her sisters would have nothing to do with the Grigori, despite the fact they carried the blood, however thin, of the giants. In the eyes of the Pelleth, the Grigori were corrupt, greedy for wealth and temporal power, and made all the more dangerous because they possessed vestiges of the great powers of their ancestors. They lurked behind every rumour of conspiracy; they broke the backs of world leaders, sacred kings and wise prophets upon the cruel, hard wheels of their complex web of power. Meggie despised the Grigori. She knew the ancient Kingdom of Cornwall was rife with them, because this was the place where their ancestors had made landfall, but she also knew they must be scattered all over the country, if not the world. The Grigori were doubtless already aware that Shemyaza had returned, and they too would be eager to draw him to them. Wizards and charlatans, power-mongers and wheeler-dealers; that was how Meggie saw the Grigori. They would want Shemyaza with them to increase their own power. Meggie's people had different ideas. Shemyaza and his colleagues had fallen from grace because of their love of humanity. The knowledge they possessed they had wanted to share. But the Grigori were jealous of their power and looked down upon those who were not of their kind. They would not want to share Shemyaza's light with

Meggie's people, or indeed any other pure-born humans. There-fore, it was the Pelleth's duty to get to Shemyaza first and protect him and his knowledge from his greedy descendants.

The kitchen was the heart of the Penhaligon house; a massive room, complete with a temperamental old range, as well as a modern, fit-ted oven and hob. An enormous table filled its centre, and this was where much of the business of the Pelleth was discussed, as well as all manner of things pertaining to the welfare of the villagers and the surrounding countryside. It was also where Meggie and Betsy held their "surgeries", when they prescribed herbal remedies, or else read the cards for tourists. The house was very old and had a sunken, relaxed appearance, its gables sway-backed like an old mare. In the summer, Meggie and Betsy, aided by a couple of girls, served cream teas in the garden, and sold strawberries grown by their own hands. Meggie liked talking to "foreigners"—as she referred to anyone not born in Cornwall—and was rarely hostile to tourists. Once, she had been asked by archaeologists to give her permission to examine the cove below the house; a request she had politely refused. There was nothing of interest there, she said, and if they did not believe her, they realised the futility of pressing the matter. As the years passed, the Pelleth knew that more and more people were paying attention to the old legends, and were waking up to the fact that once England had been known as the island of giants. Scholars were putting two and two together and coming up with ridiculous numbers, especially concerning the connection between the giants and the legends of fallen angels from the Middle East. It did not bother the Pelleth, quite the opposite, in fact. They knew that eventually, the whole world would have to wake up to this knowledge, but in the mean-time they guarded it carefully. Sometimes, if necessary, they would employ extreme means to keep their secrets, and it was not unknown for the over-curious and persistent to disappear during one of the vicious wind-storms that assailed the Cornish coast. The Pelleth regarded themselves as the Keepers of Knowledge, and knew that the time had not yet come when it could be revealed.

Tom Penhaligon was Meggie's youngest son; she had borne him in her fortieth year. Now, he was thirty-five; a lean, stooped man, who was still handsome, although he had never bothered to take a wife. Meggie knew he considered himself part of her secret work, even though he knew virtually nothing about it. It was his job to make sure the house was warm when the women came back from the beach, that the tea-urn was freshly-filled, and hot food available. He took pleasure in these tasks, and never pried into matters that did not concern him. Now he moved quietly about the kitchen, as the women divested themselves of their wet cloaks, shaking out their dripping hair, chattering and laughing amongst themselves. Meggie signalled Tom to escort the oracle, Delmar Tremayne, from the room. The boy was shivering and needed a hot bath and to change into warm clothes. Also, the women had important matters to discuss, and not even the oracle was privy to that.

Once Tom had closed the kitchen door softly behind him, Meggie and Betsy took their places at either end of the long table. Tom had already poured out steaming mugs of tea, and two plates of hot crumpets steamed enticingly before them, salty butter sliding over their crisp surfaces. For a few minutes the women drank and ate in comparative silence, their hair steaming in the warmth from the range.

Meggie was the first to speak. She put her mug down upon the table. "Well, the news we have been waiting for has been delivered. This day will be marked in our records as one of great importance."

Tamara spoke up. Although her body was voluptuous, her eyes were narrow and her lips thin; marks of the snake in an otherwise moonish face. Her long blond hair hung raggedly around her shoulders. "We know the gist of what this information means. What concerns me is what the Grigori will do about it. We can't imagine we're the only ones privy to this knowledge."

Meggie wished Tamara had not spoken the obvious. "We must draw the Hanged One to us."

Tamara shook her head and smiled. "Our psychic beacons will be forever eclipsed by the great light-houses of Grigori awareness."

Meggie had the distinct impression that Tamara was playing with words, almost as if she was initiating this argument purely for the sake of it. "We have to suppose the man, if not what he represents, will have some autonomy."

"No doubt he will want to be with his own people." Tamara threw up her hands. "We must face it, Megs, this will be a difficult task. Why should Shemyaza ally with us? We can assume his power outstrips our own. The Grigori will use him to awaken the serpent, and once that is done, they will claim its power as their own. We have tended the dreams of the serpent for generations, yet once it is free, it will be attracted to the Grigori because they carry within them a memory of their ancestors."

Meggie's eyes had become dark. "Enough!" She slapped the tabletop with her palms. "What is this useless talk? We must plan and prepare the ancient sites for the time when the serpent wakes and the Hanged One walks this soil. The task may be hard, yes, but not impossible. It is what the Pelleth was formed for. It is our function."

Tamara shrugged in a conciliatory manner. "I am not arguing with you, Megs, but merely stating the obstacles. They must be confronted."

"We all agree to that," Betsy said from the other end of the table. She spoke rarely and only when she felt she had something important to offer. "If the Hanged One is drawn to the Grigori in these parts, all to the good. It halves our work for us. When the time comes, we must lure him to us. The Shining Ones will give us the knowledge on how to do this when we need it. In the meantime, we must do as my sister suggests and prime our sacred sites in readiness. The storm-beasts gather in the clouds. They feel him drawing near." She put her hands flat upon the table, and threw back her head. "Yes. He will come to the Grigori, and in their pride, they will overlook us. The season becomes darker and the winds cry for the sun, but his spirit walks always back to the land of his people."

In the silence that followed, Agatha shyly brought forth a peg-doll from her robe pocket. Gravely, she held it over the table. It was crowned with yellow woollen hair and wore a shapeless robe of sacking. Gripping it by its waist, Agatha made it walk slowly along the tabletop before her. Its wooden legs could not bend. It was a stiff-limbed, zombie, drunken walk. All the women glanced down at it.

"Where did you get that, dear?" asked Tamara.

Agatha did not move her eyes from the stalking doll, sinister in its very simplicity: a golem. "Del made it for me," she said.

After the meeting, Tamara drove home in her red VW Golf, navigating the sharp bends of the winding cliff road with almost masculine zeal. She was suffused with a sense of hysterical excitement, but it was pricked by a nagging needle of annoyance. The Conclave was so dim-sighted! Tamara couldn't believe their naiveté. They spoke with scorn about the Grigori, maintaining an obsolete feud that was rooted only in ignorance and superstition. The time of change was imminent, and clinging to outworn beliefs and opinions could only obstruct their work. The Pelleth needed to listen to the voice of reform, a voice that Tamara firmly believed spoke clearly through her, but she knew this voice must be heard as a seductive whisper, not an ear-splitting shout. She must be patient.

Tamara had been born in Cornwall, but had spent her childhood and teens in North America. As a young girl, the Native American culture had intrigued her and she read books on the subject voraciously, filling her bedroom walls with posters of young braves on horseback and the feather and thong concoctions available at ethnic craft stores. At High School, she met a girl whose mother was of Pawnee descent, and put a lot of effort into befriending her intimately. Although the girl herself had scant interest in her heritage, Tamara saw her as a means through which she could meet the Pawnee people. Part of her hungered for this, and when, after a lot of pleading and blackmailing, her wish was granted, she was not disappointed. The memory would never fade in her mind. Her friend's grandfather had been a true medicine man, and from the moment of meeting Tamara had recognised the thirst for magic within her. Tamara had always been able to charm men, and this sage shaman had been no exception. He had been happy to teach her the things she desperately yearned to know: how to call spirits from the waterfall and the fire, how to dance the Ghost Dance. On her eighteenth birthday, he had given her a prophecy. He spoke of a great serpent that slumbered beneath the land of her father, and that in its sleep, it dreamed of her. He spoke of a great sun chief who would come to her. As priestess of the sea she must lead him to his destiny. But he warned her that her heart must be true, for only the light of love would lead the sun chief to the great serpent.

Listening to these words, in the dark, before the sparking fire that burned for her day of birth, Tamara had been filled with a sense of purpose and resolve. As soon as she was able, she left her parents and moved back across the ocean to Cornwall.

It had taken her very little time to discover the legends of the ancient land, and how they aligned with the prophecy she had been given. The serpent had chosen her. At night, she felt it stir in its sleep, and its dream voice called out to her. Her passion and her sincerity enabled her to infiltrate the Pelleth, and she had spoken openly about her experiences, sure that the women would recognise her as the sea priestess, the chosen one who would guide Shemyaza to the serpent. But while the Pelleth had been happy to initiate her into their group, they felt her passion was the misguided zeal of youth. The Pelleth were *all* chosen ones, and would guide the Hanged One together. Tamara had been bitterly disillusioned at first, and it had hardened her. She realised she'd have to play the game their way until the time came when they'd be forced to recognise what she was. Her powers as a scryer and as a shamaness far outranked that of any of her Pelleth sisters. In her mind, she was clearly destined to be Meggie's successor. But Meggie refused to acknowledge Tamara's abilities, and would not promise her succession. Tamara felt this was not because Meggie doubted her powers, but that she was, in Meggie's eyes, a foreigner. Tamara considered this discrimination small-minded and inexcusable. Surely, the welfare of the Pelleth overcame such considerations? Meggie would never admit that Tamara's upbringing in America was behind her decisions, however. She would talk about the need for experience, and point out that if Tamara's childhood absence from Cornwall was really seen as a problem by the Pelleth, she wouldn't have been initiated into their ranks at all, never mind reach the Conclave. Tamara did not believe these excuses.

Now, Meggie's opinions no longer seemed to matter. Another had come into Tamara's life, one who recognised the power within her. A dark sister had come, and in her veins ran the royal blood of angels.

Two days before, Tamara had been outside her cottage, tidying autumn debris from her garden. A woman had stopped at the gate, a tall woman wearing a pale raincoat and a headscarf, her eyes hidden by dark glasses. Tamara had felt the scrutiny before turning round, a prickle on the skin at the back of her neck. She saw the long, ungloved fingers resting on the gatepost, the red smile splitting the attenuated, white face. She had known immediately: Grigori! And her heart had convulsed within her. Like all of the Pelleth, Tamara knew where the Grigori families lived around the area, and had watched the limousines with darkened windows gliding in and out of the gates of their estates. Sometimes, she had seen tall, charismatic men and women in shops or pubs, whom she'd been sure had been Grigori. As a rule, they tended to avoid the local community, for the native Cornish were attuned to their frequency, and would undoubtedly recognise them, if not for exactly what they were, then as being unusual or fey. Quietly, Tamara had been calling out to the Grigori for some months. She'd never been truly convinced they would heed her call, but she'd had no doubt at least some of them had heard it. And now: the response. The woman at the gate knew her measure. She was a powerful creature, a daughter of a powerful family, yet here she was, in the flesh, cool and seductive as a ghost of desire. Tamara had not been afraid or filled with disgust, as Meggie might have been. No. Curiosity and excitement had bubbled up within her, and the tall woman had nodded at her, as if recognising an affinity between them.

"You are Tamara Trewlynn?" Her voice was low, beautiful. When she took off her glasses, her eyes would be large and deep as ocean pools.

Tamara's mouth had gone dry. She rubbed her soil-seamed hands on the front of her jacket. "Yes. What can I do for you?"

The woman laughed—a full, secret sound. "May I come into your garden? I'd like to talk to you."

"All right." Tamara wasn't sure the gate opened, or that the Grigori woman walked through it, but suddenly she was looking up into her face, only inches away from the heat of her body. The dark glasses were removed, and there were the eyes: full of history and forbidden knowledge. Tamara felt sucked of breath.

"We have lot in common," said the woman. "My name is Barbelo." She held out her pale hand, a giant's hand, which enfolded Tamara's grubby fingers like a muscular team of serpents. "I don't want to waste time. Let me tell you the point of this contact. My people know of the Pelleth, as they know of us. We all know the Shining One is coming to us. The Grigori look down upon the Pelleth, and the Pelleth despise the Grigori, yet we should be working together at this time. The destiny of the Hanged One affects humanity and Grigori alike. Old quarrels should be buried now. This is a crucial time."

Tamara knew her face had gone red. "But that's exactly what I feel!" she exclaimed.

"I know. That's why I'm here." Barbelo coiled an arm around Tamara's shoulder and began to lead her towards the cottage door. "I know we will be friends."

Inside the cottage, Tamara made tea while Barbelo sat at her kitchen table, seeming to fill the room with her body and her presence. She spoke openly about how she felt the Grigori had become stale and staid, almost to the point where they had forgotten the reason why Shemyaza would return. "They are obsessed with conspiracies and politics," she said. "Smug little cabals of pompous power-mongers, whose magic is bled of life."

Tamara interjected excited remarks to illustrate how her own opinions of the Pelleth mirrored Barbelo's of the Grigori. "They live in the past," she said, waving her arms for emphasis. "They hate and fear change. It is absurd, for that is exactly what Shemyaza represents."

Barbelo smiled a long, thin smile and nodded. "Oh yes! I heard your dreams, Tamara Trewlynn. I heard your lonely call. We are both renegades, and I respect your abilities. However, I do have more knowledge of this subject than you, and am prepared to help and guide you. We must work together, as outsiders in the dark."

Tamara warmed to the image conjured by these words. A Grigori woman was sitting here in her kitchen, talking to her as if they'd known one another for years. She could hardly believe it was happening. "Nothing would please me more," she said.

Barbelo put her head on one side. "Of course, our association must remain secret from both sides...for now."

Tamara nodded. "Absolutely."

"We must use them without them knowing it." Barbelo delicately took a sip of tea. "We work only for the good of the land."

Tamara's trust in Barbelo had been instant and all-consuming. After the woman had left, Tamara had felt as if she'd met someone with whom she was destined to fall in love. She'd been unable to relax, pacing her cottage like a restless cat.

Now, Tamara knew instinctively that the voice that had spoken through Delmar Tremayne that night had been the voice of Barbelo. The Pelleth, in their blind faith, hadn't even questioned where it might have come from. Meggie's talk of dead ancestors was pathetic. The Pelleth lived on the same land as Grigori, yet seemed to think they were invisible to them.

Tamara parked her car and went into her garden. She saw a light burning low in her kitchen and knew that a visitor was waiting there for her. Before she entered the house, she paused to look out upon the night, extending her senses to read the currents and vibrations that flowed through it. The dreams of the serpent were faint music in her mind. It dreamed of the sun chief and of those who would guide him to it. Tamara expelled her breath in a shuddering sigh. She was smiling when she entered her kitchen.

Chapter Two
The Temptation of Eve

Daniel Cranton slipped out of the house into the grey twilight that presaged the dawn. This was the time, for him, when ghosts walked the ageless streets of the city, and myriad overlays of past times were visible to his eyes. There was no interference, no white noise, and the traffic sounds were muted. Occasionally, a dog might bark or a cat yowl, and sometimes he had heard screams, cut off sharply, or sobbing, but mostly, he supposed these were memories replayed upon the resting air, oozing from the relaxing stones of the buildings. London thinking about its past.

The house where he was staying did not look like a house, but a hall, a gathering place. It had a double flight of steps running up to the double front doors, and railings at the front. Above the lintel were the words Moses Assembly Rooms, carved into the likeness of a folded ribbon or sash. Large, uncleaned windows reared up for three stories, while in the roof small gables peered out like squinting eyes. Daniel rarely ventured onto the top floor because it screamed at him. It was a place where heart-broken domestics had hanged themselves in the cold, stillborn children had been delivered, blood steaming in the cruel winter nights of the Victorian age, and harsh voices had uttered condemnations. Daniel could still hear the muffled echo of those words. At night, they escaped down the stairs: a man's unforgiving tone, a woman's trembling, desperate pleas. He could never make out the words, even when he left his room and stood in the hallway, listening. Altogether, it was not a good building, for it would not let go of any of its history, and most of its history was cruel. Perhaps this why the outcasts of the Grigori congregated there: the shunned seeking a shunned residence. It was like a commune or a squat, inhabited but not loved or cherished. The rotting rooms were full of finery—drapes and antique furniture—but the walls were crumbling and everywhere smelled of mildew. Daniel, the most purely human of his group of companions, did not like the people who lived there. They seemed to him to be like mannequins, sequinned and painted, but only representations of living beings. Their eyes were shallow and their movements were jerky, making them all the more eerie for their semblance of life. When any of them looked at Daniel, he could sense their hunger, but for what they hungered, he was unsure. What did they do when they were alone? Did they speak, eat or sleep, or simply sit staring at the walls? Was it his own presence, or that of Lily, Owen and Emma, which made them come alive? It scared him to think that might be true, even though he had seen clusters of them sneaking out into the night through the alley door. During the day, he had heard the front doors being opened and closed, but he liked to keep to his room then or spend time with his companions, for he was uncomfortable with the thought of running into any of the other residents. They might speak to him, and he did not want to hear what they might have to say.

What was Shem thinking of, bringing them to a place like this? It was a sideways step into the dark, and Daniel could think only of light.

Out on the streets, he could breathe more easily. He was not afraid of the Assembly Rooms, and in fact was fascinated by the dark, cavernous rooms and endless corridors. But sometimes, it stifled him.

Lime trees edged the road, leafless now. The Rooms were situated on Black Lion Square; a small quadrangle of white Georgian houses, hidden away from the bustle of city life. In its centre was a Garden of Remembrance, where a robed statue stood pointing at the sky. Sometimes strange figures in black would huddle on the benches there among the trees. Daniel would watch them from a window on the second floor. They never seemed to move, nor could their faces be seen, but they appeared to be very old. Most of the other buildings in the square housed offices; nobody lived in them now.

Daniel walked around the square, feeling cold. He wondered whether he was lonely, for his life seemed to have frozen. He was held in this place, hidden away. Several weeks ago, he and his companions had arrived at the Rooms: Emma, the rejuvenated Grigori dependant and self-appointed leader of their group; the hybrid twins, Lily and Owen Winter, and the shattered remains of the Grigori, Peverel Othman, whom they must now call Shemyaza. Daniel was sure that Shem had been to the Moses Assembly Rooms before. He seemed to know the deranged Grigori who lived there, even though he rarely talked to them. He must have visited them during the shadowy, unknown and frightening time he had lived as Peverel Othman. Neither Daniel, nor any of his companions had yet ventured beyond the square into the city itself, unless you could count the times when Emma scurried out at dawn to the news-agents a short way down the main road to buy cigarettes, or magazines and papers. Daniel supposed they had all contracted a kind of agoraphobia, perhaps because they were afraid of pursuit, although it seemed silly to fear that. Even if other Grigori had followed Shem's trail from the north and had guessed he was in London, no-one came to the Moses Assembly Rooms, no-one who wasn't wanted or invited. It was a bleak and invisible place.

After the first circuit of the square, Daniel paused at the street, which led to the outside. Already, faintly, the city was waking up, but then it never really slept. Crows roosting in the trees in the Garden began to squawk. Presently, the sun would come, heralding another day during which nothing would happen. When he'd followed Shemyaza out of the north, or more accurately allowed himself to be led, Daniel had been sure that unbelievable and wonderful things would happen to him. His life could never be the same as it was. Shemyaza had *become* and the world must change. But it seemed Shem was not going to accept what he was, which was why he was hiding himself in the feathery, powdery shadows of the Moses Assembly Rooms amongst the discarded outcasts of his kind. Soon, Daniel knew, Shemyaza would shrug off his apathy, but Daniel was not convinced he would then become anything other than what he had been before; Anakim, a madman in Grigori terms. How long would they stay here? Daniel knew that nothing was keeping him there other than his own loyalty, a loyalty to an ideal that was long dead. The candle had been ignited but the flame had fizzled out. It would take more than one attempt to keep it burning bright and true.

The side street, which led to the wider road, where the bright hoardings stood and garishly lit-shops, was dark and narrow: an effective camouflage. Who would expect to find the square with its Garden beyond it? But at its end was a small cafe, which opened very early in the morning. Sitting in the Garden on occasions, Daniel had been able to watch the side-door of the cafe and had seen people hurrying out of it to march swiftly across the square to several of the office buildings. Smartly-dressed people, whose minds were a blur of hurrying and worrying. The cafe was like a door to the outside.

Daniel had a pound's worth of change in his pocket. Unconsciously, he slipped his hand into it and fingered the coins. He could go down to the cafe, buy tea, sit among people who lived real, mundane lives, and bask in their frenetic warmth. It might be the first step to leaving the square. He did not want to stay there forever.

Inside, the cafe was full of people reading newspapers and eating breakfast. Some talked together while others sat alone. The smell of frying bacon and ketchup made Daniel salivate. He was hungry, properly hungry, almost as if his body had been on shutdown for the three weeks he'd been in the square and merely taking the step of entering the cafe had woken up his system. Daniel sat down on a stool by the window, where a shelf acted as a table. An empty plate smeared with red sauce lay beside an over-flowing ash-try. The smell of stale tobacco and fried food did not combine pleasantly. Someone had left a newspaper, folded up, next to the plate. Daniel opened it out. It felt as if he hadn't seen a paper for years for he shied away from looking at those which Emma brought back to the Rooms, in case he found some mention of their disappearance. Now, after several weeks, and away from the oppressive air of the Rooms, he dared to confront the news. Had the world moved on without him?

As he began to turn the pages a middle-aged woman in an overall came up to him. She had permed hair and red lipstick, and her scarlet nails were long and looked hard. She held a note-pad. "What'll it be?"

Daniel stared at her for a moment, wondering what significance her words held for him. Then he came to his senses and said, "A cup of tea."

The woman pulled a rueful face. "Sorry, love, it's breakfast only at this time. You'll have to order something to eat." Her pen, a nibbled Biro, was poised over the pad.

"I've only got a quid," Daniel said, realising the words were inadequate, but what else could he say?

"Toast is one pound, fifty. That's the cheapest on the menu." The woman put her pen into a pocket of her overall. Her face became harder. Presently, she would ask him to leave.

Daniel opened his mouth helplessly. He didn't want to leave yet. He wanted to remain in the warmth, amid the sense of life. He wanted to read the paper and listen to the conversations of the other patrons. "Could I have *half* a slice of toast?" He smiled hopefully.

He could see the woman was considering it, probably because he was young and pretty. He was glad he'd bothered to keep himself clean. At least he didn't look like a vagrant.

"Sorry, love." She took a step back to give him room to stand up.

Daniel gave her a wistful smile and slipped off the stool. Perhaps he could go back to the Rooms and ask Emma for money. He knew she still had some cash left, even though she had forbidden the rest of them trying to use cash-points, in case they left traces of their presence in the city. She was careful with her money, but Daniel knew she had a soft spot for him, and might give him a few pounds. Then Daniel realised that once he was back in the Rooms, the freedom spell would be broken and the idea of sitting in the cafe would no longer seem attractive. Maybe he could come back another day. Even as he was thinking this, he knew it wouldn't happen. Today, the time had been right, but something had blocked his plans. Something was blocking all of their plans, he was sure.

Just as he was about to leave, he heard a low-pitched woman's voice say, "Excuse me." And something made him pause.

The waitress turned round, dismissing Daniel from her attention, and reached for her pen again. Daniel saw an immaculately dressed young woman sitting at one of the tables smiling up at the waitress. Her voice, well-modulated and smooth as dark liquor, indicated she knew she was attractive. She said, "Give the boy toast and tea. I don't mind paying."

"You sure?" The waitress seemed to doubt the stranger's altruism.

The young woman nodded. "Yes." She turned her attention to Daniel. "Would you mind if I bought you breakfast?"

Daniel shrugged, bemused. "Er...no." Something had slipped; one of the blocks had shifted. He could feel it in his mind; huge dark slabs of impenetrable stone grinding out of place.

"Sit down," said the young woman, and gestured elegantly at a free space on her table. Two of the other places were taken by other young women, but both were intent on reading magazines. They were not with his benefactress, Daniel could tell. They were drab and empty, while she was alight with energy. Her dark tailored suit looked expensive and she smelled strongly of perfume, a sweet, exotic scent. She was very beautiful, with a long, pale, well-sculpted face and dark brows. Her hair hung straight and glossy down her back, very black.

Daniel sat down. "Thanks," he said. "I do have money at home, but it was a bit of an impulse thing coming in here."

"On your way to work?" the woman asked.

Daniel could tell by the tone of her voice that she did not believe he had a job. Indignation made him reply, "Yes."

The woman raised her brows and sipped from a mug of tea. She had an empty plate before her, on which reposed a knife and toast crumbs. A blob of marmalade remained on the edge of the plate. She was immaculate and feline, which suggested aloofness, but her crumbs and her unused marmalade warmed Daniel to her, made her seem human and approachable. "What's your line of business?" she enquired.

"I work in a conference hall." Daniel didn't feel that was absolutely untrue. At one time the Assembly Rooms must have been used as such.

"And where's that?"

Daniel wondered whether the woman was simply making conversation or had some kind of sinister interest in him. He recalled lurid stories of people who preyed on those they considered runaways, turning them into drug addicts and prostitutes. "Nearby," he answered vaguely.

The woman seemed to sense he objected to her questions. "I'm sorry, I'm not prying. I just fancy some company today."

"Oh." Daniel looked round himself, unsure of what to say. Eventually, he thought of: "Do you work round here too?"

"At the moment," she replied, nodding, the tea mug held in two hands before her face. "But I don't know how long for."

"What do you do?"

"I'm a researcher." The woman smiled widely, a smile that seemed to invite Daniel in, while excluding the rest of the world. Her friendliness and openness were quite at odds with her rather forbidding appearance. Perhaps she was a bit peculiar.

"Oh, you must work in reference libraries and places like that, then," Daniel said, hoping to sound as if he knew what he was talking about. Why, over the past three weeks, did he seem to be growing younger rather than older? At the moment, he felt about twelve, gangly and wordless, rather than eighteen, a newly matured young man.

"That's right," said the woman.

The waitress came over with Daniel's tea and toast, and handed his benefactress a bill. "Thank you," she said politely, putting it on top of her own next to her plate. "Might I have another round of toast myself?"

As the waitress went back behind the counter, Daniel's new friend took out a cigarette. "Do you mind?" She had already lit up.

Daniel smiled and shook his head. "No." It reminded him of Emma, who smoked as and when she felt like it, with little regard for whether it was permitted or not, or what other people might think.

"My name's Eve," said the woman.

"Daniel."

For a split second, a strange expression crossed the woman's face. It was almost as if Daniel had just confirmed his identity in her mind, and that she'd suspected who he was. That, surely, was impossible. He bit into his toast, and then felt his stomach churn. She must have seen the colour drop from his face.

Hadn't Emma drummed into them a thousand times that other Grigori would undoubtedly have pursued Shemyaza? Could Eve be one of his pursuers, lying in wait here, day after day, hoping one of Shem's companions might drop in? The implications were terrifying, suggesting that they knew already where Shem and his companions were.

"Are you all right?"

Daniel glanced at Eve, noticing how her brows were creased in what seemed to be genuine concern. "What?"

"You look like you just had a hideous realisation!" She laughed. "Are you thinking of how it's not very wise to get into conversations with strangers in the big, bad city?" She seemed to find it highly amusing that she might be considered a threat. Daniel attempted to extend his senses to see if he could pick up anything that smelled of danger, but he felt too confused and hectic to concentrate.

"It's nothing. I—er—just remembered something I've forgotten to do." Perhaps he should have given a false name, just to be on the safe side.

"I can tell you're not a native Londoner," Eve said, smiling, "but then neither am I. I've become very adept at spotting foreigners to the city. If you live here long enough, you change, and become like all the others." She glanced at the other women sitting opposite and lowered her voice. "*They* would never talk to strangers. Only mad people talk to one another in London if they're not already friends."

Eve's second helping of toast arrived and for a couple of minutes both of them ate in silence. Then Eve poured herself another mug of tea from the battered-looking stainless steel teapot that stood in the centre of the table. Without asking, she topped up Daniel's mug and said, "I live alone in a flat, which is on the third floor of a building, overlooking the river. There are birds living in the eaves. They never go to sleep but bicker among themselves all night. Perhaps they are starlings. I don't know much about birds."

Daniel shrugged. "Nor me."

Eve smiled. "Still, it adds character."

Perhaps she wanted Daniel to offer information about his own life. He was wary of doing that because he still did not trust her. He realised he could not remain in the cafe for much longer. He was beginning to feel uneasy. Quickly, he drained his tea. "Thanks for helping me out. It was kind of you." He stood up.

Eve tilted her head up at him. "Such good manners! Don't worry, it was a pleasure. Perhaps some time you could buy me breakfast too. I'm here most mornings."

Daniel nodded. "OK." She was becoming an oppressive presence; he was sure she wanted something from him. There was a light emanating from her eyes, which suggested she wanted him to stay, tell her things. "I must go," he said awkwardly.

Eve blinked slowly and inclined her head. "Of course. Have a nice day."

Daniel grinned and, with shrinking flesh, fled the cafe. Hurriedly, he immersed himself in the shadows of the narrow street and had to force himself not to run back to the square. At the same time, he felt strangely buoyant. Contact with someone other than the bizarre occupants of the Rooms and his damaged companions had been good for him. Perhaps he *would* return to the cafe some other morning, but part of the magic of this certain day would no doubt mean he would never see strange Eve again. He hoped his meeting with her could be seen as an omen and that, as the hours rolled out, other things might happen which would enhance the uniqueness of the day.

Daniel walked up the alley beside the Assembly Rooms and used his keys to open the two locks of the side door. Inside, the atmosphere enveloped him like an amorous monster, as if the oppressive air was thick with unseen strands of fur. Already, it was more difficult to draw breath. A four-paned window beside the door provided the only light, and it was heavily barred, as well as not having been cleaned for years. Therefore the light was bleak and dim, and stillness reigned. There were no sounds, and even the noises of the city seemed to have disappeared.

A short narrow corridor led into the house, its right side flanked by stairs. Daniel had to walk down the corridor before he could double back on himself and mount the stairs. The stairs were uncarpeted, so that Daniel's boots made a heavy sound on the rough, bare wood. The banister was sticky, as if exuding a moist, sick ichor.

When he reached the first floor, Daniel increased his pace. This was the area where he was most likely to run into someone. On the second floor, he and his companions had been given rooms to use; bare, dismal spaces that ached with old regrets. Shem's room was at the end of a dark, narrow corridor, where all the light bulbs had blown. Daniel went to see him every morning with the hope that one day, Shem might respond to him in a positive way, and say something about the future. Daniel knew that Emma had a similar ritual, but she was more likely to exhort and complain, while Daniel was content simply to sit and wait.

Reaching Shem's door, Daniel knocked politely. As usual, there was no response, so he opened the door and walked into the room. Shem never locked himself in, and did not seem to want to keep anyone out. The room was large, too large, the bare boards of the floor inadequately covered by an ancient carpet, colourless now. There was little furniture. In a dark corner reposed a sagging double bed, on which the new, paisley-covered duvet that Emma had bought lay scrunched up in a marshmallowy pile. Before the vast empty fireplace stood a sofa with broken legs, supported by old books and bricks. In front of it there was a coffee table from the "seventies—chipped—and an enormous TV, which had been manufactured in the days when colour transmission was still quite an innovative thing. The television was on, but the sound was turned down; its picture veered distinctly towards purple tones. Magazines and newspapers lay scattered around, the bright colour photographs of the glossies incongruous against the drab deadness of the room. Daniel knew Shem sent Emma out to buy them for him. Was he really interested in what went on in the world?

Shem was sitting on the floor beneath the window, almost invisible in the grey light, playing a computer game on a hand-held console, borrowed from one of the other Grigori in the house. His long legs were curled up around him and his feet were bare. His pale hair hung loose over his chest, obscuring the logo on his T-shirt. He looked up when Daniel came into the room and smiled vaguely. The sight of him always made Daniel's heart falter. It was partly caused by the shock of Shem's rather unkempt beauty, but also something else, something within the man that came out of him like an invisible fan of light.

"I've been outside," Daniel said.

Shem turned his attention back to his game. "I know. I sensed your presence on the pavement outside."

Daniel sauntered over to where Shem sat and squatted down beside him. "I mean, I went out of the square, to a cafe." He wondered whether Shem would look up in alarm, be shocked into admonishing him, but no.

"Right."

There was no scolding that he should have taken care, or not spoken to anyone. "I met a weird woman who bought me breakfast."

Shem uttered an amused snort. "Daniel, to you, all women are weird."

"Don't you think that's strange though? Someone I don't know offering to buy me breakfast?"

Shem looked up at him studiously for a moment or two, then shook his head. "No, not at all. I'm sure she would have liked to buy you more than breakfast."

"So you don't think it could mean trouble?"

Shem frowned quizzically, but did not look up. "Trouble? What kind?"

"You know, someone following us."

Shem sighed and put down the game. "Daniel, I can't be bothered with Emma's paranoia, for that is what you're talking about. She puts ideas into your head. No-one has ever caught up with me before, so why should they now?"

Daniel shrugged. "Dunno. I just wonder what would happen, though, if they did."

Shem grinned. "They'd kill me and subject you and the others to unspeakable torture." He laughed. "Don't look like that. I was joking. No-one is looking for us. Nobody cares." He stood up and plunged his hands into his hair to scratch his scalp. Then he shook himself like a dog and leaned on the windowsill to look out.

"How long must we stay here?" Daniel asked, still squatting on the floor.

"No-one's keeping you here," Shem answered shortly. "Except, perhaps, for Emma."

"Do you want us to leave you?"

Shem glanced round at him. For a few moments, he said nothing. "No, I don't, but I can't see why you should waste your life here. Especially you and Lily. Emma will stick by me because she wants the Fruit of Youth." He laughed harshly. "And Owen is not in this reality, so should probably be looked after by Emma. But you and Lily should just fly away." He raised his arms. "She could carry you in her arms and fly."

"I can't leave Owen," Daniel said. He wondered why he felt uncomfortable saying that.

Shem shook his head in what seemed to be disbelief. "Why? He's weak, Daniel. He let me use him to hurt you. You very nearly died. Get out now, and leave both of us behind. You owe us nothing but your contempt."

"Once you would not have thought that," Daniel said, sensing progress, however faint.

"You don't know that."

"I won't leave you either." Daniel stood up. "You can't stay here forever. You can't deny what you are..."

Shem raised his hands and closed his eyes. "Daniel, Daniel, please be quiet. I don't want to hear your opinions. I have been many things and will no doubt be many more, but at the moment, I don't want to be anything but an invisible creature who spends all day sucking up the media and playing computer games. I could do this for millennia. You, on the other hand, don't have such a luxury of time."

"You couldn't do it for millennia," Daniel said mulishly. "The house will fall down long before then, and the TV will definitely conk out within the next twelve months."

Shem laughed grudgingly. "I was speaking, as you well know, metaphorically. Please don't hassle me now. If you're going to keep nagging, do it outside the door where I can't hear you." He flapped his hands at Daniel. "Now, please. I want some peace."

Sighing, Daniel trudged out. He paused at the door, trying to think of something clever to say, but failed. He felt angry and frustrated. What could he do to break down Shem's reserve? He couldn't go on like this. He had to finish *becoming*. Didn't he realise he didn't have a choice about that? Hiding away here would only delay the inevitable.

Chapter Three
The Watchers

Aninka Prussoe returned to the flat around mid-day. She'd spent the morning in the West End, browsing through bookshops, checking out the card sections to see whether any of her own prints were represented there. She could never resist doing that.

When she walked through the front door, her nostrils were assailed almost immediately by the smell of marijuana smoke. It indicated Taziel hadn't moved from the flat all morning, but that was not unusual. She found him sprawled on the sofa in the living room, shrouded in a fug of smoke, reading a horror novel. She and Taziel had been sharing the flat for two weeks now, ever since Aninka had been handed the keys by her guardian, Enniel. She felt that Enniel was quietly angry with both of them for failing to entrap Peverel Othman in Little Moor. Only she mustn't think of him in those terms any more. Peverel Othman had ceased to exist; Shemyaza had *been reborn.* Enniel had assured Aninka, during the embarrassing confession of their failure at the family house in Cornwall, that he did not blame her or Taziel for Shemyaza's escape. The implication in his words was that he blamed Lahash Murkaster, his own agent, who'd accompanied them to the north. Aninka and Taziel were soft, artistic types, strangers to the world of deceit, cunning and manipulation. Lahash, on the other hand, had been trained to deal with situations like the one in Little Moor.

At first, Aninka had hoped to see more of Lahash once their "mission" was ended, but he didn't contact her, and she had no idea where he was. Sometimes she'd suspected he wasn't interested in seeing her again, then reassured herself with the thought that he too did not know her whereabouts. It was unlikely Enniel would have told him. Taziel, whom she knew thought little of Lahash, never mentioned their erstwhile companion. He didn't seem to want to talk about anything connected with what had happened to them.

Taziel had been recalled from Vienna by Enniel, forced to abandon his life there, in order to help track down the Anakim, Peverel Othman. Aninka had offered her services voluntarily, although she and Taziel were linked by a common experience. Both were ex-lovers, if that term could be used, of Peverel Othman. Both had witnessed the excesses of his behaviour. Both were scarred by it. Taziel had maintained a strong psychic link with Othman, which he had used to pinpoint the Anakim's whereabouts. What followed had been a dash to the north, in the hope of capturing Othman, alive or dead. Lahash Murkaster had carried a gun: Aninka had seen it. But the climax of their search had been beyond their imaginations. On a sacred hill in the middle of a forest, Peverel Othman had performed his last, dark ritual. He had craved power, or so they supposed, but the outcome of his rite had been the stripping away of ignorance, presumably the last thing Othman had wanted or imagined. From the ashes of Othman had come Shemyaza. It was still hard to believe what they'd seen.

Shemyaza had slipped away from them, and they'd been forced to return to Cornwall and admit their failing. Taziel said that the Parzupheim, the governing body of the Grigori families, of which Enniel was a prominent member, had always known who Othman was. Aninka wasn't sure. Would the Parzupheim have sent only three people to the north if they'd suspected the truth?

Aninka wondered why Taziel didn't return to Vienna now; he had a band waiting there for him, and, she gathered, a lover. Still, he made no attempt to go home, and as far as Aninka knew had not even telephoned his people there. But as she was out so much more than he was, perhaps he did that when he was alone. He seemed content to do nothing, just sit around, although in the evenings he and Aninka went out together to pubs and clubs, or to the cinema. They got on quite well, which surprised her. Their common bond of the failed love affairs with Peverel Othman was never alluded to. Far easier to talk about their shared interest in films and books and music. Their nights out together were more like workshops than social occasions. They talked about art, ripped it apart, stuck it back together again, even made tentative plans. Taziel wanted to write a contemporary opera, and suggested Aninka could design the sets and the costumes for it. It gave them something to think about, something on which to focus their minds, so that uncomfortable memories could not squeeze in to haunt them. Aninka felt they were living in limbo. The talk of working together was a fantasy, because their involvement with Othman, or Shemyaza, was unfinished. The episode was not over yet, but merely going through a lull. The thought made her shudder. She felt this strongly and wondered whether Taziel felt the same. Sometimes she wanted to ask him, because she felt his decision to remain in England must have something to do with it, but she sensed he'd just flare up and get angry if the subject was mentioned.

Then, on the eighth night of their occupation of the flat, Lahash had turned up at the door. He'd seemed edgy but pleased to see them. He'd bought flowers for Aninka, scentless and unnaturally blue, probably purchased from a garage on the way to the flat. Still, she appreciated the gesture.

"How did you find us?" she asked. The three of them sitting together in the low-lit living-room, conjured memories of their time together in hotel bedrooms while they had hunted for Othman, and brought with it a sense of excitement.

"It wasn't that difficult," Lahash answered, smiling slyly. He was dressed, as usual, in a smart suit, over which he wore a long raincoat. Aninka always thought he looked as if he worked for the CIA, and wondered why she found him attractive. She didn't normally fancy men with short hair, whether they were Grigori or human.

Taziel looked distinctly uncomfortable, perhaps sensing that Lahash's appearance would mean they'd have to talk about Othman, and the experiences they'd shared. Still, he did not leave the room, merely watched Lahash with narrowed eyes through a veil of sweet-smelling smoke. He was the opposite of Lahash—longhaired and scruffy, his body posture languid rather than alert.

"Are you in trouble?" Aninka asked. "What did Enniel say to you?"

Lahash shrugged. "He implied I was careless, and in the heat of remonstrations, even that I might have let the Anakim escape deliberately." He grimaced. "After all, my blood too is tainted." He referred to the fact that the Murkasters were a disgraced branch of the family.

"That's ridiculous!" Aninka exclaimed. "I did tell Enniel what happened, you know. I made sure he knew there was nothing any of us could do, and even that it was Taziel and I who wanted to give up the chase. You were the one who thought we should carry on."

"Thanks. Although I don't think your—er—testimony did much good."

"I could speak to him again," Aninka suggested.

Lahash shook his head. "No, don't do that. I don't think it's a good idea he finds out I've contacted you. As far as Enniel is concerned, you and Taz are off the case."

"We're not, you know," Aninka dared to say, not looking at Taziel. "It's not over yet, for any of us."

Lahash nodded. "That is one of the reasons I wanted to find you." He gave Aninka a significant glance, which effectively increased her heartbeat.

Taziel had not yet uttered a word to Lahash other than a surly greeting. Now, he voiced a question. "What do you want?"

Lahash glanced at him, his expression showing plainly that he expected trouble from this quarter. "I want to know where Peverel Othman is. No, I want to know where Shemyaza is. And the best way to do that is to utilise the talents of the one person who's professed to have a psychic ability to track him, namely yourself. I want him, Taz. He escaped me, because I wasn't prepared for what happened at Little Moor. Now, I know what I'm dealing with, and I can handle it. This isn't over until I deliver Shemyaza, alive or dead, to High Crag." Lahash's expression had become steely, with a hint of mania.

"So you can absolve yourself in Enniel's eyes?" Taziel laughed harshly. "Show him you're a clever boy, after all. You're pathetic! You think I'll help you? Are you so obsessed with Shemyaza you can't face an obvious truth? There's no way I want to open up that wound again. Aninka knows it, so why don't you?"

Aninka was annoyed with Taziel. The confrontational side to his nature hadn't manifested once since they'd been in the flat. "Why haven't you gone home?" she asked sharply. "If you'd really thought this business was over, surely you'd have resumed your life as it was. You don't fool me, Taz."

Taziel blinked at her, apparently surprised someone he'd considered to be an ally had turned on him. She suspected that, had they been alone, he might have talked about his feelings, but Lahash was there, so Taziel's defence screens were raised and impregnable.

"I just don't see why we should let ourselves be used, so Lahash can worm his way back into the Parzupheim's favour. You know how dangerous this is, Ninka. Shemyaza is insane and unpredictable. He must have killed thousands of people. Us, he discarded. We were lucky. There is no reason now for us to get involved. We've been paid off, and have a safe haven. You think I'm waiting here to find a way to Shemyaza? You're wrong. I'm not sure whether I can go back to Vienna. But that has nothing to do with *him*. I have a feeling that I've moved on to a new cycle in my life. Going back belongs to feeling hurt and betrayed. I want to be here now, in England."

Aninka had not expected to hear anything like that. "What about your...people you're close to in Europe?" she asked lamely.

Taziel shrugged. "I'm not in love with anyone, if that's what you mean. Peverel Othman killed that in me. There's no-one in Vienna who can't survive without me. I'm a better person here."

Lahash shifted uneasily in his chair, as if he found the honesty of Taziel's remarks painful to hear.

Aninka shook her head. "This is all too much. We mustn't argue. Anyone want a drink?" She went to the liquor cupboard and poured out the drinks in silence. When she handed Taziel a glass of rum, Lahash said,

"You know where he is, don't you, Taz?"

Taziel and Aninka froze, both their hands wrapped around the tumbler. Aninka could have slapped Lahash. Why didn't he let it drop for now? Nothing would be gained by bullying Taziel. Left alone with him, she was sure she'd be able to convince him to co-operate. How could she intimate this to Lahash before he ruined every chance?

Taziel took the drink from Aninka's hand. "Of course I do," he replied.

"What?" Aninka cried. "You do?"

Taziel nodded, took a sip. "I can't help knowing. But I do try to ignore it." He laughed at Lahash's expression: a melange of surprise, excitement and hope. "But that doesn't mean I'm going to concentrate and tell you exactly where he is. I'm sorry, Lahash. It's one ghost I've got to let rest."

"And you're quite content to live the rest of your life knowing Shemyaza is around, *feeling* him around?" Lahash shook his head. "Doesn't it bother you he has such an effect on you? It's an intrusion, isn't it, that presence in your head. Continual mental rape. I think you're a coward. You're afraid of him."

Taziel laughed again, with even less warmth than before. "Yeah. I am. And you're not? If you answer no to that question then you're not qualified to try and find him. Only a fool would not be afraid of him. He would crush you like a hollow bone."

Lahash shook his head. "Help me find him, Taz. Just tell me where he is. That's all I ask. You don't have to face him, if that's what you're scared of."

"He will kill you," Taziel replied, sipping his rum.

"Just tell me." Lahash's voice was quiet, his eyes dark and direct.

Taziel shook his head. "No."

Lahash left soon after, although in the privacy of the hall arranged to meet Aninka for lunch the following day. "I'll do what I can," she whispered as she closed the door on him. In her heart, she was afraid that Lahash's attraction to her was far outweighed by his desire to snare Shemyaza. Feeling slightly depressed by this thought, she went back into the living-room and poured herself another brandy. Taziel had turned on the TV and was now watching the ten o'clock news.

Aninka stared at him, willing him to look up, but he clearly sensed her desire and ignored her. Sighing, she sat down on the chair, which was still warm from Lahash's body. After a few minutes, Taziel said, "You'll never get Othman back, Ninka. He's dead."

Aninka shuddered. "I know. Despite what you think, I really don't want to."

Taziel glanced at her. "But you feel the same way as Lahash does. It wouldn't take much to fire you up into a search lust again, would it?"

Aninka found she was shivering. "No. I admit that. I still want him found and...contained."

Taziel shook his head slowly. "It's too dangerous, Ninka. He is Shemyaza now. If I try to find him, he'll no doubt sense it, and come crashing into my brain like a hurricane. He might want to use me again, or simply kill me to cover his tracks. I have no way of knowing which way he'd turn, and I don't want to find out. One thing I am sure of is that he won't just run away and hide. Not now. He has to be stronger now."

"Surely you could protect yourself." In her heart, Aninka felt bad about pushing the matter. She knew Taziel was right and that he'd be the person most at risk if they went along with Lahash's request. But she could not stop herself.

There was a moment's silence, then Taziel said, "He's in London. Too close."

Aninka's heart turned over. "Here? But...Taz, have you been looking for him yourself?" The last question was delivered carefully.

"Not exactly, but I pick things up."

He wouldn't say any more.

Aninka related the information to Lahash as soon as he'd sat down opposite her in the restaurant where they'd arranged to meet.

"Well done," Lahash said.

Aninka frowned. "It's not enough, and I'm not sure whether I can convince Taz to do anything more."

Lahash shook his head. "You're wrong. What you said to Taz last night smacks of the truth. He *would* have gone home if he really thought this business was over. Anything else he might say is simply an excuse. We just have to wait, that's all. You know what he's like. Be patient. Trust me."

When she got back to the flat, after a very pleasant couple of hour's conversation, some of it promisingly suggestive, she found Taziel in the kitchen, holding the dish cloth to his nose, which was bleeding profusely. "Are you all right?" she asked.

Taziel growled at her and slouched into the living room. Aninka followed. "Taz? What happened?"

Taziel removed the cloth from his nose and inspected it. The bleeding seemed to have stopped, although the lower half of his face was covered in blood. Experimentally, he sniffed. "This is what happens," he said.

Aninka rushed to his side, squatted down on the floor beside his chair. "What? What?"

"When I try too hard." He reached for Aninka's hands, squeezed them. "I don't know why I did it."

"Did what?" Aninka dared not hope.

"I have a location for you," Taziel said. "Are you satisfied now?"

She had been visiting the cafe for over a week now. From there, she could keep an eye on the Moses Assembly Rooms. Lahash knew of the place; it was a refuge for Grigori burnouts and freaks. Perhaps the most clever hiding place Shemyaza could have thought of because it was just so obvious a place to look for him.

Just as she was beginning to doubt Shemyaza, or any of his companions, were actually there, the boy had come into the cafe. The moment she laid eyes on him, she'd known he was significant. His name was Daniel, the name of Shemyaza's vizier and prophet. Coincidence? Perhaps. The boy had been wary of her, she could tell. He had secrets, and had almost confessed to living at the Assembly Rooms. Working in a conference hall? No. Aninka had watched him leave the cafe and had stood in the side street as he made his way back there, disappearing down a side alley next to the Rooms. How to win his confidence? It would not be easy. He mustn't find out who she was, although she did not feel afraid. For some moments she had stood staring at the Assembly Room's blank windows. Was Shemyaza really in there? It seemed bizarre to think she might be so close to him.

Now, she had to tell Taz she had made contact. Standing in the doorway to the living room she said, "Stage one has been completed." It was difficult not to laugh. She felt elated.

Taziel looked up at her. "What happened?"

"Daniel happened," she replied. "At least I think so."

Chapter Four
The Scrying Pool

Meggie Penhaligon, her sisters of the Council around her, gazed into the lightless surface of the pool. It was situated behind the giant's throne in their sacred cave, and when the tide was high, it replenished the pool with fresh seawater.

The women were silent, waiting for information to manifest before their eyes. The only sound was the insistent tone of a brass spirit-bowl, which Lissie held in her lap. She made it resonate by stroking its inner surface in circling motions, using a pointed wooden stick. Its eerie note eclipsed even the echoes of the sea. All concentrated hard upon the flat, dark surface of the water.

Several days had passed since the oracle had delivered his prophecy. Meggie had allowed this knowledge to settle within their minds before making further attempts to discover more. Delmar was not present this evening. He had fulfilled his function; the rest was up to the women.

Meggie's eyes began to water, and her vision dimmed from the edges inwards; a black fog surrounded her, until all that she could see was the black glitter of the water. The tone of the spirit bowl filled her whole being, and the surface of the pool began to swirl. She saw colours, fragmented images. "Lady Seference, reveal to us the Fallen One." She had no doubt that her companions were also beginning to see shapes forming upon the surface of the pool. The images flared and died. Some were quite definite, others vague. Certain images clearly had nothing whatever to do with the work in hand, and were mere psychic intrusions.

Meggie saw Shemyaza's shining face, and the diffuse but penetrating glow of his startlingly blue eyes. She had to force herself not to look away. Even to someone as old as she was, he stirred a tide of lust and longing within the body. She saw figures hovering around him, and even began to determine names: Daniel—that was prominent, then Emma, Lily, and even the other boy, Owen. This was only slightly more than Delmar had relayed to them before.

What they needed to discover was how to lure the Shining One to Cornwall. Meggie tried to draw the veils of obscurity aside, project herself into the images before her. There was a link. She could see it now, as an image of the hated house, High Crag, shivered across the pool. The Pelleth knew that Grigori lived there, and it was close to their own village. Shemyaza would be enveloped by the Grigori families. Although this could be seen as an obstacle, it also meant that he would at least be brought to Cornwall. Once he was in the vicinity, the task of the Pelleth would be so much easier. Reassured, Meggie pulled herself back to reality, and around her, felt the other women follow her lead. But for one.

Tamara still stared intently into the pool, her brow creased. The towers of High Crag wavered within the rippling surface of the pool before her. She saw the long stretch of the gardens down to the cliff-top and there, on the crumbling lip of stone, stood her prince of light, with his feet curled dangerously over the very edge of the cliff. He was ready to fly. He would fly to *her*. She heard the siren song of the mer-women who haunted the cove below. They called to him in longing and desire, hungry for his beauty, for his pale, dry flesh. Tamara listened. Their song must become her song.

Yes, jump! Fly! Fall, my beautiful god! And I will lead you before the eyes of the slumbering one. Its serpent breath will make of me a goddess, and its power shall be ours! Together, we shall unleash it upon the world!

Then the tenuous form of a dark-haired woman rose up to command her visionary perception. This interloper reached out towards Tamara's golden chief upon the cliff-top.

Oh, such love, such grace. Will Seference herself come to claim him? No, not Seference. Another goddess. She is his. He knows her as his only female love. Who is she? Cannot see her face. I can only see yours, my sun king. The light of every beacon fire shines from your eyes.

Tamara sensed that the scent and power of the dark-haired woman hung all around him. He was intoxicated with her power. Tamara felt desperate. She had to find out who this female figure was. She had to see her face. But even as she strained her concentration, the images began to break up in the pool. Only the sound of bells remained. Tamara knew the bells belonged to the dark one; gentle chimes like those worn at the ankles of sacred dancers. As she stared at the pool, it regained its normal appearance of a hard and glassy surface, like a mirror. Tamara's own entranced face stared back at her. She felt a pain begin, somewhere behind her eyes.

Although all the other women had finished their scrying some minutes earlier, Meggie, out of politeness, waited for Tamara to return to normal consciousness at her own pace. Trance was not a thing to be interrupted. Tamara seemed to become aware that her sisters were all sitting staring at her. She was breathing heavily and her limbs were shaking. She glanced up at Meggie with quick eyes. For a moment, Meggie was unnerved. There was something in Tamara's expression she didn't like, some hint of excitement or truculence, that flared out of her eyes before she could smother it.

"We shall return to the house to discuss our findings," Meggie said, still holding Tamara with her eyes. The younger woman lowered her lashes, and there was a faint smile on her face as she rose to her feet.

Tom Penhaligon had prepared tea and hot food as usual, but there was a tense air around the kitchen table that night. Meggie did not feel hungry, even though the scones before her were fresh from the oven, exuding tendrils of delicious scent. She realised she would very much have liked to down a jug of Tom's cider rather than tea. What was wrong? Agatha fidgeted and kicked her chair, a sound which filled Meggie with irritation. Tamara's cheeks were faintly flushed along the bone. She had the look of a woman who nursed a secret, who had recently come from the bed of an illicit lover.

The women discussed what they had seen within the pool. Most had picked up the names again, and had glimpsed an image of High Crag, which seemed to confirm Shemyaza would either be drawn or taken there.

Tamara listened to the discussion, but added no comments of her own. In fact, she could not have spoken if she'd wanted to. She knew she had been the only one to see the future in the pool. No-one else had seen the beautiful Shemyaza poised upon the edge of a cliff, his golden hair flying back in the claws of the wind, the waves thundering beneath him. No-one had picked up the image of a woman superimposed over Shemyaza, a woman of indescribable beauty and power; a goddess. If the goddess withdrew from the Fallen One and hovered out over the ocean, he would walk from the edge of the cliff to reach her. This was important information. Tamara relived the things she had seen and felt the stirrings of love, lust and a desire for power churn within her. As usual, the Pelleth were being too cautious. They talked of drawing Shemyaza to them once he reached Cornwall, and seemed oblivious of the fact that, if he was in the nest of the Grigori, their task might not be easy. Still, their plans were irrelevant now. Tamara knew that Barbelo would be waiting for her at home, to hear all about what happened at the scrying pool. Then, they could begin to formulate their own plans.

Meggie was talking now of preparing certain ancient sites for the advent of the Shining One. "When he comes, he will awaken the serpent, and the sites must be primed to channel this power."

"Which sites?" Tamara asked. They had many to choose from.

Meggie glanced at her sharply. "The Giant's Bed, Ezekiel's Mount and Serpent's Bower at Enoch's Hall."

"Why not the Mermaid's Cove at High Crag?" Tamara's words conjured a stiff silence.

Meggie blinked at the woman. "As you know, High Crag is forbidden territory. It belongs to the Grigori, and the cove beneath it is no different."

Tamara shrugged. "True. Which is perhaps why we should claim it for our own."

Meggie smiled, but it was clear the smile did not come easily. "No." The word was final. Around the table, other members of the Conclave murmured agreement.

Tamara made a gesture. "It was just a thought." She took a sip of tea, feeling absolved. Her sisters had refused to listen to her ideas, but at least she'd made the suggestion.

After the Conclave had all gone home, Betsy and Meggie remained seated at the table. Tom came in and made them a fresh brew, before withdrawing discreetly to his parlour.

"I am concerned about Tamara," Meggie said. She wanted her sister's opinions.

"Hot and fiery," Betsy conceded. "She has a thirst on her."

"A thirst for power. I can't keep a rein on her."

Betsy heaved her rounded shoulders in a shrug. "Time will wear the edges off. The young ones are excited by the Fallen One, and his frequency affects them all. They'll be high-spirited nags for a while."

Meggie smiled. "I'm almost sad such feelings no longer affect me."

Betsy shook her head with a frown. "I'm not." She took a sip of tea.

Barbelo was waiting in Tamara's cottage, as Tamara had expected. She was sitting at the kitchen table reading a magazine. Next to her hand lay a talisman carved from serpentine; a double-headed serpent coiled around a staff. Even before she took off her coat, Tamara felt drawn to pick it up. Energy thrummed up her arms and she dropped the talisman quickly.

Barbelo directed a swift glance at her. "You must learn to hold it, for you will use it shortly."

Tamara rubbed her hands together. "What for?"

"To overcome the guardians at Mermaid's Cove."

Tamara felt a chill course through her belly. She wondered whether Barbelo was already aware of the conversation that had taken place at Meggie's house. A thread of unease wriggled through her, but she banished it firmly. "Why would I want to do that?"

Barbelo smiled up at her. "We must construct a thought-form there, which will attract the Shining One. A thought-form of a woman."

You know! Tamara thought. *You know everything already!* "I hardly think it's worth me telling you what happened tonight," she said, "seeing as you seem to be aware of everything I saw or said!"

Barbelo laughed. "Not everything," she replied.

"Who is the woman I saw in the pool?"

"Her name, I suspect, is Ishtahar," Barbelo answered. "Sit down, Tamara. You have much to learn this night."

Chapter Five
Stone-Scrying

Emma stood in the doorway, looking, as ever like a "forties film star. Her pose elegant, one hand held up beside her chin holding a cigarette, her rolls of dark hair, her red lips. She could have been anything between thirty and forty years old. She was nearly one hundred and fifty—a Grigori dependent, once left to rot by mentors who abandoned her, now restored to vitality by Shemyaza.

"If you're not going to do anything about yourself, at least do something about the boy," she said.

Shem was lazing on the sagging sofa, listlessly staring at the TV. If the set had possessed a remote control, Emma had no doubt he'd spend the entire day just flicking from channel to channel, absorbing nothing. She was beginning to feel out of her depth, what with trying to look out for the kids and keeping her senses alert for pursuit. She feared it greatly, having seen the shadowy figures who'd emerged onto the High Place back in Little Moor, just at the time she'd managed to drag Shemyaza away. Shem dismissed her anxieties. She had guessed he simply did not care what happened to him now.

"Which boy?" he asked her, without looking away from the screen.

"You know very well which boy," Emma responded. She marched into the room and positioned herself before the TV, forcing Shem to look at her. She didn't like what she saw in his face. He looked burned out. Perhaps she'd been mad to flee Little Moor with him. There were other Grigori here who could care for her needs now. Had the time come to free herself of him? She had a responsibility towards Lily and Owen, because she'd promised their mother she'd always take care of them, but this wreck? No. His apathy made her angry. It seemed so self-indulgent. "Owen," she said.

Shem looked away from her. "There's nothing I can do."

"I don't believe you. You made him like that, so I presume you can unmake him. You are the Great Shemyaza, after all."

Shem shook his head, smiling. "You make me sound like a TV magician. I'm not anything, Emma." He picked up a magazine and began to leaf through it.

"If you stopped feeling sorry for yourself, it might help," she suggested. "Have you been to see Owen?"

"You know that I haven't."

"Well, if you did, it might prick your conscience. He's lost his mind. I have to bathe him, dress him, feed him. Sometimes, he soils himself. It's disgusting. No-one should live like that. Don't you care what it might be doing to Lily and Daniel?"

"None of them are my responsibility," Shem answered. "Nothing you can say will change my mind. Peverel Othman damaged Owen, not me. I can barely remember it."

Emma did not believe these words. "Well, let me remind you then. One Thursday night, Owen disappeared into his room with you, and didn't wake up for twenty-four hours." She struck a pose. "Now, let me see, what happened next? Ah, you took him out to the woods with you on the Friday evening. He was like an automaton, drugged perhaps. For some reason, Owen felt compelled to rape his lover for you, whom you had considerately laid out for him in a similar drugged state. Of course, I may have been hallucinating, but I swear I saw demons that night, Shem, and an attempt at a ritual sacrifice. Now, I might be wrong, but I can't help feeling the condition of those kids *are* your responsibility. Daniel escaped with his mind intact because he's—well—Daniel. Lily's attempting to blot the whole thing out of her memory and Owen is catatonic. Didn't your goddess tell you to care for the children, Shem? Have you forgotten so quickly?"

Shemyaza had listened to her speech without reacting. Emma had hoped to provoke him, but appeared to have failed. "Not me," he said. "It wasn't me. I told you that."

"You can't go on like this," Emma said.

Shem shrugged. "I can't be what you or Daniel want me to be. I wish you'd both leave me alone."

Emma made an angry noise and stormed out of the room, to secrete herself in the shadowy kitchen areas in the basement, where she had made friends with whom she could drink tea and whisky all day. She liked the Grigori that lived in the Rooms, but felt unable to confide in any of them.

Left alone, Shem put his head on his knees and covered it with his arms. He wanted to weep but couldn't. If he only had some release, his mind might clear, he could feel alive again. Neither Emma or Daniel were aware of, or understood, his torment. In one cruel stroke, he had been given awareness, and although the memories of his life as Peverel Othman were diminished, those that remained were stark in his mind, like matte black figures on a white background. He couldn't help Owen, because he couldn't bear to face the boy. Also, to reverse the process, he'd have to touch Owen, and Shemyaza felt incapable of touching anyone now. Emma had tried once or twice when they'd first arrived at the Rooms, turning up in his bedroom in the middle of the night, clothed only in perfume. She had practised her art upon his flesh, but it had been as if he were paralysed. The thought of sex conjured murky, flickering memories of dark rituals he had performed, debasement, torture, unspeakable defilement of spirit and flesh. Despite his claims of indifference, he could not disassociate himself from those events. Part of Owen lived inside him, because he had stolen it. Only by giving it back could Owen be restored, but Shem was physically incapable of achieving that at present. He had forgotten how to give.

He knew how badly Daniel wanted him to express his potential as Shemyaza, but it was more than obstinacy and resentment that made it impossible. He felt that it was a mistake, he couldn't really be this thing of power. Shemyaza had been dead for thousands of years. He exhaled, long and slowly, and lowered himself down to the sofa, stretching out his limbs, seeking comfort from the yielding yet gritty cushions. He closed his eyes, and red and purple patterns pulsed across his mind; the interference of the TV screen, flickering unheeded in the corner of the room, or the colours of his own pain. His mind drifted, and thoughts swam across his consciousness like winged dreams. He descended into semi-trance states whenever he was left alone, and then it felt as if his life as he lived it now was simply a fantasy.

What right had the universe to plant the memories of that ancient, forgotten life and subsequent torturous death in his mind? He could no longer eat meat, because he could remember the smell of his own flesh burning. Sometimes, a poignant memory

would assail his mind, such as now, when his imagination flew
free. He would expect to open his eyes, not to the crumbling
decay of the Moses Assembly Rooms, but his ancient home, with
its cool, lofty chambers and swaying draperies, and the translucent pleats of incense on the air. At any moment, his old friend
and conspirator, Salamiel, might walk into the room, put his head
on one side and say, "Are you coming, then? She's waiting for
you." And there would be a message from Ishtahar in his hands;
a single sheaf of corn bound with ribbon, a wilting flower picked
from the corn-fields. Or perhaps dark-eyed Penemue, another of
the rebel cabal, would come to his chamber and fling himself on
the bed, saying, "Listen to this," and read out his poetry; shivering lines about Ishtahar and her sisters. They had held each other
once, Shemyaza and Penemue, in the perfumed opulence of
Shemyaza's palace. They had nuzzled each other's flesh and
whispered of the delights of human women, igniting their own
desire with expectation and the excitement of taking that which
was forbidden. Penemue had been innocent, wanting only to
share his words and the ability to shape them with his human
friends. For that, his people had killed him. Not for humankind
the art of writing; they must be kept as animals, uneducated. In
prison, Shemyaza had been brought word of how Penemue's lowland woman had been stabbed through the belly by a Serafim
guard. It had, of course, killed the baby, but she had lived. They
had done something worse to her afterwards, like taking her tongue
or her eyes, but thankfully Shem had forgotten the details. His
own Ishtahar had suffered, and legends spoke of how her tears of
grief had caused the Great Flood, but his people and hers had
realised she was special. They had not maimed her.

Memories of his past life flooded his mind now, but they
were intrusions. He did not want to own them, and pushed them
away, fighting off the dream-state that seemed to want to enfold him
with bittersweet recollections. He must stay conscious and refuse
the past admission into his life.

With a cry of frustrated pain, Shemyaza sat up on the sofa,
blinked at the TV ahead of him. Peverel Othman had been demonic
in his obsessions, but he had never experienced doubt or regret.
Shem yearned for that strength of indifference now.

Shem knew, in his heart, that Emma was probably right and
that someone *was* looking for him. It was inevitable, because the

Parzupheim were greedy for Shemyaza's power, or what they believed it to be. Only by refusing to accept what he had become could he hope to hide from them. It was impossible to conceal himself physically from Grigori adepts, he knew that, but if they came to believe they were wrong about him, they might leave him alone. He realised this was probably a futile hope, but if anyone was in danger, it was only himself. The Parzupheim wouldn't be interested in Emma or the others; they were insignificant.

Let them take me, he thought, raw with unshed tears. Let them destroy my body, break it and burn it. I owe them nothing. I will not be their scapegoat again and I will not *be* for them.

Lily Winter liked living in the Moses Assembly Rooms. The other occupants, who seemed to fill Daniel with apprehension and Emma with scorn, attracted her. At one time, the Rooms had been a gathering place of Grigori adepts, and perhaps strange rituals had taken place there. Certainly the multitude of bedrooms suggested that many people used to stay there; the servants quarters alone were huge. Since its hey-day in the Victorian age, it had declined and was now nothing more than a kind of hotel for Grigori who felt estranged from their people. Lily loved its fading grandeur and was fascinated by its eccentric inhabitants, who seemed to have nothing to do other than live out their own fantasies. Its caretaker—or perhaps owner, for the details were unclear—was lean Naomi, and it was from her that Lily had learned the Rooms' history. Naomi had a twisted leg and a stooped body, as if she'd suffered some terrible accident years before. This alone was unusual, because Lily had already learned that Grigori could heal their bodies far more efficiently than humans could. It was impossible to guess Naomi's age. She painted strange, ancient patterns on delicate silk, with which she adorned her body and the crumbling walls of her room. Lily spent a lot of time with Naomi who liked to be read aloud to as she worked on her patterns. Her taste in literature was eclectic; sometimes she wanted to hear humorous fantasy tales, other times heavy, depressing modern novels, written by women who seemed to have been punished by life.

Then there was Israel, whose skin was a soft, satiny purple-black. He came from a far Grigori family whose ancestors had been worshipped as demons in the dust and heat of a famished land. His people were very enclosed, he said, which was why he'd chosen to flee them. He had travelled much about the world and had seen many strange and disturbing things. For a while, to obey some facetious urge to mimic art, he'd lived as a vampire, although admitted he didn't much like the taste of blood. Israel possessed a beautiful, foreign, stringed instrument, which he took out onto the street and played. People threw him coins. Unlike some of the other residents of the building he did not appear to have recourse to his family's assets, although the others tended to share what they had without thought.

Money, Lily had quickly learned, was never a problem for Grigori, even the outcasts. They treated it without reverence. It was as vital to them as air, but just as easily obtained. Not for them the life-long love/hate affair with the demons of lucre, the humiliating entreaties and prayers of desperation, the draining offerings of time and energy for meagre rewards, spiced by the occasional god-like yet sardonic windfalls. Lily too had money—a legacy from her mother—but Emma had told her not to try withdrawing it from her account, because it would make her easier to trace. Naomi gave her money sometimes. "Do you want this?" Offering a crumpled twenty pound note, as if it was some little bauble she'd found and did not want to keep. Lily always took these presents, feeling that one day she might need them.

Her favourite new friend among the Grigori was Johcasta, although she was perhaps the most threatening. Johcasta had a sharp tongue and often resorted to slapping people if they annoyed her, which was often. But her fiery temperament, flashing and dashing about the dour halls and corridors of the Rooms, fascinated Lily. Also, she seemed to have taken a shine to the fey hybrid twin, and asked her questions about what it was like to be half human, half Grigori. Lily could not answer with any great honesty, for she had no comparisons to make, but she made up twisted feelings and dark angst, which seemed to satisfy her friend.

Johcasta's hair looked like gold wire, and glinted metallically in artificial light. She wore it tossed up on the top of her head, where it was loosely confined with tortoise-shell combs. This abundant shining mass reminded Lily of the hair on a doll she'd possessed as a child; unreal. She'd always wished it could be possible to have hair like that.

Johcasta made divining tools from many different materials. Once, in the green darkness of her room, where the windows were occluded by coloured blinds, Johcasta had held out her white hand to Lily. A spill of semi-precious stones lay there in the dry palm, gleaming dully. Johcasta cast them onto the floor, where a fringed cloth lay.

"This," said Johcasta, picking up a dark stone, "is Mevanya. See her green veins. She has great power, but her plans are always sabotaged by her jealousy, which is insane." She placed the stone in Lily's hand.

"And this pink crystal is Marmoset, the child of love. When he touches the red flank of Garibaster, the angry, he bleeds and love turns to hate."

Lily handled Marmoset; the stone felt warm to the touch.

"And here," said Johcasta, lifting a smooth tablet of turquoise, "is Fairuzi, a lady of protection. Evil eyes close in her presence and she drains the poison of Aglax, the black stone. Falling next to him, she drives his negative influence to sleep.

"Now look at this," said Johcasta, and put a piece of cold green stone into Lily's hand. "Mark her well, for it is the guardian, Zahtumuzgi, the Serpent Lady. Scorpions, snakes and bees do her bidding, as do the spider and the lizard, for good or ill."

Lily let the stones run through her fingers.

"There are more," said Johcasta, indicating the fringed cloth. "I will tell you their stories another time. Now gather them all and cast them, and I'll read you their messages."

Lily felt nervous of doing so. She was sure Garibaster, Aglax and the less clement aspect of Zahtumuzgi would gang up against her and pronounce evil omens. Still, she was equally nervous of Johcasta's displeasure, so threw the stones onto the cloth.

"Ah," said Johcasta, peering. She rested her hand on one raised knee and leaned forward to inspect the falling. "Zahtumuzgi stands alone, although her eyes are directed towards the Maiden stone, Melandra, the lapis lazuli, which represents yourself. But the sick lover, the androgynous pearl, rolls close behind you. He is Tarturophane, and his still, stagnant waters can drag you down."

Lily had a sinking feeling. "Is there anything good there?"

Johcasta laughed. "But of course, Aglax the black gives you his power of dark manipulation, while Marmoset lingers back, wondering whether Tarturophane will wither his feathers of love. But he will wait until the androgyne swims away on a river of tears. What seems to be drained of all hope will be restored."

"Oh," said Lily. She wasn't sure how good that sounded.

Johcasta carelessly gathered up the stones and jingled them loosely in her hand. "Each day brings a new falling. Don't be depressed. You're probably affected by some crisis within your group."

"Mm," Lily said, nodding glumly. She was thinking of her twin brother, Owen. Ever since they'd left Little Moor, he'd spoken little. The bright spark of his being was eclipsed by memories so dark they could only be repressed by catatonia. Peverel Othman had destroyed Owen and ruined his relationship with Daniel. Guilt afflicted Lily, because she knew she had assisted Othman. He had seduced her and she had loved him, but that was no excuse. His dextrous love-making had concealed the message "give me your brother", and she had willingly held Owen out to Othman, saying, "take him, take him, but still be mine!" Sacrifice, desire, lust and sin; Othman's heady cocktail of subtle demands. Daniel insisted that the dark presence of Peverel Othman was gone now, although Lily was not convinced of that. She had tried to talk to Emma, who simply told her that everything would sort itself out in its own time, but Lily could not stand seeing Owen as he was now. Avoiding the sight of him, she spent as much time as possible in the company of the other Grigori in the Rooms. Sometimes she wished Shem and the others would leave, so she could stay behind with her new friends. She could imagine herself drifting into their lifestyle so that her past life would become a blur in her mind. She wanted to sit all day and do things like Naomi and Johcasta did, hiding away from the world, half-existing, but safe.

One day, after she'd been in the Rooms for about two weeks, Israel asked her about her companions. They were walking down a dusty gallery, where lighter spaces on the yellowy walls showed where paintings had once hung. The windows that ran down one side, and overlooked the square, were cracked in the corners and dusty. When the wind blew, they rattled.

Israel padded light-footed beside her, taller than Lily by over a foot. "What are you doing here?" he enquired. His voice, like his body, was dark and velvety.

Lily shrugged. She wasn't surprised at the question, only at how long it had taken someone to ask it. "We have nowhere to go."

Israel sighed. "Such is often the case. The Grigori, Shem, is your father? And the woman, Emma, your mother?"

"That's right," Lily lied. She thought it best to.

"Dangerous," said Israel, "the mating of one kind with another. It is why you are estranged, of course."

"I expect so," Lily answered. "We lived in one place for a while, but it became...difficult."

Israel frowned. "The human boy, Daniel, is your half-brother?"

Lily thought it was all getting too convenient, so decided to tell a little truth, to lend authenticity to her story. "No, he was, is, my brother's lover."

"Your brother is unwell."

"Yes," said Lily. She hoped Israel wouldn't ask what his illness entailed. "I don't know what we're going to do," she said quickly, if a little lamely. "We can't stay here for ever."

"Your father is in trouble." Israel smiled widely. "Otherwise you wouldn't be here."

Lily grinned awkwardly, but did not answer. "I would like to stay here," she said, "but not with my family."

Israel didn't know who Shem was or what he represented. If she came out with the truth and said, "He is Shemyaza, *the* Shemyaza," Israel would laugh, and believe Shem's guardians had only called him that as a child because it was a powerful name. Many Grigori were named after the fallen ones. She had learned that her own father had possessed such a name: Kashday. She had never met him, nor had any hope of doing so. She presumed he was dead, perhaps reunited with her mother, a woman who had dared to love an angel.

In Little Moor, Lily had thought she was in love with Peverel Othman, only now the infection had left her. She felt empty of love, dried out; free but somehow melancholy because of it. Shem was beautiful, the ultimate desirable object, yet she could not love him. Whatever he was now, she knew too much of his past, the killing, the deceit and corruption. She could not feel sorry for Shemyaza now. He had made himself in his own image, a warped and bitter reflection. Daniel believed Shemyaza was some kind of messiah, but Lily could not share that belief. She admired Daniel's courage and tenacity, his determination to push and bully Shemyaza into *caring* about the world and his as yet unspecified destiny, but ultimately, she thought Daniel was wasting his time. If Shemyaza was so powerful, why didn't he do something about Owen?

It was only a short time ago that Lily and Owen had learned the truth about what they were, and who their father had been. All their lives, they had listened to their mother's various tall tales about the man who had loved her and either left her or died, depending on which story she was using. She had kept back the truth, which ironically would have been the most outrageous and least credible story of all. Kashday Murkaster had been Grigori, and his family had virtually owned the village of Little Moor for centuries. Twenty years ago, Helen had gone there to work for a local farmer, and had attracted the attention of Kashday. Inevitably, perhaps, they had become lovers, but once Helen learned the truth about Kashday, she had wanted to share his Grigori power. A ritual had been enacted, which had decimated the Murkasters, and dispersed the survivors. All that had been left was the old empty house, Long Eden, and a bank account full of money for Helen and her half-breed children. Lily and Owen might have never discovered what they were, but for the arrival in Little Moor of Peverel Othman. He had sniffed them out, prompting Emma, an old dependent of the Murkaster family, to reveal the truth to the twins. Emma had demanded back her lost youth from Othman, and he had apparently given it to her without question. Lily still didn't know how he'd done this, and shrank from asking, sensing the answer would not be pleasant. Since then, Emma had appointed herself as the twins' guardian. Lily wasn't sure what the woman thought of Shemyaza, but doubted she shared Daniel's view. Probably, to Emma, Shemyaza was simply a resource, like food or water. If forced into making a choice, she would undoubtedly choose him and discard the twins. Lily didn't care.

"Israel, where do you go when you go out at night?" Lily asked. They had come to the end of the gallery. She wanted to ask him to take her with him some time.

Israel chuckled. "Nowhere, child, you would want to see."

"How do you know that?" Lily snapped. She did not like being referred to as a child.

Israel shrugged. "You are sweet," he said, which could have meant anything.

Lily sighed. She wasn't bored, because she spent most evenings with either Johcasta or Naomi, or else watching TV with Emma and Daniel, but she wanted to become part of the Grigori's lives in this place. She wanted to become strange, and wear eccentric clothes, do something unusual to her body or hair, smile like a cat.

"What would your parents think?" Israel said, and a certain tone in his voice suggested he didn't believe her story at all.

Chapter Six
Chaining the Maiden

Tamara walked the coastal path that rose from the village and snaked high above the sea. The sun was a watery halo over the dark surge of the waves and the nipping wind snatched at Tamara's long coat. The brightness of the day was unseasonal, and served only to illuminate the bleakness of the winter land, the greys, duns and muddy greens of sleeping verdure. Tamara knew that today Delmar Tremayne was not in school. She had meditated on his whereabouts only an hour earlier and discovered he was down at the shore in Quoit's Cove, grubbing through the rock-pools. Often he took Agatha with him on these forays, but today he was alone. It was almost as if Tamara had planned the whole thing, but if anything was working for her, it was synchronicity.

She made her way down the steep path, pausing to watch the boy who was sitting on the sand, his straightened legs pointing towards the waves. His hair blew around his head and shoulders, spray-dampened into weedy tendrils. Delmar was sea-born and fey, having spent too much time attuned to the goddess Seference; he seemed hardly conscious of reality. Tamara wondered how he coped among people his own age. Not every Cornish youth was aware of the strange and magical things that went on around them, and those that weren't must consider Delmar very peculiar.

She came up behind him. "Del!"

For a moment, he made no movement and then turned his head slowly towards her, fixing her with his wide, green eyes. "Hello, Tamara." Sometimes, it sounded as if words of the human language came with difficulty to his lips.

She squatted down beside him. "Will you come with me to the sacred cave?" She knew there was no point in trying to explain to Delmar what she wanted from him. Neither did she have to ask for his silence. He spoke only when spoken to, and would offer no information voluntarily to the other Pelleth.

The boy looked at her steadily, then said, "All right."

They went there in silence, for Delmar was not a person who could make light conversation. As the tide was out, they walked across the sands, climbing over rocks when necessary to reach the further coves. Tamara kept close to the cliff as they approached the Penhaligon beach. Far across the bay, miles distant, she could see the long chimneys of High Crag rearing against the clear sky. Soon, she would creep to their private cove, but first certain preparations had to be made.

Delmar ran into the cave ahead of her, as if returning to a home he loved and had missed. He jumped up onto the giant's chair and squatted there, grinning. Tamara smiled at him. The light was very dim, as no candles or lanterns were lit. The stone chair gleamed dark and wet in the gloom and the air was cold and damp against the skin. "Come, Delmar." Tamara beckoned the boy towards the scrying pool, which appeared like a puddle of black ink in the darkness beyond the chair. Delmar hunkered down on the lip of the pool and reached down with his thin hands to scoop up the water and throw it over his face. He was like a mer-boy, yearning for the touch of the sea.

Tamara settled herself down opposite him, and gestured at the pool. "Scry for me, Del. Look for the Fallen One and the lady associated with him."

Delmar scratched his head and then leaned right out over the pool, extending his neck like a snake or a cat. The ends of his hair dipped into the water, causing delicate ripples to spiral out. Tamara could scry herself, but she knew Delmar's unfettered psyche could probably achieve far more in a much shorter time. Also, she knew she needed more specific information about Shemyaza's woman. Being female, and too drawn to Shemyaza, she could not get close to the female image at the scrying pool.

As he stared at the water, Delmar became still, his whole body concentrating on what might come through to him. Tamara did not bother to focus on the pool; she watched the boy.

"He is very handsome," Delmar said at last.

"Yes," Tamara agreed. "What's he doing?"

"He's just sitting on a bed in a horrible room. He's not doing much at all. He's sad. He's very sad." Delmar frowned in empathy.

"Look into him, Del," Tamara instructed. "Find the woman inside him. Tell me her name."

Delmar concentrated for a full two minutes without speaking, which seemed like an age to Tamara. Eventually, he said, "Ishtahar."

"Good." Tamara was satisfied. Barbelo had already mentioned this name and explained that Ishtahar would be important in their plans, but Tamara had wanted to make sure she was telling the truth. The name Ishtahar was not totally unknown to her. The Pelleth called her Ishtara, or Isatar, but basically, she was the original temptress, who had lured Shemyaza away from his people, thereby instigating the Fall from grace. However, she had never figured greatly in the lore of the Pelleth. Had they made a mistake in under-estimating her significance now? "Can you see her face?" Tamara asked.

Delmar turned his head from side to side, inquisitively, like a monkey. "Yes. She's pulled back her veil to me. It's made of gold disks. I can see a big eye painted upon her belly."

Tamara was pleased. This meant Delmar could visualise Ishtahar with ease, and thereby expedite her work. She reached out to touch his face. "Thank you, Del. Now, I want you to do something more for me."

He nodded. "OK."

"Meet me tonight, at seven o'clock by the crossroads on the Hill Road. Will you remember that? I'll pick you up in my car."

Delmar nodded again, although Tamara could see he was slightly perplexed by her request. Normally, the Pelleth would only bring him to the sacred cave.

"There's something I need you to help me with. It's very important, but you mustn't tell anyone about it. Not even Agatha. Do you understand?"

Again, a sombre and uncertain nod.

Tamara ran her hand through his hair. "Don't worry, Del. I'm not asking you to do anything bad. We'll be helping Meggie and the others. It's going to be a surprise for them. That's why it's a secret."

His face brightened a little. "All right. Seven o'clock."

Tamara spent a full hour preparing herself for the ritual to come. She bathed herself in salt water, and daubed her body with protective oil. In her bedroom, she picked up from her dressing table the talisman Barbelo had given her and ran her fingers over the worn, carved contours of the double snakes. At first, the lively vibrations emanating from the talisman were almost unbearable to her, but she forced herself to hold onto it. After a few minutes, the furious, writhing energy that crawled like electricity up her arms abated to nothing more than a slight tingling sensation in her fingers. Barbelo had told her that the talisman was incredibly ancient, and had been fashioned by a member of a priesthood known as the Magians, who had been exiled from ancient Persia. The rites that the Magians had developed to enable them to use the earth energy, or serpent power, was now called magic; the word itself derived from their name. The double snake was their symbol. They had called it the Shamir, and it represented the duality of the serpent power: black magic, white magic, good, evil, truth and lies. The potential for both existed within the reach of humanity's will and life force. Tamara knew that Barbelo's people had been utilising this natural life force for millennia, and now a great source of that force lay slumbering within the earth, ready to be reawakened. Tamara gazed at the talisman, wondering whether it would make magic for her. She breathed deeply and felt the stone in her hands respond, grow hot. She began to visualise a white light seeping out of it, which rose like a veil towards her face and around her body. She wanted to create a caul of invisibility around herself, so that she wouldn't be observed about her work by those with the sight to see. The misty breath of the talisman enveloped her body and aura with its subtle vibration. She could feel its effect, almost as if her body had become lighter and insubstantial. It was almost too easy. How fortunate she was to have access to Grigori magic.

"Now, great Shamir," she said aloud, using the Grigori name for the serpent power that Barbelo had taught her. "Tell me what I must do to chain a maiden."

Images flowed into her mind. She saw her Pawnee shaman, at the time when he had taught her how to create spirit images, which the Pelleth called thought-forms.

She saw the shaman's dextrous fingers creating totems, winding coloured thread around tiny wooden stakes. Before him, on a mat upon the ground, lay a scattering of feathers and brightly-coloured beads. Once these were added to the totem, he would paint primitive features upon it. Then he would say to the girl, Tamara, "Now child, breathe upon it, give it life. It is easy for you. You are a woman, and women have the gift of creating life. Come on, now.

Create me a spirit." And she had done as he'd instructed, yearning for the approval in his old eyes.

Snapped back to the present moment, Tamara thought, Yes, a totem, but of what?

The image of the tattooed eye upon Ishtahar's belly flashed strongly within her mind. As she concentrated upon it, the eye gradually transformed into the shape of a large cowry shell, with the thunder of the sea roaring secretly within it. The cowry shell was an ancient symbol of the Watchers' eyes. It was perfect.

Tamara lifted the talisman up before her face. "Shamir, I thank you for these images." She smiled. "And did you know that I happen to have just such a shell in my possession?"

Once she was ready to leave the cottage, Tamara summoned the flame of her inner strength to glow brightly within her, then, using the talisman, folded herself within the caul of invisibility, as she'd practised earlier.

The clear day had been eclipsed by a cold, rainy evening. Wind turned the lances of the rain to blades. Tamara dressed herself in a dark robe, over which she threw a heavy, winter coat with a hood. She did not want to use light or incense, which might attract attention, but put handfuls of certain herbs into a leather pouch. There was camomile, rosemary and agnus castus, which were the plants associated with the female form, love and gentle strength. Then, there was henbane and mandrake to create the dusky, sexual power required to attract her golden prince; blackberry for the dark sweetness of her essence; rowan to create the illusion of a seeress and finally black ash, the plant of the water serpent. These ingredients she secreted, along with the cowry shell, into the deep pocket of her coat. Just before she was about to leave her cottage, the phone rang. Tamara stared at it for a moment, wondering whether to leave it ringing. Then she picked it up. Her flesh prickled with cold when she heard Meggie Penhaligon's voice at the other end of the line, although she forced her voice to remain cheerful and friendly. Meggie had rung to arrange a meeting of the Conclave for the following evening. It had to be coincidence she had called at this time, although Tamara did not underestimate the older woman's abilities, which was why she'd taken so many precautions in veiling her intentions.

Finally, she managed to end the conversation and dash out through the rain to her car. She would be a few minutes late for Delmar now, and hoped he hadn't wandered off, thinking she wasn't coming.

Her headlights picked him up at the cross-roads. He wasn't wearing a coat and was already soaked to the skin, but then cold and wet never seemed to bother Delmar. Tamara leaned over and opened the passenger's door. "Get in."

Delmar slithered into the seat like something that had crawled up off the beach. He shook his hair and sprayed her with freezing droplets.

They drove along the coast road, following the curve of several coves. The road ran close to the cliff edge here, and occasionally, there were lay-bys where tourists could pause to take in the sights or eat picnics. Tamara swung her car onto one of these and turned off the engine. A few hundred yards up the road, the imposing bulk of High Crag was visible above the boundary walls of its grounds. Lights could be seen in many of the upper windows. It looked almost as if a party was going on. Tamara was fascinated by the house and its occupants. Did Barbelo live there? The woman had not deigned to reveal that information to her, but now Tamara wondered whether Barbelo was standing at one of the lit windows, her sharp sight focused upon them. Delmar stared at the house, as a rabbit, frozen in the road, might stare at the headlights of an approaching lorry. Tamara didn't bother to comment on his obvious unease. If there were problems to come, she would deal with them when they occurred. She leaned across in front of the boy and removed a powerful torch from the glove compartment. "Come on, Del. Let's get going."

She managed to coax him out of the car, so she could lock its doors. The climb down to the beach would be tortuous, but she trusted that Seference would help them find a way. Delmar was sacrosanct; the elements and the land would not harm him until the time came when, with due ceremony, he would be given to them for eternity. The boy paused at the cliff edge, and Tamara could see he was shivering.

"We must not go here," he said. "It is forbidden."

Tamara shone her torch along the edge of the cliff. She knew there were a few narrow tracks that led down to the beach around here. "Don't worry about it, Del. We'll be safe. It's important we do this." She took his arm, and reluctantly he allowed her to lead him.

Once negotiating the cliff, some of Delmar's apprehension seemed to evaporate. He clambered down and across, leaping and scrambling, reaching back to assist Tamara over the trickiest areas. They came across dilapidated wooden signs that read: "Private" and "No Trespassing". This was Grigori land, and guardians had been placed around the cliff path to deter sightseers and those who might deliberately seek access to their domain. The guardians might toss any persistent interlopers off the cliff, although Tamara had no fear they would alert their Grigori masters. Barbelo had told her the serpent talisman would easily control the guardians. They would believe that Tamara and Delmar had a right to be at the cove. Thinking of this, and not totally confident it would work, Tamara withdrew the talisman from her pocket. She must be strong and have faith in her Grigori friend. Almost at the same time, Delmar uttered a frightened yelp and crouched down on the path ahead of her. Tamara shuddered; a vague form was taking shape before her eyes. To untrained eyes, it would be invisible, but to psychics and those who had learned how to see beyond reality, its presence seemed very real indeed. As it solidified, she could see it was a lizard creature, disturbingly human in appearance. Its eyes glowed red and its black-clawed, delicate hands gripped the slick serpentine of the cliff-face. Tamara held out the talisman, and uttered an incantation. The guardian hissed at her and made a sudden movement, as if about to pounce forward. Tamara cringed, but held her ground. Delmar scuttled back to her and hid his head in her robes, whining. Firmly, Tamara repeated the incantation and took a few steps forward, pushing Delmar ahead of her. The boy cried out in fear, but she ignored him and even kicked him to get him to move. Another lizard form dropped down from the cliff behind her. She could feel the heat of its steaming breath on her back, through her robe and coat. Only her faith in Barbelo's magic could protect her now. The guardian ahead of her put its head on one side inquisitively, one eye trained on the talisman in her outstretched hand. Tamara felt something tug at her robe and wheeled round, finding herself face to face with a lizard-man who was over eight feel tall. It raised a ruff of spines and scaly skin, hissed at her, and put out its long black tongue to lick her wrist. But it did not attempt to attack her. Tamara forced any feeling of terror back into the depths of her mind. If these creatures sensed she was afraid, she and Delmar were doomed. Gradually, she pressed forward until she was up against the first guardian. It would not move aside. Mustering all her strength, she reached out to touch it with the talisman and with raised ruff the creature leapt nimbly upwards to perch on a ledge above her head. Tamara bowed respectfully. "I thank you for granting us passage." Then she grabbed Delmar by the scruff of the neck and virtually threw him down the path ahead of her, onto the beach.

Tamara could feel the power oozing from stones of the cove. The cliffs and the surrounding rocks were all of pure serpentine. In daylight, they would be red, gold and green, but at night, the stone appeared densely black. The rocks seemed to be full of giant faces, grimacing out upon the night. Delmar stood trembling upon the windlashed beach. The house was not visible from here for the cliff overhung the shore. The black ovals of cave entrances could be seen; places where the Grigori undoubtedly conducted their own rituals at certain times of year. Tamara would have liked to explore these places, but knew that time was short. She must conduct her work and hurry away. Lingering too long might alert the Grigori to her presence.

She crouched down upon the sand and removed from her coat pocket the pouch of herbs. Hastily, she broke the contents into small pieces and placed them within the hollow of the cowry shell. Then, without hesitation, she picked up a sharp stone from the beach and made a shallow cut across her wrist. Delmar uttered a sound of distress at the sight of her blood. He was clearly unfamiliar with some of the more gruesome magical practices, and remained rigid and staring as Tamara squeezed a few drops of blood into the cowry shell. This accomplished, she spat onto the mixture, then finally added some sea-water gathered from a nearby rock-pool. Slowly, still crouching down, she began to agitate the mixture within the shell, making it move in a spiral. After a few moments, she leapt suddenly to her feet. Delmar whimpered and cringed away from her. Tamara ignored his fear. She held the shell before her, her spine erect, her hair blowing around her face from beneath her hood. "Now, Del! Send the image of Ishtahar to me!"

His jumpiness and fright were beginning to annoy her, although she could tell he was trying to overcome these feelings, so that he could concentrate on her request. His instinct now was to obey her.

"We are safe now," she told him. "Just relax. No-one knows we're here."

He nodded, although he still looked terrified. Tamara closed her eyes. Soon, the image came through, the figure of a woman, clad in blue veils, which curled around her body like smoke. Her ears and neck were hung with heavy gold jewellery and her eyes were painted thickly with kohl in the Egyptian fashion. Tamara visualised this figure standing upon the beach directly in front of her. Then she opened her eyes and, holding the cowry shell aloft, poured the potent libation around them in a small, tight circle, all the while chanting in a guttural whisper: "Sitar, Ishtahar, Abdur Sitar, Ashur Sitar, Ishtahar." She spiralled lithely around the circle, each step executed with the purpose and precision of a trained dancer. Then she halted in the centre of the circle and poured the residue of the libation onto the sand, breathing heavily. Gripping the shell in one hand, she held out the talisman in the other, and willed the carved serpents to release their breath, so that the form of Ishtahar could take shape within it. Within her grasp, the talisman began to grow hot. Fine, snaky fronds of smoking energy rose up from the serpents' open mouths and slowly crept upon the air, until they found the serrated folds of the cowry shell and slipped within it.

Satisfied her intentions were taking effect, Tamara asked Delmar to dig a hole in the sand between them. She sat down opposite him, and watched his fingers scrabbling away, until he had dug down for about eighteen inches. Then she placed the shell in the hole, and together she and Delmar filled it in once more. There would be no outward sign that the shell was buried there. The tide would wash away all signs of their libation. If Tamara wanted to remove the shell, she would have to use psychic means to locate it. She reached for Delmar's gritty hands, and instructed him to meditate further on the image of Shemyaza's woman. Tamara was unnerved by the thought of closing her eyes for the meditation. Her heart had begun to beat quickly; she would not be sorry to leave this place.

A sudden gust of wind blew Tamara's hood back from her head and sprayed her hair across her face in stinging tendrils. She heard the howl and roar of sea grow momentarily furious and wild, and could not help opening her eyes quickly, convinced that an enormous wave was about to crash down upon her. But the sea was merely restless and seething, its waves lashing fretfully at least twenty yards from where they sat.

"Come Del, we must leave." She was on her feet in an instant, the flesh along her spine crawling in apprehension. The knowledge that she would have to empower the thought-form of Ishtahar a few more times yet did not please her. It wouldn't be so bad if they could work by daylight, but the risks attached to that were too great.

On the climb back up the cliff, Tamara felt the guardians' presence around them. Their clawed, spectral fingers reached for her coat as she struggled and scrabbled on the treacherous path. Delmar uttered a monotonous keening sound, and by the time they crawled back onto the concrete surface of the lay-by, he was twitching and gibbering like a lunatic. Tamara had never seen a person so afraid. Now that the deed was done, she herself felt light-headed and disorientated with shock and fear. They had dared to invade Grigori territory! Her unease was blended with a sense of triumph. With shaking fingers, she unlocked the car and bundled Delmar into the passenger seat. She dared not look back over her shoulder as she threw herself in through the driver's door. Her car skidded on the tarmac as she turned it back onto the Hill Road. Delmar had put his face in his hands. When the lights of the village were visible below them, Tamara reached out and pressed her cold fingers on the back of the boy's neck.

"Hush," she soothed. "It's over."

For now.

Chapter Seven
Dream Talking

On the day following her initial meeting with Daniel, Aninka arrived at the cafe near Red Lion Square very early, around six-thirty in the morning, convinced the boy would call in again. She sat there all the way through until nine, earning suspicious looks off the waitress. Perhaps her tension was evident in her posture. Had she frightened Daniel off the previous morning? She couldn't remember saying anything too pushy or interrogative, but the boy was psychic, after all. Perhaps he'd guessed who and what she was, and Shemyaza and the others had already fled the Assembly Rooms.

Standing at the threshold of the cafe, Aninka considered walking boldly up to the main entrance of the Assembly Rooms, and simply knocking on the door. Shemyaza *knew* her, she had been his lover. Would he attack her now? It was impossible to guess his state of mind. She kept reminding herself that Peverel Othman was no more. What lived in his body now was alien and ancient, and perhaps would not even recognise her.

Back at the flat, she confided her fears to Taziel. "Have we missed our chance?"

He scoffed at her question. "I wouldn't put it that way. If Shemyaza has fled London, it's a narrow escape for us, if anything."

"Can you tell if he's still around?" Aninka sprawled on the sofa and lit a cigarette.

Taziel shrugged. "I think so. I don't think Daniel guessed who you were, otherwise I'm sure there would have been more..." he grinned, "...*impact*."

"What do you mean?" Aninka asked stiffly.

"The Anakim would have had us," he answered shortly, then grimaced. "Perhaps a gentle prod or two won't go amiss. I'll see what I can do."

"Gentle prod?" Aninka sounded unsure.

"Perhaps your friend Daniel needs to be reminded it's a good idea to get out of the house now and again."

Daniel had in fact thought about going to the cafe again that morning, but had decided against it at the last moment. It was mainly inspired by a fear that his new friend Eve would not be there. As he'd roamed the house in the grey pre-dawn, he'd come across Lily, barefoot and wraith-like. It was as if they hadn't seen one another for years, but it had been only two days. She asked if he'd been to see Owen at all, to which Daniel had to reply that he hadn't. Lily obviously felt they should talk and insisted on dragging him to Naomi's room with her, where the hours sped by as they sat around drinking tea and chatting. He realised how easy it would be to end up frittering away his life in this place.

Daniel went to bed early, feeling lethargic and bored, unable to think of anything interesting to do. He tossed and turned for what seemed like hours on his lumpy mattress. Noises from outside intruded into his dreams, calling him to wakefulness, ordering him to sleep. He awoke, or thought he did, to sense a presence in the room. This was not unusual in the Assembly Rooms; it had already happened to him several times, and on each occasion, he'd ignored the visitor and returned to sleep. Awareness of presences was something he'd lived with all his life; it did not unnerve him particularly. But this time, as he turned his back against the darkness between himself and the blanketed window, his spine crawled with unease. He resisted the urge to turn over and open his eyes, willing himself to relax.

There was a pressure on the bed.

Daniel was alert instantly. It felt as if someone had sat down beside him. He froze, wondering whether another member of the household had crept into the room without him hearing, although in his heart he sensed this was not the explanation. The presence was not corporeal, but was it threatening or not? In his mind, Daniel conjured a glowing caul of protection around himself, a cocoon of light. He formed a silent question. *"What do you want?"* There was no immediate response, although he sensed a quickening of interest behind him, and an intensifying of the pressure against his protective ether as if a hand was pressed against it. He sensed the presence did not intend him harm. Reassured, he turned over, but could see nothing in the faint light seeping between the ragged curtains. He closed his eyes, willing an image to form in his mind. *"Who are you?"* The Assembly Rooms might be haunted by dozens of spirits. Perhaps one of them had homed in on him. He felt very calm.

Without warning, a rush of sensation assaulted Daniel's mind and body. He felt as if he'd been caught up in powerful arms, held against a body of light and cloud, absorbed by it. He was flooded by a hungry desire and an awareness of heat and strength. His breath came out in a gasp of pleasure and shock. At first, he thought it must be Shem, giving in to the urge for contact, but nothing about this entity was redolent of Shemyaza. Neither was it a ghost. He could sense, however, that it was male; a tall Grigori, eager with need. Daniel opened his eyes and the air was full of blue sparks. He felt he was suspended a foot above the bed, gripped in the invisible arms.

The sensation fled as quickly as it had come. Daniel found himself panting and gasping upon the bed, gazing up into a spiralling void that was closing in on itself even as he looked at it. Whoever had come to him had vanished. Daniel sat up. Who had it been, and why had they come? He had seen nothing physical, but felt sure he would recognise the visitor's face should he ever find it.

He got out of bed and walked over the window, looked out over the square. He didn't know what he expected to see.

In the shadow of the trees, standing against the railing was a line of dark shapes. He could make out no detail of their features or clothing, only that they were very tall.

Daniel let the curtain fall back. His first instinct was to go and tell Shem what he'd seen and experienced, or perhaps Emma, but as nothing had threatened him, it seemed like more paranoia. Emma would leap on it, and Shem would scoff. Easier to remain quiet. Sighing, he went back to his bed and crawled under the duvet. Perhaps the visitor had been nothing more than a manifestation of his own desires. His body throbbed with a need to be held close by enfolding arms. His lips burned because no other lips pressed against them. A fierce and reckless thought sped through his mind: he wanted freedom, the liberty to explore the world and find himself a lover, someone who, at the very least, was aware of his existence. Owen was dead to him. Strange how easy it was to think that, now. Almost comforting. Daniel turned onto his side and closed his eyes.

In the dream, Daniel opened his eyes to find that he floated upon calm water. Moonlight fell down upon his naked body and the sea-perfumed air was warm against his skin. In the distance, he could hear a call, like whale-song. He bobbed upon the thick waters, utterly relaxed. The shore was about a mile away; he could see rugged cliffs, which reminded him of the Cornish coast, where he had spent summers as a child. He turned over, wallowing in the womb-like waters, and saw a shape against the moon, a tall, sinuous figure walking upon the moonlit water towards him. A woman. Even though the light was behind her, he could discern her features, for it seemed as if she was full of a soft cerulean shimmer, which radiated out from her. She was beautiful, clad in wafting blue veils and her long dark hair seethed around her head as if she were underwater. Upon her belly, visible through the veils, was the image of an enormous eye. He realised then that he knew her. It was the goddess who had appeared to them at the High Place in Little Moor on that fateful last night. Shem's woman. "Ishtahar!" At the sound of the name, she held a slender finger to her lips in a request for silence.

Daniel dog-paddled in the water, trying to reach her. She was walking towards him, but seemed to draw no closer. "Ishtahar, I need your help!"

She was still smiling, her long, graceful feet dancing upon the moonlit waves.

"Ishtahar, Shemyaza will not listen to me. He will not *become*. Help me."

She paused. "Daniel, beloved, I am powerless to affect the destiny of the divine in flesh. The time of resurrection is at hand. I can only lament for the loss of his light but I am she who is eternally with you."

"But what can I do?"

"Swim to shore." With these words, she vanished, and there was only white moonlight falling on his face where once her shadow had hung.

Daniel woke up, dazzled by moonlight, yet none fell into the room. Without pausing to think, he struggled into a T-shirt and hurried from his room. He could no longer keep silent. Not now!

He entered Shemyaza's room without knocking. Shem lay asleep, half in, half out of the bed, his long, pale limbs illumined by the flickering colours emanating from the silent TV. Daniel paused, momentarily taken aback. Shem looked so vulnerable lying there. He could be killed so easily. Daniel padded softly towards the bed, wondering how close he could get before Shem woke up. Before he was within three feet of the trailing duvet, Shem cast it back and said, "Are you frightened? Are you cold? Get in."

Daniel was neither of these things, but slipped into the hot nest. He wondered why Shem's reserves were down tonight. Normally, he would let none of them get so close. Daniel decided not to question this matter, for fear of invoking Shem's distancing cold. He put an arm around Shem's body, and conjured no rebuff. Shem merely sighed deeply, lying on his back.

"I had a dream," Daniel said.

"Only that?" Shem reached out and stroked his hair. "I never dream now."

"I saw her, Shem. I saw Ishtahar." He felt Shemyaza's arms stiffen, the slight sense of withdrawal.

"It was just a dream. Forget it."

"I can't. I think it was important. I was floating in the sea. I think it was Cornwall, and she walked towards me across the water. She told me to swim to the shore. But I woke up."

"There is no Ishtahar," Shemyaza said. "She's dead. Dead and gone a long time ago. Whereas you...my faithful Daniel, you have followed me across the deserts of time, kept at my heels, remained faithful in life and death. And here you are now. Where is the woman? Gone." He leaned over Daniel in the bed, and Daniel was flooded with a sense of remembrance, from a life long past. He could almost smell the incense and the clear air of the forgotten country. It was springtime, and the air was balmy. Ishtahar lay in the future, an undreamed-of threat. He closed his eyes, waiting for the kiss, the long-fingered hand upon his waist, but it did not come. Shemyaza sighed and lay back down. Daniel sat up and found himself looking at a fierce grin.

"I am castrated by my own delinquencies," Shem said. "Not even with you can I overcome them. The thought even of a kiss turns my stomach, yet you are a lovely creature."

Daniel lay down with his head upon Shem's chest. He curled his fingers in the long strands of pale hair that lay there, damp against the skin. "Just sleep," he said. "It doesn't matter." In his heart, he knew that it did. Impotency was just another part of the murky hinterland that was once the light of his soul.

Shemyaza lay awake for a long time, staring at the ceiling. He suppressed any thought of Ishtahar, and tried to concentrate on the lithe, young body against him. Why couldn't he find succour in communion of the flesh? At one time, it had been his gift to humanity, and theirs to him. Now, he was empty of feeling and could not even draw comfort from the warmth of arms around him. Brief, tantalising images surfaced in his mind: Ishtahar's laughter ringing out, the smell of corn, the fierce heat of the sun against his naked skin. He pushed these memories back down into the deepest recesses of his brain. Then came the unbidden recollection of the original Daniel; their heat, their oiled bodies sliding against one another in the perfumed shadows of the great, cool house, which once had been home. *Why can't I recapture that now in reality?*

He ran his hand down Daniel's sleeping flank, and in his memory felt a surge of lust, but in the present moment, felt nothing. Fretfully, he rolled Daniel onto his back and pressed his lips against Daniel's own, but it was like putting his mouth against yielding cloth. There was no exchange of feeling. Daniel murmured in his sleep and frowned, then rolled onto his side. Shemyaza watched him for a moment, then lay back down, his arms behind his head. If this was the way it was to be, he could do nothing about it. His head ached with the desire to recapture sleep, and slowly, fitfully, it came to him.

She was waiting there for him, beyond the threshold of wakefulness: a young woman, dark of skin and hair, robed in blue, with small gold beads chinking in her braided hair. She sat upon a shingled beach, her slim, brown arms encircling her raised knees. The froth-cuffed waves lapped at her bare toes. Bright sunlight gleamed against her skin. Ishtahar: as lovely as a man could imagine or a woman could fear. As she saw Shemyaza walking towards her, she raised a hand in casual greeting and smiled.

He did not return the signal, afraid she would disappear or mutate into something hideous the moment he acknowledged her. Still, her image did not flicker or fade as he drew near. She appeared to be as relaxed as if they'd only recently parted and this was a planned meeting.

Shemyaza cast his shadow over her. He could smell a musky scent emanating from her body, and the languorous curves of her limbs murmured to him in a silent language of sensual promise. She was a witch, like a drug, a poison. His whole body ached at the sight of her.

"Hello, Shem," she said. "How are you?"

He sensed amusement behind her words, or perhaps, even now, it was bitterness.

"I am broken, but I'd have thought you'd know this. Why torment me?"

She squinted up at him, shielding her black-rimmed eyes with one henna-patterned hand. "You speak of torment? Ah, the selfishness of men! Can't you think of anyone's anguish but your own?"

He sighed impatiently. "Is this why I am here? For you to scold me?" He thought to himself: I am dreaming, and this vision is my own creation.

Ishtahar, however, seemed oblivious to the fact she might not be real. "Scold you?" She uttered an indignant sound. "Can't you stop for a moment, and consider *my* torment? You dwell in the realm of flesh, and walk upon the breast and body of the earth. Your light is hers to absorb. Yet, where am I? Nowhere and everywhere. Oh, I can tell you of torment!" She leaned back on straight arms, gazing out to sea.

Shemyaza hunkered down beside her. He wanted to speak, yet there were too many words in his head to choose from. Most of them seemed inappropriate.

Perhaps taking his silence as contrition, Ishtahar spoke again. "I have had an eternity to ponder our time together. Sometimes I used to wonder what it all meant, but that was when I still had flesh about my soul. You were taken from me by the war that your angry heart waged against your brethren, supposedly for the enlightenment of my *primitive* people. What was I meant to feel about that? Serenity? Acceptance?" She shook her head, and the gold beads flew around her. "I hated the world for the sacrifice it had demanded. I hated my captors, who called themselves guardians. They told me my tears created a flood to purge the world of sin and blame, but I was purged of nothing. All of it remained inside me, heavy like a child that would not be born." She sighed deeply. "Now, beyond life, I have been made a goddess, and my grief is eternal. I did not ask for what happened after I met you. Perhaps I was wrong to lie with you; perhaps we were both foolish to believe it would have no repercussions. I was simply a woman in love, who had no idea what tragedies that love would spawn."

There was a silence, then Shem said, "I should not have come to you then. Now, I wish I hadn't."

Ishtahar laughed coldly. "Oh, but what a different place your world of men would be if you had not!"

Shem grimaced. "I am sick of the world of men!"

Ishtahar put her head on one side. "But it is a world you chose! Can't you remember? You took your punishment gladly, sacrificed yourself to seek the light of redemption."

Shem shook his head. "There was more to it than that. I was young and ignorant. I was betrayed. Now I am ruined. I want only to end it all."

Ishtahar looked away from him. "From the ashes of ruin comes the phoenix of fire to herald a new dawn." It seemed she was quoting from something. She smiled and glanced at him again. "You live as a man now, Shem, but it is only as a god that you can end it."

"Right, I shall deify myself this instant!" He smiled sadly. "Ishti, what is this? Why are we here talking like this? How can it change things? Do we have anything to share apart from bitterness or recriminations?"

She shrugged. "I like to think so, but if you refuse to take what I say seriously, then there is little hope. Believe me: you must be more than a man."

"Don't you think I haven't tried that?" he said angrily. "My life as Peverel Othman was dedicated to that, in a perverse fashion! And what good did that do?"

"Misguided," Ishtahar replied. "You concentrated on clawing open the stargate, thinking that finding access to the Source would empower you. Wrong. The redemption you need and truly seek lies within yourself already. That is where you'll find godhead. And even now, despite your flippant words, you hunger for it."

Shem fixed her with a burning stare. "I hunger only for you."

She smiled tightly. "Remember, I am a goddess now. Only as a god may you return to me. That is the way of things."

"Then tell me how!"

"I just have!"

Shem shook his head. "No, what you said means nothing in real terms. Look inside myself?" He made a scoffing sound and pressed a closed fist against his chest. "There's only darkness inside me, and I can't see the way!"

Ishtahar regarded him steadily for a few moments. Shem wondered why he couldn't just reach out and take her in his arms. This interaction of words seemed meaningless. In the past, their strength had been in physical communion. But it seemed as if an invisible barrier lay between them. He dared not attempt to breach it, sensing that if he did, Ishtahar would vanish.

After a while, she spoke. "I have been thinking how I might help you. You must understand it's difficult for me, there are constraints about me. However, I can at least tell you this. Your vizier knows the place of your ancestors and descendants. He hears its call. Listen to him. Let him be your guiding light. I know there is still much darkness ahead."

"My ancestors? My descendants? Why? Where?"

Ishtahar leaned forward, clasping her knees once more. Her voice took on a lilting tone, as if she recited poetry. "Come, gaze upon this water, for it is the ocean of my tears. A part of you lies sleeping deep within the belly of these serpent rocks. It is ready to be reawakened. Keep the light of the truth that I have spoken strong within you. And do not be tempted by my image again, until my time for flesh is come."

Shem knew then that he had reached the end of his dream. The waves crashed upon the shore, drowning out any further words Ishtahar might have spoken, and presently he was sitting alone, gazing up at the sky, where dark masses of cloud moved quickly, inexorably to obscure the sun.

In the morning, Shemyaza awoke late, to find Daniel standing over him holding a mug of tea. "Kiss me," Shem said.

Daniel put down the tea on the floor and knelt beside the bed. His eyes looked faintly troubled, but he put his hands upon Shem's shoulders and leaned forward to kiss him briefly.

It was a start, Daniel supposed, though for some reason he felt unhappy doing it. Shem's lips were unresponsive beneath his own, but at least they were warm.

"Was it Cornwall?" Shem asked him.

Daniel knelt upright, his hands plunged between his thighs. "In the dream? Yes, I think so."

"Are you sure?"

Daniel frowned. "As much as I can be."

Shem nodded. "Thank you."

Daniel said nothing more, but offered the mug to Shem again. He took it. Daniel watched him drink, the movement in his long throat. Was his question significant? Could it possibly mean Shem was considering acting upon it? He dared not hope, and was frightened of asking questions for fear of killing any recently born purpose before it could take a hold in Shem's mind.

Chapter Eight
Meeting at High Crag

A long, green limousine stood in the rain before the columned por-
tico of High Crag House. The Cornish weather was at its most fierce,
battering the long windows of the house with spears of rain. There
were no stars visible in the sky, but merely the shadows of boiling
cloud. Wind howled about the chimneys. The limousine had brought
a visitor to High Crag; a seat of Grigori power, home of the Prussoes,
where Aninka had grown up.

Enniel Prussoe received the woman, Sofia, in his office, where
the long curtains were drawn against the night, fretted only slightly
by the most persistent of breezes which fought their way in around
the window-frames. Warm light bloomed discreetly from a number
of Tiffany lamps, and the fire was banked high. The room smelled
of leather and pine, its high walls adorned with tapestries and paintings. Enniel stood before his desk, a perfect example of the cream
of his race: tall, his long, red hair confined neatly at his neck, his
clothes casual yet expensive. He appeared to be a man in his early
thirties, yet he had lived through two centuries already and was still
young in Grigori terms. His fine-boned face was composed in a
bland expression. He was not looking forward to this interview.

Sofia was ancient, a tall matriarch of Grigori. Her clothes
were of classic cut and could have fitted comfortably into the haute
couture of any period during the last thirty years. She wore a long,
cream-coloured coat of soft wool, gloves and a hat, which she removed with stately precision, and placed into the waiting hands of
one of Enniel's staff, who stood quietly at the door.

Enniel was slightly unnerved by her. He was himself a salient
figure within the inner circles of Grigori administration, but Sofia outranked him in experience, and he suspected her network of contacts
was far more comprehensive than his own. It was rumoured she dipped
her fingers into the most distant, hidden pools of Grigori knowledge.
For the past two weeks she had been working on a problem for Enniel—
namely discovering the whereabouts of the erstwhile Peverel Othman.

Enniel had been given this task some months before, when his ward, Aninka, had unwittingly become involved with the Anakim, thereby finding herself in an unsavoury position and implicated in murder. The Parzupheim, of which Enniel was a member, were the governing body of the Grigori. They were anxious to secure Peverel Othman. They had their suspicions about him, which they needed to prove or refute once and for all. The Parzupheim were far from impressed that Enniel's plan to capture the Anakim had failed. After all, Enniel's agents had had Othman in their sights. It was clearly Enniel's choice of operative that had jeopardised the mission. Enniel could not find it within himself to blame Aninka or Taziel Levantine for this failure, although he was furious with Lahash Murkaster, whom he had trusted. Since then, the Parzupheim had designated other agents to work on the problem, and Enniel was working with them only as advisor. He was unused to embarrassment, and was still pondering how best to punish Lahash for his incompetence. Lahash, as a member of the disgraced Murkaster family, was indentured to the Parzupheim for a millennium. This blot on his performance would do little to change anybody's mind about his worth.

Sofia, aside from her considerable political influence, was also one of the most powerful psychics known to the Grigori community. Enniel knew little of her other than her status, and that she was rumoured to have a base in India. He wondered whether his Parzupheim colleagues had deliberately sought her help, or whether she'd decided to become involved herself. It was unlikely she'd admit to either. Now she sat composed on a leather sofa alongside Enniel's desk, and politely inclined her head when he enquired whether she wished to partake of a measure of brandy.

"It is an inclement night," she said, as if to stem any risk of Enniel concluding she drank alcohol for pleasure. She was a frightening creature to behold—her skin white and as translucent as tissue paper, her brows highly arched and sketched lightly as if with an artist's finest brush. Her lips were thin and coloured with matte, dark-red lipstick. Her teeth, when she chose to bare them in a smile, were faintly yellow. She carried her centuries with her and around her like a stole, and her beauty was fragile, like that of a fabulous relic discovered in the tomb of king who had lived long before the Egyptians had learned to be civilised.

Enniel poured out the drinks into cut crystal globes, treating himself to a generous measure.

Sofia sipped delicately but quickly from her glass. Then she placed the empty globe on a table beside the sofa and put her brief-case onto her lap. From this, she withdrew a sheaf of papers. The whiteness of the pages was dulled by the proximity of her bloodless skin. With the fingernails of one hand, she tapped the pages. "This is my report."

Enniel nodded. "Good, good. May I ask what conclusion you have reached?"

Sofia frowned a little, pulled down the corners of her mouth. "There is no doubt in my mind that the Grigori known as Peverel Othman carries within him the psychic profile of the one named Shemyaza. I have made several avenues of investigation into this matter to reinforce my findings. First, I read the transcript of the interview with your ward, Aninka Prussoe. It seems quite clear that Peverel Othman was attempting to reopen the stargate, to gain access to the Source, the ancient and lost knowledge of our people. The stargate was closed to us over ten millennia ago, entirely because of Shemyaza's misconduct."

"I am aware of the history," Enniel interrupted.

Sofia clearly did not approve of the interruption, but chose to ignore it. "I have had a team of psychics working on investigating the periphery of the stargate, at considerable risk to themselves, and it does appear to have been tampered with. They were able to approach it quite closely and noted a great deal of etheric disturbance. However, none of them were able to pass through it. Two days ago, I put myself in trance and sought to witness a re-enactment of what might have happened. Whoever had been there had been careless. There were no safe-guards and no erasure of events. I was able to pick up times and even names. A human boy named Daniel Cranton freed the soul of Shemyaza from bondage in the constellation of Orion. It was plain to see. Residue of what had occurred was left float-ing around all over the place." She grimaced. "Very messy. The ritual Cranton had employed was crude, and entirely sexual in nature. He worked with a Grigori half-breed named Owen Winter, whom we have since discovered is related to Lahash Murkaster. You sent Murkaster to Little Moor to deal with the problem, didn't you?"

Enniel frowned. "Neither I, nor Lahash, know of this con-nection. Perhaps you'd better explain."

"Of course. Twenty years ago, the Grigori family Murkaster was resident in Little Moor, the place to which your operatives tracked Othman down. It is common knowledge what happened to the Murkasters, namely that a human woman sought to re-enact certain ancient rituals, which coincidentally involved the legend of Shemyaza, his human mistress, Ishtahar, and the opening of the stargate. Naturally, this ritual failed, and the Murkasters were dealt with by the Parzupheim for their transgressions. However, the human woman was never taken into custody, and it appears she bore twins, of whom Kashday Murkaster was the father. These twins lived hidden in Little Moor for nearly twenty years. When Othman fled there, escaping what had occurred in Cresterfield, he naturally sniffed them out, and sought to use them, and any other Grigori dependants, for his own purposes. A young psychic human named Daniel Cranton was involved. We are as yet unsure of the exact details, but it seems that while in Little Moor, Othman was made aware of exactly who and what he was. There is no doubt that Othman performed profane rites in the Little Moor area, for my people have visited it, and have picked up much of what went on, although it all seems very confused. We do know that Othman— or Shemyaza as we must now refer to him, I suppose—escaped Little Moor with the Winter twins, Daniel Cranton and someone else who is most probably a human dependent of his. Physically, they have hidden themselves well. We could trace no financial transactions. But psychically, none of them are trained, and Shemyaza himself seems not to care about precautions. We have tracked them to an establishment in London, long regarded as a hideout for Grigori misfits and renegades. I have examined Shemyaza as best I can, and can only conclude he is no threat in his present condition. He is apathetic, confused, his energies scattered. He is a great maelstrom of potential, however, and I'm sure I don't need to tell you that we must secure him as soon as possible, before someone else takes an interest."

"Is that likely?" Enniel enquired.

Sofia directed a scornful glance at him. "But of course. There are many cabals and factions within the Grigori community around the world, who would covet Shemyaza's power. It is highly probable that at least some of these groups are already aware that something is afoot. They will have their own psychics scanning the etheric world. Some of these groups are very dangerous, and there's no telling what might happen should they get their hands on the Anakim."

Enniel, who had business dealings with some of the darker cabals of Grigori society, was unsettled by Sofia's remarks. "Then what do you recommend? Shall we simply march up to this establishment you have discovered and take Shemyaza into custody, or is it likely we will meet resistance, and will need to employ more subtle means?"

Neither Sofia nor Enniel had to say aloud that some sort of skirmish was undesirable, especially in a city centre where humans abounded.

Sofia nodded thoughtfully. "I have been considering this dilemma. If it were not for the urgency of securing Shemyaza, I would suggest infiltration of the group by one of my operatives. I would prefer to gain the trust of one of Shemyaza's followers, and use them to lure the Anakim out. However, we don't have that much time. Most of the buildings around the Moses Assembly Rooms are offices. Therefore, I propose a night-time convergence on the premises by Parzupheim personnel. We must take Shemyaza, and take him soon. Can you organise your agents by tomorrow night?"

Enniel realised the situation was more urgent than Sofia was admitting. Tomorrow? That soon? "Who exactly do you suspect is after Shemyaza?" Would she dare to keep the information from him?

Sofia considered for a moment, then came to a decision. "Old vendettas can persist for millennia, Enniel. You can imagine that, all those centuries ago, when the business with the renegade Watchers blew apart, there were many casualties at very high levels within the Grigori community. A nest of corruption was uncovered, with many respected Watchers being implicated. Shemyaza, in comparison, did not hold that much power. He was a romantic and adored by many. His death sentence was contentious at the time, although no-one dared speak for him. The High Lord Anu was enraged, and all feared for their lives. Shemyaza died horribly, as an example, but many others lost their power and their lands, and were driven into exile. Their children were murdered by Anu's militia. Others were driven mad and destroyed one another. We can only imagine what those times must have been like, but there are others, older even than myself and my peers, for whom those days of war and disruption are actual memories."

"Is that possible?" Enniel snapped. "You're telling me there are still Grigori around from those days?"

Sofia blinked slowly and nodded. "That is exactly what I am telling you. And those people have been waiting a long time to regain their power. The centuries have embittered them. They care nothing for Grigori or humankind. Shemyaza, a foolish idealist in life, has become a spiritual icon in death, more powerful as an archetype than he could ever have been as a living entity. The stargate, once his prison, is also his domain. He can be used to control it. Our enemies want the ability to reopen the stargate and seek out the Source, in the hope of discovering some vestige of Anu and the cosmic power, over which only he held dominion. Then, they will exact their revenge, and you can be sure this will have fatal repercussions for this world and its civilisation."

Enniel took another sip of brandy, then tapped his lips with steepled fingers. He was frowning. Sofia waited politely for his response. "I appreciate the urgency," he said at last. "But one thing has occurred to me. If these enemies exist, they are unlikely to cease searching for Shemyaza once he is safe with us. I assume we can expect trouble from this direction?"

Sofia nodded. "Precisely. The only course of action we have is to take Shemyaza to a safe house, keep him under surveillance, and coax him into fulfilling his role. Once he has acquired a sense of responsibility and some control over his potential, the enemies will be no match for him." She raised a hand before her face and slowly clenched it into a fist. "He must be *ours,* Enniel. Entirely ours. The end of the millennium approaches and great changes are heralded. These changes must be beneficial for our race, rather than otherwise. The responsibility is upon us, the agents of the Parzupheim, to ensure that no other influence takes control."

"Lahash Murkaster is in London," Enniel said. "I shall contact him immediately. He is hoping for a chance to redress his failings." His hand was already reaching for the telephone.

"No!" Sofia said. "No Murkaster is to be trusted. They are tainted by the same base urges that caused the Fall of our race in the first place. We can use only the purest, untouched bloodlines in this venture. Call upon your Serafim, no-one else."

Later, in the elegant guest-room, to where Enniel's staff had conducted her, Sofia lounged upon the canopied bed, before a hungry fire that illuminated the frowning faces of the stone angels that supported the mantle-piece, in an otherwise darkened room. Thoughtfully, she kicked off her shoes and caressed one long shinbone with a silk-sheathed foot. She put her hands behind her head and stretched. High Crag. At last. She had already organised a residence for herself in the area, but Enniel did not know about that. Neither did the other members of the Parzupheim, who believed they employed her. Not even Sofia's true employers knew all of her activities. She liked to believe that ultimately she was governed solely by herself.

Outside the wind wrestled with the chimneys of the house, sending mournful, elemental notes careering around the high towers. Sofia knew that down the coast road, on the outskirts of the village, her unwitting protege dreamed before her own high-banked fire. Tamara Trewlynn; dreaming of gleaming serpents of the sun and a lover with a shining face, dreaming of a friend named Barbelo, who would lead her to an angelic lover. Sofia smiled and writhed in secret pleasure upon the thick quilt. Tamara believed her, as Barbelo, to be a young Grigori woman of the Prussoe clan. She would never learn the truth.

Sofia's plans were like a garden in spring. She had planted and fertilised and was now awaiting the first delicate shoots. Shemyaza had so much more potential than Enniel, or any of his pompous confederates, imagined. Sofia had a fecund imagination. She had been preparing for this time for centuries. The power of the Shining One would be hers, and in their greed, all the others who hungered for him would let her use them. They would be blind to anything but their desires.

Chapter Nine
The Dance of Desire

Aninka waited in the cafe, smoking cigarettes and drinking tea. She felt nervous, as if waiting for a lover. Today, surely, Daniel would show up. If he didn't, then he never would, and some other tactic would have to be adopted.

She hadn't seen Lahash since they'd met for lunch, and she sensed he did not wholly trust her. Perhaps she was foolish to become involved in his schemes. Shemyaza had escaped them once, and was quite likely to do so again. She realised that what really drew her to the cafe each morning was the chance to speak to someone who had spent time with the man she had known as Peverel Othman. Was Daniel his lover now? Taziel had sensed many presences around Shemyaza. Any one of them could be warming his bed. Aninka, in moments of cold stability, rebuked herself for wondering about these things. Othman had abused and used her. As far as he was concerned she might well have been dead, another naked body amongst all the other bodies in the house in Cresterfield, where Othman's dark ritual had gone awry. Or not. Maybe he had planned the whole thing. Aninka shrank from re-experiencing that night and refused to replay her memories. It was all too vile. And yet Othman had been such a good lover to her, undemanding, intelligent, inventive. As a companion, he was equally as entertaining in a restaurant as he was in bed. *Do not think of his hands*, she told herself as she signalled the waitress to order more tea.

Daniel came in just as she was about to pour herself a fresh cup.

Aninka didn't notice him at first, then registered that someone was standing at her table. She was sure that, when she looked up, her face had coloured. She tried to appear normal. "Well! We meet again." Feeble. Couldn't she have thought of something more intriguing to say?

The boy sat down, brushed his hair from his forehead. If Aninka leaned forward, would she be able to smell Pev on him?

Her hands shook slightly as she set down the tea-pot. He still hadn't said anything. She smiled at him, a smile that felt too tight and strained. He was watching her carefully, wondering what she was after. She could sense it on him.

The waitress came over and Daniel ordered toast and tea. "Do you want anything?" he asked Aninka.

She shook her head, and gestured at her cup on the table. "Too late." It was difficult to think of something to say. The first time had been easy, but now, knowing too well who he was, her conversation had dried up.

Daniel, sitting opposite, thought that Eve was far from pleased to see him. She appeared chilly and unwelcoming. He should have known better than to come here again. His first instincts had been right; his last meeting with her had been a one-off. Events in the night had unsettled him, to the point where he really wanted to get out of the Assembly Rooms and breathe some fresh air.

"You look tired," Eve said at last, looking at him over her tea-cup. She was dressed, as before, in a smart, dark suit, but this time there was something dishevelled about her appearance, something that came from her eyes and posture rather than her clothes or hair, which lay like hanks of black satin around her shoulders. Daniel picked up a sense of tension within her. Perhaps it was nothing to do with him. She might have had an argument with a lover, a friend or someone she worked with. Perhaps she was dreading going to work that day.

"I am tired," he answered. "Bad night."

Eve pulled a sympathetic face and nodded. "Must be planetary. I've not slept well myself."

"Planetary?"

Eve shrugged. "Astrology. You know, planets moving around the zodiac. I believe it affects people."

"Oh." Daniel's tea and toast arrived. He had asked Lily for money, which she'd been happy to donate, although he hadn't told her what he was going to do with it. There was a moment's silence, as both sipped tea. Then someone came into the cafe behind Daniel, and Eve looked up. Her face registered both shock and annoyance. Daniel turned round, presuming that whoever had just come in was someone Eve knew. An extremely tall, good-looking young man with long tawny hair was making his way between the tables towards them. At first, Daniel was sure he knew this person, but the impression was fleeting, and after only a moment, he realised the newcomer was a stranger. His interest was pricked by the man's attractiveness, but he also felt disappointed that his private meeting with Eve was curtailed. This might even be her lover.

"Hi!" Eve said nervously. "What are you doing here?"

The young man sat down between them. "Just passing. Thought you'd be here." He pushed his hair behind his ears and picked up the menu, at which he frowned. Eve continued to regard him in surprise. Daniel wondered whether he should leave. The tension was too great.

"This is Daniel," Eve announced. Daniel sensed a certain pointedness about the remark. The young man looked at him then, apparently for the first time. Daniel felt a flush creep up his face. The look was too direct, too assessing.

"I work near here," he mumbled, to indicate his presence at Eve's table was not illicit.

"Yeah? I'm Jack. A colleague of the lady here." He directed his attention back to the menu.

"It is rare that Jack sees this time of day," Eve said, rather acidly. "We are honoured by his presence." She lit a cigarette, narrowed her eyes through the smoke. It was then that Daniel picked up the distinct impression that Eve thought Jack was an intrusion. She didn't want him there, because she wanted to be alone with Daniel. This intrigued him. What exactly did she want from him?

Jack spoke about how he'd come to give Eve a message, which she clearly did not believe. He told her that the "boss" wanted to meet her for lunch. Something to do with an overdue report. He ordered a full breakfast, then mentioned that he'd offered to "help out" with her work, seeing as she appeared to be having problems with it. Daniel sensed a sub-text to their conversation, and picked up a sense of extreme annoyance simmering beneath Eve's cool reserve. "You seemed to have little interest in the project," she said in an icy voice.

Jack shrugged and smiled, lacing his fingers together on the table. "Well, I've reviewed it and have changed my mind."

Eve shook her head and, much to Daniel's surprise, started to smile. He sensed more was being said than he could understand. It was a code between them. "OK, get on with it then. I'll wait to be impressed by your expertise."

To Daniel's horror, she picked up her bag, which was stowed under her seat and stood up. She was, Daniel realised, incredibly tall for a woman. "See you later."

"You're going," Daniel said, inadequately.

"Yes, sorry. Sit and chat to Jack. I'm sure you'll find him entertaining." She moved fluidly towards the counter to pay her bill.

Daniel gulped down his tea, intent on leaving too. Jack seemed to guess this.

"Don't go," he said. "Keep me company."

"I don't know you," Daniel blurted.

Jack laughed at him. "Of course not. But if you stay, you can begin to. Tell him I won't eat him, Eve!"

Eve looked back over her shoulder with a quick, bright smile. "Stay, Daniel."

Daniel's heart had begun to beat faster. He sensed a conspiracy. Why would this perfect stranger want his company? Had Eve told Jack about him? If so, why? A memory came back to him of the weird experience he'd had in the night, and the silent figures standing vigilantly in the darkness outside the Rooms. He stood up. "I don't think...I mean, I have things to do." The pair of them were staring at him, almost without expression, but with a sense of waiting.

Then Jack laughed and applied himself to his breakfast, which had just been placed before him. "Yeah, you're right. Piss off. I'm bad company."

Daniel glanced at Eve. Her expression was intent. She mouthed a single, silent word, *"Please!"* Daniel frowned at her, unsure of her meaning. He wondered exactly what was going on between these two. Something to do with their work?

Eve came towards him, put one pale hand on his arm. "You would be doing me a favour keeping him occupied," she said lightly. Her eyes said more than that, however. "I'll see you here tomorrow morning, shall I?" she added. "Then you can buy me breakfast like you promised."

Reluctantly, Daniel gave in and sat down again. "All right."

Eve leaned down and kissed him lightly on the cheek. "Thanks." He could smell her perfume, sense her warmth; both of which were quite intoxicating.

Looking back, Daniel could see that he was seduced from the start. He couldn't remember exactly how Jack had engineered it, but somehow they spent the day together. He took Daniel out into the city, into the real city, the back streets and hidden shops, the bars known only to natives. Daniel had fifteen pounds in his jacket pocket. He wondered whether he could buy himself something, but in the event spent it all on beer and food.

They ended up spending most of the afternoon in an empty pub, where Daniel established that Jack was not Eve's lover as he'd thought. He risked asking why Eve wanted him to stay with Jack in the cafe.

Jack grinned, took a swig from the bottle he held, leaning back in his chair. "She thinks it's therapy for me."

"Oh? Why?"

Jack leaned forward and put his arms on the tabletop. "I've had a bit of hassle, that's all. Emotional fuck-up. Eve's doing the mother hen bit. Perhaps she thought you'd be good for me."

Daniel, inexperienced in the ways of world but nonetheless perceptive, drew back. "Why would she think that?"

Jack shrugged. "She likes you. She has good taste."

How do I handle this? Daniel wondered, unsure whether he was picking up the right signals. Was this man making a pass at him, partly engineered by Eve? How could she make such assumptions upon such short acquaintance? Was it written all over him that he preferred men to women? He considered himself to be free of all obvious signs, and didn't know now whether to feel offended or complimented. "Eve doesn't know me very well. We've only just met."

Jack pulled a wry face, shrugged. Without further preamble, he asked Daniel if he'd like to go out clubbing later on. Daniel was unsure. A mild flirtation in daylight was one thing, the possibility of getting drunk and irresponsible in a club late at night another. "Oh, I don't know." He paused. "I don't have much money."

Jack rolled his eyes. "Well I have. What's the matter? You really don't trust me, do you?"

Daniel risked a partial confession. "Look, I haven't been in the city long. I hardly know anyone. I hardly know you. It's just..."

"Then bring a friend with you, if you have one, and if it'll make you feel safer, although I swear I haven't murdered anyone in my life yet. I have considered it a few times, and have accomplished maiming, but little else." He smiled disarmingly.

Daniel considered. Lily had talked of wanting to get out at night. Maybe she would come. "Well, there's a girl I know. She might be into it. I'll ask her."

At lunchtime, Aninka met Lahash at their appointed place, an expensive bistro. She was unsure whether to be angry with him or not. "Did you send Taz to the cafe this morning?"

Lahash shrugged. "Taz suggested it himself. It seemed sensible."

"A planned seduction, is that it? I gather that was the innuendo behind his words."

"I wouldn't go so far as to say that." Lahash poured icy white wine into a tall glass for her. She sat rigidly, poised behind a spray of white carnations that stood between them on the table in a crystal flute. Lahash looked achingly handsome, clever and cunning. Aninka recognised the warning signs. Perhaps it would be wiser to back off. "So what are your plans, then? We've established contact with Daniel. When do we move in?"

Lahash smiled in a fashion Aninka did not like. Disturbingly, he often looked like an assassin, with his smart suits and heavy overcoats. A secret agent with a gun beneath his arm. "That depends on Taz. We need information. I just hope he's reliable."

Aninka grimaced and took a drink of wine. "You should know he is not." She twirled the stem of her glass between her fingers. Lahash was now examining the menu. "What kind of information do you want?"

Lahash did not meet her eyes. "How many people in the house. Shemyaza's frame of mind, that kind of thing. Also, whether any of them are armed."

Aninka shivered. She had a vision of Peverel Othman lying slumped against a wall, his guts spilled out across the floor. "Do you suppose the Parzupheim are on to him?"

"Of course they are. I just hope they've opted to be circumspect." He leaned forward. "We have to take him soon, Ninka, or rather, I do."

Aninka felt suffused by a sudden, overwhelming depression. The odds seemed too high. What were they playing at? "Perhaps we should just leave them to it—the Parzupheim, I mean."

Lahash scowled. "No! I can't let him beat me."

"It's too much of a personal vendetta for you!"

Lahash raised an eyebrow. "And it's not for you?"

She shook her head. "I don't know any more. I fear for Taz. What if Shemyaza should find out he's tampering with Daniel? What if he's just lying in wait?" She paused. "Do you think Taz'd be stupid enough to go into the Assembly Rooms without you?"

"No," Lahash answered, summoning a waiter. "He just wants to fuck the boy that Shemyaza fucks, that's all. Perhaps getting his own back?"

Aninka uttered a disgusted sound. "You're wrong. Taziel, for all his ways, is not an animal. I think he just finds the idea of playing at sleuths amusing."

The atmosphere during the meal was strained. Aninka picked at her food, wondering why Lahash had become so aggressive and bitter. Perhaps Enniel had given him a harder time than she'd thought. It seemed impossible to imagine that Lahash could care for her now. The time in Little Moor, and what happened afterwards, when they'd closed ranks in the draughty halls of High Crag to face Enniel, seemed insubstantial, as if it hadn't really happened. A runnel of anger seethed through her and she dropped her fork onto her plate, where her steak lay virtually untouched.

Lahash glanced at her, forking rare meat into his mouth, an expression of enquiry on his face.

"I must go," Aninka said.

Lahash frowned. "Why? You haven't finished your meal."

She gestured helplessly with stiff fingers. "It's all wrong. None of this feels right." She lowered her hands, composed herself. "I don't think you're telling me everything."

Lahash made an abrupt move, rubbed one hand through his hair. By that, Aninka guessed she'd hit on the truth.

"What could I possibly not be telling you?"

She shook her head. "I don't know. But there is something. Lahash, why won't you confide in me? Are you just using me? I had hoped that was not the case."

Lahash regarded her without expression for a few moments, then admitted bluntly, "I've been watched."

Aninka made a small move upon her seat, but otherwise remained outwardly calm. "By whom? The Parzupheim?"

Lahash shrugged. "I don't know. I don't think so. I'm just not sure, but the feeling's...well, not good."

"You mean bad," Aninka said. "I think that's the word you're looking for. How do you know? Have you seen these people?"

He blinked at her. "Ninka, I *do* know my business. There have been figures in the porches of the houses opposite my room. Occasionally, I've been aware of being followed. Noises on the line of my phone by day and in the static of my head at night. Believe me, someone is watching."

Aninka leaned towards him, spoke softly but urgently, suddenly aware that these unseen pursuers could be here with them in the restaurant. "Then you must forget about Shemyaza. Leave him to those who can match his power. Why risk your life—or your sanity?"

Lahash clasped his hands together, closed his eyes briefly, rubbed his long nose with his thumbs. He sighed. "I can't let this go, Ninka. Things could go badly for me if I don't redeem myself with Enniel. He holds the keys of my life." He straightened up. "Look, there's no need for you to be involved. I understand your feelings, your anxieties."

"Then I'll just walk out of here," she said, gambling. "Like I wanted to before we started this conversation."

"Please don't." Lahash tried a boyish smile on her. "I want you to stay."

Aninka picked up her fork again, toyed with her food, staring at her plate. "I remember a conversation that seems to have taken place such a long time ago, when you said that one day we'd sit in a restaurant, and you'd tell me the story of your life. Things were different then, weren't they?"

He stared at her for a moment. "Not that different, no. I'm sorry. Perhaps I seem obsessed. Let's spend the day together, enjoy ourselves. I want to do that, Ninka, I've always wanted to. You are very beautiful, and I care about you a great deal."

"I'm surprised to hear you say that. I've had no inkling."

"I know. Perhaps I assumed too much, or expected you to be psychic like Taz. Well, will you spend the day with me?"

Aninka nodded. "OK. We'll see how it goes." She shook her head sadly. "What am I letting myself in for? Perhaps I'm being presumptuous here, but I couldn't bear to get involved with you only to lose you in some horrible, life-shattering way."

"I'll do my best to avoid that happening," Lahash said.

They went for a walk in the cold air, strolling through the West End. Lahash bought flowers for Aninka from a road-side stand. She smelled them, and they had hardly any perfume. Twice he had given her scentless flowers. An archaic gesture, perhaps, and now she had to carry them round with her for the entire afternoon.

As the day became smoky and blue-grey, they wandered into a cafe and drank espresso coffee. The city was lighting up around them; buses and taxis roared down Charing Cross Road. Their conversation skirted the issues of Shemyaza, Little Moor, Cresterfield, the past. Aninka was astounded there was so much trivia to talk about. At five o'clock, she looked at her watch. "Well, I'd better get back to the flat. You coming?"

He nodded. "Yes. We should see how Taz got on."

He helped her into her coat, and leaned forward to kiss her hair. "Have you had a good time?"

She turned her head and smiled up at him, tightly. "Yes." She wished it could be true.

Taziel was uncharacteristically energetic, prowling the apartment, eating cole slaw from a tub. Aninka regarded this transformation with suspicion. She felt her heart grow heavy, slide down within her. *He fancies Daniel,* she thought. *He really does.*

"How was it?" she asked, rather too acidly.

"Fine," Taz replied. "I'm meeting him again tonight."

"What information did you get out of him?" Lahash demanded.

Taz frowned. "Nothing yet. I can't push it. He's very wary."

"We must all talk to Daniel later," Lahash said. "You must bring him back here."

"We're going to a club," Taz said. "It'll be late."

"I'm sure Aninka and I can find something to do to amuse ourselves."

Aninka regarded Taziel speculatively. She could swear that he'd somehow decided to keep Daniel for himself, but she wasn't sure of his reasons for that. Simple altruism just didn't ring true. "What time do you want us back?" she asked him.

"Around three."

"That *is* late."

Taz shrugged. "I know. But I want him to be settled comfortably here before you arrive. I'll pave the way."

"Is that wise?" Lahash said. "He might flee."

"Trust me," Taz answered. "We're both psychics after all. I'm sure I can intrigue him enough to get him back here without scaring him off. Once he's here, the bolt'll be across the door, don't worry."

"Taz, be careful!" Aninka warned. "You don't know what link he might have with Shemyaza. If you kidnap the boy, Shemyaza might come raging to the rescue. I don't want to come home to a wrecked flat, strewn with bits of your vital equipment!"

"It won't be kidnap, I promise," Taz said, grinning, and from the width of the grin, Aninka gathered only too well what Taz hoped it would be.

"Once I get the information from the boy, I'm going hunting," Lahash said. "It must be tonight."

"What will you do with him?" Aninka was alarmed it would be this soon.

"Get him to High Crag as soon as possible."

"He might be frisky," Taziel said. "Do you know what you'll be facing?"

"Hopefully, yes. After I've talked to the boy."

Aninka threw herself down in a chair, one leg hooked over the arm. "You're assuming Daniel will talk. Why should he? The minute he finds out who and what we are, the chances are he'll be hostile, wouldn't you say?" Out of the corner of her eyes, she noticed Taziel stiffen. Hadn't he thought of that?

Lahash put his hands into his coat pockets, which could be stuffed with instruments of torture for all Aninka knew. "Don't worry. He'll talk."

Aninka sighed, scrubbed at her hair with her hands. "I hate this!"

"You don't have to be here later if you don't want to be," Lahash said. "You could wait at my place, although it's hardly palatial."

Aninka realised that he was trying to sound considerate. It only depressed her.

Chapter Ten
The Night of Cankered Stars

The corridor was long, stretching away into infinity, into darkness. At the end of it, behind a door presently hidden in shadow, a blind star blazed. Daniel trudged down the corridor with aching calves; his legs were reluctant to make this visit never mind his mind, his heart. What lived in the room was never far from Daniel's mind. It lurked there, like something he didn't want to do and had forcibly forgotten, or something to be faced in the future that he dreaded. What lived there was the ghost of his first love.

The door handle was beneath his hand; he turned it.

The room behind was dingy and empty but for a mattress set upon the floor against one of the walls. On this, Owen Winter sat like a pale, carven effigy, his white-gold hair upon his shoulders, his body clad in white, in the way Emma was keen on dressing him. He stared at the door with his dark eyes, but seemed to see nothing.

Daniel, Owen's erstwhile lover, came into the room. Owen neither blinked nor stirred.

"How are you?" Daniel asked, venturing into the brown light, which contained the blazing star.

Owen said nothing.

Daniel squatted down on the floor before the bed. He looked up at Owen's chiselled features, his radiant, angelic beauty, and the past came back. He remembered the time Owen had come to pick him up from school in his old car—it seemed centuries before Peverel Othman had ruined their lives. Daniel recalled walking toward the car, drinking in the sight of Owen's long, liquid body draped against the bonnet. Daniel's heart had hammered in desire and fear, because he had not known then that Owen loved him. He remembered the first time they had truly made love, and the visions of Shemyaza that had come to him, vistas of ancient history opening before his eyes, ignited by passion. He thought of these things, but then, because it came afterward, he remembered the dark ritual enacted upon the High

Place in the woods, when Owen had become a stranger, who could rape and witness murder without a thought. Othman had done something to Owen, something bad. If the essence of Owen lived in the body still, it was hidden very deep. Daniel had tried to reach out and in to Owen's mind, to retrieve the spirit of the one he loved, but the barriers were beyond his penetration. Now, he could hardly bear to look upon Owen's face, because he was still, in his autism, so lovely.

"I had to come and talk to you," Daniel said. He did not wait now for responses. "I've met someone—a man—and tonight I'm going out with them. I don't know what will happen, or whether I really want this. It felt good today, talking to him. I'm sorry, O', I think I have to do this. You've left me, and there's nothing I can do about that." He wanted to lean forward and kiss Owen's bloodless mouth, but couldn't force himself to. He was afraid the flesh would be cold and stiff. This corpse lived.

Because there was nothing more to say, and he felt he had performed his penance, Daniel left the room.

For a while, nothing changed in the dim, brown room. Then a glister came to the cheek of Owen Winter, and a single tear rolled down it to fall upon his listless hands where they lay in his lap. A single tear, nothing more. But the room shook to the etheric echo of a silent, agonised scream.

Daniel found Lily in Johcasta's room, having her hair plaited with ribbons and beads. Lily glanced at Daniel in the mirror. "Did you do it?"

Daniel nodded and sat glumly on the end of Johcasta's bed. He could tell Lily was excited about their proposed night out, although it had been she who'd suggested that Daniel should visit Owen beforehand. "Something is happening at last," she'd said when Daniel had nervously asked her if she'd like to go out for the evening. "And it gives me an excuse to ask Israel out."

Daniel did not relish having to spend time in the company of Israel, who scared him, but realised that Israel was part of the deal if Lily was to be his chaperone. She seemed less interested in the fact that Daniel had met a man, than that it had allowed her diversions of her own.

"Have you told Emma?" Lily asked.

Daniel shook his head. "No. She'd object."

Lily nodded. "Yeah, best not to say anything." Johcasta had lent her a red velvet dress, which virtually swept the floor. Radiant in the candlelight of Johcasta's room, Lily looked like a medieval princess, some enchanted creature awoken from sorcerous sleep. Daniel wished he could share her enthusiasm. Now, he regretted having agreed to meet Jack, and felt on edge and embarrassed. Yet hadn't his strange experience the night before presaged that he wanted or needed physical comfort? For a moment, in the cafe that morning, he'd felt he'd recognised Jack. Perhaps his body was calling out for a lover, and coincidence had aligned to allow Jack to walk into his life. Despite this admission, he still couldn't dispel his uneasiness. What the hell am I doing? he wondered, and blamed the beer at lunchtime.

Israel made an appearance in Johcasta's room at eight, bearing bottles of red wine. He was resplendent in black leather trousers and a minimal black T-shirt, the dark skin of his arms gleaming dully like forbidden fruit. His eyes burned with a speculative light as he contemplated casually the vision of Lily in the glass. She looked so small before him that Daniel worried for her. He saw Israel as a demon, who could break her neck like the stem of a flower.

Before they left, Johcasta insisted on casting her stones for them. Daniel had consumed two large glasses of wine too quickly, which had succeeded only in burning his stomach, while leaving his head untouched. He felt sick with nerves.

The others in the room seemed oblivious of his condition, as Lily excitedly rubbed the handful of stones between her palms. When they fell, Johcasta let out an awed gasp.

"What is it?" Lily pleaded. "Tell me!"

Johcasta grinned and gestured with outspread fingers at the fallen stones. "Tonight will be a time of great happenings," she pronounced. "Marmoset the lover lies close to Zahtumuzgi, the queen of serpents. Exciting secrets wait to be discovered in the trance of passion."

Daniel let out a groan, prompting a quizzical glance from Israel. "The boy's fretting," he said and laughed. There was a moment's awkward silence, then Israel said. "Here, will this help?" He held out what looked like a joint.

Daniel grimaced. "Not with wine, no."

"It's not what you think," Israel told him. "Try it." He lit the roll-up and a sweet, herby scent swirled around him, more perfumed than marijuana.

"What is it?" Lily asked.

"Haoma," Israel answered, "an old intoxicant of our people." He offered the joint to Daniel. "Go on, it'll settle your stomach *and* your mind."

Daniel snatched it off him and drew in a large lungful. For a moment, the air sparkled before his eyes, then a languorous wave swept through his blood, like loving hands reaching up to cup his mind.

"Better already!" Israel said.

Daniel had arranged to meet Jack in The Black Dolphin, a pub close to the square. By the time they'd made the short walk to the place, Daniel's spirits had lifted, which he supposed was the gift of the haoma. He also felt slightly unsteady on his feet, and his mind hummed, as if he was on the verge of hallucinating. The pub was quite full, and for a moment, Daniel panicked, wondering whether he'd actually recognise Jack again. It was Lily who spotted the figure with his back to them, leaning against the bar. "Long hair," she whispered. "That him?"

"Um—I think so." Daniel wasn't convinced.

Lily swept up to the bar, leaving Israel standing by the door with Daniel. "Hmm!" Israel murmured. He sounded faintly perplexed or displeased.

"What is it?" Daniel asked him.

Israel shrugged and glanced down his nose at Daniel. "Has a scent to him, that one."

"What do you mean?"

Israel shook his head. "Don't know. Yet." He smiled.

Daniel noticed Lily inspecting the male figure at the bar discreetly as she ordered their drinks. Then she tapped him on the shoulder and spoke. The man turned round quickly. It was Jack.

"Grigori!" Israel hissed.

And Daniel answered, "No, no he's not. I'd know, Israel. I really would." He didn't want to say "I'm psychic", because it would sound absurdly melodramatic. Also, it would be too much of a coincidence meeting another Grigori so quickly, unless...No, he mustn't think that. Shem was probably right. There was no-one chasing them. "He's just tall. Not every tall person's Grigori, you know!"

Israel shrugged and smiled. "Maybe he's human, then. The sweet weed's playing tricks. Perhaps."

Jack came over with Lily, carrying a drink, which he handed to Daniel. Daniel noticed the quick, intense glance Jack directed at Israel. Was there a hint of nervousness there, the fear of recognition? No, get a grip! Daniel scolded himself. He felt small in the circle of towering people. He wasn't short, but the other three were unnaturally tall. Now, he wished he hadn't been so greedy with the haoma. It was clearly warping his perceptions.

After five minutes of stilted introductions, Jack skilfully put the group at ease. He spoke with a sly, compelling wit, flashing his eyes flirtatiously at Lily. *He is perfect,* Daniel thought. There were elements of Owen in Jack; the litheness, the clever sarcasm, the apartness from Daniel that meant only *later you'll be mine.* But a faint, barely discernible alarm was ringing in his head. Had Israel caused that with his suspicions, which only served to augment Emma's paranoia? Last night, Daniel had been convinced that someone had found them, but perhaps that had been only a presentiment of what was to come. He could not be sure he'd seen dark figures motionless beneath the trees below his window.

Jack took them to a club that was hidden away down a side-alley, far from the hissing main roads of the city. Ancient warehouses loomed high to either side. At ground level, it could be seen that they were now all nightclubs, but the windows of the upper storeys were occluded. Lights could not be seen, nor the throb of music heard. Jack led them to a narrow doorway, where gleams of purple light spilled out onto the street. Shadowy figures skulked there, some hunched against the wall, sitting down. It was named The Holy City Zoo.

Inside, Jack insisted on paying entrance for all four of them. They paused at a red-lit booth, where a girl in predatory drag clawed money through a wire mesh. Daniel pulled an agonised face as he heard the price, but said nothing. Jack, after all, had claimed he could afford it.

The club comprised a series of linked rooms, none of which were very large, all of which were full of dry ice, or the lighting was so low it was impossible to see anything but the bar. Heavy ambient dub oozed from the sound system like molasses over stones. The clientele was mixed: a jumble of nearly every youth sub-culture.

Lily was eager to dance, her body moving involuntarily to the summoning of the music. She was a tawny cat slinking and stretching before the pantherine grace of Israel, who watched her with a smiling, feline eye. Daniel felt an urge to warn her. He was trying to enjoy himself and relinquish the nagging sense of unease, but it was fixed to him like a parasite.

The group gathered in a booth against one of the walls. Daniel sipped his beer, but didn't feel like drinking. Lily and Israel kept the conversation going, and Jack joined in, but Daniel could tell he was perplexed by Daniel's mood. When Lily and Israel got up to dance, Jack addressed the situation. "What's up?" There was accusation in the question as well as wariness.

Daniel shrugged. "I'm just not in the right mood for this." He forced himself to smile. "It's not your fault, I mean, it's nothing to do with you."

"So what are your problems?"

You don't really want to know, Daniel thought. *This is just a line.* "Nothing really." He was assaulted by a vision of Owen left alone in the Assembly Rooms, while Emma and Shem watched TV together in terse silence. Suddenly, they all seemed so vulnerable. An urge to get back there swept through him. He almost stood up. "I think I want to go home..."

"Don't," Jack said, and the word sounded like a command. When Daniel looked at him, he'd softened it with a conciliatory smile. "Just give it a chance, OK? An hour?"

Daniel sighed. "All right." He hoped he could bear this feeling of anxiety for an hour. He glanced at Jack, and saw the potential just waiting to be taken. This might never happen again.

The next hour passed quickly, as Daniel drank steadily in an attempt to quell his uneasiness. Jack chatted smoothly about music, films and clubs he'd frequented, taking care to ask Daniel questions about his own tastes. To Daniel, it seemed absurdly to have been scripted, as if they were actors on celluloid, moving towards the bedroom scene, when the audience's hopes and hungers would be gratified. Only Daniel intended for there to be no bedroom scene. He had no desire for it, felt too sick.

Lily and Israel seemed to be getting on very well, performing the dance of flirtation to mutual satisfaction. Occasionally, they'd come back to the table and drink hurriedly, before moving back to the dance floor, which was beginning to fill up with shadowy figures. More dry ice puffed into the air, until Daniel could believe that he and Jack were the only people in the room.

"Something's gone off-key since this afternoon," Jack said.

"You're too impatient." Daniel couldn't keep the sharpness from his voice. "We've only just met. What do you want from me?"

Jack recoiled. "Was that called for?"

Daniel shook his head. "I'm sorry. I don't know this world. It's alien to me." Jack couldn't possibly guess he was referring to casual relationships, the careless use of the bodies of others.

Jack slumped back on his seat, scowling, a bottle of beer nursed in his lap.

You are beautiful, Daniel thought, *but empty. I thought I wanted to touch you, but I don't. You won't let me reach the places I want to touch.* With this thought, he glanced at his watch. The hour was nearly up. The only problem he had was how to find his way back to the square without an A-Z street guide. Perhaps Lily and Israel would accompany him, although he doubted that. They were too engrossed in their own mating ritual. Daniel began to compose his departure speech. One or two mordant remarks wouldn't go amiss.

Then Jack raised his head. "Don't bother thinking of the excuses. I've made a mess of this. Sorry."

"What?" Daniel felt unnerved.

"What you were thinking. You want to leave. You do fancy me a bit, although you also think I'm an airhead. The only thing that's keeping you here is that you don't think you can find your way back to the square without an A-Z and Lily's having too good a time to go home yet." Jack grinned at Daniel's shocked expression. "That's right. I'm psychic. Like you are. Do you still want to go home?"

Daniel shook his head slowly, his eyes round. "Not yet. Not now. I *can't* go home now. How did you know about me?"

Jack laughed. "I told you, I'm psychic! Like calls to like, as they say. Want more proof? You had a lover called Owen, who's very ill now. Breakdown?" He shrugged at Daniel's stunned stillness. "You haven't got a job and you live in a weird old place that feels very...temporary."

"Stop it," Daniel said. "Don't do this. It's an abuse."

"I'm not prying, just trying to convince you. Your secrets are safe, I promise."

Daniel put down his drink. "This is weird. I've never met anyone who can do this. I mean, I know other psychic people, and sometimes, under *certain* conditions, I've experienced things with Owen, but this..." He shook his head. "I'm not sure I like it."

Jack put up his hands. "I'll back off, OK. I'll keep my ears closed."

"Good."

Jack was silent for a few moments, then took a deep breath and said, "I've been through hell, Daniel. I think we can help each other."

Daniel glanced at him cautiously. "What makes you think I've been through hell?"

Jack just shrugged significantly.

Daniel didn't think Jack's hell could be anything like his own. Neither could he imagine ever confiding his experiences to a comparative stranger. He wasn't sure whether he wanted to take this on. He had enough problems of his own without someone else leeching off his emotional energy. But still, Jack was before him, splendid. This just needed thinking about. There would be plenty of time.

"Let's go for a walk," Jack said, and stood up.

They ventured into another room, where the light was red. Here, they sat against the wall, drinking in silence, watching the dancers writhe. Then, Jack put down his bottle, which was empty. "Come on, let's dance." He was on his feet before Daniel had finished swallowing his drink.

They moved in among the moving bodies, and Daniel let the music take him. It was easier than he thought it would be. There was no break in the music; one track flowed into another; tribal rhythms, electronic throbbing. Daniel danced with his eyes closed, feeling the liquor swirl round his brain. It felt good now, as if he'd drunk more than he had. Perhaps the haoma was partly responsible. He was relaxed. Someone put their arms around him, and he opened his eyes. Jack. For a moment, he panicked, glancing round himself, but no-one was looking. No-one cared. They danced together, bodies close, belly-grinding to the rhythm, invoking the demands of lust. Jack pulled Daniel closer, sought his mouth in a kiss. They stopped dancing. A girl came and threw her arms around them both. "You're beautiful!" she screamed. "I love you!"

Jack grinned and mouthed, "Happy drug!" They moved to the side of the dance floor.

Daniel realised he was extremely drunk and began to laugh in a high, uncontrollable way. Jack pushed him against the wall again and slid down to sit beside him. He looked dazed, not altogether happy. Daniel touched his face, and Jack glanced at him, took his hand in his own.

"We have to talk, Daniel."

His voice was too serious. Daniel's body was still hot with desire. He hadn't expected this. "We can talk anytime." Strange how the roles reversed, back and forth, back and forth. He wanted to devour Jack and didn't care for conversation.

"No, we can't. This is urgent. But we can't talk here."

"Then where?"

"My place?"

Daniel was silent for a moment, then grinned. The moment of decision. "If you like."

After a hurried explanation to Lily, who clearly didn't care what Daniel did that night, they hailed a cab and drove through the city to Jack's apartment. He lived in Docklands, which hardly surprised Daniel. "What do you do to earn money?" he asked.

"Scrounge," Jack answered, and smothered any further questions with a kiss. Daniel was conscious of the cab driver in front of them, and in his intoxicated state, it only inflamed his lust.

"You must be good at scrounging," Daniel said as he spilled out of the cab into the street.

Jack laughed. "Yeah, I am. Very."

Jack's apartment was spacious and modern, a converted docks building. Daniel wandered around the enormous living space while Jack poured drinks. Daniel fell onto a sofa, which was covered with an ethnic print rug. Jack summoned him.

"Not here. My room. More private."

Daniel frowned. "You said you lived alone."

"A lie. I share. A small lie. Come on."

Jack's room was bare and sleek; stripped pine and floor cushions. The bed, unmade, was a mattress on the floor, but lacked all the connotations of poverty associated with the floor mattresses at the Assembly Rooms. CDs were scattered everywhere, out of their cases. Jack selected one from a pile and slotted into his CD player, which Daniel noticed was filmed with a layer of dust. Soft, ambient music filled the room.

"Why are you sober?" Daniel complained, accepting another glass of bourbon off Jack.

"I'm not. Well, some thoughts just make you sober." Jack sat down beside him on the bed. Daniel slumped down and put his head in Jack's lap, gazing up at his face.

"Don't be so serious."

Jack stroked his face, summoned a smile. "Sorry." He paused, then said, "Daniel, I want you to know about what happened to me, how I ended up half crazy..."

"Don't!" Daniel put his hands over his ears, closed his eyes. "Please don't. Not now."

"But it's important...relevant. Look, my name's not Jack, it's Taziel, Taziel Levantine."

Daniel felt the name should mean something, but it didn't. "So? Why did you pretend to be someone else?"

"You've not heard the name before?"

Daniel frowned and shook his head. "I don't think so." He grinned. "Why, should I have?"

Taziel shrugged uneasily. "Well...I don't know. I thought, maybe, you'd picked my name up psychically." His voice was lame, but Daniel failed to register it.

"Look, I don't care. I don't get a bad feeling off you. I feel safe."

"This isn't you talking. You're off your face!"

Daniel laughed. "True, but it makes no difference. Look, Jack, Taziel, whatever, I don't want your angst. You can hear my thoughts! Don't you know what that means to me? I want to touch you. I want to live this moment to its ultimate potential." If there were alarm bells ringing within him, the drink and the smoke had soundproofed them out. All he could think about was the freedom of being away from Shem and the others and being able to do as he liked.

Taziel sighed and reached out to stroke his face. "OK. We'll talk later when you've sobered up."

"Take advantage of me," Daniel said. "You have my permission." He wriggled upwards and pushed Taziel back onto the bed.

"We share certain things, in our pasts," Taziel said.

A glimmer of understanding flashed across Daniel's mind. "Don't," he said. "Not yet." He didn't want to know, because he was afraid it would change everything. He lay on top of Taziel, looking into his face, which was tawny in the lamplight. "Don't spoil everything. This is my first night of freedom in a long time."

"The last time you had sex, you were raped."

"Stop it!"

"No, I can see that, don't you understand? I know!"

"It's over. Whatever happened to either of us is over. I want to forget it. Help me do that. Didn't you say we could help each other?"

Taziel closed his eyes, reached up to Daniel's face with his long hands. "Oh yes. I did. And we can. But I don't want you to end up hating me."

"I won't. Why should I?"

Taziel blinked and smiled sadly. "It happens," he said.

"Whatever you've lived through, whoever you are, I promise not to hate you," Daniel said, and before Taziel could say anything else, covered his mouth with his own. Silent words passed into Daniel's throat. He would not recognise them. They could not possibly feel like the shape of Peverel Othman's name.

Chapter Eleven
Prey Down

Aninka and Lahash left Taziel at around eight o'clock. He was in the process of taking great care in readying himself for his night out. Aninka felt uneasy. She knew that Taziel wasn't as tough as he made out, and that he, of all of them, had probably suffered the most damage at the hands of Peverel Othman. She realised that, despite Lahash's misgivings, she'd have to be present when he spoke to Daniel, if only to look after Taziel. It was unlikely she could exert any control over Lahash, but perhaps her mere presence might temper his methods of extracting information from the boy.

The evening grovelled by, minute after endless minute. Lahash had taken Aninka to a small, avant garde theatre, but she could not concentrate on the play. The actors spoke incomprehensible gibberish in a manner she supposed was meaningful, but to her it was too contrived. Angst over modern relationships meant nothing in the face of monstrous realities like the existence of Shemyaza. Even now, she found it hard to believe, and suspected, even hoped, that when Shemyaza was found, it would simply be Peverel Othman; a little more insane, and certainly more dangerous, but nothing more powerful than he had been before. If the spirit of such a great archetype was to reincarnate, why would it choose the corrupt body of Othman? Shemyaza had died for love: Othman could only murder for it.

At eleven, Lahash took her to a cramped, private drinking club, situated above a Greek restaurant. It was owned and frequented by city Grigori, some of whom Lahash appeared to have a slight acquaintance with, although none of them invaded the space of their table, huddled beside a narrow window. A candle glowed in a glass globe between them as they sipped an antique brandy. Below, gangs of young people surged up and down the narrow street; their noise was aggressive, threatening, but perhaps they were simply enjoying themselves. Aninka nodded in the right places as Lahash talked about the play. She realised, dully, that he had hoped to impress her with his knowledge of the arts. Presumably, although she could not remember, she must have told him that she and Taz spent most of their evenings this way. With Taz, she might have enjoyed the production. They would certainly have enjoyed bitching about it afterwards.

At half past midnight, Lahash suggested they seek out a Chinese cafe he frequented, and eat. Aninka agreed to this, thinking that soon this mimicry of entertainment would finish, and the grisly business would begin. She was beginning to feel nauseous.

However, at the threshold of the cafe, which was not far from the club they'd just left, Lahash paused.

"What's the matter?" Aninka asked too quickly, remembering his earlier words about surveillance. She glanced around herself tensely.

Lahash looked at her. "Nothing. Look, I think we should go back to your place now."

"It's not time," Aninka said.

"I know, but we should still go back."

"Taz won't be pleased if we get there before him."

Lahash smiled. "That is precisely why I think we should go now. I have an idea of what Taz is up to, and it could be dangerous for him."

Aninka considered for a moment, then nodded. "Yes. Let's get a cab."

At first, Aninka thought that Taziel had left all the lights on in the main room by mistake. When she and Taz went out for the evening, they always left one lamp burning, just to discourage house-breakers, but when she and Lahash entered the hall, she could see that the whole flat was lit up. She took off her jacket and put it down on the sofa, along with her shoulder bag.

"He's already here," Lahash said pointing at the floor behind the sofa.

Aninka peered over the furniture and saw Taziel's leather jacket lying on the carpet. It looked absurdly vulnerable, like a discarded skin. "They must be in his room," she said.

Lahash pulled an exasperated face. "I thought as much. Lead the way."

Aninka hesitated. "Do we have to? I mean, I don't relish the idea of barging in on something intimate."

Lahash grinned at her. "Don't be squeamish. We *do* have to. As I said, Taz is putting himself at risk."

Aninka huffed a sigh, and led the way down the short corridor to Taz's room. *Taz is doing this because Daniel's psychic,* she thought. *That has to be the reason. A meeting of souls. The meeting of bodies must be something wondrous.* She realised the futility of confiding these thoughts to Lahash, who would be unsympathetic at best.

When they stood before Taz's door, she pointed and mouthed, "There." Let Lahash be the one to intrude. She just couldn't do it.

Lahash clearly had no scruples about what he was doing; he virtually kicked the door open.

A dim lamp threw golden brown light over them where they lay on the bed. They were only half clothed, entwined together, and gazing at each other as if a kiss had just ended. For a split second, Aninka experienced an enormous grief, and then Lahash was in the room, hauling Daniel from Taz's arms, and everything broke up into chaos.

Daniel swore, wriggled and clawed in Lahash's hold as Lahash attempted to drag the boy from the bed.

Taziel uttered a succinct curse, his eyes fixed on Aninka. He thought she'd betrayed him. "What the hell are you doing?" he screamed at Lahash.

Lahash had retreated to the door, the struggling Daniel held firmly in his hands.

"Is this really necessary?" Aninka asked lamely, her voice unheard through the cacophony of Daniel's complaints and Taziel's furious questions. Lahash disappeared out of the door, hauling Daniel along the carpet.

By the time Aninka and Taziel reached the living room, Lahash had thrown Daniel down onto the sofa. Now, he leaned over the boy and Aninka's worst fears seemed about to be realised. Lahash held the dull, black muzzle of a gun against Daniel's hair. Daniel was curled up, his arms over his head, making no sound. He wore only a pair of black jeans. To Aninka, he seemed all bones and ribs, his skin stretched tightly over his body. His slim naked feet looked fragile. Aninka swallowed, thought *Shem's boy.* And understood immediately the root of Taz's desire. Shemyaza had touched this creature; part of him lived in Daniel.

"Did Shemyaza send you?" Lahash demanded.

Taziel ran over to the sofa, doing up his belt. His naked chest was pimpled with cold or shock. "Are you mad, Lahash? Put that gun away! Get real!" Aninka could see he was frightened.

Lahash ignored him, nudged the cold nose of the gun against Daniel's neck, making him whimper. "Answer. Did Shemyaza send you."

"No!" Daniel squeaked. "No! No!"

"You know he didn't!" Taziel shouted. "For fuck's sake, Lahash, let him go."

Lahash, apparently satisfied, straightened up, although he did not slide the gun back into its nest within his jacket. "I know no such thing. You blithely believe the boy is here because of you, but it's quite possible Shemyaza is aware of us, as we are aware of him.

Daniel slowly uncurled and glanced fearfully at Lahash, while modestly rezipping his trousers. "Who *are* you?"

"Friends of Peverel Othman," Lahash answered.

"Who?"

Lahash glanced theatrically at the ceiling. "Don't bother lying to us, Daniel. We know you're holed up in the Moses Assembly Rooms with the erstwhile Othman."

"He had no friends," Daniel said. "You're Grigori, aren't you." He glanced at Taziel. "I knew! Fuck, I knew! I'm so fucking stupid!" He balled his hands into fists and rolled his eyes in exasperation. Aninka's heart went out to him.

"It's not your concern what we are," Lahash said. "We just want answers."

Daniel shook his head wearily. "What do you want with me? If you think you can hold me hostage to get at Shem, you're wasting your time."

"That is not our intention," Lahash answered.

Daniel sat up straight, glanced round at Taziel again. His eyes said much, although his thoughts remained silent. "Then, what is your intention?"

Lahash sat down on the arm of the sofa, the gun held carelessly in one hand in his lap. "We just want to talk to you. We need information."

Daniel snarled at Taziel, "You bastard."

"I tried to tell you, didn't I?" Taziel said. "You wouldn't let me." He gestured at Lahash in apparent contempt. "This is not my idea, believe me."

Daniel looked at Aninka, as if for the first time. "Eve," he said, and smiled bitterly. "I walked right into it. Both of you! My God, why didn't I listen to Israel? He spotted what 'Jack' was straight away!" Daniel realised, miserably, that tonight was the last time he would ignore the voice of his intuition—supposing he had another chance to hear it.

"Daniel, you're not in any danger," Aninka said, sitting down on his other side. "We've had to be underhand, yes, but you don't know how important it is that Shemyaza is looked after by his own kind. He could be a very dangerous man."

"Daniel knows that," Taziel interjected.

"Will you kill him?" Daniel asked. He seemed calm, but Aninka could see he was shaking.

"No," she answered firmly. "I don't know how much you know about him, Daniel, but he's a special kind of person. He needs to be with people who appreciate that, otherwise he's a danger to himself and to others. Yes, we are all Grigori, and we are very concerned about Shemyaza. There are people waiting to meet him, to talk to him about what he is and try to help him. You care about him, don't you?"

Daniel was silent for a moment. "He could be something...marvellous."

"We know that," Aninka said. "We have been looking for him, and need to talk to you before we take any action."

"He doesn't care," Daniel said, and began to laugh. "You didn't have to lie to me. You could have walked right in there and taken him. He wouldn't have stopped you."

Aninka glanced at Lahash, whose posture had become alert. "What is his state of mind?" she asked carefully.

Daniel looked at her from beneath a fringe of hair. "I suppose if I don't tell you what you want to know, I'll get hurt?" He shook his head. "Eve, why didn't you tell me from the beginning?"

"No-one's going to hurt you, Daniel. I'm sorry we had to deceive you, but we had no way of knowing how you'd react to us. Now please, tell us what we want to know. It's very important."

Lahash uttered a scornful sound. "Don't be taken in, Ninka. This could just be a front." He prodded Daniel. "How many people are with him, and do they have weapons?"

"If I'm such an unknown quantity, how do you know I'll tell the truth?" Daniel said. He shook his head. "There are no weapons.

This is real life. Shemyaza is a broken man, and he's accompanied by an emotional cripple, a dream-eyed girl and a Grigori dependent who's over a hundred years old. That's our deadly fellowship." He laughed. "Scared?"

Lahash did not respond to Daniel's scorn. "Who else? There are other people there."

Daniel shrugged. "A bunch of weirdos. I hardly know them." He shot a hard glance at Taziel. "You met one tonight. Israel."

"Harmless," Taziel pronounced.

"How do we get into the Assembly Rooms?" Lahash asked.

Daniel's face clouded. Aninka wanted to reach out and touch him. At that moment, he seemed to have realised Lahash really meant to go to the Assembly Rooms and take Shemyaza away. "I don't know," he said lamely.

"Not good enough," Lahash said. "Is it locked up? Do you have keys?"

"Lily has them," Daniel said.

Lahash glanced at Taziel. "Where's his coat?"

Silently, Taziel picked up Daniel's leather jacket from the floor and handed it to Lahash. The keys were in an inside pocket. Lahash sneered, held them out and examined them. "These presumably open doors in Little Moor?"

"Yes," Daniel said. "I brought them with me from home."

Lahash grinned. "Of course you did." He glanced at Aninka, his eyes alight with the kind of excitement she did not want to see. "I must get over there."

Aninka stood up. "Then, I'm coming with you."

Lahash frowned. "Is that wise? We can't be sure the boy's telling the truth."

"I'm not letting you go alone." Aninka did not trust Lahash to try and take Shemyaza alive. Even now, she felt sick at what might have happened if she hadn't come back to the flat with him.

Lahash pointed a stiff finger at Taziel. "Keep the boy here. Are you capable of that?"

Daniel was sitting staring at his hands, his expression unreadable. Taziel sighed. "Yeah. Just get going."

Aninka did not envy Taziel's predicament, or the explanations he would now have to make.

"We need the car," Lahash said as they stepped from the building. "But it might be dangerous for me to fetch it."

"Then I'll go," Aninka said. "But don't think you can sneak off to the Assembly Rooms without me. Wait nearby. Where's the car parked?"

It required a short tube journey to reach the car park where Lahash kept his vehicle. He waited outside, while she rode the lift to the correct floor. She stepped out from the lift into an echoing vault, which was nearly empty of vehicles. Aninka recognised Lahash's sleek limousine immediately; it was the same car they had used to go to Little Moor. Nervously, she walked quickly towards it through the echoing car park. She held the car keys ready in her hand, and her eyes swivelled this way and that, alert for signs of pursuit, of shadows becoming real and hard and predatory. Her hands shook as she activated the central locking system and slid into the driving seat. For a brief, electrifying moment, she thought she'd forgotten how to drive, then reality kicked in and she sent the car squealing down to the street.

Outside, Lahash jumped into the passenger seat and snapped directions at Aninka. Much to her chagrin, she felt excitement begin to fizz up through her mind and limbs. She pressed her foot hard against the accelerator.

"Steady!" Lahash said. "Don't get done for speeding on the way there."

They seemed to reach Black Lion Square too quickly. When Aninka turned into it, she could not remember any details of the journey there. The square was empty, street-lamps shedding inadequate light. Aninka drove right up to the door of the Assembly Rooms and turned off the engine.

Lahash had Daniel's keys in his hand as he got out of the car. "Don't lock it," he said, as Aninka pointed the car keys to activate the locking system.

Aninka realised he was concerned they might need to get away quickly.

The front doors looked as if they hadn't been opened for years. There was only a large keyhole, which could not be unlocked with any of the small keys they had taken from Daniel. Lahash went to investigate the side alley, Aninka following. When they found the door, Lahash started experimenting with the keys.

"This place is enormous," Aninka said in a whisper. "He could be anywhere inside."

"Don't come with me if you're afraid," Lahash answered, and the door clicked open onto darkness. "Ladies first?"

Knowing he wanted her to decline, Aninka took her courage in her hands and walked through the door. Lahash made a quiet, approving sound and followed her.

Neither of them perceived the shadowy shapes standing motionless in the alley behind them.

Emma was arguing with Shem again. She had already imparted the information that Daniel and Lily had gone out; a circumstance of which she disapproved. Predictably, Shemyaza appeared to have no interest in the matter. He sat listening to her complaints with a pained expression on his face. "Why are you telling me this? What do you expect me to do?" His hands curved on the air, parting the wreath of smoke from Emma's cigarette.

"We must move on soon," Emma said. There, she had voiced it, though she would give him no reasons. If she told Shem about how her nerves were jumping, how she was feeling increasingly edgy, he would only smile.

Shem looked up at her. "Go where you like."

She ignored this remark. "Perhaps we could go abroad. You must know of other Grigori haunts."

Shem shrugged, and even opened his mouth to speak, but Emma silenced him with a raised hand. "Sssh! What was that?"

He put his head on one side. "What was what?"

"A noise!"

"This place is crawling with noises. Sit down, Emma. Have some wine." He was happy to let her play the role of guardian. All evening, he'd been aware of a sense of approach, and knew that people were coming for him. Since the dream of Ishtahar, it had been inevitable. He had let the future into his life.

Emma ignored his knowing smile and slunk to the door, her body stooped and tense. She felt it would be futile to tell Shem of her suspicions. Ever since leaving Little Moor, she'd been nervous of pursuit, and now her instincts were screaming in her mind. She wanted to get into her car and drive, anywhere, but she could not do it alone. Her promise to Helen Winter bound her to Lily and Owen, and sweet Lily had decided to abscond for the evening. Shem and the others seemed so sluggish, indifferent to the dangers of their position. They should have left this place days ago.

She opened the door as quietly as possible and went out into the dim corridor beyond. All seemed normal, but her spinal cord flexed in its column, an irrefutable warning. She ground out her cigarette beneath the sole of her shoe and, one hand touching the wall, advanced cautiously down the corridor. Meagre light illumined the landing beyond. There was no sound.

She bumped into the stranger on the stairs. He seemed as surprised as she was, for he took a step back. He was dressed in a well-cut suit, fairish hair falling over his shoulders. His long white hand lay upon the banister, his nails long and curved, dark like eagle claws.

Neither spoke. Emma looked into the pale eyes of the stranger and saw only relentless purpose looking back. She knew it was pointless to try and converse with this creature. Now, she did not feel afraid or nervous.

With one expertly aimed kick, she sent the interloper plummeting down the stairs.

Pausing only to glance down and see him writhing and curling on the next landing, Emma retreated up the corridor. As she did so, she heard the sound of soft footsteps running up the stairs. Many of them. They were upon her before she could draw breath to call for Shem. Blond-haired, all of them. It seemed like there were a dozen of them, pushing her against the wall. They spoke in whispers to one another, in a language she did not know. She knew they would kill her. Claws raked her cheek, her throat. She felt the fabric of her dress tear. She tried to cry out, but one of them stuffed sharp-pointed fingers into her mouth, and the sound came out muffled, gurgling. She tried to kick, but her feet could not make contact with flesh. They were too quick, swarming round her like a multitude of tiny things; grouping and regrouping. Yet the impression of smallness was insane; every one of them was as tall as she was.

Then the night splintered into sound and light: a dull crack, a sulphurous flare. Emma's assailants made a new noise, high and keening. They dropped to the floor and scurried back along the corridor on all fours, leaving her dazed and stiff with shock against the wall. She looked down and saw that one of them lay just beyond her feet, his angel face streaked with thin trails of blood. He was dead, shot through the brow.

The sound of gunfire came again, and again. Emma ran back up the corridor to Shem's room. They must get out. Perhaps through the window.

She was surprised to find Shem on his feet, staring at the door. Not as apathetic as he liked to make out then. She used her moment. "We have company. We have to escape. Now."

It satisfied her to see the expression on his face change. Surely he wouldn't simply sit there and wait for them? "Are you all right?" he asked her.

She nodded tersely. "Yes. The window."

He followed her across the room. "What happened?"

"Some *things* came for me. Someone started shooting them. I don't know who or why. We have to get out."

They were on the second floor; a sheer wall dropped away from them. No time to gather possessions or even the rest of their party. Shem shook his head and laughed at Emma as she climbed up onto the sill, ducking beneath the looming sash. "Shem, I'm not joking. There are monsters out there!" She experienced a thrill of emotional pain as she thought of Owen, sightless and vulnerable, sitting on his bed. Would they find him? Perhaps they would think he was Shem. That might give them some time. She hated herself for that thought. Lily and Daniel would have to look out for themselves as best they could.

"Emma, calm down," Shem said. "They are no more monsters than I am."

Emma ignored his remark. "I'll probably break my leg," she said. "We have no choice but to jump."

The door swung open before she could find the courage.

"Don't move!"

Emma looked up in alarm, expecting to see one of the blond things. A tall man stepped into the room, but his hair was very dark. He wore a raincoat, which hung open. He carried a gun. She thought she recognised him, but perhaps that was just because he was Grigori. There was no doubt about that.

Emma looked back at Shem. They could still make it through the window if they were quick, but Shem was standing with folded arms, staring placidly at the interloper. The gun did not appear to worry him.

The stranger moved towards them, his weapon held high. "Get back down, woman," he said. "If you jump, you'll die, or a bullet might get you first."

She hesitated, then Shem held out his arm and pulled her back into the room. His voice was calm, silky. "And who are you exactly? Might I ask what you want?"

"We want *you*," said the man.

"And who am I?" Shem asked.

Emma wanted to laugh. Shem radiated power. It was obvious what he was.

The man did not lower the gun. "You are Shemyaza. I've been looking for you."

"I believe I have a cult following," Shem said dryly.

Outside the door, Aninka heard the exchange of words. It would take guts to enter the room. The familiarity of Pev's voice came at her like a slap across the mouth. She felt afraid and nervous of seeing him, her heart was beating too fast. Her body and mind convulsed with the memories of grief and pointless love. For a moment, she considered running from the building, but even the thought of that was folly. She knew she had to see him again.

When she finally entered the room, everything seemed so still, as if time had slowed down.

He was there, beside the window, a woman standing against him. It was hard to believe she had actually found him now, but his presence was undeniable. He didn't look that different. She could tell that he recognised her, but also that he wasn't quite sure from where. The past, which meant so much to her, was clearly only partly remembered by him. Then he said her name, with some wonderment. "Aninka?"

Yes, she thought. *I have hunted you down.*

"Pev," she answered, unable to call him anything else. She could hear the pain in her voice; it sounded small in the room. What could she say to him, this man who had nearly destroyed her?

The woman standing at Shem's side said, "*You know her?*"

Lahash gestured with his gun. "No time for introductions, get moving. They'll be back soon. I only scattered them."

At Lahash's words, Shem seemed to gather himself up. Perhaps it was the instinct to survive. "They? I sensed only the two of you!" He towered like a reed of light in the room, shivering with power.

Aninka felt the hairs on her neck raise. *He doesn't have to go with anyone if he doesn't want to...*"They are weird people," she said. "Dangerous." She pointed at Emma's scratched face and neck. "They had your friend."

"So?" Shem said. "What are they? The hounds of the Parzupheim? Insects! Why should I go anywhere with you?"

"It would be best to," Aninka answered coolly. "At least you'll be safe with us."

"Safe? You have no idea..."

"I do," she said.

"There's a car outside," Lahash said. "Let's go."

Shem would not move. "Where do you want to take me?"

"Cornwall," Aninka said. "High Crag House. You're expected." *He won't come with us,* she thought. *He'll put up a fight, and Lahash might kill him.*

"Cornwall," Shem echoed and tapped his lips with a forefinger thoughtfully.

He seemed amused, as if he was playing with them. Aninka suspected he was on the verge of complying with their request, but then Lahash decided to take action. Without warning, he leapt across the room and slammed Shem against the wall. It was the kind of thing Aninka had feared might happen. She cried out in warning, yelled at Lahash to stand back.

Shem uttered an indignant roar, and the room filled with a blaze of light. The woman beside him let out a stifled scream. Lahash was tossed backwards, to land in a heap at Aninka's feet. She feared he was dead, but he uttered a shocked groan and rolled onto his side. It was a miracle the gun hadn't gone off.

Shem stood against the wall with his arms held high. His face was radiant with infernal power. His whole body emanated a spectral glow. Aninka swallowed reflexively. What stood before her now was more than a man, more than Grigori.

"Stop this!" she cried harshly. "You must come with us! My guardian, Enniel Prussoe, is a member of the Parzupheim. They only want to help you. They *know* what you are. So, it seems, does someone else. We want you alive, but others might want you dead. For your own sake, you must come with us!" She was still unsure whether the creatures outside the room had been sent by Enniel or not, but felt she had to convince Shem the Parzupheim would not harm him.

Shem flexed his hands into fists and hissed. "To Cornwall?" Sparks of light seemed to crackle in his hair.

Aninka nodded. "Yes. My guardian has a stronghold there. Nothing will be able to get to you."

The room seemed to hold its breath, then Shem relaxed a little and the glow faded from his eyes. He smiled affably and said, "All right."

For a few moments, nobody said a word. Then Emma began to laugh, a sound tinged with hysteria.

It can't be this easy, Aninka thought. Shem now looked tired and thin, drained by the burst of energy he'd directed at his attacker. The light in the room had become dim, as if the bulbs had been sucked of power.

Lahash got gingerly to his feet and rubbed his arms as if they were numb. Shem stared at him scornfully. "I said I'll come with you. What are you waiting for?"

Aninka half expected another attack. "Well, let's go then."

They began to move towards the door, then Shem hesitated. *Here it comes,* Aninka thought. *He'll back off again.* But she was wrong.

"Daniel..." Shem said. "The twins..."

"Don't worry," Aninka told him hurriedly. "Daniel's with us. Once we get to my guardian, we'll do what we can for your other companions." She still expected another excuse to emerge.

Shem directed a single, penetrating glance at her. "You have been busy," he said coolly. "Lead on."

Chapter Twelve
The Lord of Terrors

In a high room, opposite the Moses Assembly Rooms, Sofia awaited developments. She held a pair of night-sight binoculars to her face and behind her, two women in black stood like caryatids of stone. They were Serafim; Grigori warriors. The room was empty, an attic smelling of must. Spiritual presences, long enchained within the wood and stone of the building, clustered towards the light of Sofia's soul, but she burned them away with her indifference. All her attention was focused on the building in front of her. Nearby, at strategic points, other Serafim waited in vehicles or on foot. The etheric Kerubim, savage Grigori predators, awaited Sofia's summons, although she hoped she would not need them. All was prepared.

Half an hour before, Sofia had been ready to send in her people and use whatever method possible to entrap Shemyaza. Then, Lahash Murkaster's car had drawn up on the road outside, and she'd recognised Enniel's ward Aninka. Had Enniel sent her? That was possible. Within the inner cabals of the Grigori, trust was virtually unknown. Enniel might suspect Sofia's motives. She smiled. No, he wasn't that clever. Othman had once been Aninka Prussoe's lover. It seemed most likely that she had her own agenda. The scorned huntress. Her search for Othman, which had culminated in Little Moor, had ended in failure. Perhaps now, she aimed for success. Sofia sighed. Love and desire: what fatal arrows they were. She watched Aninka and Murkaster sniffing round the building opposite, and decided to observe what happened. She had no fear for Shemyaza's life, confident that his power would protect him. Anyone else was expendable.

It was possible that Aninka and Murkaster might jeopardise her own plans, but she doubted it. Let them do the work for her. She could intercept them afterwards. Also, it seemed most likely Aninka's involvement meant only that they intended to take the Anakim to Enniel.

Then Sofia's skin had prickled a warning.

Across the road in the Assembly Rooms, something alien had manifested in the echoing, empty rooms and the bare, neglected stair-cases. Intruders. Sofia sensed them as chaotic forms. They were Grigori, but transformed, like Kerubim, into beings that were monstrous. They did not have the psychic feel of creatures that had been sent by the Parzupheim. Was some other faction acting without her sanction? Then, as more information poured into her mind, her lips peeled back from her teeth in a grin. So, another of her proteges was making his presence felt. She recognised the intruders as Emim, and knew of only one person in this country who had recourse to such demons. She herself had helped him shape them. *Fool!* she thought. *You think you can get to him before I do?*

She summoned one of the Serafim women. "Semili, please go and position yourself upon the roof of the Assembly Rooms. Await a message from me."

The Serafim inclined her head and melted from the room like a half-seen shadow.

Sofia turned to the remaining aide. "Agnestis, go and start the car."

Left alone, Sofia extended her finely tuned senses towards the building opposite. She could sense the black flame of Shemyaza, and the other bright points of light, which indicated the positions of living souls. He eclipsed them all. Her hands curled into fists. *Murkaster, get him out now!* Alien presences were slithering over the stairs, hanging from the rafters, dropping down like spores. They possessed a doorway of some kind, a portal that enabled them to travel between space and time. If Murkaster didn't move quickly, he would be engulfed, and Sofia didn't trust that the owner of the Emim could control them completely. Shemyaza might get damaged.

Movement alerted her. She saw Semili's fluid shape flowing over the rooftops. The Serafim would gaze down chimneys, hang from eaves to peer into attic rooms. Sofia directed a message to her. *What do you feel? What do you see?*

I feel the presence of chaos, Mother, but I see nothing.

Wait, then. Sofia put down the binoculars, closed her eyes, and concentrated entirely with her mind on what was happening in the Assembly Rooms. She could sense argument and confusion, all enwrapped by the sinister presence of the *others*. Perhaps she should act overtly, call in the Kerubim, flood the building with them. Then, a spear of thought pierced her mind. Semili.

They are moving.

Sofia opened her eyes and raised the binoculars once more. She saw dark shapes hurrying down the alley: one of them, female, running on ahead. That must be Aninka. Shemyaza was instantly recognisable. She could not make out the details of his features, but he was surrounded by a golden aura. Sofia counted heads: four. Shemyaza must have one of his followers with him. She wondered what had happened to the others. They too would have their uses.

Sofia contacted Agnestis. *I am coming down.*

They would follow Murkaster and Aninka to Cornwall, and if they tried to go anywhere else, they would have to get past the Serafim first. The master of the Emim she would deal with later.

"Do you think it was all right to let Daniel go off with that guy?" Lily asked, as she walked arm in arm with Israel up the side street that led to the square. Now that they'd left the club, some of her euphoria had evaporated. The dance-sweat had dried on her back; her skin was cold. She felt nervous of Israel's hot proximity.

Israel made a palliative sound. "He'll be fine."

Lily, conscious of this Grigori's strength and height beside her, fought for words. "But he's...inexperienced."

"Don't be afraid," Israel said.

They walked into the square and Lily could hear birds calling in the trees of the Garden of Remembrance, even though it was still the middle of the night. The city was like that, she thought, mixed up in time. During the dark hours, many things happened that belonged to the light of day, or vice versa.

"Let's cut through the gardens," Lily suggested.

They walked through the creaking iron gate and onto the path, strewn with wet, papery leaves, which were slippery underfoot. The bare branches of the trees gripped the sky above them, and a few stars could be seen through the orange haze of the city lights. Lily sighed. She felt momentarily sad; one of those moments when time condenses and the past and the future seem to come together in the heart in one melancholy spasm. Only a few weeks ago, she'd been able to predict the course of her life from day to day. Now, the illusion had been shattered. There was no routine, and her belief in one had been misguided. Always the gift of her heritage had been waiting for her, waiting to pounce and tear the fabric of her reality to shreds.

Israel put his arm around her shoulder. "Don't worry about Daniel."

"I'm not." Lily wondered whether she was about to cry. It was absurd, but her emotions seemed outside of herself; she could observe them with a cool eye.

Israel made her stop walking and put his dark hands upon her arms. She looked up into his inscrutable face. *He's not human.* The thought seemed inconceivable. But how could she think that? She'd never been completely human herself.

Israel lifted her bodily in his arms until her face was level with his own. Then he kissed her, and Lily opened her eyes to the vague, occluded stars. She felt her body was a void, empty of light, but stretching into infinity. She thought of Ishtahar, and the time-lessness of love, its eternally damned patience. She thought of Owen and the way they had once been lovers, drawn to one another because there was no-one else of their kind to turn to.

When Israel released her, Lily sat down upon one of the wooden seats beside the path, hugging her arms because she felt cold. Israel sat down beside her and touched her cool cheek with his fingers. She shivered, prompting him to withdraw his hand.

"No!" she said, shaking her head, and turned towards him. "Touch me again."

He reached out and slid his long, dark hand beneath her hair. Lily leaned against him. She felt lonely, yet weirdly happy. She wanted this Grigori male. It was his duty to obey her desire.

On the wet mat of leaves behind the bench, Lily lay back upon her shawl and lifted the red folds of her borrowed gown. She parted her legs with her knees raised, and Israel knelt between them. They said nothing to each other as he unzipped his trousers. Lily closed her eyes and stretched her arms along the ground, high over her head. She parted her legs wider, feeling the cold air moving against her moist sex. She still felt weirdly removed from herself. Her instinct was that of lust, and her body was responding to it, but her mind seemed up among the stars.

Israel touched her gently between the legs, opening her up with his long fingers. Coolly, she felt the lust grow hotter in her loins, the hungry contraction of muscles that desired only something to grip, something male and hard and alive. His dextrous strok-ing, which he must see as foreplay for her own pleasure, only teased her. It was agony because she wanted all of his body, and there was pleasure in prolonging that agony, in not voicing the command for him to enter her.

She was almost at the point of orgasm by the time she felt his thick Grigori penis begin to push into her. She was used to their size, for she had slept with Othman, but Israel seemed concerned about causing her pain and moved only slowly. Were Grigori women any larger than human girls? Was that why he was so careful? She didn't care. She wanted to feel her flesh stretching to accommodate him. In an attempt to encourage him, she curled her legs around his back, pressing down with her heels to pull him into her. She felt him shudder with desire, and could hear his breath becoming harsher. His hands were upon her breasts as he strained his upper body against the constriction of her encircling thighs, but she gripped him only harder. She was still the empty void and she sucked him into her. In, out: the long fist of his sex pumped her body. Her skin was hypersensitive, registering in abnormal detail each fraction of his movements. Then, she sensed a ball of light spinning in the void, getting larger, drawing nearer, bringing with it a tail of fire. She thrust her legs high into the air as the orgasm crashed through her body. She felt it in her arms, her legs, her fingers, her toes, her eyelashes, her tongue, the depths of her ears. Her hair seemed to stand on end. Then, in the pulsing aftermath, she felt Israel's seed gouting into her, soaking into the soil of her womb.

With tangled hair, and leaf-strewn clothes, they ambled down the pavement towards the Assembly Rooms, beneath the shuttered eyes of the dark, looming buildings. Few words had passed between them. They had stood up, brushed themselves down, and resumed their walk home. Their communion had seemed a necessary thing, an act of love for the world, something which ensured the sun would rise tomorrow. She would sleep with Israel tonight, and before they slept, they would make love again and again.

When Lily saw the dim lights in the windows of the Assembly Rooms, alarm stabbed unexpectedly through her belly. The light looked different, although she couldn't understand how. She sensed danger, and without realising it, became rooted to the spot.

"What is it?" Israel asked.

"There's something...something feels *wrong.*" She wondered why Israel couldn't sense the strangeness all around them. He was pure-born Grigori and should surely be more sensitive than she was.

Israel only peered at her, waiting for her to explain.

Lily tried to find the words, but found that the feeling had ebbed. It had been like a brief waking dream. She shrugged and began walking again. "I don't know what it was," she said lamely, but in her head was a blazing image of Owen. She felt worried about him. They had left him alone.

Once they reached the side alley, Israel retrieved his keys from his jacket pocket, but after he put the first of them in the lock, he made a sound of consternation. "The door's open." He glanced at Lily, and she felt her skin crawl with dread once more.

"Owen," she said, and pushed past Israel into the building.

The moment she stepped into the place, she felt the change. Something had happened here, or was still happening.

"Wait, Lily." Israel's hand clamped on her arm. His voice was low.

"You sense it?" She was shivering now.

"Let me go first."

"Owen's room," Lily said. "Please!"

Israel glanced back at her, made a soothing gesture. "OK."

They went up the back stairs. On the second landing, Lily stifled a cry of disgust. There was blood on the threadbare carpet, wet and shiny in the dim light. Israel swore softly. "Is this because of your friend Shem, do you think?"

"I don't know." She risked a partial honesty. "Probably." She wondered how much Israel had worked out about her and her companions.

Israel shook his head and padded up the next flight of stairs, Lily following some distance behind. She felt very much afraid now, her fear condensing in her chest, clogging her breath. She wanted to turn around and run from the house, but the image of Owen held her feet to the climb.

The strangers dropped down upon them before Lily and Israel even noticed they were there. Uncanny creatures: their bodies as skinny as birds, and their floating hair like feathers. They seemed to drift down from the dark corners of the ceiling, or from an upper storey, like webs of gauze, but once they struck they became hard teeth and claws, possessed by the strength of eagles.

Lily uttered a cry of horror. She saw the flash of white faces, with dark, burning eyes, but they moved so quickly, she could barely isolate their images. She was aware of slender limbs encircling her body with preternatural strength.   They did not attempt to hurt her, but their smell was unliving and it frightened her.

Israel gasped out a cry of pain, and Lily realised the creatures were not being so solicitous with him.   She tried to utter a protest and struggled to go to his aid, but the blurred, shimmering assailants held her firmly in their grip.   She could not see Israel for his body was completely covered in the flickering creatures. "Don't hurt him!"   Her cry was ignored.   She realised then that the sinister pursuers, whom Emma had always feared, had become a hideous reality.   These creatures had come for Shem.   Lily cursed herself.   If both she and Daniel had been here, their heightened awareness would have felt these creatures coming.   As if sensing her thoughts, one of them stopped shimmering before her eyes and she was able to look into his face.   He was beautiful, with small features, heavy-lidded dark eyes and a pointed jaw, but he was slightly less tall than Grigori normally were, and silent.   "Who are you?" Lily murmured, her voice a husky fragile sound.

The creature's lips did not move, but she heard the word, "Emim.   We are the Terrors."

There had been blood upon the stairs.   Whose?

Israel was still trying to put up a fight—she could hear him cursing—whereas she was capable only of standing against the wall, helpless.   She understood there was no point in fighting.

"Lily!"

Her body stiffened at the sound of her name.   She looked up and saw Johcasta running towards her on the landing above.   Her clothes were in disarray and her face was bruised and bloody.   Behind her came a pair of grinning Emim.   They stalked her without haste, aware she had nowhere to run.

The Emim around Lily broke away from her, and swarmed up the stairs to engulf Johcasta in a melee of dark limbs.   "Lily!"

Lily put her hands over her ears.   She felt utterly numb, incapable even of fear.   Johcasta managed to struggle free a little and threw something down the stairs, which landed at Lily's feet. It was a small leather pouch.   Lily stared at this object for a few moments, unable to identify it.   Then she realised it contained Johcasta's divining stones.   She glanced up the stairs as Johcasta uttered an agonised, despairing groan.   There was no clear sight of the Grigori woman now, just a dark, twitching huddle, and the pale heads of the Emim, dipping and swaying above their victim.   One white face came up and snarled silently at Lily. Blood dribbled from its mouth. Lily felt nausea rise within her, yet she couldn't be sick. This was all too unreal. Her limbs had become sluggish. She could not decide what to do, although she did not feel as if she was in any physical danger herself. These creatures had come for Shem; they had come for all of them. Slowly, she sank down the wall, and squatted against it, with her hands still clasped around her ears. This did nothing to blot out the hideous sounds around her: the bubbling cries of Israel and Johcasta, the crunch of bone and the tear of flesh. She closed her eyes and began humming loudly to herself, in an attempt to isolate herself from what was happening. She did not think of Israel. He was lost to her now: she knew that. Hadn't the intensity of their love-making in the garden somehow foreseen this moment? She couldn't feel shock or grief, because in some way she had known this was to happen. The price for loving her was death. She thought of Ishtahar again, and a blue calm came into her mind. *I am going mad,* she thought. *Madness is no pain.* But it didn't feel like madness.

Gradually, everything subsided to quiet. Lily, with her eyes screwed tightly shut, wondered whether she had stepped out of reality. If she opened her eyes now, would she find herself somewhere completely unknown? Something nudged her foot, and she flinched, reluctantly opening her eyes. One of the pale-skinned Emim stood over her, his hands and face seamed with blood. He gestured for her to rise. Holding the Emim's eyes with her own, Lily reached out and grabbed hold of the pouch Johcasta had thrown to her, which she slipped into one of the deep pockets of the red gown. Then she rose slowly to her feet. She didn't want to look to left or right for fear of seeing what had happened to Israel and Johcasta. The Emim nodded in apparent approval, then began to ascend the stairs. Lily shrank against the banister and followed him. Out of the corner of her eye she saw a splash of bright, gold-embroidered fabric on the floor: the corner of Johcasta's skirt.

Lily followed the Emim into one of the rooms upstairs. It was a bare chamber, furnished only by an ancient table, which still gleamed with French polish beneath the light of the street-lamps coming in from outside. Here, a tall, red-haired figure sat, his legs crossed casually, his pale, long-boned hands resting gracefully upon his raised knee. Even in the dim light, his features were plain to see, as if his skin glowed from within. She knew he was Grigori. No humans were ever that beautiful.

"You are Lily Winter," he said. His voice was soft yet sharp, like light dancing upon ice cubes.

Lily nodded. She knew then that these creatures had not found Shem, and were about to question her about it. Shem had gone. He had abandoned her, and there was nothing she could tell his pursuers that would help them.

The red-haired man blinked slowly, as if he'd heard her thoughts. "You don't know where he is." There was no hint of enquiry in his voice.

Lily shook her head. She felt too numb to speak, and yet if she said nothing, they might kill her because she was of no use to them. Her only thought was that at least Daniel was safe somewhere, and because of this she was not totally alone. If she could only survive this night, she too would be safe. "Who are you?" The words came out separately, as if they had no meaning.

The red-haired man re-crossed his legs and drew in his breath through his nose. "I am Salamiel," he said. "A friend of Azazel, whom you know."

She shook her head. "No I don't. Who is he?" She knew she was playing for time, but it was so difficult because her mind felt disconnected from the present moment.

Salamiel laughed, but made almost no sound. His head simply went back and his mouth dropped open. A series of coughing sighs came out of him. "You *do* know him," he said. "He has touched you, enfolded you. You are his."

Lily frowned. "I don't know what you mean."

"You call him Shemyaza," Salamiel explained. "That is one of his names, but he has many. Shemyaza means, literally, the name of Azza, and that is but a form of Azazel, the scapegoat." He pulled a scornful face. "But you know none of this, of course. You simply accept what you see, and have no interest in the truth behind the name." He smiled and held out his hands. "To me, he is Azazel, and always will be. It is his dark side, and one that the Parzupheim wish dearly to contain. But I am his brother, and his dark soul calls to me. I seek him because of this yearning. You are his creature and you must lure him to me."

"I don't know where he is," Lily said helplessly.

"The boy, Daniel, will know." Salamiel's eyes burned with a vivid orange light. He had the eyes of a red cat.

Lily felt she was witnessing the true face of the Grigori, more so than those she had met before, like Israel and Johcasta. This was Shem's equal.

"Azazel will not abandon his vizier," Salamiel said. "He will summon him, one way or another."

"Daniel's not here," Lily said lamely.

Salamiel stood up and made a gesture of irritation. "I know that, as I know exactly what he is doing at this moment. Oh, it is all of no consequence! The Parzupheim will take Azazel to their sanctuary in Cornwall. Of that, I have no doubt. It is the only place to take him, because that is where his work must begin." He turned and looked at Lily. "It is an inconvenience that he's been taken by them, not least because some of my Emim have suffered. Still, at least I have you..."

Lily could not prevent an image of Owen flashing through her mind.

Salamiel smiled. "And the damaged boy, of course." He gestured towards the door, where two of his Emim were waiting. "Would you like to see him?"

Lily felt a thrill of alarm course through her belly. *I must guard my thoughts.* But of course, it was too late.

"How little you know of the history of your race," Salamiel said in a conversational tone, as he led the way to Owen's room. "Have you no curiosity about it?"

Lily shrugged. "Yes. I haven't had time..."

"I have seen so much about you." Salamiel placed a cold hand on her shoulder. "The little village, your little life, and what happened to you when Azazel came upon you. Don't you realise how privileged you are?"

Lily wanted to say "Nothing good happened," but kept silent, realising Salamiel would not want to hear that. "He told us very little," she said.

"We have all the time in the world," Salamiel said. "Do you know that? And yet we have no time at all." They had come to Owen's door. Salamiel put one hand flat against the flaking paint and said, "Your brother is sacred." Then he pushed open the door, splintered the wood, shattered the rim lock.

Inside, the room was a forest of candles. Here they had built a temporary shrine. Owen sat naked upon his mattress, his eyes staring sightlessly at the door. His flesh was scored as if by the point of a very sharp knife, with swirling patterns and hieroglyphs. The blood had not run, but lay in beads along the cuts, catching the light. One of the Emim lay with his head in Owen's lap, sucking away at the fruit of maleness that grew there.

"O'!" Lily made to run to him, but Salamiel held her back.

"You must not disturb them," he said. "Azazel has absorbed part of the boy into himself. Therefore, part of Azazel resides within the boy. A small, silent part, but present nonetheless. We pay homage to this residue and draw out the essence of Shemyaza with flesh."

Lily saw Owen's body convulse, his head thrown back. He made a wordless noise, which sounded almost like a question. The Emim rose from his lap and spat into a glass vessel that was held out to him by one of his companions.

"We must keep the seed," Salamiel said casually, "for it has great power."

Lily made a disgusted sound and turned her head away.

Salamiel made a small noise of surprise. "You are shocked by this? Why? You and Azazel have shared far rarer pleasures."

"Let him go," Lily said. "He's ill. He doesn't know what's happening."

Salamiel nodded. "True. It is disappointing, but only to be expected. Azazel can restore him, and for this reason, surely, you should want my assistance."

"He won't do it," Lily said. "Everyone's tried to persuade him. He won't. He's not what you think."

"He is the greatest Grigori that ever lived, or ever shall," Salamiel remarked. "The sacrifice he became on behalf of our race made him so. Nothing is beyond him. If he has not become aware of himself, that is only the fault of those around him, who cannot appreciate his power." He reached out to touch Lily's hair, but she jerked away from him.

"What are you going to do to us?"

"Fear not, pretty maiden. My plans for you are all congenial." He sighed and walked towards his companions. "We must leave now. Dress the boy." He turned to Lily. "Are there any belongings you wish to take with you?"

"With me where?" Lily asked in a whisper.

"My house," Salamiel answered. "You are to be my guests for a while. We have so much to discuss."

Chapter Thirteen
Coast Flight

Daniel sat on the sofa in Taziel's living room, refusing to speak.
Taziel had tried, on numerous occasions during the last hour, to initiate a discussion, and had explained himself in several different
ways. Daniel knew that Taziel's explanations were all valid and
without artifice, but still felt betrayed and angry. How stupid he had
been to fall for Taziel's seduction. He realised now that he had been
the victim of a Grigori plot since the moment he'd met "Eve" in the
cafe. The presence that had come to him in the night, held him in
etheric arms, had been Taziel, paving the way for a later conquest.
Daniel knew he had been used, and no matter how much Taziel
insisted he respected and felt genuinely attracted to him, Daniel could
not bring himself to utter forgiveness. He realised this was more
because he was angry with himself, but the effect was the same.

"We are doing the best thing for Shemyaza," Taziel said, but
Daniel could tell he still hated and adored the image of Peverel
Othman, and that he didn't really care what was best for Shem, only
what was best for Taziel. He wanted revenge, if only to speak his
mind to the person he believed had ruined him. But, no matter how
much he denied it to himself, Taziel also wanted reconciliation.
Daniel could see the wistful colours of it in Taziel's aura as he stalked
around the room, talking quickly, his arms snaking on the air. By
this time, Daniel had heard the story of what Peverel Othman had
done to Taziel at least three times. He admitted to himself that if
he'd experienced such traumas as Taziel had, he'd probably feel the
same way, but was physically unable to commiserate. He wanted
Taziel to suffer because he had lied.

"I tried to tell you, but you wouldn't let me," Taziel said,
lighting a cigarette. "You were too interested in sex."

If that was supposed to provoke a response, Daniel refused
to rise to it. He turned his head towards the window, then considered lying down. If he pretended to go to sleep, that would infuriate

Taziel even more. How long must he stay here? He presumed the other two would come back once they had persuaded or threatened Shemyaza to accompany them. He could imagine Shem's response. There would be no resistance, of this he was sure. Shem didn't care. He would find their interest in him mildly amusing, that was all. Emma might not be so compliant, but ultimately she would follow Shem's lead.

Daniel stretched himself out on the sofa and put his hands under his head. Taziel made an irritated sound, but Daniel would not look at him. He closed his eyes, wondering whether this would provoke Taziel enough for him to get violent. With the room blotted out, Daniel became aware of his body, how it still tingled with the fading rhythm of sex and desire. It seemed obscene now, and yet part of him still wanted it. He presumed this was because of the drug Israel had given him earlier. How would Taziel react if Daniel just sat up now and demanded that they make love? The thought made him smile, although he had no intention of doing anything about it.

"What's so funny?" Taziel asked.

Daniel felt his weight as he sat down on the end of the sofa. He considered saying something to Taziel at last, something cruel and witty, but before he could decide on the words, a cramp of incredible pain lanced through his body. He cried out in shock and curled instinctively into a tight ball.

"What is it?" Taziel asked in an urgent voice.

Daniel could not speak, but managed to utter a choked groan. Images flashed through his mind: blood, terror, pale creatures dropping down in darkness to devour and tear. He saw Lily's white face, screaming silently, her mouth an enormous dark oval. He saw Israel's head hanging from his ruined body, his open eyes filmed with blood. "No!" Daniel leapt upright and staggered across the room, only to fall down in increasing waves of pain.

Taziel was beside him in an instant, his hands on Daniel's shuddering shoulders. "What's happened?"

Daniel tried to regulate his breathing. It felt as if sharp knives were scoring his skin in whirling patterns. He sensed his suffering was sympathetic, and that he must take control of it; the agony was not his. He slapped Taziel's fluttering hands away and managed to pull himself into a sitting position, clutching his belly. Gradually, he pushed the sensations of pain away, calmed himself with deep breathing. "Something's happened. Israel is dead. Something attacked them."

Taziel's eyes grew wider. "Tell me."

Daniel shook his head. "I don't want to go back into that. It wasn't...too pleasant." He rubbed his face. "Lily and Owen are alive, I feel this. I think Shem and the others are OK too, but some have died. There's a presence, a red hot presence, and it can sense me. I must shield myself." A metallic, grinding, humming noise was beginning to fill his head, accompanied by a shrill ache. Daniel shook his head again vigorously. His eyes were watering.

Taziel said nothing more, but sat back on the floor opposite Daniel. To Daniel's intense relief, he began to conjure a cone of white light around the room, to protect them from any malign influences. The force of Taziel's mind was so great, the effect took place almost at once. Daniel felt the hideous sensations fade away. He could do nothing but fall into Taziel's waiting arms, needing the reassuring, physical presence of another body.

For a few moments they sat there hugging one another, unable to speak. Then the phone began to ring. Taziel leapt up and answered it. Daniel heard him say, "Ninka! What's happened?" He said nothing more, but kept nodding and uttering small urgent sounds of encouragement. Finally he said, "Let me speak to Lahash."

"What's happened?" Daniel asked, but Taziel only raised a hand for silence.

"OK, we'll do that." Taziel put down the phone. "They were on the mobile, in the car. They have Shem and the woman, Emma. You were right. There was trouble. Another Grigori faction beat them to it, but Lahash, with his macho weapons, managed to get them out alive."

"Are they coming here?"

Taziel shook his head. "No, too dangerous. We'll have to follow them to Cornwall. In view of what you just experienced, I think we should go sooner rather than later. We might be in danger ourselves."

"Do people really want Shem so badly?"

Taziel shook his head in disbelief. "Daniel, are you mad? You know what Shem's potential is. He is the herald of the New Age. Hell, he *is* the New Age. But if the wrong people get hold of him, the New Age could be worse than the old."

"All this, yet he is still Peverel Othman to you, and you want to tell him how much he hurt you."

Taziel looked away. "Yeah, well. It's all relative. Are you OK to travel now?"

"How? On the train?"

Taziel smiled and picked up the phone. "Don't be ridiculous. I'll call us a hire car. Grigori money can buy anything at any time of day or night."

As Taziel punched in the number, Daniel asked. "They got Lily and Owen out as well then?"

Taziel flicked him a furtive glance. "Er...no. They left without seeing either of them."

Daniel leapt to his feet. "Taz, we must go there! We can't just leave them!" Then he slumped down to the floor again. "No, too late, too late."

He put his head in his hands as Taziel ordered the car. He sensed that Lily and Owen were alive, but they had been seized by the same creatures that had killed Israel. And whatever had taken them wanted him, too. It was collecting Shem's followers. The name "Azazel" came into Daniel's mind. Was that who was behind the abduction? He remembered dimly that it might be the name of one of the other Watchers, which he and Owen had picked up when they'd been researching the Grigori in Little Moor.

Taziel put down the phone. "Half an hour," he said. "I'd better get some things together."

He went into the bedroom, and Daniel followed him. "Does the name "Azazel" mean anything to you?"

Taziel was pulling clothes off a rail in the corner of the room. "Yeah, in some versions of our history he was supposed to be Shemyaza's right hand man. In others, it's simply another name for Shemyaza himself."

Daniel nodded. "Right. Well, I think that someone called Azazel is behind what's happened. I picked the name up a short while ago. It can't be Shem...I don't know. It might be that someone is just using the name."

"I don't want to find out just yet," Taziel said, stuffing clothes into a canvas carrier. "Let's get to Cornwall as soon as we can. We'll be safe there. It's a Grigori stronghold."

Daniel raised his arms helplessly. "But what about Lily and Owen? We can't just leave them."

"What else can we do? If you think this character is looking for you too, we have to get you to a sanctuary as soon as possible."

Daniel shuddered. He suddenly felt very cold, and an image flashed across his mind, of pale, crawling creatures with long white hair swarming over the roof of Taziel's apartment, dropping down the chimneys, scratching their way in through the windows. They were physical creatures and no cone of light could keep them out.

"I'm afraid," he said.

Taziel zipped up the bag and came to take Daniel's shaking body in his arms. He kissed the top of Daniel's head. "I want to protect you," he said.

The next half hour seemed to take an age to pass. Daniel frantically paced the apartment, checking every window, expecting to see ghostly white faces at every one. He jumped whenever he heard a strange noise, thinking it was something on the roof.

"We're fine," Taziel said. "They haven't found us. They're just looking." He shared Daniel's discomfort, but knew that if they both gave in to fear, it would act like a beacon of light to those who were hunting them. Taziel tried to shroud Daniel's worried thoughts with a blanket of calm.

Taziel turned out all the lights and watched at the long front window for the car. When it finally arrived, five minutes late, he and Daniel fled the flat. Outside, the night seemed alive with presences, and whispered voices seemed to hiss in Daniel's ears as he threw himself into the back of the car.

"This must look very suspicious," Taziel remarked to the driver, "but please drive us to Cornwall as fast as you can. Drive as if the dukes of Hell were after us."

The driver laughed, probably thinking they were involved in some kind of criminal activity and put his foot down. Daniel curled against Taziel's side, and listened to the rapid beat of his heart.

The car hissed through the night, filled with the sound of a late night radio station. Taziel chain-smoked, gazing out of the window. Occasionally, the driver tried to make conversation, but Taziel replied in monosyllables to discourage him.

"Say if you want to stop for anything," said the driver.

"We don't want to stop," Taziel replied.

Soon the city was left behind, and the road stretched out ahead into darkness. The miles flickered by; sleeping towns and dreaming fields. As they drew nearer to Cornwall, the countryside became wilder and more empty. Fields gave way to wilderness and moorland.

On a lonely road, a pale figure materialised on the grass verge. "Hitch-hiker at this time?" said the driver, incredulous.

"I don't think so," Taziel replied calmly, "don't slow down."

"But it's a girl! We can't just..."

"Put your foot down, will you!" Taziel could see the pale face, the dark holes of the eyes, the long, floating white hair, the slender body leaning into the rain.

The driver made a disgruntled noise, but stepped on the accelerator. As they passed the pale figure, it launched itself at the windscreen. The car lurched violently as the driver applied the brakes in terror. The vehicle slewed across the wet tarmac, and slid to a halt, half-facing the direction from which they'd come. There was no sign of the strange, leaping figure. The driver made to open his door, but Taziel barked a command. "Don't you dare! Just get going again!"

"But, for fuck's sake, the kid's probably lying half dead on the road."

"It's no kid and it's not on the road!" Taziel yelled. "It's on the fucking roof!"

Daniel had woken up, murmuring, "What's going on?"

Taziel hit the driver in the back. "Just get moving will you? Are the doors all locked?"

"Fucking hell!" The driver sounded frightened now.

"I said the dukes of Hell, I meant the dukes of Hell," Taziel said. "We have to shake that thing off. Put your damn foot down!"

The car screeched forward, and Taziel heard the unmistakable scrabble of diamond hard claws on the car's roof. At this sound, the driver uttered a panicked string of profanities. How long would the thing keep a grip? Presumably, it intended to take a ride with them, see where they ended up. If it had wanted to attack it would have done so by now. But what if there were more of them further ahead? Taziel wiped sweat from his upper lip. Daniel's face was white and tense, his eyes round as he looked up into Taziel's face.

Taziel forced a smile. "Trust me. We'll be fine."

They reached a straight stretch of road, where Taziel instructed the driver to increase their speed. When the speedometer reached ninety, he said. "Now stop."

"What?" There was an edge of hysteria in the driver's voice.

"Emergency stop? Remember?"

"It'll fucking kill us!"

"Just do it!" He pulled Daniel forward off the seat. "Down. Curl up." They both huddled onto the floor behind the front seats.

The car had slowed a little, but the jolt when it came was bone-breaking. They heard something bump on the road in front of them, followed by a strange, high-pitched scream.

"Now step on it again!" Taziel cried, scrambling back into his seat.

He peered out of the side window as the car streaked forward, and saw the pale, crouching figure on the tarmac; it stared at him malevolently. The image of the white face seemed to zoom towards him, even though they were travelling swiftly away from it.

As they drove further onto the moors, thick, glutinous fog swirled across the road, as if someone was operating a gigantic dry ice machine somewhere out in the darkness. The driver was forced to slow down, despite Taziel's entreaties for speed. Eerie balls of light streaked out of the mist, flashing over the road in front of them. Attenuated phantom figures scurried backwards and forwards across the tarmac, their clawed hands held high, their starved ghost faces screaming in fury. Daniel could not stand the sight of them and covered his face with his hands. Then, an enormous black shape formed itself from the fog and leapt at the car windscreen. Taziel saw the snarling jaws of a great panther. The driver, who had been making an effort to be brave, now lost control. He uttered a cracked scream and the car skidded off the road to land in a ditch. Taziel and Daniel were thrown about in the back like rags.

Taziel summoned his inner strength to clear his head. The car hung at an angle over the ditch. There was no way they could reverse out without leaving the safety of the vehicle and physically pushing it. The driver seemed to be weeping. He was hunched over the steering wheel, his head resting on his hands. Taziel couldn't feel sorry for the man. He wished they'd hired a Grigori driver, someone who wouldn't freak out at strange phenomena. He squinted out of the window at the swirling fog. All seemed quiet now, but that might not last. This was clearly what their pursuers intended to happen. Taziel prodded the driver on the shoulder. "Don't crack up. We're not out of this yet. Daniel and I will have to try and push this thing out of the ditch. You steer, OK?"

The driver raised his head and nodded miserably, although Taziel was unconvinced he'd be much help. Taziel picked up the impression that the man was thinking about his family and whether he'd ever see them again.

"Go out there?" Daniel queried, his voice full of misgivings.

Taziel opened the door. "What else can we do?"

"Wait until morning?" Daniel didn't have much hope.

Taziel sighed in disgust and got out of the car. Daniel followed him. "It's not that bad," Taziel said. He pressed his back against the front bumper. "Come on, Daniel. Help me, will you."

At first, Daniel thought the car would never move. It felt as if strong, unseen hands had reached out of the earth and were clinging onto the axle. "Perhaps it's damaged underneath?" he suggested.

"Just keep pushing! It's tangled with the gorse bushes, that's all."

The undergrowth pulled and scratched at Daniel's body as he flexed his muscles against the car. Slowly, the vehicle began to move backwards. If anything was holding onto the car from beneath, it released its grip. "What's that?" Daniel asked.

Taziel looked out into the fog. He saw a large ball of white light hovering some distance away from them, although it was impossible to tell how far. "We're nearly there," he said in a calm voice. "Don't look at that thing."

The car suddenly bounced backwards onto the road, and Taziel grabbed hold of Daniel. Even though they had only a few feet to cross, it seemed to take minutes before the car door was beneath Taziel's hand. The ball of light came screaming towards them.

"In!" Taziel yelled and threw Daniel into the back seat. He just managed to scramble inside and shut the door before the light-ball exploded against the car's flank. There was a sound of grating metal and the stink of burning paint.

The driver, saying nothing, started the car and set off at speed into the thick fog. The only sound in the car was that of panting breath. Taziel reached out a shaking hand and gripped the driver's shoulder. "You've done great," he said. "Don't worry. Nothing will get us. It's mainly all for show."

The driver gibbered a soft sound, and Taziel patted his shoulder a few more times, before leaning back in his seat.

Daniel was kneeling on the seat, looking out of the back window. "There's a light following us," he said.

Taziel looked round. "So there is."

"It's like the film "Close Encounters'," Daniel said, his tone a mixture of terror and wonder.

"Not much," Taziel said. "If that thing decides to engulf us, we'll lose rather more than a few hours of our life."

Daniel sat down again. "Whoever's after us must be very powerful."

Taziel pushed his hair out of his face. "Yes."

"Will we make it?"

Taziel looked at Daniel, and reached for his hand. He seemed so young and vulnerable. "Yes, I think so. We'd have been finished off by now if they meant to kill us. You're important, Daniel, you're Shemyaza's vizier. They want you in their clutches, but they won't risk your death."

It seemed as if the weird denizens of the moor had given up trying to frighten them. The ball of light trailed them for a few miles before veering off to the left of the road. Gradually, the fog dissipated. The driver uttered a shaky laugh. "I dunno what you geezers are into," he said, "but I've never seen shit like this before. I could use a drink right now."

"You'll be well paid for this," Taziel said. The driver would be dining out on the story of this night for several months to come.

Chapter Fourteen
Coming Home

The minute Shemyaza walked through High Crag's front door, he felt he had returned home. This was absurd because he had never set foot in the place before. Still, all Grigori family houses shared a certain ambience and decor; he could now be in any one of them.

The journey down had been strained to say the least. Aninka had done most of the driving, nervously tapping the steering wheel with her fingernails. On occasion, she narrowly missed causing an accident. Shemyaza could sense her tension and excitement. It was bizarre to him, for he barely remembered her. His life as Peverel Othman had become fragmented in his memory. It was as if he'd been drunk and acting out of character. There were one or two recollections that still burned vividly in his head; sitting in a dim-lit apartment drinking iced wine before the television; a visit to an art gallery. But that was all. He could tell from Aninka's attitude that she had witnessed him doing sublime as well as horrifying things. Deeply, hidden, she still loved him. Now she felt torn, unable to reconcile the image of Shemyaza with the frightening memory of Peverel Othman.

Shemyaza had slumped back in his seat, listening to Emma confer in a clipped voice with Lahash. They talked about Shem as if he wasn't there for a few minutes, and then went on to discuss the white-haired creatures that had appeared in the Assembly Rooms. Who had sent them? Would they try to get at Shem again?

Shemyaza felt a faint stirring of recollection as he listened to their conversation. Deep within him, something uncurled and woke up, pricked its ears. His mind skittered briefly across the thought of Lily and Owen. They had been left at the mercy of those creatures. And where was Daniel? Suddenly Shemyaza felt chillingly alone. His vizier had been left behind. How could he have been so blind as to ignore Daniel's importance? He leaned forward, tapped Lahash on the shoulder. "You are sure that Daniel Cranton is safe?"

Lahash glanced round nervously, the memory of being flung across the room by Shem's power clearly still fresh in his mind. "Yes. He's at Aninka's apartment. You heard me talk to Taziel on the phone as we were leaving London."

"Taziel." Shem hadn't really listened to the phone call. He'd simply climbed into the back of the car and gone into shutdown. The name: Taziel. He knew it should mean something to him.

"Taziel Levantine," Aninka said sharply. "Surely you remember him?"

The words sent a shock through Shem's mind, but didn't quite connect with a memory. "Obviously, you think I should," he said. "I'm sorry. I can't remember everything that happened to me before."

Aninka made a disgusted sound. "Vienna," she said coldly. "A band, Azliel X. You managed them, fucked Taziel, then fucked him up. Badly."

A faint but discomforting image of a screaming face surfaced in Shem's mind. "I think I remember," he said cautiously and then added lightly. "Is there an army of ex-lovers out for my blood now?"

Nobody laughed at this remark, although Emma did smirk a little.

"Is Daniel coming to Cornwall?" Shem asked. "I don't want him to stay with this Taziel. I want him with me."

"He's coming," Lahash said.

Aninka suddenly expelled a staccato burst of laughter, which prompted Lahash to say, "Can it, Ninka."

Shem knew there was something they weren't telling him, something about Daniel. Games, just games. Daniel was coming to him. Whatever else these people thought or felt was irrelevant.

Enniel Prussoe was typical of the Parzupheim: urbane, condescending, immaculate. Shemyaza felt wary of him at once. He saw cold ambition in Enniel's dark glittering eyes, and something else: humiliated anger. Still, he was politeness itself, ushering Shem into a seat in his study, offering wine or brandy to his guests. Shem could almost see Enniel's fingers twitching, as if he longed to get hold of Shem, incarcerate him, flay him, peel his secrets and power from him. The Parzupheim were dangerous, with far-reaching influence. Peverel Othman had always treated them with wary respect, haunting the periphery of their territories. Shemyaza, for all his rebirth and the fanfare of his second coming, would be wise to remember that. He accepted a globe of brandy from Enniel, their fingers touching as the glass exchanged hands. The ends of Enniel's fingers were burning hot. Shemyaza exuded a thought, *All right. At your convenience.* And Enniel withdrew a few feet as if scalded. Shem smiled into his glass, took a luxurious sip of the liquor. Emma, Lahash, Aninka: they were all shadowy figures on the boundary of this meeting. It was no longer the light versus the dark, but one spectrum of light against another. *You want mine,* Shem thought. *But maybe I don't want yours. You can't make me be anything I don't want to be.*

He kept these thoughts veiled, but guessed Enniel knew the gist of his feelings. "You must appreciate why it is so important for you to be here with us," Enniel said aloud. "I have heard reports of the *interference* at the Moses Assembly Rooms."

Shemyaza met his eyes, noticed with amusement how uncomfortable Enniel was with that. "The twins, Lily and Owen Winter. Before I agree to do anything for, with or to you, I want your assurance that you will send people to help them—wherever they are." He remembered some of Ishtahar's last words to him then, the time when she had come to him on the hill outside Little Moor. *These are our children, Shem. Love them and care for them.* It had only been a cruel illusion. He had resigned himself to the thought that it was unlikely Ishtahar and he would be reunited in this life, but if there was some vague essence of her floating around him, he hoped to appease it.

Enniel sucked his upper lip. "I will, of course, see what I can do."

"I would appreciate rather more commitment than that." Shemyaza took another sip of brandy.

Emma came to sit beside him on the couch and put her arm along his shoulder. Shemyaza drew strength from her presence, knowing they presented a united front to Enniel. Impulsively, he turned and kissed Emma's cheek.

Enniel regarded them coolly. "I will do *everything* I can," he said, "but I won't make promises I can't keep. I don't know what's happened to the twins, or who was behind the raid on the Assembly Rooms. I can only hope the Winters are of more use alive to their captors than dead."

Shemyaza nodded. "I shall work upon discerning their whereabouts as soon as I've rested. But I shall need Daniel for that."

"He is on his way," Enniel said.

"Good."

There was a moment's silence, then Enniel leaned back against his desk and said, "I would like to talk to you alone."

Shemyaza nodded. "As you wish."

Enniel smiled at Aninka and Lahash. "You have done well," he said. "We shall talk in the morning." A more curt dismissal was difficult to imagine.

Aninka directed one last, burning glance at Shemyaza before uttering a chilled "good night."

"Take Shemyaza's companion with you," Enniel said. "Rooms have been prepared. My staff will take you to them."

"Do you want me to stay here with you?" Emma asked Shem.

He laid a hand over her own and shook his head. "I'm sure I'll be fine. I'll see you later."

Enniel waited until the three of them had left the room, then picked up the brandy decanter and sauntered over to the couch. Shem held out his glass for a refill.

"I find it hard to believe you are here," Enniel said. "Are you really what everyone thinks you are?"

"You see what looks like a man," Shem answered, "as do I whenever I look in a mirror. The answer is: I don't know. It's cosy to think there is an explanation—and perhaps a tenuous justification—for the way I behaved as Peverel Othman. Memories of being burned alive are more vivid to me than, for example, those of making love to your charming ward, Aninka." He raised one eyebrow and shrugged. "But nothing is really clear to me. I feel as if I've been hypnotised or brainwashed. It's as if other people have forced me to be what I am, to fulfil their own fantasies and yearnings."

"I appreciate your honesty," Enniel said.

Shem could tell he was surprised at how communicative he was being. What had he expected? A confrontation of wizards, complete with bolts of purple light and threatening incantations?

"What are your plans?" Enniel asked.

Shem gave him a dry glance. "You mean I have a choice?" He smiled. "I have no plans. You tell me what you'd like me to do." He made it quite clear from his tone there was no guarantee he'd fulfil those wishes.

Enniel moved away from him. "Let me explain what I think you are."

"Please do. It will interest me greatly."

Enniel leaned back against his desk, his hands gripping its polished edged. He seemed to be at ease, but the way his knuckles pushed against the taut skin of his hands betrayed his tension. "Shemyaza is an archetype of our people, our progenitor, our beloved king, our long-awaited Messiah, and also our dark lord. How can you really have come back to us? Is this possible?" Enniel raised his arms, pulled a quizzical face. "Rationally, it does not seem likely. Did Shemyaza's soul really hang in the constellation of Orion awaiting the reawakening? Or was that just a metaphor for the hopes and fears of our people? I have always thought the latter. Then, I am told of your Second Coming. People above me, of greater experience and knowledge, believe in it passionately. Who am I to refute their heartfelt claims? Shemyaza is among us in flesh, they said. I naturally balked at such a belief. They told me of Peverel Othman, an amoral monster who murdered and played with the hearts and souls of others. Peverel Othman is the sleeping form of Shemyaza, they said. Again, this sounded like fantasy. Very soon afterwards, I listened to the pitiful outpourings of my "charming ward," as you refer to her. I heard all the sordid details of your activities. Was this evidence to support the claims of my elders? I did not think so. I did not want to think so. I wanted to believe you were simply Anakim; a force that should be culled. But I followed orders, as I am used to doing. If Lahash and his colleagues had been successful in finding you there, you would have been brought here a lot earlier, which might have been better for everyone concerned. However, this was not to be. Then I was told of the events that took place in Little Moor. The Parzupheim had psychically scoured the whole area, and scooped up the residue of your little ritual. I know what you did there, and also what you tried to do. You attempted to open the stargate by force, using your beloved vizier, Daniel, as bait for the demon of falsehood—Ahriman. Hearing of these things, I am half convinced, against my will, of what you are supposed to be. And yet, I see you sitting there, and you are tired and anxious, no matter how much you try to hide it. Would the great Shemyaza suffer such mortal frailties? You are frightened and confused. Shemyaza has been burning alive among the stars for millennia. Having endured such torment, surely fear is unknown to

him. So, are you merely Peverel Othman; Anakim?" Enniel paused
and shook his head. "I don't think you are. You are more than that.
I can see it in your eyes, beyond your weariness and confusion. So
how can this be? How can legends be made flesh?"

He waited for an answer. Shem shrugged. "You tell me."

Enniel smiled. "Maybe we have *made* you happen. Maybe
the collective desires of humanity and Grigori have forged you into
being, and Peverel Othman was the suitable scapegoat for this wish
fulfilment. He was the outcast, the Anakim, the destroyer. He offered up what was dearest to him, the sacrificial son, and some blithe
angel somewhere intervened. My sources tell me it was a goddess,
the memory of your lost love, Ishtahar. But Ishtahar no longer wears
flesh, whereas Daniel lives and you need him for your work. Somehow, in Little Moor, Othman was transformed into a being of light
and love. If we suppose, for now, that these assumptions are correct, where do we go from here?"

Shem snickered into the silence that followed Enniel's words.
He was conscious of the beat of his heart, the wings of fear beginning to flutter within the blood-bound cage of his ribs. He felt that
Daniel should be here to speak for him now, with his determination
to believe in wondrous possibilities. At one time, he had been prepared to sacrifice the boy, but Daniel believed in the reality of
Shemyaza, as an ideal, and had forgiven him for the deeds of Peverel
Othman. Shem felt wrung of words. His fingers passed nervously
across his dry lips, and he said again. "You tell me."

"One would suppose the knowledge would reside within
yourself."

"The knowledge of what?" Enniel's words held a disturbing
echo of certain things Ishtahar had told Shem in his dream of her.

"Your purpose. You are supposed to be the saviour of the
world. Don't you know what it needs?"

Shem shook his head. "I'm not playing with you, Enniel.
This is not a game to me. Don't believe I'm possessed of ultimate knowledge and being coy with you about it. I don't know
what my purpose is, or even if I have one. The thought of it is all
too exhausting. You want me to work some magic? Heal the
world? Stop war and famine? Make people *like* one another?
Shall I create a world of women to rid the planet of aggression?
Tell me how to do it." He laughed coldly. "I don't know what's
happened to me. I remember the life of Shemyaza, his loves, his

hates, his torments and ambitions. It seems real to me, but it's so far away, so tiny. It's irrelevant now, like someone remembering their childhood, and acting upon long forgotten conflicts and fears. The life in between has been sucked out, and surely that is what is important."

"They say the personality is forged in childhood," Enniel said.

Shem turned his eyes briefly towards the ceiling in exasperation. "I know you people won't leave me alone. I also know that others want a piece of me too. There is no escape for me, that is obvious. But I cannot comply with you, because I have no faith in your beliefs. If I truly am Shemyaza, then I am a bitter husk, a man who was murdered for daring to love and to teach. I have brought all that anger with me into this time, all that resentment for what was done to me. Why should I help you, or anyone? No-one dared to help me. My soul has been imprisoned for millennia, quietly going mad out there among the stars. What possible incentive do I have for helping you now? Altruism?" He sneered. "I don't care."

"Ishtahar," Enniel said, slipping the word into Shem's consciousness like a knife.

Shem felt himself wince as the blade turned. He dropped his eyes. "A human woman, long dead. I have created illusions of her that have even spoken to me, but they all came from my own head. Through her image, I speak to myself." He pulled his mouth down into a grimace, and nodded. "True, that part of myself talks about love and creation, but it is only a small part. It barely breaks out of my dreams."

"In dreams, the soul speaks most freely," Enniel said.

"You speak in platitudes and clichés," Shem answered sharply. "Spare me that. I don't think you believe in it any more than I do." He shook his head. "I think you all want me to be the scapegoat, to fall from the highest cliff and atone for your sins. You all want to kill me again, make me a sacrificial king. But unless the king believes in the power of redemption in his death, it can't work, and I refuse, *refuse*, to be a part of that." He held out his empty brandy glass. "I would appreciate a refill."

Enniel complied with this request in silence, then said, "Others will speak to you over the next few days."

"They can speak as much as they like!"

"I understand the way you feel."

Shem stared at him in a cool fury. "I cannot believe you dared to say that. Understand how I feel? I wish you did!"

"I'm sorry."

Shem saw that the apology was genuine. He made a careless gesture. "It doesn't matter."

"Would you like to sleep now?" Enniel glanced at his watch. "It's almost dawn."

Shem guessed that Enniel had had enough of him for now. "Yes. I would like to rest. Please keep everyone away from me, including my assistant, Ms Manden. The only person I want to see is Daniel Cranton."

"As you wish." Enniel rang for his bottelier, Austin, who came in looking half asleep.

Shem smiled to think of what must be going on below stairs in this grand establishment at present: the assumptions, rumours and gossip. People had been kept up all night for him. Cars arriving in the middle of the night. Hushed private interviews.

Enniel gestured towards the door. "Austin will show you to the rooms we've made ready for you. You'll find everything you need in there. We'll leave you undisturbed until one o'clock tomorrow."

After Enniel had dismissed them from his study, and Emma had been taken to her room, Lahash and Aninka stood in the corridor outside the suites they'd been given. Aninka guessed that Lahash wanted her to invite him into her room, but didn't feel like conversation, never mind anything else. Her mind and heart were numb. She couldn't help thinking that the man who had accompanied them from London was Peverel Othman, despite what everyone said about who and what he had become. He had looked like Pev to her, down to the heart-breakingly familiar mannerisms. He had looked as beautiful as she remembered him, yet he had all but forgotten her.

Lahash reached out and squeezed her arm. "Are you all right?"

She saw the concern in his eyes and felt irritated by it. "Yes. I'm just tired."

"But it must have felt...disturbing to see him tonight."

Aninka ran a hand through her hair. "I really don't want to talk about it now."

"That's OK," Lahash said softly.

Don't humour me! Aninka thought.

Lahash rubbed his neck. "I couldn't have taken him if he hadn't wanted to come. We didn't have to persuade him. He'd already made up his mind."

"I had nothing to do with that."

"I know."

Aninka turned away, put her hand upon the door-knob to her room. "Thanks for reminding me."

Lahash made an anguished noise. "I'm sorry...I didn't mean to..." he paused. "You're still in love with him."

Aninka laughed harshly, opened the door to her room. "In love with the memory of a man who didn't even exist. Pointless." A surge of anger threshed through her. "I like you, Lahash. I find you attractive. Yet I look at you beside him, and you are like a pinprick of light to his sun. That is the legacy of having loved him." She could have continued, but realisation of the cruelty of her words stemmed the anger.

"One cannot gaze at the sun too long, remember," Lahash said bitterly. He opened the door to his room and went inside.

"Lahash!" Aninka clawed her head, stared at his closed door. "Damn!" She considered for a moment, going after him then abandoned the impulse. She had meant what she said, although she knew that Lahash would take her rejection to heart. She had sacrificed a potential relationship for the sake of a dream that could never be real.

Chapter Fifteen
The Star of Life

Grey dawn was breaking in the eastern sky as Taziel's hired car turned onto the gravel drive of High Crag. Daniel had dozed against Taziel's side for most of the latter stages of their journey, but after the horrors of the night flight, Taziel had been unable to close his eyes. Whenever he dropped off, he saw hideous, white-haired figures clawing at the windows of the car or peeling open the roof as if it were a flimsy tin can.

High Crag was magnificent against the paling sky, its forest of chimneys rearing like a crown above its frowning eaves. Taziel roused Daniel. "Wake up. We're here."

Daniel rubbed his face and yawned, turned to peer out of the window. "Wow! It's a stately home!" He smiled at Taziel. "Like Long Eden back...back home."

Taziel noted with concern Daniel's pale face, the dark circles beneath his eyes. "Just like Long Eden," he said. "Both of them are Grigori haunts."

Daniel sat up and stretched. "They must all be rich then." He grinned archly. "Like you."

Taziel smiled thinly in reply.

The driver brought his vehicle to a halt before the front doors. Lahash's car was parked nearby, along with an array of four-wheel drive vehicles that belonged to the family. The driver turned in his seat and gave Taziel a sickly smile. "Well, we made it."

"Yeah. Thanks. You were great." Taziel opened the car door. "Shall we go in?" They would have to offer the driver food and rest before he drove back to London.

Taziel had to ring the doorbell several times before a sleepy member of Enniel's staff came to answer it—some underling of Austin's who'd been instructed to wait up for them. Yawning, he invited them inside. The driver's eyes were very round as they entered the grand hallway. Taziel made a brief explanation and asked that their driver be given hospitality. "But don't worry about us. We'll crash out in the drawing-room for a couple of hours." The servant knew Taziel from the time he'd been down before with Aninka, and grudgingly allowed him to lead Daniel off down the corridor.

Daniel stared about himself with weary amazement. This was what Long Eden would have looked like in its prime: dark, gleaming wood; tapestries and paintings; heavy furniture and muted light. Taziel opened a door and led him into a spacious room where long, stained glass windows overlooked the garden. The curtains hung open, admitting the wan dawn light. They could hear the crash of the sea from here. A clock ticked richly within the room. "Take the sofa by the hearth," Taziel said. "The fire's still glowing."

In a daze, Daniel stumbled towards the long, well-cushioned couch and threw himself down. The luxury of straightening his body out on the comfortable upholstery was almost too blissful to bear. He was racked by cramps and aches from the car journey.

Taziel went over to an ornate sideboard and picked up a bottle. "Enniel always has good brandy," he said, lifting two fat globes by the stems in the fingers of his other hand. "In every room."

Daniel laughed weakly. "Is that true?"

Taziel sat down on the end of the sofa. "Absolutely." The thick sound of pouring liquor could be heard. "Here, a night-cap, or a dawn-cap. You look like you need it."

Daniel rolled onto his back and took the proffered glass. When he sipped the brandy, it burned his mouth and throat, but it was comforting heat. He closed his eyes and rested his head against the cushions. "This...feels...so...good." He heard Taziel lean back at the end of the couch.

"Yeah." He sighed. "Daniel, I can't tell you how sorry I am about what happened tonight."

"Try." Daniel opened his eyes. He wasn't about to forgive Taziel for his part in the deception. "Your friend is a thug."

"Well, as I told you in the car, he's an exiled Murkaster," Taziel said. "From Little Moor. You should know their reputation."

Daniel nodded. "Lily will be amazed to find out one of her relatives is still around. I hope she's all right. I don't think she is, but what can I do?"

Taziel reached for Daniel's booted foot and rotated his ankle. "Nothing at the moment. We'll talk to Enniel tomorrow. He might be able to help."

"Is Shem here?" Daniel asked.

Taziel looked into the embers of the fire. "Lahash's car was out front, so I suppose so."

"I should find him," Daniel said and rose up off the cushions.

"Not now," Taziel said sharply. "We are in Enniel's house and must play by his rules. We must wait to see what he's done with...Shemyaza."

Daniel slumped back. "I can't just lie here doing nothing. I'm worried about Lily and Owen, and about Shem and Emma."

"They'll survive without you for a few hours." Taziel ran his hand up Daniel's shin. "I wish I could go back in time and relive this night. I would have played it differently."

Daniel stared at him without expression, wanting to push his hand away, wanting to take hold of it and squeeze the fingers tightly, guide them to his face. It was hard to stay angry with Taziel. Since they'd met, they'd shared some weird experiences, and on the nightmare journey down to Cornwall, Taziel had succeeded in keeping Daniel safe. "What were those things that were after us?" he asked.

Taziel shook his head. "I don't know. Grigori have many specialised mutations. Still, we're safe from them here."

"I hope so." Daniel put his half-finished brandy down on the carpet, and pulled a heavy tartan blanket down from the back of the couch.

"You're cold," Taziel said, and tried to arrange the blanket around him.

Daniel shook his head and pushed Taziel's hands away. "Not really. But I will be once I've taken my clothes off. Will you see to my boots?"

Taziel stared at him speculatively for a moment, then said, "OK." He began to unlace the left boot, his fingers not entirely steady.

Awareness of Taziel's nervousness rekindled a flame of lust in Daniel's belly. He felt exhausted but sensual, and beyond being angry with Taziel's lies. They were all in this together now, come good or bad. He knew Taziel wouldn't take the initiative now, because he was wary of rebuff, but he could tell Taziel was thinking of their interrupted passion. Daniel waited until both boots were off before saying, "We have something to finish, haven't we?"

Taziel paused before answering, still anticipating scorn and refusal. "Whatever you want."

"I want," Daniel said.

Taziel nodded abstractedly and stood up. He turned his back on Daniel and slowly removed his clothes. Daniel had to admit that it was quite a performance. He thought, *Shem is here in this house. Can he sense this?* And the thought of that intensified his desire. He struggled out of his jacket and T-shirt, and opened the top of his jeans. Taziel turned to him, an erotic silhouette in the twilight. Without words, he leaned over Daniel and slid his hands inside his jeans, pulling them down in one dextrous movement, slipping them over Daniel's feet. *You're too practised,* Daniel thought dispassionately. *How many times have you done that? Did you do it to Peverel Othman?*

Taziel laid his warm body over Daniel's cooler skin; their flesh was throbbing to the same insistent demands. Daniel thought of Owen's timid, respectful love-making, the memory of how they had discovered carnal pleasures together for the first time. This Grigori male was experienced and confident. It was different and arousing, but not altogether more pleasing. *Too many have passed this way,* Daniel thought. Owen's inexperience had been special and pure. Was it lost forever now? Taziel kissed him like a serpent, invasive and muscular. This was not the anxious person, harbouring secrets, who had lain beside Daniel in the apartment in London. The truth was out between them now and, sure of Daniel's compliance, Taziel no longer felt diffident. For a moment, Daniel experienced panic, felt overwhelmed and out of control. Then Taziel's skilful fingers were sliding over his flat belly, playing lightly across his groin, pausing to squeeze, pull, massage, before running delicately along his inner thighs. He seemed to want nothing in return.

The light was pale and grainy in the room, and sea-birds outside were beginning to scream for the morning. Daniel felt himself becoming delirious with pleasure. His body was an instrument, and each stroke and caress of Taziel's hands conjured a new, exquisite chord of sensation. It seemed as if the sofa was swallowing them both. *I'm not really here,* Daniel thought, and stared dazedly at the silvery sky beyond the windows. One moment he was drifting on the ocean of Taziel's caresses, the next Taziel was pushing inside him. It happened so smoothly. Daniel expelled a moaning sigh and pressed his head back into the cushions, his legs curling around Taziel's lean back. Their movements were slow, languorous, slippery. *How does he do this?* Daniel thought. *It's so comfortable.* The light of new day filled his eyes like tears. And there was a tall, dark shape against the windows, indistinct and shadowy. Only its eyes were visible; vaporous blue lights, burning like neon. Daniel tried to concentrate on it, aware of it, yet distant from its presence. He sensed its focused attention, yet could not gauge whether it was hostile or not. He wanted to tell Taziel about it, but could not speak. It seemed as if he lay there for hours, moving with unnatural slithery slowness, staring at the silent, watchful figure. Daniel felt that, as Taziel moved inside him, the sun rose and fell a hundred times, while quick, buzzing figures went about their daily business invisibly in this room, unable to see the lovers on the couch because they moved to a different rhythm in space and time—far slower, removed and tranquil. Only the tall shape before the window could see them, and it could see right inside them to the pulsing, bloody core. A tide of feeling was building up within Daniel's belly and soon it would crash through him in a dazzling foam. When it crested, it would banish the sight of that sentinel figure. Nothing else could.

Only the onset of orgasm enabled Daniel to close his eyes. Reality crept back in. He was aware of Taziel's heart beating hard and furious against his own. The feelings within him had accelerated, like a film of an ocean shore on fast forward. Waves sizzled up the beach with unnatural speed and withdrew in a frothing, lacy spume. His head ached slightly and his eyes felt gritty. He turned his head upon the cushions, blinking back sparks of light, and the crescendo of coming gushed through him; uninvited and immediate. It filled all the darkest pools of his spirit, then drew back its watery, weedy tendrils, leaving a flotsam of sparkling shells and darting creatures, before threshing back up the shore of him again. It was like drowning rather than surfing the wave.

Taziel waited for Daniel's feelings to subside, before gently withdrawing. Daniel realised Taziel had climaxed some minutes before. The cushions beneath them were wet with their mingled seed. Sleepily, Daniel wondered whether they should try to do something about that to avoid embarrassing explanations later in the day, then yawned and thought, *Oh, so what.* They both turned on their sides and pulled the blanket over them. Already their sweat was cooling. Daniel could hear his own heart thumping in his ears. Taziel curled against Daniel's spine and curved an arm around Daniel's chest, briefly kissing the back of his neck.

"Are you OK?" he whispered.

Daniel nodded. Suddenly, he felt like crying. "Shem was here," he said. "I saw him."

He felt Taziel's body stiffen, become alert. "No, no he wasn't. You were imagining it."

"I saw him," Daniel said, yawning. "By the window. He watched us. He's gone now."

Taziel shivered, but said nothing. Daniel slept long before Taziel dared to close his eyes.

Chapter Sixteen
In the House of Light

Lily woke up believing she was eight years old. She was on holiday with her mother and Owen, and the room around her was the small, rather Spartan bedroom in the boarding house beside the sea, which they visited every year. There was the old, scratched night table beside her bed, covered in a yellowed lace doily. A huge, shapeless wardrobe of dark wood dominated the left wall. Without looking over the side of the bed, she knew the carpet would be almost colourless and threadbare. She could hear gulls outside and the faint roar of the ocean. The air smelled of the past, of childhood; the briny perfume of sand stuck to bare legs with the brackish liquor of stagnant rock pools. Lily shivered and turned over in the high, creaking bed. Then she remembered the events of the night before, and it came with a jolt. She sat up in the bed and the thin, white counterpane fell away from her body. She was fully dressed and the mattress beneath her, covered inadequately by an ancient flannelette sheet, was damp. No-one had slept here for years and this was not a seaside boarding-house.

Lily got out of bed and went over to one of the two small windows. She looked out upon a bleak landscape, a grey sky. The house was positioned in the centre of a flat garden of gravel paths and symmetrical lawns. Two hundred yards away from the building, a grey stone wall enclosed the garden boundary. Somewhere nearby the sea lunged hungrily at the land, heard but not seen. Lily rubbed her arms: she felt so cold. She glanced at her watch: two o'clock. It seemed inconceivable that less than a day ago she had been in London with Daniel, getting ready for a night out. Why had there been no presentiment to warn her what would happen? "Daniel." She said his name aloud and touched the windowpane. Was he safe? Had the Emim waited at the Assembly Rooms for his return?

A memory flashed into her mind: the day Daniel had walked into her cottage in Little Moor, bringing an invitation for her and

Owen to go for dinner at his father's house. She had not liked him then, because she'd felt jealous, aware of the seeds that he and Owen had planted between them, which even at that early stage, had been pushing their way to the light through the fertile soil of their needs. She had felt excluded, resentful. Now, she realised she had come to depend upon Daniel. He didn't have to do anything to prove his protective power; just his mere presence was enough to create a sanctuary around her. He was strength and light; no wonder Owen had loved him.

Escaping Little Moor with Shemyaza had seemed the climax of an unreal and terrifying time in her life. How foolish. Events in the north had been only a foretaste of what was to come. Once Peverel Othman had come into their lives and made them aware of their Grigori blood, they had been doomed. There was no going back, no safe normality to retreat to. Now what? Dare she open the door to this room—presuming it wasn't locked— and explore the boundaries of her prison? Should she just wait here until someone came?

The previous night, she and Owen had been bundled into the back of a van outside the Assembly Rooms and driven away from London. Salamiel had allowed Lily to gather a few belongings together. Under the eyes of two watchful Emim, she had torn Johcasta's dress from her body, uncaring that they saw her breasts and knickers. They were not men, and she sensed their drives had no human parallel. She had clothed herself in jeans and a holey black jumper and pushed her feet into a pair of Owen's dilapidated biker boots. She thought about leaving behind the small pouch Johcasta had thrown to her, but at the last moment thrust it into her canvas bag. She knew it contained her dead friend's divining stones. There was a dull clink as they rubbed together inside the cloth. The Emim had simply watched her preparations. Neither of them spoke to her or interfered.

In the van, she had hugged Owen's listless body closely, kissed his hair, his face. It was like he was brain-damaged. *He will never be well,* Lily had thought then. *Someone will always have to care for him.* This was accompanied by a brief, savage surge of anger towards Shem. Why hadn't he helped Owen? How could he have just left her brother like this? Lily resolved to tell Salamiel anything he wanted to know. She had no loyalty to Shem. If she could save her own skin, and that of her brother, she would betray the one who had used and abandoned them. She cried then, for a while. When she slept, fitfully, leaning against the musty cushions provided for their comfort, Lily dreamed of Israel's death. Only it was not in the Assembly Rooms, but out in the garden. He was making love to her, and the Emim dropped down from the trees, ripping his handsome head from his body, even as he still pumped into her. Lily screamed, showered with blood. The headless body ejaculated and the Emim danced around her, giggling, swinging Israel's staring head by the hair.

Lily woke up, gasping. All she could think was *Thank God, it wasn't Owen. Thank God it wasn't Daniel.* She was slightly appalled by the fact she felt so removed from what she had witnessed on the stairs in the Assembly Rooms. Surely she should feel furious, grief-stricken, terrified, sick? Instead, she felt only a mild sense of frustration, an indignant annoyance at the waste of life. Yet moments before his death, Israel had been as close to her as it is possible for a person to get. *Is this numbness the flower of the Grigori within me?* she thought. *The amorality, the legacy of Shemyaza?*

Owen moved feebly against her, making a faint, whimpering sound. Perhaps he had sensed the horror that had seethed in her sleeping mind or the cold dispassion of her waking thoughts.

Before dawn, they'd reached their destination. In the darkness, it had been difficult to discern any detail, but Lily could tell the house before her was large. She had also seen the name of it: a floodlit ribbon of stone above the door bore the single word: Pharos. Two Emim had taken them inside. The hall was flagged in rough stone and the walls were unplastered. It would have looked primitive and neglected, but for the array of ornate Far Eastern-looking masks that adorned the walls and the heavy chandeliers swinging overhead, and the thick rugs upon the flagstones. Salamiel had been nowhere in sight. An Emim had taken Lily up several flights of stairs to the top of the house, where she'd been shown to her room. It was not a guest's room, for she could sense that servants had once slept here. She had a feeling Owen had been accommodated in more comfortable quarters. Perhaps the Emim would fawn over him all night, hoping for a taste of Shemyaza's memory in his flesh. She had slept surprisingly well; the sleep of the exhausted, the defeated.

Fools, Lily thought, turning away from the window and the bleak landscape. She lay down again resignedly on the lumpy bed.

Salamiel and his Emim were blind to the fact that Lily herself was far more potent a tool than Owen. She had melded with the essence of Shemyaza's lost love, Ishtahar. She had risen up through the ground of the High Place in the belly of a goddess. She had been reborn Shem's daughter. Owen was mindless, ruined. Salamiel had not picked up on this. He was too obsessed with Shemyaza. Perhaps this could be used to her advantage. Salamiel would expect her to try and escape, or to at least leave her room. She did not want to try the door and find it locked. She would not give her captors that satisfaction. She would be patient and wait. If there were games to be played, she wanted to invent some of her own rules.

Some hours before Lily awoke, Salamiel took a late breakfast in his heated conservatory at the back of his house. It was to here that one of his servants conducted a visitor. Salamiel had just poured himself a cup of Lapsang Souchong tea and spread a hot muffin with bitter marmalade. He did not particularly want to speak to anyone, as he needed to think. The servant knew he did not have to announce the visitor. She treated this place as her own, and Salamiel deferred to her.

She stalked into the conservatory and removed her hat and coat. Salamiel looked up at her with some discomfort and annoyance. "Sofia."

"Good morning, Salamiel." She smiled tightly and signalled to the servant. "Bring me a cup of coffee. I can't stand that poisonous pond-water he drinks!" She sat down in a wicker chair.

The servant bowed and departed. Sofia stretched out her long legs and crossed them at the ankles. Leaning back in the chair, with her be-ringed fingers interlaced on her flat belly, she looked very masculine. Because of her demure, lady-like appearance, the effect of this body posture was all the more unnerving. It spoke of a certain callousness and pitiless strength.

"Well?" Sofia said.

Salamiel refused to look away from her hard, dark eyes. "We have the Winter twins. Azazel was too slippery. He had assistance. I presume the Parzupheim was involved."

Sofia put her head on one side. "I know all this. You should not have interfered, Salamiel. Your disgusting little Emim were crawling all over the Moses Assembly Rooms. Blood was spilt, lives were lost. Those lives could so easily have been the wrong ones.

Why did you do that? My orders to you were specific. You should not have acted until Azazel was safe in High Crag."

Salamiel shrugged and sipped his tea. "I was unprepared to wait. Azazel must come to me, Sofia. This you know. I don't want him contaminated by the Parzupheim's lies and machinations."

"What you want is irrelevant," Sofia said in an icy voice. "You are a mote, Salamiel, my dear, as are Enniel and his bunch of family conspirators. I speak for echelons too high for you to comprehend."

"I'm not interested," Salamiel replied silkily. "You need me as much as you need Azazel. We are brothers."

Sofia laughed politely. "You, my dear, are a side-kick. You always were in the past, and you are now. Azazel has the power, not you. Do not make the mistake of over-estimating your value."

Salamiel stared at her blandly. Her satiny insults meant he had ruffled her feathers more than she cared to admit. "Have you been to High Crag?"

Sofia withdrew an enamelled cigarette case from her purse and took out a black cigarette. She did not answer him until she'd lit it and taken a satisfying lungful of smoke. "Not yet, no. I am prolonging the moment of revelation."

Salamiel smiled. "You're not afraid, are you?"

She rolled her eyes scornfully. "Terrified, naturally."

"What will you say to him?"

She shrugged gracefully. "I don't know. I shall wait until I've seen him before formulating a strategy." She took another draw of smoke. "The Parzupheim have not yet realised how Azazel may be used in this locality. That is to our advantage, because consequently, they cannot interfere with our plans."

"Others know of the potentials," Salamiel pointed out.

Sofia pulled a sour face. "Small fry! They are of no consequence."

Salamiel stuck out his lower lip and nodded thoughtfully. "Perhaps, but I never make the mistake of under-estimating rivals and competitors. That kind of pride makes you vulnerable."

Sofia smiled sweetly. "Well, that is a sensible attitude for someone of your status."

Salamiel blinked slowly. It was pointless to lock horns with this female.

She relented. "So, what have you done with the twins?"

"The girl is sleeping." He frowned. "The boy is badly damaged. He has retreated inside himself."

"I am not surprised. He has undergone the trauma of Grigorian tantra." Sofia leaned forward. "I suppose it is best you should know. Azazel attempted to open the stargate in Little Moor. He invoked the demon god, Ahriman, into himself, but before that had taken the Winter boy into his power. There is very potent and dangerous ritual, whereby a magician incites a person to assault them sexually..."

Salamiel interrupted her. "And, of course, what the attacker doesn't realise is that the event is preordained. In the act of violating their supposed victim, they surrender their soul to the magician's power. Don't patronise me, Sofia. I am aware of these practices."

Sofia sniffed. "Whatever. That, in any case, is my estimation of what has happened to Owen Winter. He has become the victim of violation, raped of his soul essence and personality. If Azazel had wanted to restore him, he would have done so by now. We can only assume Winter is useless for our purposes."

Salamiel's servant padded silently back into the conservatory, bearing a silver tray on which a wide china cup of coffee wobbled precariously. Sofia took this from him and sipped with pleasure. "The girl, Lily, is more important."

Salamiel frowned. "How? Azazel, in this life, has acted through the male principle. He would work with only one female vibration, and that belongs to Ishtahar, who unfortunately is beyond our control techniques."

"Precisely," Sofia agreed. "But Lily is in tune with that vibration."

Salamiel looked uncertain. "What do you recommend I do with her?"

Sofia smiled. "Make her trust you. Teach her. Azazel will need her very soon, and we don't want our plans delayed by any childish petulance on Miss Winter's part. Also, we will need Azazel's vizier. The boy is a powerful psychic, and gains in strength with each day that passes."

"Daniel Cranton."

"Yes. He should be at High Crag as well by now." She narrowed her eyes at Salamiel. "You look furtive, my dear. I do hope you haven't done any interfering in that quarter as well."

He shook his head, averting his eyes, unwilling to admit to the occult display he'd put on for Cranton's benefit during his journey down to Cornwall. "I don't have Daniel Cranton. As far as I know, he is at High Crag."

Sofia nodded curtly. "And the Emim? I don't want them running around loose. They are at best an unpredictable force."

"The Emim have been put to rest," Salamiel answered. "They sleep below the house."

"Good!" Sofia finished her coffee in one elegant gulp. "Now, I have some shopping to do in Newquay. This afternoon, I shall visit High Crag and introduce myself to Azazel. Of course, I shall say nothing at this stage of my connection with you, or even of your existence. Let him believe I work solely for the Parzupheim. I want to see how the land lies, what condition he is in."

"When do you anticipate he'll be ready to come to me?"

"Patience! How can I answer that yet? I shall report my findings to you later, when I come here for dinner this evening."

"Did we have an arrangement?" Salamiel smiled widely.

"No, but we have now. It will please me to meet Lily Winter, so have her ready to be presented to me. Say nothing of my station to her. I must simply be a friend." She stood. "I have some very fine lamb in my freezer. I'll send one of my people down with it. If I'm to dine here, I might as well ensure the meal will be palatable."

Salamiel wouldn't have been surprised if she'd offered to lend her cook as well. Sofia had a very dim view of Salamiel's establishment and staff. He stood politely as she retrieved her hat and coat. "Until later, then."

Sofia smiled fiercely, breathed "Goodbye!" and sailed regally back into the house.

Salamiel sat down and finished his breakfast. He thought about what Sofia had said to him. Most of the time he ignored her scorn because he realised she possessed far greater power and knowledge than he did, but occasionally her autocratic manner grated on his nerves. They had waited centuries for this time to come, and he had put up with her insults and put-downs because he knew he needed her help. But he felt she was too confident of her own power. She was wrong about Owen Winter for a start. Salamiel did not dismiss Sofia's opinions about Lily, but he felt sure the twins needed to work as a pair to be useful.

At half past two, Salamiel considered sending a servant up to Lily's room to let her out. Then, on impulse, he appropriated the key and went there himself. If he was to win her trust, he must begin immediately. He found her lying on her bed with an array of coloured stones spread out on the mildewed counterpane before her. She looked up in alarm when he entered the room. He saw her throat convulse in a nervous swallow, but she forced herself to look back down at the stones, to move a few around each other.

"They are pretty," Salamiel said. Pointedly, he put the key to the door down on Lily's bedside table. She would realise that he intended to leave it there.

"Your monsters murdered the woman who gave them to me," Lily said.

Salamiel sighed. "I am sorry. The trouble is, my dear, you are mixed up in something far too big for you to understand."

She looked up at him again, greasy rags of red hair hanging over her face. Some of them were still entwined with ribbons. "If you want Shem, you can have him!" The outburst seemed heartfelt. The poor girl felt betrayed. Salamiel decided to ignore it.

"You must be hungry. Come down and I'll get you something to eat."

"I'm not hungry." She was lying.

"Lily, I am on your side," he said. "When you fight me, you are only fighting yourself. Come now. I know you feel angry and hurt, but there's nothing to be gained by punishing yourself. It feels horrible to be hungry, I know."

"I don't want to see any of the disgusting *things* that killed my friends!"

Salamiel's voice remained soothing. "The Emim are gone, Lily. You have nothing to fear."

Lily pushed a few more of the stones around the bed. Then she sighed. "All right, but I want to see Owen first."

"Of course."

Salamiel led her to the first floor room where Owen had been put to bed. Its appointments were grand; the huge four-poster bed stood upon a plinth, surrounded by tapestry drapes. A window-seat looked out upon the gardens to the rear of the house and the rugged cliff top. "This room is much nicer than mine," Lily said, "but I expected that."

"Preparations were hasty last night," Salamiel said smoothly. "You can choose a new room today, whichever one you like. I have many."

"I want to be here with Owen," she said and walked towards the bed.

"Very well." Salamiel followed her. The boy was sitting upright, clad in paisley-patterned pyjamas. His pale hair glowed in the dim light of the room. His skin looked like stone, the skin of a statue. Lily sat down on the bed and picked up one of Owen's white hands. She leaned forward and stroked strands of fluffy, freshly washed hair from his face. "O'," she said. "Can you hear me?"

Her brother did not even blink.

Salamiel gently laid a hand on her shoulder. "Perhaps we can do something to help Owen," he said.

Lily glanced round at him. "Can you?" Her face fell into a sneer. "I don't believe you. Why should you do anything? You're like *him*; a sweet-talking liar!"

"I'm glad you think I'm like Azazel," Salamiel said. "But neither of us follow the lie. Owen was used for something very special, and he will recover. You mustn't judge us, Lily, for you do not yet understand our purpose."

"I don't care!" Lily said. "I just want Owen back to how he was."

"Of course you do. Now, you can see that he's comfortable, so why not come downstairs with me. What would you like to eat? How about a full breakfast?"

He could see the mention of food stimulated Lily's appetite. She hadn't eaten anything since the previous day. "All right." Her consent was grudging.

He took her down into the spacious kitchen, which threw his servants into a panic, for normally he never ventured below stairs. Ignoring their furious attempts to appear busy and efficient, he sat down at the head of the kitchen table and gestured for Lily to sit beside him. Looking around herself like a wary cat, she did so, and pushed her hair back behind her ears. Salamiel gave his people instructions to prepare Lily a meal, then folded his hands on his stomach and smiled at her. She peered at him defensively.

"After you've eaten, you can take a bath. I'll send out for some clean clothes if you like."

She shrugged. "Whatever." She rubbed her face. "How long will you keep us here? What do you want with us?"

"I'm keeping you here for Azazel," he said. "I'm looking after you until he arrives."

"Why do you keep calling him that?" she asked. "He's Shemyaza. I know that's his name."

"He has many names," Salamiel answered, "but Azazel is the one I prefer. Shemyaza is a hopeless martyr, whereas Azazel is a god."

"You've not met him yet," Lily said. "When you do, I think you'll realise why he's called Shemyaza. There's nothing sacred in him. He's selfish and lazy. He doesn't care what happens to any of us."

Salamiel shook his head. "Don't be deceived. He's undergone a terrific shock, but he'll soon be himself again; the person I knew a long time ago."

"You're like him, then? Reborn?"

The smell of frying bacon filled the kitchen. The scent seemed to do Lily good, for she was already more responsive. *I will give you meat*, Salamiel thought, *and once you eat of my offerings, you will be mine*. He smiled. "Unlike Azazel, I never died," he said. "I was imprisoned and tortured for millennia, and eventually forgotten about. I was weak and without power, but some years ago, a Grigori adept found me and brought me back to consciousness."

Lily laughed. "It's like a horror film. You're like a vampire or something."

Salamiel smiled, a conspirator to her joke. "I suppose I am— a little." In fact, he was nothing like that at all.

"I can't believe you're that old," Lily said. She was daring to tease him now.

"Neither can I," he answered.

Lily frowned. "Now that I'm away from Shem, I don't really want to see him again. I loved him once, but he's changed. I think it was easier to love him when he was evil, because he..." she struggled for words. "He *cared* about people, in a weird sort of way. I know he loved Owen and me, no matter what he did to us. Peverel Othman would have restored Owen after his ritual, but Shemyaza is not the person we knew before. Now, he's a husk, and his indifference is worse than anything else."

"He was never what you would call evil, Lily," Salamiel said.

Lily glanced at him. "You weren't there! He took control of people and destroyed them. But never us. I thought we were safe, Owen and I."

"You're safe now."

Lily shook her head. "How can I believe you? Look what happened in the Assembly Rooms."

Salamiel could tell she wanted to believe him, for she felt lost and insecure. She wanted to believe she might have found an ally. "I'm sorry for what happened. We were desperate to secure Azazel, and because of that, lives were lost. It was not my fault, but that of the Grigori who were also intent on capturing Azazel, the ones who succeeded in doing so."

"Is he in danger?"

Salamiel shook his head. "No-one can hurt Azazel now. He is too powerful."

"I wouldn't be too sure about that." She spoke with such conviction that Salamiel, for a moment, experienced doubt and fear.

"Later, someone is coming to meet you," he said. "Her name is Sofia. This afternoon, she is meeting with Azazel. He's quite nearby, Lily, but just with the wrong people. Your friend Daniel is with him too. You will all be reunited soon."

"Is Shem being held against his will?" she asked.

Salamiel shook his head. "I don't believe so. He needs guidance, that's all. As yet, he is unaware of me. Once he realises I am near, he will leave the stronghold of the Parzupheim and come to me. If anyone tries to stop him, he will destroy them."

"You don't sound very sure," Lily said.

Salamiel risked a partial confession. "This is a delicate time. Of course, I am anxious and will remain so until Azazel is safely beside me."

"Are you in love with him too? Most people who meet him seem to be."

"I love him," Salamiel said, "but that is not the same as being *in* love, is it."

Presently, Lily's meal was laid before her and Salamiel watched in satisfaction as she devoured it. She was not just hungry, she was starving.

As she was eating, Salamiel summoned his secretary, a human dependant named Nina. From her appearance, she appeared to be stuck in the "sixties; a bright creature of enthusiasms, who wore a white crocheted mini-skirt and pale lipstick. But perhaps she was just a victim of the most recent fashions. Salamiel instructed her to go into the nearest town and buy Lily some clothes. "Something smart, but comfortable and feminine," he said.

Lily just smirked, shovelling fried egg into her mouth.

When she'd satisfied her hunger, he took her back upstairs and left her in his personal bathroom while he attended to some mail at his bedroom desk. He could hear her splashing around in the bath next door. Her youth and her vitality were intoxicating. He realised he liked her. Would Azazel approve of this? He hoped so.

Lily came to find him, swathed in his black towelling bathrobe, her wet hair hanging around her shoulders. She wasn't afraid of him now, but trust was still some distance away. She smelled fresh and clean and her bare feet left wet prints on the thick carpet.

"Would you like some coffee or tea?" Salamiel asked her.

"Yes please. Tea." She sat on his bed as he picked up the phone extension. "This is a wonderful house. My father lived in a house like this, but I never explored it properly. It was all shut up and abandoned by the time I was born. Do you know my father?"

Salamiel uttered a terse order to the servant on the end of the line, then turned in his seat as he replaced the phone. "Who is he?"

Lily wrinkled her nose. "I'm not even sure he's still alive. His name was Kashday Murkaster."

Salamiel stared at her with round eyes. Kashday? Was it possible this was the living daughter of one of his brethren? Kashday had been a confederate of Azazel's, caught and punished for his misdemeanours thousands of years ago. It was possible this girl's father had merely been named as a child for the renegade Watcher, but the idea that it might *really* be Kashday was too alluring to ignore. Salamiel was a firm believer in the power of coincidence or synchronicity. "I think I might have known him," he managed to say.

"I can see that in your face," Lily said. "It was like you saw a ghost."

Salamiel was annoyed that Sofia hadn't seen fit to apprise him of this morsel of knowledge. He had no doubt the woman was aware of Lily's heritage. Sofia would think it was none of his business for it had no bearing on his present task. "Kashday was a colleague of Azazel's," he said.

Lily nodded. "I know. It's weird my father has the same name."

"Perhaps not."

Lily flicked him a sharp glance. "No-one knows where he is now. He's probably dead."

"Maybe we can think about that another time," Salamiel said, smiling. "For now, we have to concentrate on getting Azazel and his followers together again."

Shemyaza did not sleep despite his exhaustion. As Enniel's soft-footed bottelier had led him up to the grand guestroom provided for his use, he had sensed Daniel's approach to the house. Dismissing Austin as soon as he'd entered the room, Shem turned out all the dim lamps and went to open the curtains. Outside, the sky was pearly grey, and the lights of a car shone on the gravel driveway. He could sense that Daniel was in the car, but there were others around him. Shem sent out a beam of thought to Daniel, requesting the boy to seek him out as soon as he could get away from his companions, but then he realised, with some alarm, the thought did not make contact. Someone was monopolising Daniel's attention, physically and psychically. It could only be the one named Taziel, the other inconvenient relic from Peverel Othman's past. Shem sighed and turned away from the window. He sat on his bed cross-legged, and concentrated on following Daniel's progress into and through the house. He took great care to shield himself from Taziel's awareness, for he could sense it was keen and acutely attuned to him. There was a familiarity about Taziel's etheric body, which Shem realised he had picked up on vaguely in the Assembly Rooms. So Enniel had used this past lover to track him down. Aninka and Taziel; the avenging angels. Aninka was no problem—she was too hurt by Othman's betrayal—but Taziel was another matter. He sought to control Daniel. Shem smiled to himself even as he thought of this. There was no way he'd let that happen.

Consequently, Daniel's behaviour in the drawing room was a great shock to Shem. It was so unexpected. He had believed Daniel would not contaminate himself with others. He had thought that Daniel, with his strong morals and sense of loyalty, would remain true to Owen, despite the condition he was in. Had he misjudged Daniel? Where had this provocative, sensual creature come from? Was it a product of what had happened at the High Place in Little Moor? Daniel had been so innocent before then, almost like a child. *My fault, my fault,* Shem thought, as he forced himself to witness every crucifying detail of what Daniel did with Taziel. He knew that Daniel could sense his astral presence in the room, yet it didn't stop him making love to this interloper. Where was the modesty that had been such a part of him? Gone, ripped from him by terror and dark knowledge.

Shem had to force himself to tear his awareness out of the room. He sat gasping upon his bed, feeling as if he'd been punched in the stomach. There were tears on his face, but he began to laugh softly. He wiped his eyes. *Daniel, you have reached me. Wasn't this what you wanted? Haven't you been nagging me to wake up?* Still, he wished it could have happened in a different way.

He spent the next six hours or so trying to gather his thoughts and his strength. As he meditated, he became aware of resources within himself that he'd previously been unaware of. It was like discovering new limbs. He did not yet know how to use them, or even how strong they were, but simply observing their existence was enough for now.

At one o'clock precisely, Austin came tapping at his door. Shem informed the man he would not be coming downstairs just yet, and requested a light meal. "Please bring me a pen and some paper," he said.

When the meal arrived, the writing utensils were on the tray. Austin brought the food up himself. "Your colleague, Miss Manden, has asked to see you."

"Convey my apologies. She'll have to wait a while."

Austin raised one eyebrow and almost smiled. "She was most insistent."

"I'm sure you can handle her. I don't wish to see either of my colleagues at present." He wrote hurriedly on a piece of paper and folded it in half before handing it to Austin. "Please give this to Daniel Cranton." The bottelier inclined his head and departed.

At three o'clock, Austin returned. "Lord Enniel requests your presence in his study. There is a visitor who wishes to meet you."

Shem was still sitting on the bed. "I do not intend to leave this room. If anyone wishes to see me, they must see me here."

"I shall convey your feelings to Lord Enniel." Austin withdrew once more.

Shem gripped his feet and placed his head on his thighs. He felt in turmoil, despite the meditations. He felt tired, but unable to sleep. He felt hungry, but sick. Only a few minutes elapsed before someone knocked sharply on his door once more. Shem did not call out, but the door opened anyway and Enniel came into the room. He was followed by a fearsome-looking female, whose heavy-lidded eyes seemed to look straight into Shem's soul. Enniel seemed nervous, which was interesting.

"Shemyaza, this is Sofia."

The woman inclined her head and smiled in a dangerous way, walking past Enniel to confront him. She held out her hand. "I've been *so* looking forward to this meeting," she said.

After lunch, Emma went for a walk around the grounds with Aninka, while the men sat in the drawing room to read the daily papers. It seemed as if all the occupants of the house were avoiding them, for no-one else came to sit in the room. Daniel was feeling more and more disoriented. He felt as if he'd accidentally stepped into another life, and was a normal houseguest, down for the weekend with his lover, to sample the opulence of Enniel Prussoe's house. What was he doing sitting reading a paper? It was absurd. The words on the page swam before his eyes. He wanted to see Shem. Why hadn't he been sent for? When the note came, Daniel almost tore it in half in his urgency to read it. This had to be the summons.

"What is it?" Taziel asked sharply.

Daniel read the note before answering. He looked at Taziel in bewilderment. "He won't see me."

"Show me." Taziel held out his hand.

"No." Daniel couldn't bear to think of Taziel reading it. He was also aware of Lahash's attention, even though he appeared engrossed in his paper. "I'll show you later."

Taziel stood up. "I want to know now."

Daniel sighed. "All right." He didn't want to lie about what Shem had written.

Taziel read it and laughed. "He's got a fucking nerve! Who does he think he is?"

"I think we both know the answer to that," Daniel said dryly.

"Will you do what he says?" The question was a challenge.

Daniel felt torn. Where did his loyalties lie now? Where *should* they lie? He dropped his eyes from Taziel's furious gaze. "Yes," he said simply. "I have to. This is nothing to do with relationships. It's more important."

"Nothing to do with relationships? Hah!" Taziel read the note aloud, much to Daniel's distress. "Daniel, you have polluted yourself. You cannot come to me until you have been purified. Abstain from the greeds of the flesh for three days, then send me word. We shall meet at this time. Bollocks!" Taziel ripped the note up. "You really jump to his tune, don't you!"

Daniel choked back a cry and raised his hands to his face as the fragments of torn paper rained down on his head. "Taz, I only met you yesterday. Why are you behaving like this? You knew of my connection with Shem. It was the reason you seduced me in the first place!"

Lahash cleared his throat to remind them he was there. Taziel uttered an angry sound and stalked from the room. Daniel sat with his face in his hands, thinking only, "Fuck, fuck, fuck."

"It didn't say three days from today," Lahash remarked, shaking his paper to straighten the page.

Daniel looked at him through a cage of fingers. "That's true," he said.

Emma knew that Aninka Prussoe was curious about her. As they walked through the bedraggled, leafless gardens of High Crag, she sensed the multitude of questions that Aninka could barely contain. This Grigori woman had loved Peverel Othman very much; Emma could see that in her face. What a silly bitch! Emma had never deluded herself that Othman could be an ordinary lover. Still, there was a wistful, vulnerable quality about Aninka that endeared her to Emma. Also, she did not treat Emma with condescension, a trait exhibited by most Grigori in human company.

As they strolled towards the broken-down wall that marked the boundary with the cliff edge, Aninka told Emma about Lahash. "He is a Murkaster, you know. He lived in Little Moor at one time."

Emma nodded. "I thought he looked familiar. I didn't know him personally, but then the Murkasters were a large family, relatives were always coming and going."

"You have given up a lot to be with Shemyaza."

Emma smiled. At last, Aninka had dared to broach the subject. "Not much. Without the Murkasters I was dying. You should have seen me a couple of months ago. I looked like a hag."

Aninka cast her an amused glance. "That is very hard to believe!"

Emma shrugged. "To be honest, I feel rather adrift now. In Little Moor, I had a role, as Lily and Owen's protectress. And it was me who organised everything to get Shem and the others to safety." She grinned at Aninka. "Well, relative safety. Now..." she sighed. "I don't seem to have a purpose. Lily and Owen have vanished, and Shem and Daniel certainly don't need me."

Aninka gently touched Emma's shoulder. "Oh, I'm sure that's not true."

"Don't humour me," Emma said lightly. "It's quite true." She walked to the wall and put her hands upon the slick, rough stones. The wind was hungry here, grabbing at their clothes and hair. Emma took a deep breath. "Look at the sea. It's alive."

Aninka leaned on the wall beside her, her long black hair flying back like a sinister flag. The waves were a grey-green maelstrom far below, furious breakers collared with foam. "I grew up here," Aninka said. "For a while I wanted only to escape. Now I can appreciate it again."

"You are lucky," Emma said dryly.

Aninka pursed her lips, then said, "Enniel will find the Winter twins, I'm sure."

"I hope so. I made a promise to their mother that I'd look out for them."

"I'd like to meet them," Aninka said. "I'm sure we have a lot in common."

Emma gave her a wry glance. "I expect so. You'd like Lily. She's a lovely girl. And Owen—well, if he ever gets back to normal, he's quite a stunner."

Aninka smiled, then glanced at Emma speculatively. "Would you tell me what happened in Little Moor? I mean, do you mind?"

Emma pulled a rueful face. "No, I don't mind."

Aninka stared straight ahead, her gaze fixed on the sea as Emma related all she could remember: Othman's arrival, her rejuvenation, how she assisted him to take control of the village. "He wanted to enact a ritual at the High Place, which is a sacred mound outside the village. The Murkasters used it, and so have magically inclined humans. For centuries. He would have killed Daniel, you know. He had no sentimentality about it." She frowned. "But something happened. A goddess came." She paused, then spoke the name. "Ishtahar. She was Shemyaza's lover, the human woman who seduced him thousands of years ago. Only she's something rather more than human now." Glancing at Aninka, she could see that the woman looked crestfallen.

"Ishtahar stopped him," Aninka said in a dull voice.

Emma nodded. "Yes. I saw it. They will be together again one day, Ninka. You must forget about him."

Aninka laughed nervously. "Am I that transparent?"

Emma was quite surprised Aninka wasn't offended by the frankness of her remarks. Grigori wouldn't normally take criticism or censure from a human, no matter how gently worded. "I do understand," she said. "I know the effect Shem has on people."

"I wanted to be different," Aninka said hotly. "I wanted to stand out from the adoring masses. Is that so bad?"

Emma shook her head. "No. I would have felt the same."

"Ah, but you didn't."

Emma turned away from the sea. "I'm not Grigori," she said.

Aninka's face assumed a determined expression. She reached out briefly and touched Emma's arm. "I will help you find the twins," she said.

Chapter Seventeen
Rites of Truth and Passage

When Sofia arrived at Pharos for dinner, she was still high from her meeting during the afternoon. Her heart continued to beat faster than normal, and there were spots of colour along her sharp cheekbones. She felt slightly out of breath and unnaturally joyous. The experience of seeing Azazel in the flesh had affected her more than she would have believed possible. There was no doubt he was everything they thought him to be.

Salamiel's secretary showed her into the library, where a fire burned in medieval splendour and the indigo drapes were drawn against the night. Sofia demanded a gin and tonic and Nina moved obediently to the sideboard to mix one. Sofia stood before the fire, taking quick, thirsty sips and staring into the flames.

"Sofia."

She turned to the sound of her name and put her empty glass down on the mantle-piece. Salamiel had come into the room and upon his arm was a beautiful young woman. Lily Winter. It had to be. Her long red hair fell softly over her breasts, confined only by tortoiseshell combs behind her ears. She wore a long dinner dress of green fabric that looked rather too old for her. Sofia was slightly annoyed Salamiel was not alone, for some things she did not want to discuss in front of the girl. Collecting herself, she glided towards Salamiel, put her hands upon his shoulders and kissed the air beside his left cheek. "Sal! How lovely to see you!" She withdrew and smiled at Lily. "And you must be Salamiel's visitor, Miss Lily Winter."

The girl smiled awkwardly and wriggled her shoulders. "Hi." She appeared to feel uncomfortable in her matron's gown. Sofia did not blame her. Salamiel had obviously chosen it for her. Stupid creature! No taste!

"How pretty you are," Sofia drawled.

Lily blushed. Sofia drew in her breath and turned to Salamiel. "Sal, darling, I really must have a few minutes alone with you before dinner. I've had a horrible letter from my broker again. Would you look at it for me?"

"With pleasure." Salamiel disengaged Lily from his arm. "Sit here for a while will you, my dear? Nina will get you a drink."

"I do apologise for whisking him off like this," Sofia trilled at Lily, "but I simply can't digest my meal until my mind's at rest."

"That's OK," Lily said, moving towards the couch.

Salamiel smiled at her. "Thank you, Lily. We shan't be long." He virtually dragged Sofia from the room.

Outside, with the library door shut, Salamiel and Sofia held onto each other's arms, their relative status forgotten in the intensity of the moment. The light was dim around them. Only their eyes glittered and the jewels at Sofia's throat. "Well?" Salamiel hissed.

"Yes!" Sofia exhaled. She was shaking. "He lives!"

Salamiel let her go and briefly closed his eyes, a delighted grin spreading across his face. He took hold of her arm again. "My study. Come."

They ran down the corridor, creatures far removed from the masks they wore in human, and occasionally each other's, company. Their tall shadows flickered along the walls. Sofia looked like the Witch Queen from a fairy tale, with her long, black gown and gleaming hair and eyes. Salamiel looked like what he was; a son of angels, crowned with a fiery mane, his eyes glowing like coals. They stopped before the door behind which Salamiel's private office could be found. Sofia followed him into the room and threw herself into a leather chair, her gown spreading out around her feet like a pool of India ink. "I saw it in his face the minute I walked into his room," she said, breathlessly. Her eyes were like black gems in their deep sockets, her flesh like powdered tissue. Her breath even steamed a little on the warm air.

"How did he appear?" Salamiel leaned on the desk beside her, his hair hanging over his chest. His face was in shadow, but for his pale cheekbones and the wet gleam of his eyes.

"Magnificent! He is tired and troubled, but underneath it all, I feel he is in control. He is playing with Enniel and his cronies. He's just waiting to see what they are offering."

Salamiel watched her breast rising and falling. The physical manifestation of her excitement fascinated him, although he was equally shocked by it. "What did you discuss?"

Sofia shrugged and shook her head. "Hardly anything. I dropped a few morsels of bait, subtle ones. It remains to be seen whether he picks them up." She rubbed her hands together; her fingers were like polished bones, the skin deathly pale. "I need a drink. Have you anything in here?"

Salamiel nodded and went around the desk to open a drawer. "What are Enniel's plans?"

"Oh, the Parzupheim will meet at High Crag during the next few days. They'll pussy-foot around Azazel, because they haven't got his measure. Now they have him in their claws, but in truth, I don't think they have a clue what to do with him." She smiled in a brittle fashion and accepted a small tumbler of whisky from Salamiel. "Which is all to our advantage. I shall need to speak to him alone, of course, and in the very near future. I don't want to risk Enniel getting any hooks into him."

She seemed to be calming down, as if her feverish excitement had only been a desperate need to expel in words some of what she'd seen that afternoon. Salamiel was amused by her condition. She had not anticipated the force of Azazel's presence, his overwhelming charisma. Salamiel was glad it had winded her. "What was your impression though? Do you think he'll come to us without any trouble?"

She nodded. "If I intrigue him enough, yes." Her hands still shook a little as she put the tumbler to her lips. Before she spoke, she wiped her mouth with the back of her hand. "I want to begin work by the winter solstice. Azazel must initiate the preliminaries to awakening the Shamir."

"That gives us very little time."

She sneered, took another drink. "Enough!" She narrowed her eyes. "I need to establish what Azazel wants, and then offer it to him. I suspect he desires only solitude and peace, in which case, it will be easy. If he comes to us, we shall give him a citadel in which to hide, somewhere where no other Grigori can molest him."

"Azazel was never a one for peace and quiet," Salamiel remarked. He wasn't sure whether the anxiety he felt was inspired by suspicion or perplexity.

Sofia directed a sharp glance at him, apparently in command of her composure once more. "There are bound to be changes! What do you expect? If you think he's going to come bouncing into Pharos like a long-lost friend, ready for a party, forget it!"

"But is his mind...intact?"

Sofia inhaled impatiently through her nose. "It's impossible to tell at this stage, but he certainly didn't look or sound like a lunatic."

"I was not thinking of anything so extreme. I was thinking of instability, depression, confusion."

Sofia leaned forward in her chair. "Listen, Salamiel. Azazel is like a man who's been kept hostage in a hostile country for a long, long time. Freedom must be a frightening thing to him at the moment. He's bound to be disorientated and unsure. We must be patient and understanding."

Salamiel's expression was bleak. "He's worse than you're saying, isn't he."

Sofia shook her head. "I can't make any firm judgements on what I've seen so far."

"Describe him."

"I can't." Her voice was hoarse. She sipped the whisky, staring Salamiel in the eye. "He possesses a beauty beyond words. To see him is to desire him. That, of course, is part of his power. He is a prince of light, my dear, and we must take care, for fear of being blinded by him."

Salamiel felt a shiver of apprehension fizz down his spine. He was sure he'd lived this moment before.

Back in the library, Lily sipped gin while she waited for Salamiel and his friend to return. Nina attempted to keep her occupied by talking about clothes and make-up; topics in which Lily had scant interest. She was thinking about Salamiel and his visitor, Sofia. They had been surrounded by a thick fog of tension, which had suggested the presence of secrets and excitement. Sofia had been desperate to talk to Salamiel. She had claimed she wanted advice about a letter, but there had been no letter in her hand when she'd left the room, and her hand-bag still lay beside the sofa. Lily considered these things, while nodding and smiling at Nina, who appeared oblivious of her lack of attention. Then, she remembered what Salamiel had said to her earlier. *Sofia had seen Shem that afternoon.* The woman's frenetic air confirmed it. He had cast his spell on her. But why did Sofia need to speak to Salamiel alone? What were they keeping from her? Lily realised she must be firm with herself, and not trust Salamiel, nor his strange friend, too easily.

At High Crag, Shemyaza ate alone in his room. He too thought about the meeting with Sofia that afternoon. She was typical of her kind; high-ranking Grigori were all very similar. The realm of conspiracy and intrigue was her home territory. He had known at once that she was rather more than a representative of the Parzupheim, and also that Enniel was unaware of her true nature. Ultimately, Sofia represented only herself. A sub-text had passed between them. She had seemed to be making an offer: whatever he desired in exchange for the use of his powers. She had told him that his first act must be to awaken the Shamir, the serpent power in the land. He knew nothing about this, although talk of the subject kindled uncomfortable feelings within him that were almost like memories. Shem noticed that Enniel seemed surprised by Sofia's words. Clearly, she had not spoken to him first, but he tried to hide the fact. "I think we need to discuss this matter with the Parzupheim before any decisions are made," Enniel had said stiffly. "Perhaps Shemyaza isn't yet ready to take on such a potentially dangerous task."

Sofia had ignored him. "The Shamir waits," she had said, curling one of her elegant hands into a fist before her, "and by awakening it, you will initiate the dawn of a new age."

Shem had felt faintly embarrassed by such talk. Sofia believed him to be more aware and in control of his strengths than he actually was, but he realised this was probably a fortunate misconception. He had no doubt that should she get the faintest inkling she could exploit him, or the slightest whiff of weakness, she'd pounce, dig her teeth into the back of his neck and never let go. Peverel Othman had locked horns with such people in the past, and won, but Shemyaza did not yet feel strong enough to deal with a similar situation. Othman had invaded the darkest, deepest cabals of the Grigori. In such places he had learned of ancient, forbidden rituals, which he'd subsequently employed in Cresterfield and Little Moor. Shem knew that Sofia was familiar with all those unhallowed practices, and could smell their residue on him. She was the one whom the Parzupheim had sent to Little Moor after he'd fled. Therefore, it was safe to assume she'd been able to visualise everything that had happened there. Shem could tell that, unlike Enniel, she did not disapprove of his actions. It was clear to him that she was a creature who felt very little emotion, and who understood that Othman had done only what he'd felt was necessary and right. Whether he agreed with her judgement, Shem was not quite sure. Was he capable of perpetrating the cruelties that Othman had dispensed so casually? Could he sacrifice Daniel to a demon now?

Perhaps Sofia was the least of his considerations at present. He'd abandoned the twins to an unknown fate, which now pricked at his conscience. He needed Daniel to help find them again, and Daniel must be brought to heel.

Daniel knew he should take heed of Shemyaza's words, not for his own sake, or even for Shem's, but for the sake of some greater purpose. Playing games now was a waste of valuable time. He could sense the evaporating hours, slipping away like sand through a narrow waist of glass. He could sense dark, purply power moving in, gathering in a cloud of bruising storms above High Crag. Yet part of him, a new rebellious part, felt annoyed that Shem thought he could order him around, select his lovers, apportion his time. Daniel did not like feeling owned. For this reason, although he felt uncomfortable about it, he sought Taziel out and apologised to him. Taziel was hurt, spoke of the way Peverel Othman had damaged him and implied further damage was imminent. Daniel acted contrite, affectionate. While conscious at every moment of Shemyaza's presence within the house, he cajoled Taziel into the room they'd been given and offered himself unreservedly. Taziel seemed convinced by this display, although even as they writhed together on the bed, Daniel knew the magic of what had occurred between them that morning had been ephemeral, doomed to a single experience. Now it was only hungry struggling, the gratification of shallow appetites. He wondered whether Taziel was aware of this. Like Daniel, he was extremely sensitive to atmospheres. It seemed they were acting out a play, and the lines they spoke to one another failed to connect, did not make up an entire conversation.

In the evening, after they had eaten, Taziel dozed on the bed, while Daniel lay awake, his heart beating in what felt like panic. Shem had done this, crushed the fragile shoot of their relationship before it could take root. They had glimpsed the promise that morning, now it had been poisoned. Daniel could smell the scent of Owen's body in the room, and knew that Shem had projected it. *Leave me alone!* he cried in his mind. *Let me experience life! You have lived through so much. Would you deny me the same opportunities?*

He could almost hear Shem's reply. *Daniel, you have to make sacrifices. This dalliance is a waste of your time. You are destined for better things. Cast him off. Come to me. We have work to do.*

Daniel knew it was only a matter of time before he gave in.

He awoke in the middle of the night with a start, as if someone had poked him. For a moment, he lay breathing hard, blinking at the darkness. Taziel snored softly beside him, his tangled hair spread across the pillow. Looking at him, Daniel experienced a pang of emotion. He leaned over to kiss him, but before his lips made contact, a bolt of blue radiance filled his eyes.

Throwing himself back against the wall, Daniel saw a spinning ball of azure light hanging over the end of the bed. It was so bright it was painful to look at. The room was rendered black and white by its brilliance. It spat out sparkler motes. Yet Taziel did not wake up. Daniel managed to gasp, "Shem! No!"

A low-pitched female voice answered him. "No, my Daniel. Not Shem."

The light condensed until a shape was visible within it; a woman sitting with her knees raised, her arms curled around her ankles. She was young, her hair was black and she wore a string of gold disks around her brow. "Ishtahar." Daniel breathed the name like a prayer.

She nodded at him, smiling. "I am she. Listen, Daniel, for I have no strength here and cannot stay long. You must quell the torment within you and return to the inner silence that used to be your guide. A wild and judgmental storm is gathering around Shemyaza, and dark sisters move close to breathe the mist of their will around him. Go back to him, and give yourself to him completely. This will teach him how to give again. An important lesson, for there is much that Shem must give before the storm abates. But go to him as an equal and teach him humility."

Daniel gulped air; it had become difficult to breathe. "Give myself to him as an equal? How? Must I leave Taziel?"

Ishtahar closed her eyes for a moment, the blink of a smiling cat. "The path of the seer is the loneliest of paths, my Daniel, but its rewards can be great. The time of your initiation has long past; it has never been dealt with. You must take control of your own heart, body and vitality, and let no other dominate them. When this is done, the time to reclaim your birthright will be upon you."

"My birthright? What is it?"

"You will know. For now, you must go to Shem, and go to him soon. He needs your strength. He attempts to control you, because he is used to power, to those who must obey. But you cannot let his ways muddy your clear sight. Let him think you dance to his sacred music. Ultimately, you are beyond his control. But there is one thing you must do before the dawn light lifts from the sea. When you go to Shem, go to him as an adult, not as a child. Undertake this rite of passage before the night shies before the sun. Do you hear me?"

Daniel nodded slowly. "Yes, but you must tell me how."

"No time." She seemed to be receding in his sight, becoming smaller. Now it appeared she was at the end of a dark tunnel. "There can be no tall candles, no sweet incense, no ritual chant for this ceremony, for your time is short. Listen to your blood, Daniel Cranton. This is not the time for hearts or minds."

There was a crack of blinding blue light, then darkness. Daniel found he was leaning over Taziel, as he had been the moment before Ishtahar appeared. He felt disorientated, unsure of whether he'd been dreaming or hallucinating, or whether Shemyaza's woman really had revealed herself to him.

Taziel made a small, sleepy sound, then awoke. He jumped to find Daniel leaning over him. "What is it?"

Daniel almost told him what had happened, but then only put a finger against his lips and murmured, "Ssh."

Taziel looked afraid, as if he'd sensed something peculiar had occurred. Daniel put his hands upon Taziel's shoulders, pushed him against the bed.

"You look weird," Taziel said. "Stop it."

Daniel could feel the cold air on his naked back and the beat of blood in his loins. *Listen to your blood.* He drew in his breath, his head hanging between his shoulders.

"Daniel?"

He raised his head, and could barely see, for his vision was broken up with spinning motes of grey light. "Owen, Shemyaza, you," he said slowly. "All of you have taken me as your boy, drunk from me like a vessel. Surrender to me, Taziel. Let me be a man for you."

Taziel blinked at him. "What's the matter? Have you been dreaming?"

Daniel shook his head. "No. I am awake." He reached out and cupped Taziel's jaw with one hand, bent down to kiss him fiercely. There was some small protest to begin with, but it was swiftly quenched.

Daniel thought, *Do I want this branch of fire? Will it change me?* But he submitted his will to the tide of his blood. There were no visions before his eyes, no shifts of awareness, just the animal thrust of masculinity.

Afterwards, he got up and went to stand in the window. It overlooked the garden, which led to the sea. Behind him, he heard Taziel light a cigarette, inhale deeply. "What time is it?" Daniel asked.

He heard Taziel pick up his watch from the bedside table. "Two twenty-five. Why?"

"No reason."

Taziel was silent for a moment, then said. "You have begun the countdown haven't you. At two twenty-six, in three days' time, you will be at his door."

Daniel shivered, but said nothing.

"He was *in* you earlier, wasn't he," Taziel said. "That wasn't you. It was *him*. You disgust me."

Daniel turned then. "You're very selfish. I have work to do. Why should that mean our friendship is over? Can't you wait three days?"

Taziel stared at him, took a few long draws off the cigarette, then said resignedly. "He won't let you come back to me. If you think otherwise, you're deluding yourself."

Daniel didn't recognise the gruff, aggressive voice that burst out of his mouth. "If I don't come back to you, it'll be my own choice! OK?"

Taziel's eyes had widened slightly. Daniel didn't often sound harsh or raise his voice. "Come back to me now," he said quietly.

Daniel shook his head. "No. I can't. If you have any respect for me, you'll stand by me now, not drive me away."

"Respect you?" Taziel laughed bitterly. "Daniel, I *love* you."

"Don't say that!" Daniel turned away, leaned on the windowsill. "You hardly know me. Don't bind me with words!"

"You are human," Taziel said coldly. "Only that. Why the hell should I tell a mere human I love it, unless I mean what I say?"

Daniel did not respond but dressed himself quickly. Taziel tried to stop him as he left the room, and called him back, but Daniel kept on walking. He went out into the garden through the French windows in the drawing room where he'd spent the dregs of the previous night. Outside the night was alive with elemental presences that tumbled in the wind and the salt perfume of the sea. Spectral fingers plucked at his hair, half-heard laughter tickled his ears. Daniel stood upon the wet lawn and took several deep breaths. He felt angry and confused, and it manifested as a desire to hit out at something. *I am a man,* he thought. *Oh God, it is vile!*

Chapter Eighteen
Casting the Stones

Sofia, Lily decided, was a person-eater. Not just a man-eater, although she'd undoubtedly gnawed a few masculine bones in her time. She was also a liar. Lily was intrigued by her, but also wary and a little frightened.

At dinner, Lily sat across from Sofia, who rested her elbows on the table, her raised white hands drooping before her, like the paws of a praying mantis, in mid-air. In fact, she was much like a praying mantis all over. The triangular head, the large eyes, the long, thin body, the general air of watchful hunger. Lily wanted to ask her about Shem, but kept her mouth shut in case anything was asked of her in return. She had a feeling Sofia would utter very personal and embarrassing questions. So the three of them sat and made painful small talk.

Lily was intrigued by the relationship between Sofia and Salamiel. They started off amicably enough, but halfway through the first course, Sofia became waspish with him. First, she complained about the temperature of the soup. When the fish arrived, she pulled a sour face after her first sip of wine and made disparaging comments about Salamiel's knowledge and tastes. The fish she dissected carefully but refused to eat. Her silence on its texture and appearance were eloquent enough to reveal her opinions. By the time the meat arrived at the table, Lily was squirming in discomfort. Sofia felt that Salamiel's cook had murdered the meat. Why had she been so foolish as to waste it on him?

Lily thought everything about the meal was fine, which perhaps only revealed her ignorance about food. She wasn't used to eating well. It amazed her how Salamiel was not offended by Sofia's moaning. Mid-way through one of Sofia's caustic diatribes, while she poked at the tender lamb with her fork, Salamiel caught Lily's eye and winked. Lily smiled back at him, puzzled by the warmth that his private gesture had kindled within her. He was a strange, confusing creature. Last night, he had terrified her, as commander of an army of ghouls. Not only had he apparently condoned the murder of Johcasta and Israel, and perhaps other residents of the Assembly Rooms, he had also kidnapped her and Owen. He'd spoken vaguely of saving them from the clutches of the "other" Grigori, and keeping them safe for Shem, but Lily wondered whether he had other motives as well. She thought she should mistrust and despise him, treat him, in fact, in the same way Sofia did, but that would not be a natural reaction. Neither, she had to admit, did she possess the skill. Today, he had shown her a vulnerable side, which she'd lapped up, and as a result had spoken to him far too candidly. She felt annoyed with herself for being so open, so ready to give him the benefit of the doubt.

Earlier that day, after Lily's bath in Salamiel's private rooms, he had given her the clothes that Nina had been out to buy. Thankfully, the plain black leggings and thick jumpers were far more to her taste than the hideous evening gown she'd be obliged to wear later on. Then Salamiel had shown her around Pharos, leading her through high, echoing rooms with bare stone walls, long galleries where dim paintings hung, and out to his conservatory of forced lush greenery and unseasonal heat. The house was stuffed with ancient artefacts: statues, books, talismans. As they walked, Salamiel told her stories about how he'd acquired some of his possessions. He had unearthed the strange, elongated stone head that sat on a polished marble plinth from a desert tomb; he had bartered in a bazaar in a Middle Eastern land for the worn statuette of a goddess, which now resided on top of a bookcase. Masks of the Watchers adorned the walls; attenuated features and slitted eyes.

"You have travelled a lot," said Lily, thinking of Peverel Othman.

He nodded. "Yes. I had a lot of catching up to do. The world has changed so much." If Salamiel really had walked the earth in the days of Enoch and Noah, this understatement seemed farcical.

"Surprising you didn't run into Pev somewhere." She smiled. "That is *Azazel.*"

Salamiel smiled bleakly. "I would have known if I had."

Lily glanced at him as they walked into the conservatory. She tried to imagine him desiccated and inanimate, buried for thousands of years, beneath a ton of rocks in the earth. He seemed far too sane, too whole and too youthful for that to be true. He was certainly not ordinary, but then he was Grigori, so that was inevitable. Lily found herself wondering whether his story was genuine. Perhaps he only wanted it to be. A sad chord sounded in her heart. She felt sorry for him. He seemed at once lonely and deluded, waiting for the saviour he called Azazel. Lily felt Shem would only laugh at him. *No,* she thought bitterly. *He'll seduce him, then laugh.*

Now, as he dealt graciously with Sofia's complaints at the dinner table, he seemed world-weary and ancient, but it was not evident from his appearance. It was something indefinable, perhaps archaic, in his manner. *Damn,* Lily thought. *I'm getting too interested.* He was attractive, as all Grigori were attractive to her. She felt angry with herself about this. The surface meant nothing. What was underneath that perfect face and body might be horrifying. She had only to think of Peverel Othman to realise that.

After dinner, they returned to the lounge. Salamiel opened a bottle of red wine, which of course Sofia detested. Lily thought it was wonderful, being used to supermarket plonk. Still no mention had been made of why she was there, or of Shem. After one glass of the wine, which warmly accentuated the effects of the alcohol consumed at table, Lily decided to say something herself.

"I'd like to talk about what I'm doing here."

Her remark silenced Sofia, and Lily was immediately scared. Sofia's face changed, as if she'd removed a mask. This was no twittering, silly female, but a creature of passionless power. Lily wished she'd kept her mouth shut.

"My dear, you are here because you belong to Azazel. Soon he will be with us and you must be here waiting for him."

"I don't belong to anyone," Lily said lamely. She glanced at Salamiel in appeal, but he was staring into his wine glass, slumped in his chair, his long legs stretched out before him, crossed at the ankles. She was disheartened by his lack of support.

Sofia laughed, but it was not the infuriating trilling with which she'd punctuated the meal. This was a low, cruel sound. "You *are* his, Lily Winter. You know it. I know it. Why deny this ultimate truth?"

Lily blushed. She wanted to say, "Shem does not believe in ultimate truth", but knew Sofia would only have a response to her remark which she could not counter. "What are you going to do with him?" she asked.

"Help him rediscover his destiny," Sofia answered, almost casually. She took a sip of wine, grimaced, and pointedly put down her glass on an occasional table. "He will need you for this."

Lily scratched her left ear, uncomfortable. She had visions of herself spread out on a slab in the cellar, Shemyaza transformed into a demon, fucking her life away. She thought of Daniel, and experienced a pang of love and need. She needed to divert the conversation. "You've seen him, haven't you."

Sofia paused for a moment before answering. "Yes. You are a very fortunate young woman."

A thought passed through Lily's mind. *I don't want him to rediscover his power. It will be terrible. He'll become something hideous, like the ultimate weapon.* She heard Sofia laugh softly.

"You are so transparent, my dear, and so innocent. You must learn to take hold of the shadows and command them. You must learn about your own power too." She gestured with one hand. "Why be frightened? Don't you feel the presence of Ishtahar within you?"

Lily glanced up at Sofia and couldn't help saying, "You know about her?" which seemed ridiculous. Anyone with knowledge of Grigori history knew about Ishtahar.

"I know about what happened in Little Moor," Sofia said. "And that Ishtahar used you as a channel."

Lily shook her head. "No, it wasn't like that. She was just...there."

"Wrong," said Sofia. "You simply don't understand what happened. Your presence enabled Ishtahar to manifest and speak to Azazel. We need that influence here too, and you will provide it."

Anger shivered through Lily's body and she spoke without thinking. "No! Ishtahar has no place here with you! She is absolute love and serenity. She is nothing like you, nothing like Azazel. She loves Shem, not the thing you want him to be!"

Sofia raised her eyebrows. "Poor child," she said, turning to Salamiel. "She simply cannot understand that Ishtahar is a sexual influence, who can lead the beast from the labyrinth." She looked back at Lily. "Ishtahar was a manifestation of the Maiden, whose filmy veils fan the fires of masculine desire. Azazel will smell her sex and be drawn by it."

"That's disgusting!" Lily said, but a part of her understood exactly what Sofia meant. She remembered Peverel Othman coming to her cottage in Little Moor, the way his eyes had seemed to stroke her flesh, reach right into her and take hold of her artless lust. She remembered the smell of him, the feel of his warm skin against hers, his hair like a banner across her thighs as his serpent tongue teased the most secret parts of her. A tingling sensation ignited between her legs. Sofia could sense it too. Lily hung her head so her hair covered her face. She wanted to weep with shame, yet at the same time was possessed by a longing to run from the house, into the wild winter elements outside. She wanted to scream with rapture and leap into the air. *He was coming to her...*

Sofia reached out and patted Lily's knotted hands. "You must relax, my dear." She stood up. "I must be off now, Sal. I have a desire to take a glass of good wine before bedtime and I'll not get that here."

Lily sat with a numb, blank mind while Salamiel escorted Sofia to the front door. When he returned, he began to speak to her, but Lily interrupted him.

"I don't want to talk about it. Please, take me to Owen. I want to go to bed."

Salamiel looked rather disapproving but slowly nodded. "As you wish. Can you remember where the room is?"

"No." Lily stood up. She felt very drunk now, and slightly sick.

"Then I'll show you. Come." Salamiel offered her his arm.

The stairs seemed like a dark, threatening void ahead of them, the hall far too cavernous and draughty. They passed into the shadows, beyond the inadequate pools of light in the hall, and the chandelier overhead tinkled in a spectral breeze. Lily shivered, her fingers hooked as lightly as possible through Salamiel's elbow. As they mounted the stairs, he said to her, "Sofia has frightened you."

"I said I didn't want to..."

"Hush!" Salamiel interrupted. "I'm not going to talk about it at length, but there are a couple of things you must know. Don't be frightened. No harm will come to you. You are worried that Sofia and I want to shape Azazel into a dark god, but that's not so. I know him better than Sofia."

Lily made a disgruntled noise. She sensed a sub-text to Salamiel's words, which suggested his ideas and Sofia's were perhaps not in accord. "I don't trust you," she said. "You have to earn that."

"And maybe there are things you have to earn as well," he answered.

Lily realised he felt offended. They continued their walk to the bedroom in silence, through the shadows of the house.

Once in the room, Lily wished she hadn't suggested sleeping with Owen. He was still sitting upright in the bed, staring at the door, clearly not seeing anything at all. Two lamps burned dimly in the room, and Owen's skin seemed shockingly white against the darkness of the wooden headboard.

Salamiel, perhaps sensing Lily's feelings and deciding she needed to be punished in some way, said goodnight curtly and left the room. Lily stood against the carved panels of the door, looking at her brother. She could not bear the thought of lying beside him, while he sat there staring. Yet it would be worse if he made some movement or looked at her. Owen was not himself any more. She dreaded to think what he might be.

There was a wide window-seat, upholstered as a couch, and it was here that Lily spent the night. She removed the thick top quilt from the bed, her stomach turning over as Owen's dead white hands moved bonelessly against it, and wrapped herself up in it, fully dressed. She could not face turning out the lights, but shuffled over to the window-seat and lay down. The wind howled close to her ear, and she was afraid that if she paid too much attention she would hear words in it. She pulled the quilt over her head, creating a hot but uncomfortable nest for herself. Then she started having disturbing thoughts about how, now that her head was covered, Owen had turned his face towards her, his eyes burning. He had become the creature that had raped Daniel at the High Place and was getting out of the bed, padding towards her on silent feet, getting ready to rip the quilt from her back and...she threw back the quilt and looked at Owen in terror, but he hadn't moved. Her sleep, that night, was fragmented, and tortured by fleeting nightmares.

Chapter Nineteen
Learning to Fly

Daniel wrote a note for Shem in the afternoon of the third day. Austin delivered it to Shem's room, and waited to see if there would be a reply. Shem laughed as he read the note, and shook his head. "No reply. I don't believe one is needed." The note consisted of two short sentences. "Two twenty-six a.m. Be awake."

Shem did not eat after two in the afternoon. When night fell, he moved all the furniture in his room out to the edges and created a circle for himself in the centre. Austin had brought him two packets of white candles and two dozen candlesticks. "Tonight, I have a visitor," Shem explained. "I want romantic light." He did not think it would be a good idea to advertise to Enniel that he planned some magical work. After Austin had left, Shem ran himself a bath, to which he added a palmful of salt from the cellar on his supper tray. After bathing, he dried his hair and dressed himself in a loose towelling robe. Then he arranged the candlesticks around the room. They were all of different shapes and sizes, made of glass and wood and metal. Some were very ancient and had clearly been used in magical rites before. Shem allowed himself the shivering light of a single candle, but left the others unlit.

Daniel and he must begin work immediately the boy arrived. First, they would have to track down Lily and Owen. After that, Daniel would have to concentrate on what this Sofia woman really wanted, and whether the Parzupheim had any hidden agenda. Then, they must think about what to do next. Tomorrow, he would put Emma out of her misery and summon her to him, but first he had to speak to Daniel. Shem moved his untouched supper tray onto the dressing table. Later, he might need to eat.

The hours ticked by, each stretched to its limit. Shem listened to the movements of the house, the faint voices. He heard the lights click off, one by one. People paused beyond his door, wondering. He could sense their thoughts. One was angry, another curious, a third leaden with sadness. He heard Emma's breath outside, but she did not knock or call to him. The house sensed something was to happen this night and its tension affected its inhabitants.

At eleven o'clock, Enniel walked into the room without knocking. Shem wished he'd been able to lock the door, but he didn't intend to move from the centre of his circle when Daniel arrived.

"What are you doing?" Enniel asked, his face bland.

Shem was sitting cross-legged on the floor within the ring of unlit candles. "What you want me to do."

"Which is?"

"Concentrating upon my new form, getting to know it. The day after tomorrow I shall meet with your colleagues, if you're agreeable."

Enniel's face softened. "That is good news. I shall call them tonight."

"Now, if you would leave me in peace. I need solitude."

Enniel nodded, began to walk to the door, then paused. "I hear you are expecting a visitor."

Shem smiled. "Yes. My vizier, Daniel. We work together."

Enniel smirked a little. "I see. Well, I'll leave you to it then."

Shem exhaled a sigh of relief. Why were these people so easy to fool?

At two fifteen, Shem pressed his fingers against his temples. He felt an ache behind his eyes; the last thing he needed. He got up and lit the candles, then composed himself once more within the circle. A digital clock on the table beside the door, which earlier he'd synchronised with the speaking clock on the telephone, flicked away the seconds in red light. *I will give him what he wants,* Shem thought. *His unconscious desires. The urge to fly. It must happen now.*

He glanced at the clock. Two twenty-seven. He felt as if all the clocks in all the world stopped at that very moment. Would Daniel dare not to come to him?

In her bed, Aninka tossed and groaned. Her sleeping body kicked back the duvet, for she was too hot, yet her sweat cooled immediately in the freezing air.

Further down the corridor, Emma sat before her own candle. Something was happening; she sensed it. Something was approaching fast.

Taziel and Lahash sat in Lahash's room playing cards and drinking a bottle of brandy. Taziel was very drunk and kept losing.

Lahash watched him carefully, wishing he was the kind of person who could get Taziel to talk about his problems.

Daniel sat in his own room, looking at the clock. At two-thirty, he thought he'd let Shem suffer enough and got up.

The house held its breath.

Shem was frozen, his watering, unblinking eyes fixed on the clock. He faced the door.

Outside, Daniel pressed his hands against the wooden panels. He tried to think of what he would say when he went through the door. *Be in control. Be his equal. Don't let him bully you.* He had no idea, really, what Shem would ask of him. He was afraid to go in, but found he had opened the door without thinking. The room was a blaze of candlelight.

Shem saw a stranger in the doorway. Daniel was harder, wiser, older. The clock flicked onto two, thirty-two. Shem felt a finger of foreboding touch his heart, for he could see that time had already passed for Daniel. Age. Humanity. Brief candles.

For a moment, they stared at one another like hostile cats, then Daniel came to stand at the edge of the circle. Shem wanted to scold him and then get down to work. He wanted to appear business-like and cool. But the sight of this slim, confident young man, with his dark, shadowed eyes and serious face destroyed all his plans. He simply said, "Daniel, fly with me."

And Daniel stepped into the circle. Like Shem, he'd had a barrage of clever words to say, but none of them seemed relevant now. This was not the broken man who'd lounged around the Assembly Rooms. This was Peverel Othman, with all his poise and power, reborn, renewed. There was no dark taint to him now. How had it happened? "You can teach me to fly?" he said.

Shem nodded. "Yes."

At first, Daniel thought that this was a game of words, something he was used to. Then he realised it wasn't. His heart said, "*Crawl into his arms*," and his mind objected, "*Wait*," but Daniel had already sunk down into Shem's lap and put his arms around his neck. Shem felt warm, alive and smelled of soap.

Angel, demon, man, ghost: what are you?

Shem enfolded Daniel in his arms and rocked him like a child. He uttered a low, monotonous groan, as if in pain, then words spilled out of him like blood.

"Daniel, it is lonely, so empty. I am burning. I am cold. I

can't contain all the things that I am inside. It is bursting out. Take it from me. Daniel, pour your light into me. Make me feel, bring me faith. Heal me. Be one with me. Banish my eternal void. Give unto me your wisdom, as you always have. I will listen with humility. Take from me the burden of salvation. Still for me the endless procession of spinning stars and unfold for me the path of my destiny, but please walk with me along the way."

Daniel looked up into Shem's face. "Give me the knowledge." The words came unbidden to his lips.

Shem stroked the hair from Daniel's brow. "Ah, how young you are, how beautiful. I can't bear to think of what will happen to you. I can't bear the thought of watching you wither."

"Give me the knowledge," Daniel repeated. "How can I walk beside you without the fruit of eternal knowledge within me?"

Shem kissed his hair, rocked him in his lap. "*She* said those words to me," he whispered. "And I gave her the knowledge, all that was forbidden to her race. But what good came of it?" He closed his eyes, and tears leaked out between his lashes to fall onto Daniel's face.

"Look at me," Daniel said.

"I cannot. All I see is the future." He opened his eyes. "We have given the curse of longevity to those who have worked for us, but it is a corrupting force. I could give you that, Daniel, but it would ruin you."

"You said I could learn to fly."

"It is not the same. You are asking for the fruit of the tree, but you ask in ignorance."

Slowly, the realisation of what this exchange was about became clear in Daniel's mind. He could be like Emma, his life extended. But he knew that the dissolution, when it came, could be worse than any natural ageing. Shem was putting the request into Daniel's mouth, but it was his own idea. He had not thought about it until Daniel walked into the room. He had seen Daniel older and wiser and he had begun to be afraid. He feared he could not survive in this world without his vizier, and inevitably, because Daniel was human, he would eventually forsake his master for the hand of death.

"I will sacrifice my mortality for you," Daniel said. "If that is what you want." *You impart the gift,* he thought, *yet it seems the other way around.*

"It will not be long enough," Shem said, then sighed, "but scant time is better than none. I want you, Daniel, to be with me. Taste the fatal apple; I have held it for eternity. It is humanity's curse, but if you want the knowledge, you can't avoid plucking the forbidden fruit."

"Give it to me," Daniel said.

There was a pause. "Are you sure?"

"Yes." Daniel had no idea what to expect. He knew vaguely that Grigori could summon a kind of etheric force from their bodies, which when supped or otherwise absorbed by human flesh, bequeathed the longevity.

"You are so fragile," Shem said. His eyes were glowing as if he looked upon moonlit water. There was a shift of light within them.

"I am not a child," Daniel answered. "I am strong enough to withstand whatever happens.

Shem's brow was creased. He looked unsure. Then, as Daniel watched, the frown smoothed itself away. The light became steady in Shem's eyes, but harder, a smoking blue. A shred of unease entered Daniel's mind.

In a sudden movement, Shem dropped Daniel's body, but almost immediately his hands shot out and gripped Daniel's head. He pulled Daniel upwards, stretching his neck painfully. Still holding his face in the vice of his fingers, Shem kissed him deeply. Daniel knew this was not part of the process, but something Shem felt he had to do. Perhaps a benediction or a protection. Then he let Daniel fall back onto the floor. He hung over the boy, a stooped, carnivorous shadow. Daniel felt a sudden surge of alarm. What had he agreed to? Shem no longer looked remotely human. He had become Shemyaza, the Hanged One, full of bitterness and fire. His eyes had become vaporous orbs, burning with intense blue light, and his features were dark and indistinct. His pale hair glowed like the reflection of moonlight on virgin snow, moving languorously around his shoulders as if lifted by a breeze.

Daniel scrabbled backwards, still on his back. *This is the truth of it. They look like us, but they are not. No sight for human eyes!*

Shemyaza took off his robe. His body was corded with taut muscle, which seemed to writhe like serpents beneath his skin.

"No!" Daniel was terrified now.

Shemyaza lunged forward and gripped Daniel's face between his hands again. His voice was low and booming. "You must trust me, for you will experience intense pain."

"No!" Daniel tried to escape, but his neck felt as if it would break.

"There is no going back. You have signed the contract with your will and your desire." Shemyaza, fallen angel; he seemed to be eight feet tall with the pale hair whipping around his shoulders. He snarled like a demon, and ripped Daniel's clothes from his body. The fabric tore into Daniel's flesh, skinned the back of his neck, his hips. Shemyaza reared up, Daniel dangling helplessly from his armpits between the powerful hands.

"This is what you asked for," Shemyaza said. His face was like an enormous grotesque mask before Daniel's stinging eyes. Daniel could not look away. "I came to you as a shower of gold, yet you asked to see my true face. Now you see it. Are you dying, Daniel? Are you burning up?"

Daniel uttered a strangled whine, sure he was about to lose his life. Shemyaza had gone insane. He closed his eyes, tried to call for Taziel, but Shemyaza jerked his boneless body in the air and impaled him upon a spear of fire.

Daniel screamed, and felt the whole building shake to his terror and pain. The screaming went on and on, until a black void, spinning faster than the speed of light, enveloped him in darkness.

The pit, the abyss, the endless chasm of despair. A graveyard of stars and of the light of hope. Daniel dropped through it, weightless, yet heavier than lead. There was no time in this place, yet Daniel was still aware of time, because he ached with horror that this descent might be his eternal fate.

Then, slowly, light bloomed around him.

Daniel blinked. He was enveloped in cold, white light; a radiance that bleached colour and shape from the world. Slowly, he realised he was curled up on the ground, but it was a place far removed from High Crag. He sensed he was lying upon pebbled turf, but it was indistinct to his eyes. He was whimpering, naked, but could barely feel his body.

Shemyaza stood some distance away from him, at the edge of a cliff. He was dressed in a white robe, belted with gold. Around his neck, he wore the bony filigree of a serpent's spine, and he was cloaked from shoulder to ankle in black feathers. His waving hair was woven with long, white plumes, tassels of corn and soft thongs of leather.

"Daniel, get up!" Shemyaza's voice was so loud, it could hardly be heard. It was the voice of the thunder, the storm, the planets spinning in the void.

"I can't."

"Get up. Come to me."

Daniel found he was on his feet, swaying as if his body had no substance. With shaking steps, he walked towards the edge of the cliff.

"Where am I?" Daniel asked. "What are you showing me?"

Shemyaza did not answer the questions but merely said, "Look down."

Fearfully, Daniel did so. He gasped and wobbled, nearly fell. There was no end to the abyss below, only a seethe of clouds, shot with bloody streaks of light.

"Take my hand."

Daniel had turned his head away, closed his eyes, but he reached out for Shemyaza's hand.

"Do you trust me?"

Daniel dared to open his eyes, look up into the face of the angel. He could not answer.

Shemyaza removed his cloak of feathers and placed it around Daniel's shoulders, making sure the clasp was fastened firmly at his neck. "Fly for me, Daniel," Shemyaza said. "Jump."

Daniel glanced down into the abyss, winced and groaned.

"Do it. Jump. I will be with you."

Daniel gripped Shemyaza's fingers hard. This was the moment of ultimate decision. He did not hesitate, but uttered a roar that reverberated deep within his chest. Still screaming, he threw himself from the cliff.

The clouds rushed up to meet him and fingers of fire spat out of them, stinking of burning meat. Daniel felt as if his heart had stopped beating. He had died of fright already. Then he was soaring above the tumbling, curdled clouds, and up and up, towards a peak on the other side of the abyss. He was as mighty as the great vulture kings, hovering on the thermals of the astral plane, as the shamans of old had flown. He flew with the wings of the griffin, a wingspan of thirteen feet. But he flew alone. Shemyaza was not beside him.

Up to the peaks and down to the fabled lands. He saw the Sphinx, a mere cub in time, its face freshly carved. It stood upon an island in the middle of a blue lake. He saw the Tower of Babel reaching for the sky, and the tiny people working upon it, dragging stone and wood. He soared across the lowlands, where the little people toiled and bred and fought and died. He saw the Ark, and the sons of Noah looking towards Hermon's Mount, where Enoch spoke with the Sons of God. He saw the lofty temples rise and fall, and mighty armies surge across the land. He saw the great king, Solomon, taking wisdom from the Shining Ones, and flew through the heart of the most secret arcana known to humanity or gods. Then the Garden was before him, its terraces rearing up towards the High House where Lord Anu ruled the land. He was at home again. Had he ever left?

Now the flight was over and he wore the skin of a child. Memories of his life as Daniel Cranton seemed but a dream. He was playing in the garden, and his mother was coming out to him from the shady coolness of their dwelling. He was ten years old. "Daniel. It is time. Say your good-byes now."

Time to go. To leave home. Take up the position.

He was walking upon a mountain path, up to a great house formed from immense blocks of smooth, white stone, with cedar trees all around it. A tall figure stood waiting for him. And his mother was behind him, pushing him forward. "He is there, Daniel. Your master. Work well for him and be loyal."

Your master. Shemyaza.

The master reached out for him and took his little hand. "Come, Daniel. This is your home now."

The vision ended and his consciousness jerked away. He was flying again, into a mist. The mountain peaks around him faded away, and his wings beat upon a moist, occluding fog. The motion of flight and the deep, heavy beat of his feathers lulled him into a semi-hypnotic state. Then, the mist was clearing, and his eyes blinked against bright sunlight. He was flying over the sea, towards land. The coastline undulated green, red and gold like the scales of a great serpent. Cornwall: the Lizard. He was back. He saw the image of an immense lion naturally formed in the cliff-face, which he recognised as a guardian. As he drew nearer to land, he could feel the flexing of the serpent power beneath the rock as the presence of Shemyaza, so close, disturbed its sleep.

Daniel hung over the cliff-top, absorbing the impressions that came to him. The serpent was a chained creature, which needed to be free. But how to wake it? How to set it free? A voice whispered in his head. *You wear the wings of the shaman. You must go the underworld and reawaken the Shamir.*

But these are not my wings, Daniel thought. Beating them slowly, he descended before the face of the lion. Now, he could see that it was a giant sphinx, whose eyes were closed, and that between its paws, which reached towards the ocean, there was a columned portal. He alighted upon the rocks, and the eyes of the sphinx opened, expelling a fierce red light.

Have you come to sing the lament for Serapis?

Daniel did not understand the riddle. He knew an answer was required of him before the guardian would allow him entrance to the underworld, but was unsure of what to say. "I come to seek the Shamir," he said, with forced confidence. "For the good of the king. For the good of the land."

The columned portal began to glow faintly. Daniel could make out the convolutions of strange glyphs, geometric shapes carved into the stone. A series of triangles, circles, lines and dots flickered before him. He thought they were the marks of some ancient written language, although he did not recognise it. Was he supposed to translate these markings to gain access to the underworld? Perhaps the Lament for Serapis was written in the stone.

His eyes scanned the alien shapes upon the smooth stele, back and forth, back and forth, as if by staring at them their meaning would somehow become clear to him. As he fixed his concentration upon the marks, a deep, resonant hum began to fill his head. It gradually grew in pitch, until it was unbearably loud and shrill; it seemed to vibrate within each individual fibre of his body. Beneath his feet, the rocks trembled, and below the humming shriek in his ears, he heard the groaning clack of tortured stone grinding against itself.

Daniel was suffused with a terrible sense of doubt. The elation of flight had fled from his mind and body. He had begun the process, but was ignorant of how to continue. Was he in danger? "Shem," he cried. "Where are you? What am I supposed to do?"

No-one answered his plea.

Cautiously, Daniel reached out to the stone portal. He would just have to act on instinct. As his fingertips made contact, the shrill humming around him abruptly ceased. The silence that followed it seemed absolute, but as Daniel's senses adjusted, he realised a new sound had started up: a deep and even booming. As he listened, it gradually grew louder, and he realised it was the beat of his own heart, amplified by the stone. In his mind, he formed the intention of wanting to enter through the portal beyond the slick rocks and into the dark tunnel that lay behind them.

Daniel closed his eyes, and threw back his head. "Let me through!" he called. "I am Daniel of the Lion and I am worthy!" He projected his intention at the guardian.

The sound of his heartbeat receded, as if it moved away from him, deep into the cliff-face, and down, down beneath the earth. Daniel stood in the tense silence that followed its retreat. Then, he extended his inner vision, and thrust his senses through the portal. Beyond, all was in thick darkness. He could not smell or hear anything, but his perception soared down the lightless tunnel, trying to keep up with the fleeting sound of his own heart-beat, which still seemed to fly ahead of him. Then, at the very perimeter of his perception, he perceived a tiny ball of light. He could not ascertain its speed, but he could tell it was approaching him, pulsing nearer and nearer, growing brighter and larger.

Outside the portal, Daniel was filled with alarm. He withdrew his senses from the tunnel, and knew he should fly away from the approaching light, but his body was frozen. He could not avoid the inevitable collision.

He sensed that the light was now a massive sphere, hovering just behind the two stone stele of the portal. Perhaps it would stay there, as a warning. Perhaps he could just creep away.

But before he could move, the light exploded from the cliff-face. Daniel felt the thunderous roar of its vibration engulf him, paralysing him with cold fire. His body was hurled backwards and upwards.

Frantically, Daniel tried to beat his borrowed wings, but a searing hurricane held him in its grip. He was travelling up above the earth at great speed, up and up, towards the stars. Then, the constellation of Orion hung before him. It was empty of captives now. Shemyaza's soul had once hung here for ten millennia. It was a part of him. Surely he could hear Daniel's inner voice in this place?

"Shem, where are you? You said you would be with me. You knew I would fail, but you still used me to test the water. Do you feel nothing for me? Or are you just afraid of these lonely stars, which could be your prison once more? If I could wake the Shamir for you, my king, I would, but I know now that the serpent will allow no other but you before its eyes."

As if in response, the stars of Orion grew blindingly bright, and Daniel felt himself being repelled by an invisible thrust of force. It sent him plummeting downwards, and as he fell, his body filled up with liquid fire. His feathers were scorched away. He could feel his vitals burning, devoured by the caustic fluid.

Daniel screamed and fell. Stars rushed by him, and the mocking laughter of invisible entities rang through the void. He saw blazing angels rise up, shrieking, in a maelstrom of oily wings, and then the great deluge engulfed the world.

He sank into the fiery flood and his head hit stone. He closed his eyes, roaring with pain and fear. Light. Flames. Screams. Darkness.

Silence.

"Hush now. It's over."

Daniel opened his eyes to the blaze of a host of candles, in Shem's room at High Crag. He felt like vomiting and doubled up, clutching his stomach. Shem's hand lay upon his shoulder as he choked and writhed upon the carpet.

"I'm sorry, Daniel. I knew it would be bad for you, because of your gift of sight. But it's over now. Straighten up. There's no pain."

He looked up into Shem's face and saw in it both sorrow and repletion. How could Shem have taken satisfaction from his agony? It was obscene.

"Peverel Othman is not dead in you," he gasped and crawled towards the bed. He wanted to lie down on his belly on something soft and yielding.

Shem helped him climb up. "I'll run you a hot bath. Lie there for now."

Daniel laughed weakly. This was absurd. Moments ago, he had soared in another world. Now it was necessary to see to frail human needs. Daniel realised, for the first time, what a hindrance flesh could be.

When the bath was ready, Shem lifted Daniel in his arms and carried him to the water. "I didn't want to see you like that," Daniel said. "It isn't really you."

Shem lowered him gently into the bath. "Daniel, you must face the fact that it is part of me."

When the warm water touched his skin, Daniel could not repress a cry of pain. "It's too hot! You're burning me!"

Shem lifted him just above the water. "No, it's not, Daniel. It's just an effect of the transference. For a while, your senses will be heightened, but this will pass."

Daniel dug his fingers into Shem's arms as his body entered the water. His eyes spun with light and the room revolved around him, as if he was drunk. He glanced at the sparkling taps, and it seemed they were alive. He could see the soul of the metal. Smells assaulted his senses; the overpowering aroma of the soap, the animal products within it stinking of dung and rancid fat; the scent of the water itself, describing the nature of its elementals.

Shem held onto him. "Ride it, Daniel. Absorb it. Take control. The first time is always like this, at least for those who truly deserve the fruit."

Daniel closed his eyes, panting for breath. He leaned over the side of the bath so that Shem could hold him. "It's horrible! I can't live like this!"

Shem stroked his hair. "Take deep breaths, come on. It'll pass. I promise you."

Daniel hung gasping in Shem's arms for half an hour before the sensations began to subside. Gradually, he was able to repress the images and information that came to him. It was, he realised, like experiencing a visualisation in reality. The water had gone cold, but he pushed himself away from Shem's arms and lay back in the bath. He felt as if his skin was covered in grit and mud and blood. Shem turned on the hot tap and scorching water gushed over Daniel's feet. He winced and laughed, and Shem stirred the water with his hands.

"Relax," Shem said. He stroked Daniel's hair one last time, then stood up and went to the washbasin. As if they were ordinary people in an ordinary life, he began to clean his teeth. Daniel chuckled uncontrollably at this sight.

Shem spat into the basin. "You look young again," he said, which sobered Daniel up.

"I'm not though," he answered.

Shem wiped his mouth on a towel, then came to sit on the end of the bath again. "Tell me what you saw when you were flying."

Daniel took a sponge off the side of the bath, and dunked it into the water. He squeezed it out over his chest, watching the shining streams. He wasn't sure whether he wanted to talk about what he'd seen.

Shem reached for one of his feet, squeezed it. "Daniel. Tell me."

"All right. I saw the Garden, Kharsag. I was a child and I lived there, but my mother sent me to work for you. What does that mean?"

Shem sat on the edge of the bath. "You have always been my vizier. We lived together in Kharsag a long, long time ago. I thought you knew this."

Daniel rubbed water over his chest. "Sort of. But, in that case, I can't have been human."

Shem stood up. "No." He appeared uncomfortable. "You were Grigori."

"Then why am I human now?"

Shem laughed coldly. "Fate's mordant humour, I expect. As Ishtahar is kept from me, so are you, in a different kind of way." He sat down again. "But I have done a little tonight towards fighting that."

"Longevity is not being Grigori," Daniel said.

"It is the best we can do," Shem replied. "What else did you see?"

Daniel told him as much as he could remember. "You passed the feathered cloak to me. Why?"

Shem shrugged. "You needed it to fly."

Daniel shook his head slowly. "No, you wanted to pass responsibility to me. I can't be you, Shem. I am your vizier, but I cannot undertake your tasks. What is all this serpent business anyway?"

Shem sighed. "Something the Parzupheim wants me to do. I expect we'll find out soon."

"Well, when we do, don't send me in first like a canary to test the air. It won't work."

Shem smiled. "I can't help it. I sometimes think you're more powerful than I'll ever be."

Daniel pulled a scornful face. "Don't be ridiculous. And don't be lazy." He winced. "God, I ache."

After the bath, Daniel sat on the bed, wrapped in a towel, helping Shem eat his supper. They talked about Owen and Lily, what should be done. Daniel was privately amazed Shem had become concerned about the twins again, although he took care not to show his feelings. Only a few days ago, Shem hadn't appeared bothered whether any of them lived or died, but now he seemed to have forgotten the way he'd behaved in the Assembly Rooms. Daniel spoke candidly about Taziel, and what had happened on the night they'd left London. Shem agreed that another Grigori faction must have taken the twins, and that for the moment, they were not in any danger. But that might change. "You must try to find them," Shem said. "Call to Lily. I'm sure she will hear you."

Daniel noticed that when they spoke of the Winters, only Lily was mentioned by name. He found he didn't want to talk about Owen, which troubled him. It was wrong to blame Owen for all that had happened in Little Moor. Othman had been the perpetrator, Owen a victim. Yet here Daniel sat, gazing at the monster himself, full of love and awe, while Owen lay in a stupor somewhere, his mind in ruins. Daniel realised he was angry that Owen had been too weak to resist Othman's dominion. Did some cruel part of him now believe that Owen deserved what had happened to him? Since fleeing the north, Daniel had spent little time thinking deeply about the past or his feelings about it. Taking a deep breath, he asked. "How much can you remember of Peverel Othman?"

Shem gave him a shrewd glance. "I can remember most of what happened in Little Moor, although more as an observer than a participant. Before that..." he shrugged. "It's fragmented. Peverel Othman didn't want to admit who you were."

"I know. You wanted to kill me because you feared I would make you remember who you really were, although I don't think you realised that at the time."

Shem shook his head. "No, Daniel, you are wrong. I didn't *want* to kill you. Your death was simply a necessary component of a particular ritual, as was Owen's role. There were no deeper motives, no real excuse or explanation. I needed a sacrificial victim, and you were the most suitable candidate, that's all."

Daniel did not wholly agree, but elected not to argue about it. "But for Ishtahar, I would be dead now."

Shem made an angry sound. "But for Ishtahar?" He shook his head. "I'm not sure about that. Why did she call us to this place? What is it she wants of us here? If she lives, where is she now?"

"I've seen her," Daniel said. "She speaks to me in dreams and it was she who persuaded me to come to you. A few days ago, I was angry with you, and confused, but Ishtahar told me what I should do. After seeing her, all the negative feelings I had seemed petty and trivial."

"I might have projected all that to you," Shem said. "The part of myself that despised Peverel Othman might also have conjured her up in Little Moor. An illusion to prevent me doing the unspeakable."

Daniel reached for his hand. "I don't believe so. Shem, she *will* be there for you one day. I think she's there for you now, but not as a woman of flesh and blood."

Shem touched his face with the ends of his fingers. "Kind Daniel," he said sadly. "I know you want to believe that for me, but at the moment, I have only you. Of course I want you both, but how many people are lucky enough to have their desires fulfilled? I can see and touch you. Ishtahar is only a beautiful ghost." He sighed. "By Anu, I have no right to touch you, no right to accept your love and loyalty. If you had any sense, you'd spit on me now."

Daniel couldn't repress a laugh. "You don't mean that! As you pointed out a short time ago, the dark side is a part of you I have to accept."

Shem took both of Daniel's hands in his own. "You have always been there for me Daniel. I don't deserve it. Your spirit has waited to be reborn into this time to help me. Part of me feels I should deny myself any closeness with you, because I want to punish myself for what I did, but..." he shook his head and smiled. "Please come here." He pulled Daniel into his arms and held him close. "You feel so alive."

"Less so than I was before I came here," Daniel said dryly. "You hurt me, Shem."

"I couldn't help it."

"Then I want you to make me a promise." He pulled away a little. "You must never hurt me again. Never. Will you promise me that? No matter what instincts and compulsions burst out of Shemyaza, Shem must remember his word."

Shem nodded. "I will never hurt you."

Daniel wasn't entirely convinced by this, but felt it had been necessary to make Shem aware he was not wholly submissive. He felt a little like the keeper of an unpredictable wild beast, beautiful in its unchained splendour, purring and rubbing against him, but liable to turn on him without warning.

Shem sighed and rested his cheek on Daniel's head. "I wanted to begin work tonight, but mentally I'm too exhausted. How do you feel?"

"I think we should sleep," Daniel answered, "and start searching for Lily and Owen tomorrow."

Daniel got into bed and Shem blew out all the candles. The room was full of drifting skeins of smoke, visible in the soft moonlight that came in through the gaps in the curtains. The air reeked of the temple aroma of wax. Looking at Shem's slim white body coming towards him, Daniel thought, *I cannot believe I have some influence over this being. I can speak to him and touch him. He is here, with me, and he needs me.* Ishtahar must have had thoughts like these, all those thousands of years ago.

Shem got into the bed and took Daniel in his arms. "You have healed me," he said. "Only a short while ago, merely the thought of touching someone seemed to scald me."

"You've healed yourself," Daniel said.

"I want to make love to you properly."

"Well you can't, and you've only yourself to blame."

Shem laughed. "You are saying "no" to me. How unusual. Do you really want to deny yourself pleasure?"

"I want to deny myself discomfort."

"Daniel, you've suffered from having only unimaginative lovers. Let me teach you a little."

"I will, but not now."

Shem laughed. "You are fighting me. I can feel your desire." But he did not push the matter.

Chapter Twenty
Revealing the Viper

The Conclave of the Pelleth sat around the table in the Penhaligon kitchen. The atmosphere was tense, and there was a significant absence. The place where Tamara usually sat was empty. Meggie and Betsy had convened a meeting and had deliberately refrained from inviting Tamara.

"We have a sad business to attend to," Meggie said.

Lissie, Rachel and Jessie glanced at the empty seat, their faces set in grim expressions to express their loyalty to the elders of the Conclave and to show plainly they were no part of Tamara's rebellion. Agatha sat with her chin resting virtually on her chest. She looked afraid. Meggie thought that perhaps the child was too young to have to cope with problems such as this, but as she was a member of the Conclave, her presence was mandatory. The laws of the Pelleth decreed it.

Meggie laced her fingers together on the tabletop. "The matter is this. Tamara Trewlynn has betrayed us."

The company uttered soft sounds of shock, although none of them were really surprised by Meggie's statement.

"What's happened?" Jessie asked, her eyes round. Everyone felt guilty, even those who were innocent. That was the trouble with dishonesty, its taint spread wide. It bred distrust.

"Betsy had a dream," Meggie said. "In it, she saw Tamara cavorting with Grigori. She heard her revile the Pelleth and curse our names. We have consulted the cards and the crystal on this matter, and there is no doubt in our minds that Tamara has her own plans for the Shining One. She has been a quick, little viper among us, and now has slipped free."

"What must we do?" Lissie asked. "Should we bind her?" There was sinister implication behind her words.

Meggie shook her head. "We shall protect ourselves, but other than that, we must turn our backs on the traitor. I feel she is deluding herself and is no threat to our plans. Let her go her own way. It will accomplish nothing, other than to burn her fingers down to the bone."

"Have you confronted her?" asked Lissie.

"No. I would not give her that much satisfaction. From this moment forth, Tamara Trewlynn is a stranger to us. I must forbid any of you to make contact with her, or even acknowledge her should she cross your paths."

All the company nodded, even Agatha, whose small face was composed in a solemn and uncannily understanding expression.

"There is more," Betsy intoned from the other end of the table.

Meggie sighed. "Yes, I'm afraid there is. It seems that Tamara has beguiled Delmar. He's been working for her."

All the women voiced their disgust. "What?"

"But how!"

"That's appalling!"

Agatha uttered a wail, "No, not Del!"

Meggie let them rant for a few seconds, then raised her hands for quiet. "There is nothing we can do. He is contaminated now, poor mite."

"How did you find out about it?" asked Jessie.

"Well, I did have a word with him," Meggie replied. "I've had suspicions for a while that he's not been quite right, and asked him what was bothering him. He acted dumb and confused, but I could smell his fear. So I pressed him further. He panicked and blabbered something about "it's to be a surprise. It's for you." Then he said the thing that shocked me most. "I don't like the salamanders, though. They scare me." Naturally, I questioned him further and he clammed up, but let drop enough for me to work out that the little viper has been working in Mermaid's Cove and taking Delmar with her."

This revelation conjured a further shocked ripple of sound around the table.

"She suggested working there not long ago!" Rachel said.

Meggie nodded. "Yes. When we disagreed with her suggestion, she obviously decided to follow it up on her own."

"Fool!" Rachel said. "She'll be in terrible danger. The Grigori guardians will attach themselves to her like dark elementals. They'll destroy her."

Again Meggie nodded. "That is a distinct possibility. Anyway, I did wonder whether we could save Delmar, bring him back to us, and followed him several times after school. On each occasion he went straight to Tamara's cottage. I can only assume he goes there every day." She sighed. "Poor lamb. I pity him. He's innocent, caught up in something he can't understand. But because he has worked on Grigori soil and has Tamara's paw prints all over him, I cannot risk having him work with us any longer. We must have no link with the deserter. Delmar is lost to us, my sisters."

"But we can't be without an oracle!" Jessie exclaimed.

"I know," Meggie answered. "But we must trust in the Shining Ones. They will provide for us. Until then, we must continue to prime the sites in readiness for the Advent. Shemyaza is very close to us now, and the night of the solstice draws nigh. We mustn't lose heart because some of our number are abandoning us. This is perhaps a natural result of Shemyaza's frequency. He is Change, and the effect of his proximity is that our weakest links will be broken away. We must comfort ourselves with the knowledge that we are best rid of them."

The women glanced at one another fearfully, wondering if any of them would also prove to be weak links.

Agatha's high voice broke the silence. "But Gran, Del is my friend."

Meggie sighed. "Aye, I know, love. But sometimes we have hard burdens to bear. I'm sorry. You must forget about him."

Agatha swallowed, clearly close to tears. "I will!" she said fiercely. "Oh, how could he have been so stupid!"

The women looked with tenderness upon Agatha. Tamara had changed the girl's future for her. Agatha's destiny had been linked with Delmar's. In a few years' time, she was to have taken him as her lover for a few scant nights before he was sacrificed to the elements. Now this sacrament, this flowered path to womanhood, had been snatched away from her.

"Come now," Meggie said. "We have work to do this night. Bolster's Bed awaits our attentions! Put any thoughts of Delmar or Tamara from your minds. They are no longer our concern, although I shall do my best to keep a weather eye on the boy. Tamara's own actions will give birth to her punishment." She picked up her mug of tea. "Drink up, now. It's a cold night and we've a long walk ahead of us."

The Pelleth had been preparing the ancient sacred sites for some time, doing what they could to prime them for the solstice night, when they believed Shemyaza would awaken the serpent, and all the sites would be flooded with energy. They drove in two cars up to the edge of the moorland, and then proceeded on foot to Bolster's Bed, a fogou, or underground artificial burial chamber, where the body of Bolster the Giant was reputed to lie. Each woman carried a bag containing her ritual equipment. They were all dressed in black cloaks, beneath which they wore their ritual robes. The night was dark, so several of the company carried electric torches, gliding silently past darkened farms and drowsing sheep. Meggie thought about how, in the old days, they would have walked by the wavering light of hurricane lamps, or candle jars, but even the ancient order of Cornish witches had to make concessions to the century. Now that the population of "outsiders" had grown, and there were more tourists about, it was more practical to carry lights that could be switched on and off with speed and the minimum of fuss. The Pelleth were adept at melting away into the darkness, if necessary.

The fogou was set into a hillside, its entrance flanked by listing stones, topped by a cracked lintel. A curving passageway led to the chamber itself, and the women had to walk in single file along it. The ceiling was so low, they had to stoop, and as they eased their way forward, they were surrounded by an intense perfume of earth. Meggie was depressed by the evidence of mindless humanity that littered the floor of the passage: crumpled sweet wrappers, an empty Coke can. She gestured for one of the company to pick up the offending items and place them in a carrier bag brought for that purpose.

When they reached the chamber, Rachel set up a circle of candles and lit them. Lissie prepared the incense, lighting a charcoal and sprinkling a few fragrant grains upon its glowing core. Jessie unpacked the spirit bowl, while Betsy uncapped a wide glass jar of herbal unguent. With her bare fingers, she scooped out a large handful of the mixture and transferred it to a silver dish. Meggie took the dish from her and smeared the unguent at the four elemental quarters, representing air, fire, water and earth. When the site was finally empowered by the serpent, the unguent would help open the channels for the energy to flow.

When all was ready, the women sat down in a circle. Lissie held the spirit bowl in her lap, and began to stroke its inner surface with the sounding stick, conjuring a ringing resonance in the low chamber. The rest of the women whispered a soft chant and concentrated on the image of their goddess, Seference: "Om Sefer, Tu Sefer, Sefer, Sefer, Sahar." Gradually, their voices rose in timbre and the song of the spirit bowl rang out, enhancing the inherent energies of the site. As their chant intensified, the Conclave felt the tired, latent dynamism around them start to hum and wake up. Soon it vibrated throughout their bodies. Their actions were not enough to awaken the serpent fully, but they could make it shift in its sleep.

As the energy and sound swirled around them, Meggie addressed the ancient Giant king who was buried there. "You will soon awaken, Ancient One. Your time is near."

"Your time is near!" echoed the company.

The women didn't stay long at the Penhaligons that night, and the cheerful banter that usually took place around the table after a night's work was absent. Although the Conclave had succeeded in forgetting their dilemmas during their ritual, gloom descended upon them once the work was done. Meggie felt weary herself, and beyond chivvying the rest of them into lighter spirits.

After the rest of the women left, and Agatha had gone to bed, Meggie and Betsy sat alone at either end of the table. They drank strong, sweet tea in silence, each lost in her own thoughts. Then Betsy said, "Megs, we must see to the matter of the oracle."

Meggie nodded. "I know." She sighed. "We must find a replacement for Delmar very soon."

"Tonight," Betsy said.

Meggie looked into her sister's face. "The mirror?"

Betsy nodded. "Aye."

That night, before retiring, Meggie and Betsy took out their velvet-wrapped scrying mirror. The two women had already put on their nightgowns and their long grey hair was braided down their backs. Meggie wore a heavy, fringed shawl of scarlet wool against the nip of the night-air, while Betsy was buttoned to the neck in a housecoat of thick pink velour. In a dark corner of Betsy's bedroom, which smelled of old face powder, they sat down upon two stools with the mirror between them. Their bent heads were almost touching.

"Seference, show us the face of he who comes after," Betsy said. "Show us the face of the oracle, he who must be ours."

The dark surface of the mirror seemed to be the portal to a bottomless void. The suggestion of faint, distant stars spun in its depths.

"There," Betsy said. "I see a boy. Ah, he is beautiful, and he has the way of wyrd within him."

Meggie's eyes were watering, and the image of the boy in the glass seemed to be in soft focus to her. "It is Shemyaza's vizier," she breathed. "The one named Daniel." She glanced up at Betsy who was still concentrating on the image. "But how can we bring *him* to us?"

"Through the woman, his protectress," Betsy answered. "She has been given extended life."

"Emilia!" Meggie exclaimed.

Betsy narrowed her eyes at the mirror. "She calls herself Emma now."

Meggie shook her head. "But they are both connected with the Grigori! I don't like this."

"Don't doubt Seference," Betsy said without rancour. "She would never speak false. The opportunity will come to us. I've a feeling, because of Miss Trewlynn mucking around, Daniel Cranton will want to work with us."

"Tamara won't have that much influence," Meggie said. "She's no threat to anyone."

Betsy shook her head. "She will cause tremors in the earth and the aether. Like a midge, she'll buzz in our ears and be too quick for us to swat."

"Perhaps," Meggie murmured, shaking her head. "But if this Daniel is Shemyaza's vizier, he will have great sight. He will know how the office of oracle must end. He won't want to offer up his life for us."

"We must reach him through the woman," Betsy repeated. "When the serpent wakes, every man and woman in the land will become aware of their destiny, and if that is to be sacrifice, so be it. Everyone will accept their portion."

Meggy frowned, still staring into the mirror. "I don't like the idea of attracting Grigori followers. We have always shunned the Grigori and their kind."

Betsy nodded. "True. But this is a changing time, Megs. We have to make good use of the tools that fall in our lap, no matter how sharp they seem to our clumsy fingers." She turned the mirror over and reached for its velvet wrap. "The time will come, you'll see. We'll need to expend no effort to bring the boy to us."

Chapter Twenty-One
The Parzupheim

The Parzupheim in Great Britain and Ireland consisted of representatives from twelve Grigori families. Enniel Prussoe administered the ancient kingdom of Cornwall, while his colleagues held sway in other parts of England, Ireland, Scotland and Wales. To the Grigori, all of the countries and islands around England were one, known as the empire of Albion.

They began arriving at High Crag around mid-day, when Austin came to wake Shemyaza with a tray of lunch. Having not gone to sleep until well past five in the morning, neither Daniel nor Shem felt like facing an interrogation from the Parzupheim. Shem insisted he wanted Daniel to accompany him to the meeting, although privately Daniel wondered whether Enniel would allow that. Even though he was now officially a dependent of the Grigori, having been bestowed longevity, he was still only human. Austin brought them clean clothes, presumably donated by Enniel. Daniel, wanting to make a good impression, dressed himself in a loose white shirt and black trousers, but Shem pointedly donned the clothes he had arrived in; ripped black jeans and a faded T-shirt. His hair hung in a matted, pale tangle nearly to his waist.

"If the way I look bothers them, they don't deserve my attention," he said in response to Daniel's critical glances.

At two o'clock, Enniel himself came up to Shem's room. As Daniel had anticipated, he seemed reluctant to allow anyone but Shemyaza to attend the meeting, but Shem was adamant. "If Daniel doesn't come, neither do I." Grudgingly, Enniel gave his consent, and led them to a meeting chamber on the first floor

Daniel was afraid of running into Taziel, but they saw no-one as they walked along the hushed corridors, past many closed doors. Enniel halted before a pair of double-doors, carved with stylised representations of the peacock angel. He glanced back at Shem. "Are you ready?"

Shem shrugged. "As I'll ever be, I suppose."

Enniel flung the doors wide and they went into the room beyond. It was a high-ceilinged chamber, with long, stained-glass windows flanked by heavy drapes. Natural light came only dimly into the room.

The Parzupheim were seated around a round table. Daniel counted twelve men and one woman.

"That's Sofia," Shem murmured. "The mother spider, but I don't think they realise it."

Every head, but for Sofia's, turned or looked up to regard Shem as he walked towards them. Sofia concentrated on lighting a cigarette. Daniel was immediately wary of her. He sensed her power, and the darkness of it.

"Shemyaza has requested that his vizier attend this meeting," Enniel said, as he gestured for Shem and Daniel to take a seat facing the window.

Daniel sat down nervously. His position made it difficult to see clearly the faces of those sitting opposite him.

Sofia exhaled a curling serpent of smoke. "That is reasonable enough." She smiled at Daniel, but he couldn't manage to return it.

Once everyone was seated, Austin came round with small blue bottles of mineral water and glasses, which he placed before each attendee. A pen and a note-pad, embellished with the Prussoe seal, already lay before every place. The mundanity of it was unnerving. There was a hushed, expectant atmosphere in the room; people spoke in whispers. Daniel poured himself some water for his throat was dry. A residue of the effects of last night's ritual still shimmered around him; he could taste the history of the water as he drank it. Over the rim of glass, he inspected the Grigori around the table. Beautiful men, like models or actors, but whose eyes burned with cold fire. *They are angels,* Daniel thought. *This is a host of angels.*

Enniel took his seat last and cleared his throat. He made a small speech about welcoming Shemyaza to High Crag and introduced his colleagues. While he spoke, Daniel watched Sofia. When it was her turn to be introduced, she smiled at the table. It appeared she was based in India and had been allowed admittance as a "foreigner" only because of her involvement with the case. "Also," she interrupted Enniel's explanation, "because Shemyaza's advent affects the whole world, not just the empire of Albion. I sit here as an agent of other Parzupheim."

And not just that, Daniel thought.

She gestured languidly at the men. "Of course, we all appreciate Shemyaza's work must be initiated here, in these isles."

"Really!" Shem leaned back in his seat with his arms folded. "I'm most interested to hear how!"

Sofia gave him an appreciative glance. Daniel realised that she thought Shem and herself were conspirators. "That, I suppose, is another reason why I am here." She glanced around the table. "May I tell Shemyaza of the suggestions that have been discussed?"

All assented, although not without reluctance. Daniel guessed the Parzupheim were uncomfortable with an outsider taking a leading role in this business. But Sofia made it known, from her cool glances to her very body posture, that she had been sent by Grigori who outranked these men; it shone from her aura as amused defiance.

Sofia smiled at Shem. "It is my opinion, and that of my colleagues abroad, that you must begin your work by reawakening the sacred sites, or holy omphali, of these lands."

Almost immediately, Enniel interrupted. "We are aware of that, Sofia. But surely, Shemyaza's first task is to become familiar with..." he glanced at Shem in faint apology. "Forgive me, but I feel you need to understand yourself before you can extend your powers out into the world."

Sofia uttered a small gust of a sigh. "I feel you under-estimate your guest."

All waited for Shem to respond, but he only lifted his shoulders in a shrug.

Daniel felt as if the cloak of feathers had just dropped heavily onto his shoulders again. He realised then exactly why Shem had wanted him there. "We need to hear all that you have to say before decisions are made," he said.

One of the Parzupheim expelled a cough of sarcastic laughter. "We?" He looked at Enniel. "This boy is merely a dependent. I am not comfortable with this 'we'. The involvement of humanity in Grigori affairs brings only confusion and greed."

Daniel fought a blush of embarrassment. He knew he had to hold his own in front of these people. Before Enniel could answer, he said, "I am Shemyaza's vizier, his adviser. The age of this body has little to do with the maturity of my soul, or the fact that once I lived in Grigori flesh."

Still, Shem did not speak. Daniel would have appreciated at
least some support, but knew it would not be forthcoming.

Surprisingly, Sofia said, "I can vouch for Daniel's presence
here."

Daniel's antagonist pulled a disapproving face, then shrugged
resignedly. "I would not presume to argue with *you*, Sofia."

Not openly, anyway, Daniel thought.

Sofia directed caustic smiles around the table. "So, may I
continue?" She waited for comments, but none came, then directed
her attention back to Daniel. "For many centuries, the rituals of the
Grigori have been stagnant, for the life force of the land is dormant.
The same conditions prevail around the world, to greater or lesser
degrees. We cannot call upon the power of the land with the same
success as once we could. It is essential that the power is made
available to us, so that we may guide the civilisations of earth into
the new age. Eventually, we hope to regain access to the star-gate,
and find our way back to the source." She laced her hands before
her on the table and looked at Shem. "Shemyaza, many thousands
of years ago, your actions caused the Anannage, our ancestors, to
withdraw from this world. They closed the star-gate to us, effectively cut us off from the influence this world knows as god, or
gods. It is your task to help us reclaim our heritage. And you can
begin here. Beneath this land, a great force lies slumbering. Only
you can reawaken it. Once you do, energy will course along the
corridors of ancient sites from here to all corners of Albion."

"Just a moment." One of the Parzupheim interrupted her.
He stood up, a pale man with a shock of thick black hair and dark
green eyes. "Why should Shemyaza begin work here? It is surely
more sensible for him to reawaken the power in the mid-shires, the
very centre of the empire?"

Another stood, whose long brown hair was held back at his
neck. "No! The sacred soil of Eire is where his work should begin.
The energy has stirred in its sleep more regularly there, and would
require less effort to revive."

Suddenly, the whole company were on their feet, all arguing
about where Shemyaza should begin, each championing his own
area as the most likely location. Sofia remained seated, as did Daniel
and Shem. Sofia shook her head in private amusement.

Eventually, Enniel's voice thundered louder than all the rest.
"Be seated! Are we a mindless rabble to bicker this way? No.

Listen to me. Where was it that our ancestors first made land-fall, when they arrived from Phoenicia? Where did they emplace the serpent?" Everyone had quietened down and was resuming their seats with disgruntled mumbles.

"Here!" Enniel said, his eyes sparking. "Their first steps were upon Cornish soil. How can you argue about the location for Shemyaza's work? It is here, it has to be! If all goes well in this place, Shemyaza need never set foot on any other part of this country. The alignments and the energy matrix itself will see to that."

"He is right," Sofia said softly into the silence that followed.

Then tumult broke out again. Daniel glanced at Shem, who raised a single, scornful eyebrow. He reached out and touched Daniel's face, as if they were alone in the room. Daniel could not help but derive a certain amount of satisfaction from the gesture.

Shemyaza's caress effectively stemmed the argument around them. All eyes turned towards Shem with indignant surprise. There were times and places for dalliance with human dependants, and a meeting of the Parzupheim was not one of them.

"What do you think?" Sofia asked him.

He shrugged and looked at Daniel, who picked up the cue. "Seeing as Shem is here already, it does seem sensible that should he do anything, it might as well be in Cornwall. Perhaps we need to hear more." He did not want to tell them about his visions of the night before. Let them all think he lacked knowledge. Beneath the table, Shem pressed his thigh against Daniel's own to signal his approval.

Sofia expressed her gratitude with a narrow smile. "So, then, is everyone in agreement? The gate to the underworld lies here, and Shemyaza must enter it."

Most of the company nodded, although one or two still appeared truculent. Daniel glanced at Shem and wished he'd stir himself to ask at least a few of the questions.

"What does that mean, in real terms?" Daniel demanded. "You talk of power being left beneath the land and Shem having to awaken it. But can you explain to us exactly how he must do this? What will happen once the serpent is awake?"

The Parzupheim still looked at him with stern disapproval. To them, he would remain an interloping concubine. Only Sofia smiled.

"Beneath the land is a network of caverns and tunnels," she said. "Within them lies a deep, pulsing energy, or entity, which was planted there by our ancestors, who came from ancient Sumeria. It is known as the serpent power, or the Shamir, and it lies slumbering, protected by guardians. There are now twelve Grigori strongholds in the empire, and the Shamir is their legacy. They must be the ones to control it. The serpent has been dormant since the times of the Persian Magians, who are remembered as the druids. They maintained the sacred omphali and the energy matrix of the land."

Daniel wrinkled his nose. "Omphali? What's that?"

Sofia nodded. "Right. An omphalos is a sacred centre of a settlement or community. Humans tended to utilise or build structures around these natural fountains of life force, such as beacon fire hills, stone circles, stone quoits, standing stones, holy wells and springs, and in this millennium, churches and cathedrals."

Daniel nodded. "I see. Carry on."

Sofia directed a rather arch glance at him, then smiled and resumed her explanation. "Our ancestors set up a corridor of sacred sites—shrines, temples, henges, and other such structures—which ranges from the southernmost tip of Cornwall, up to the north-east reaches of Norfolk. At this point, other corridors join with it like a rail network, which stretches to all corners of the land, and across the sea to Ireland and the smaller isles. The sacred sites along these alignments were used as enhancers of ritual by shamans, druids, and early Christian mystics alike. Look upon the sites as the ancient equivalent of power stations. But with the fall of the druids, the power stations closed down. When the energy is reawakened, all of these sites, which are like electrical appliances waiting to be plugged in, will come alive, empowered by the force. Ancient peoples believed that their survival was ensured if the sacred sites of a country were energised and used efficiently; the sick would be healed, crops would grow, communities would flourish and the seasons turn in their proper manner. Whoever controls the destiny of the omphali controls the destiny of the people who live around them." She looked at Shem. "The Grigori must have this control. Humans would not know how to use it and could cause only destruction."

"Why does Shemyaza have to be the one to awaken this energy?" Daniel asked. "Why can't any one of you do it?"

"Because he is the divine king," Enniel replied. "Only he is worthy of the gaze of the serpent." The words fell like a prophecy into the room. Daniel felt Shem stir uncomfortably beside him.

"And how will he do this? In trance or in actuality?"

Enniel glanced around the table. "That is yet to be decided." Daniel noticed he shot one furtive glance at Sofia, perhaps suspecting the woman had already made up her mind about it. But she remained silent. Daniel wondered whether Shem had some subconscious inkling of what was required of him. The previous night's vision of the sphinx was clearly connected with gaining access to the underworld and the serpent. Daniel knew that Shem would quite happily let his vizier take on the task rather than attend to it himself, but Daniel was unsure why. Was Shem lazy, afraid, indifferent, or simply lacking in confidence? Last night, he'd appeared to be ready to take action, assume responsibility, but now, he was making absolutely no contribution to the meeting, and appeared to be lost in his own thoughts. Daniel also sensed that, despite the Parzupheim's outward appearances of arrogance and calm, they were nervous and wary of Shem, as if they feared he might leap from his chair at any moment and proclaim himself their king, or perhaps destroy them. *They don't know him,* Daniel thought. In his opinion, Shem was still reeling from the transformation he'd undergone in Little Moor. He wondered himself whether Shem was capable of doing what the Parzupheim required of him.

While the discussion took place around him, Shemyaza found his mind drifting. It was hard to concentrate on what was being said. Let Daniel deal with it—it was his function after all. Shem stared at the stained-glass window ahead of him. He thought he could hear some faint, far-off music, the sound of a woman singing. Was it calling to him? He thought of Ishtahar, but dismissed it. He mustn't think that way. It might weaken him. Last night, he'd almost convinced himself he would do whatever the Parzupheim required of him. But now he felt drained and listless, perhaps because of the energy he'd expended in bestowing longevity on Daniel. The talk around the table meant nothing to him. He wanted to leave the room, walk out into the gardens to feel the elements around him. The room was stifling him.

"Shemyaza?" The sharply spoken word sliced into his awareness.

"What?" He looked at Enniel, saw immediately that Enniel knew he'd been paying no attention.

"We feel that you should undergo the ceremony of coronation. The land must recognise you as its spiritual king."

Shem laughed. "King?" He looked at Daniel. "Did you hear that?" Then he spread out his arms at the gathering. "Do I look like a king?"

"It is merely a formality," Sofia said.

"Rather more than that!" Enniel snapped. "Shemyaza, it is your duty and your right. Take the peacock crown. It has always been yours."

"Your co-operation will make them very happy," Sofia drawled. Daniel noticed she excluded herself from the remark.

"Crown Daniel," Shem said. "He will be your king."

"I think you fail to appreciate the solemnity of this offer," Enniel said, clearly having trouble controlling his voice. "Whatever his capabilities, Daniel cannot assume the mantle of the divine king. He is your vizier, but he is not you."

Daniel was astounded that Shem could have suggested such a thing. He recalled, uncomfortably, the ritual at the High Place in Little Moor, when Peverel Othman had offered him to a demon. Was this really any different? "Do it, Shem," he said.

Shem raised an eyebrow at the sharpness of Daniel's tone.

"I believe your *vizier* has just advised you," one of the Parzupheim murmured, conjuring a ripple of soft remarks around the table.

Shem shrugged. "All right, if I must."

Enniel seemed far from happy with his attitude. "We shall enact the ritual this evening." He glanced around the table. "Shall we break for refreshment now?"

After the company had risen and spread out around the room, Austin led in a retinue of servants pushing trolleys laden with food and drink. Daniel stood with Shem and Enniel by the fire-place. He felt angry with Shem, and weirdly betrayed. Enniel tried to make conversation, but could elicit only monosyllables from Shem, and clearly thought it beneath him to try and talk to Daniel. When Sofia stalked over, he excused himself and went to attend to other guests. Sofia touched Shem on the arm, "You have ruffled their feathers."

Shem shrugged. "I find it hard to take all this seriously."

Sofia nodded and lowered her voice confidentially. "They are a stuffy lot, and rather too fond of pomp and circumstance." She paused. "Why don't the three of us go out into the garden for a reviving breath of air?"

Outside, Sofia lit a cigarette and walked in silence. No-one wanted to speak, yet the lack of conversation was comfortable, rather than otherwise. Daniel still did not trust Sofia, but wondered whether he was being too harsh in his judgement. She alone seemed to appreciate how Shem felt, and was prepared to accept Daniel in the role where Shem had placed him. They walked to a gazebo, which was surrounded by dead rosevines. Here, Sofia sat down upon a carved stone bench that might have come from the sands of Sumer. Daniel sat beside her, but Shem remained standing, staring out over the garden to the cliff-top.

"Shemyaza, you really must put aside your impatience with the Parzupheim and oblige them," Sofia said, and took in a lungful of smoke. "They are your people, after all."

Shem glanced down at her. "I'm no fool. Don't think I'm not aware that 'divine king' equates with 'sacrificial king'. I've had enough of that. I will not be a scapegoat."

"Perhaps you are right, but there are others who see you in quite a different light."

"Others?" Daniel interrupted.

Sofia looked at him askance. "Yes. The Parzupheim aren't the only Grigori power-wielders in this country." She patted the seat beside her. "Shemyaza, please sit down. There is something I must tell you."

Shem hesitated a moment, then complied with her request. Daniel noticed that Sofia swallowed involuntarily as Shem's body touched her.

"Then tell me," Shem said.

She nodded. "I'll get straight to the point. The Parzupheim are relative small fry in the scheme of things. Tell me, if you had the choice, who would you be working with now?"

"Daniel," Shem answered shortly.

"Yes," Sofia said, "but who else, of your own blood?"

Shem frowned out at the garden. "No-one."

"Not even your brothers?"

Shem turned his head to look at her intently. "What do you mean?"

"You are not the only one to survive," Sofia said. "I do not want the Parzupheim to know about it, but Salamiel is nearby. He is waiting for you, Shemyaza."

"Salamiel?" Shem peered at her, his expression puzzled. "He is here?"

Sofia nodded, clearly holding excitement in check. "Yes, very near. Like you, his consciousness has survived into this time. He awaits your command. Soon, if you are agreeable, I will take you to him, perhaps after this charade of a coronation has taken place."

Shem's face had broken into a smile. "I would like to see him," he said.

Daniel felt extremely on edge, and his mistrust of Sofia seethed back in full force. He was uncomfortable with the idea of Shem meeting with this person Sofia had secreted away. The name Salamiel meant nothing to him, but he was wary of it. "What about Shem's work with the Parzupheim? Are you suggesting he do something else, without their sanction?"

"My, you are jumping on ahead," Sofia said dryly. "Did I say any such thing?"

"No," Daniel replied, "but the feeling's there."

Sofia shrugged. "Actually, what the Parzupheim want is what I want, and what I want is the best for Shemyaza. It was I who suggested he should reawaken the Shamir. The only thing I've not seen fit to reveal to Enniel's cronies is that Salamiel should also be involved."

"Why not?" Daniel insisted. "Why can't you tell them about this other person?"

Sofia sighed. "It's very complicated, Daniel. Politics, you know. If the Parzupheim thought that Shemyaza had allies, they'd worry that they wouldn't be able to control him as efficiently."

"You don't have that fear."

"No," Sofia said, grinding out her cigarette on the stone patio. "I don't." She paused for a moment, clearly coming to a decision about something. "There is also another matter I'd like to mention. It should be of especial interest to you, Daniel."

"What?" Daniel's suspicions were engorged. He was frightened of being seduced by this woman into believing she had their welfare at heart.

"Your friends, Lily and Owen Winter, are with Salamiel now. He is caring for them. We thought it best to keep them away from the hubbub here."

"That's good news," Shem said.

Daniel said nothing. He remembered the visions that had come to him in Taziel's apartment, and their horrifying flight to Cornwall. He knew then, with utter conviction, that this Salamiel had been behind all that. Salamiel and Sofia. He would have to speak to Shem privately about this. How could he be taken in by this woman? Couldn't he smell the danger? Realising some kind of response was appropriate, Daniel said, "Are they all right?"

Sofia nodded enthusiastically. "Oh yes. Soon, we shall restore Owen for you, Daniel."

The implications were not lost on Daniel. Sofia hoped to distract him a little, prise him away from Shemyaza's side, thus allowing herself freedom of access. She did underestimate him, but not as much as he'd thought. He tried to smile. "I'd like to see Lily and Owen very much. I've missed them."

Sofia touched his hair, and he had to force himself not to recoil. "I know you have! Don't worry, everything will work out fine. It will just take a little time, that's all."

When they returned to Enniel, Daniel was disturbed by the fact that Shem seemed more animated. Clearly, Sofia's news had pleased him. He wondered whether his misgivings were caused only by jealousy, the revelation that someone who'd been close to Shem in the past had reappeared, someone who might possibly take on some of Daniel's position. Had he become greedy and protective of his status and power? The thought did not please him. He knew that power was a corrupting force, and that Grigori power was more corrupting than most.

Before dinner, Daniel wandered off into the house, ostensibly to look for Emma and let her know what was happening, but he knew in his heart he had to confront Taziel. He found Emma watching TV with Aninka in one of the drawing rooms. He was aware that Aninka was a close friend of Taziel's and suspected she now harboured some hard feelings for him. His friend, "Eve', seemed to have disappeared completely. When he asked her where Taziel was, she replied. "You're too late. He's upstairs, getting ready to leave. Lahash is driving him back to London. Perhaps it would be best if you just left him alone now."

Daniel offered no response, but went directly up to the room he had shared with Taziel. When he entered the room, Taziel was lying on the bed, wearing only a towel, his wet hair spread out around him. Daniel couldn't help thinking it all looked too premeditated, as if Taziel had hoped he would come.

"I hear you're leaving," Daniel said. "I'm sorry if..."

Before he could finish his apology, Taziel interrupted him. "I heard you scream. Was it pain or pleasure? Hard to tell which with that creature, isn't it?"

Daniel sighed. He didn't want to argue. "It's a shame if we have to part this way, Taz, but if that's how you want it to be..."

"You are full of him," Taziel said, "I can see his glow on you."

Daniel guessed Taziel wanted a full-scale row that could end in sex and reconciliation, but Daniel couldn't be bothered. With only a curt "goodbye', he left the room. The incident left him feeling depressed and uneasy, as if he'd closed the door on unfinished business, which might come back to haunt him one day.

At seven-thirty precisely, Austin rang the gong in the hallway of High Crag to announce that dinner was ready. Daniel had not had chance to speak to Shemyaza alone, which he suspected owed rather more to Enniel's design than it appeared. Sofia had monopolised Daniel's attention, quietly interrogating him about his life. He felt something brewing in the air, and found it difficult to eat. He found himself looking at faces that he'd never seen before, Prussoes who had emerged from the shadowy nooks of High Crag. Aninka picked at her meal, occasionally directing caustic glances at both Daniel and Shemyaza. At one point, Shem, who was sitting opposite and a few places down the table from her, leaned across the silver-starred snowy linen and said, "Aninka, you look very beautiful."

Daniel thought Aninka would go berserk, stab Shem with her knife, hurl her wine over him, but she remained tight-lipped, if a little crimson along the cheekbones.

Shem withdrew, apparently without having taken offence at her hostile silence. "Perhaps, one day, you will forgive me."

Daniel saw Emma, who was sitting next to Aninka, whisper something in her ear. Aninka smiled tightly at her plate and resumed eating.

After dinner, Enniel took Shemyaza off somewhere, presumably to prepare for the ritual to come, while the Parzupheim, along with Sofia and Daniel made their way to a temple in the heart of the house. Sofia was quick to point out that this would not be the family temple, used for various religious celebrations and festivals. No, this was the Parzupheim's domain, and used only rarely. Daniel assumed that when it was used, the land around the house must feel it. Only the most important rituals would take place there.

A silent servant of Enniel's ushered Daniel and Sofia through an enormous set of double doors. From here, they were conducted down the side of the darkened temple and up a curving wooden staircase, which led to a small gallery at the back of the hall. Here, they sat down upon hard wooden seats, and the servant departed. It was difficult to see through the fog of sandalwood incense, but Daniel could tell that the room was huge, perhaps three stories high. The gallery was positioned about twelve feet from the ground. Sofia began to cough discreetly behind her hand, then shrugged and got out her cigarettes, whispering to Daniel that no-one could possibly notice she was smoking. It amused Daniel to see her flicking ash onto the floor of the gallery.

The temple was magnificent, its atmosphere at once solemn and electric. Its floor was of dark, polished wood, into which had been laid a great circle of black and white tiles. The walls were covered in wooden panelling, and the room should have appeared large, plain and simple, a ballroom perhaps. However, what was contained within the unadorned wooden walls was something from a mad architect's dream. It looked as if it belonged out in the open air, on some wild Far Eastern hilltop, or else hidden within the aromatic darkness of an ancient forest. Not here in a rugged labyrinth of a house in Cornwall.

Around the circle on the floor were positioned twelve ornate, stone pillars, that must have been at least fifteen feet high, supporting an arched, domed canopy. The pillars were covered in representations of serpents, most of which were winged. Others were half human, or half Grigori; a woman's torso rising from a thick ophidian coil; a man with twin snakes for legs whose gaping maw devoured a child with a viper's head. The dome above the columns was inlaid with a complex mosaic of blue, white and mauve tiles: a circling frieze of winged beings, depicted enacting weird and arcane ceremonies. At the far end of the temple, opposite the gallery, stood the altar, a huge block of stone, weathered and pitted, but covered in carvings. A further two pillars reared just before it, supporting a section of the canopy, which extended out over the altar itself. Around the walls, tall brass censers on tripod legs exuded down-drifting clouds of sandalwood fumes. Light came from long, red candles, held in ornate iron sconces that were fixed to the wooden panelling. There were round windows, high up, composed of the stained glass so beloved of Grigori, but soon after Sofia and Daniel sat down, soft black drapes whispered down from some high place to cover them. The only sound was the soft pad of sandalled feet as a couple of dark-robed servants moved elegantly round the temple, making sure that the candles and incense were burning correctly, and adjusting the placement of items on the altar. Then the last of their pattering steps receded from the hall, and all was silent.

Sofia smiled at Daniel's awed examination of his surroundings. "It is supposed to be just like Solomon's temple," she said in a soft voice. The acoustics of the place would ensure that sound travelled far.

Daniel shook his head, gazing up at the imposing dome. "It's incredible." He glanced at Sofia. "This seems weird, because I've never been here before, but I *recognise* it."

Sofia took a puff off her cigarette. "That's not weird, Daniel. Think back. Relax. Where have you seen this place before?"

Daniel surrendered his mind to the flock of images that had come to flap against his consciousness. It seemed Sofia's words had unleashed them. He closed his eyes. "They have made a copy of an ancient temple that now is lost. The layout is the same." He opened his eyes and glanced at Sofia nervously. "Did I once *work* within it, in another life?"

She nodded encouragingly. "Perhaps. What was its name?"

Again, Daniel closed his eyes to concentrate. "It was the Temple of the Royal Flame at Tak...Takti el Sulamain.

"Persia," said Sofia.

"Yes. It was a fire temple. And I served a great king there." He screwed up his face with effort—the memories were fleeting and vague, mere ghosts across his mind. "Darius, his name was Darius, King of Persia."

"Ah," said Sofia. "The true Solomon and his temple."

Daniel shook his head. "This is so strange. I've never had impressions like this before."

"Oh well," Sofia remarked. "There's a time and place for everything, and you are surely in the right place at the moment."

Daniel gazed around the temple. "So many of these fittings are original, aren't they, plundered..."

"Not exactly," Sofia replied. "Look at the altar. Carved from a single block of stone. It wasn't plundered, but salvaged, from an old Persian fire temple at the time of the foundation of Islam. All the old temples were being destroyed back then, because they were seen as pagan and heretical monuments." The altar was intricately carved with symbols, but a single image dominated the side that faced them. It was of an equal-armed cross, cut to resemble the ripples of moving water. "You see that cross?" Sofia said, pointing. "It represents the four rivers of Paradise."

Various ritual items were laid out upon the surface of the altar, in readiness for the ritual to come. There was an elaborate crown, designed to mimic the tail of a peacock. Each feather painstakingly fashioned from solid gold, its shimmering eyes set with polished stones of lapis lazuli and amethyst. To the left of the crown, stood a silver chalice. Sofia explained that it was filled with haoma juice, and Daniel recalled the time he had smoked haoma in the Moses Assembly Rooms. It seemed an eternity ago now. To the right of the crown lay a silver platter, containing an arrangement of pomegranates. A mound of red, purple and white flowers were heaped beside the platter.

"What's going to happen?" Daniel asked. "Where is everybody?"

Well, here's Enniel," Sofia murmured, and gestured for Daniel to be quiet.

Enniel had emerged from the left side of the altar. He was dressed in a deep crimson robe, over which he wore a feathered apron, adorned with the symbol of the all-seeing eye, picked out in rubies, emeralds and beads of gold. "The apron signifies he is to be Master of Ceremonies," Sofia whispered.

The Parzupheim began to file into the temple with slow steps, and took up silent positions between the pillars around the circle. They were adorned with robes of vibrant colours—red, blue, yellow, purple, green, orange—that represented the spheres of celestial influence. They too wore short aprons over their robes, fashioned from shining black and white vulture feathers. Their hair hung unbound down their backs. Sloughed of their city clothing, the Grigori looked primal and shamanic, their aquiline features full of the secrets of their ancient ancestors.

For a few moments, all was still and silent, and then a low keening arose from the throats of the assembled Parzupheim. The doors to the temple opened, and there stood Shemyaza, flanked by two Grigori youths Daniel had not seen before. The youths took hold of Shemyaza's arms and led him forward. They were dressed only in feathered kilts, and their lithe adolescent bodies were anointed with oil, so that their taut flesh gleamed like polished marble in the soft candlelight. Shemyaza himself was clad in a simple white robe of rough-spun cotton that was belted at the waist with a gold cord. He looked tired and stooped, and Daniel thought with some discomfort that all he lacked was a crown of thorns.

When Shemyaza reached the centre of the circle, Enniel bade him kneel down. The Grigori boys stepped back into the shadows beyond the circle's perimeter. Shemyaza seemed dazed or drugged. His white-gold hair hung forward over his breast. Some trick of the light conjured beams of peacock blue radiance to enhalo Shemyaza's bowed head. He was, to Daniel, already a Divine King, and any ritual to proclaim him so was merely perfunctory.

Daniel had expected the Parzupheim to enact some fierce shamanic ceremony, with stamping, drums and shouted invocations, but he was disappointed. They stood rigidly erect and motionless, and the chant they uttered was monotonous, although it gradually rose in pitch and speed. All the while Shem remained upon his knees in the centre of the circle, his head drooping forward, perhaps hypnotised by the chant. Daniel himself felt weirdly affected by it. "Asha, merediska, vohu mainya! Asha, merediska, vohu mainya!" After a few minutes, he was repeating it himself, beneath his breath. He knew in his heart what it meant: truth and the spirit of love. Occasionally, the Parzupheim inserted other short phrases into the chant, but Daniel could not hear what they were. The words all seemed to flow into one another, as if the Grigori did not need to draw breath while intoning the chant. The vibration of it filled Daniel's head. It bored through to the most sensitive parts of his brain, blurring his senses and shifting his perception onto a different level. He felt his body sway, and for a moment feared he was about to pass out.

Then Sofia's cool hand was on his arm. "Look Daniel, pay attention. The Passing of Flowers Ceremony is about to begin."

Her touch seemed to bring Daniel back to reality, and the chant no longer rattled round his brain nor commanded his tongue.

He watched as Enniel lifted the flowers from the altar. They spilled over his arms in a riot of fresh colour. The Parzupheim all held up their hands before their chests, the palms pressed together in an attitude of prayer and, while the intonation continued, began to pass the flowers round the circle. The way they did this was strange and fluid. One Grigori would grip a flower stem between the tips of his fingers, roll it down between his palms and turn to his neighbour on the left, who would cover the flower-holder's palms with his own, and somehow transfer the bloom to his own hands, before passing it on. The movement was like a dance, rippling and graceful.

"What are they doing?" Daniel mumbled in a slurred voice.

Sofia's whisper sounded absurdly clipped. "It signifies a cleansing to purity, and the sharing of energies and intentions."

When the flowers had been passed for a single circuit of the circle, they were placed around the kneeling figure of Shemyaza at the centre. Once all the blooms were emplaced, the chanting ceased abruptly. Then, the Parzupheim changed positions, moving one pillar to the left around the circle.

Enniel stepped forward and stood before the kneeling figure in the centre. He placed his hands upon Shemyaza's shoulders. The silence in the temple seemed almost deafening. Nobody moved or made a sound. Peacock light blossomed around Enniel and Shemyaza, dying their skins an impossible purply-blue. Daniel wondered what communion was occurring between them. Did they speak in thoughts? What was in their minds as they stood and knelt there so silently?

After a few minutes, Enniel took a step back and signalled to the two adolescent attendants, who were stationed beyond the circle. They bowed to him, and glided forward between the pillars. Standing behind Shemyaza, they deftly removed his flimsy robe, revealing the flawless lines of his naked body. He looked so vulnerable, huddled there, clothed only in his hair.

Enniel gestured with both hands for Shemyaza to arise. Gracefully, he lifted his head and unfolded upwards from the floor like a column of white cloud, mottled with beams of the peacock light. Erect, he towered over the figure of Enniel, obscuring him from Daniel's view. Shem's body looked so perfect, it could have been an idealised statue of male beauty. Daniel heard Sofia utter a lascivious, appreciative murmur, and a blade of pure jealousy sliced through his belly. She would want a piece of Shem. Everyone did.

Shemyaza appeared mindless, because Enniel had to take hold of one of his arms to lead him from the circle. He was ushered to a stone chair, which stood on a raised dais behind the altar. Here, Enniel stood him in position, facing out towards the temple. Shemyaza made no move to resist, or even assist. He was like a magnificent sacrificial animal, docile and obedient.

Enniel went back to the altar and here opened the lid of a gilded chest that stood beside the great, stone cube. Carefully, he withdrew an enormous cloak, which hung heavily in his arms. It was adorned with beads and the feathers of many exotic birds; crimson, purple, gold and electric blue. This he carried back to the stone chair and draped around Shemyaza's shoulders. The cloak hung to the ground, a shimmering maelstrom of colour, hemmed with peacock feather eyes. Shemyaza stood unaffected, as if barely aware he'd been clothed again. Gently, Enniel helped him to sit down upon the throne. At the same precise moment, the assembled Grigori sank down as a single unit, to kneel around the circle.

Daniel stared hard across the smoky reaches of the temple, trying to catch Shemyaza's eyes, hoping to recognise some flicker of mordant humour there. But Shem looked like a stranger, beautiful beyond measure and distant as the dawn horizon. His eyes gazed blankly straight ahead and his jaw was set rigidly. His glorious hair tumbled down over the scintillant feathers that curled around his neck. Daniel wondered whether Shem's faraway eyes gazed upon distant visions of his ancient home, upon kingships long past. Or did he ponder more recent events in his long soul existence, memories of death and callous destruction?

Enniel approached the altar and lifted the silver chalice of haoma juice, which he carried smoothly to the throne. Here, he held the brimming vessel aloft and spoke in a ringing voice. "In the name of Darius the Mede, I obsecrate thee, Holy One, to state thy divinity and claim us unto your spirit, and the spirit of thy father Anu, through thy own royal blood."

Enniel pressed the chalice to Shemyaza's lips. He appeared to sip from it with detached co-operation. Then, Enniel leaned forward and parted the front of Shemyaza's cloak. He poured a measure of the dark red, sticky liquid onto Shem's exposed breast, where it spread over his heart like a stain of blood.

Enniel turned to face the kneeling Parzupheim. "Behold! For this is his blood, within which dwells the light of truth!" He handed the chalice to the Grigori nearest to him, who took an eager sip from it, before passing it to the celebrant on his left. The chalice was passed from hand to hand around the circle, each member of the Parzupheim taking their measure in restrained eagerness. Finally, the chalice was passed back to Enniel, who replaced it upon the altar.

Next, Enniel took up the platter of pomegranates and laid it before Shemyaza's feet. Reverently, he lifted one fruit, and held it before Shem's inexpressive face.

"Sacred Father, recall to us the state of thy wound upon the eve of thy sacrifice, when your most holy body lay bent and broken from thy treacherous flight."

He held the fruit to Shemyaza's mouth. As it touched his lips, Shem took a firm but delicate bite, slicing into the leathery skin. Purple juice trickled down his chin, and onto his chest, to mingle with the blood-like stain over his heart.

Enniel turned once more towards the waiting Parzupheim and held aloft the dripping fruit. "Behold, the flesh of his body, within which dwells the food of salvation!"

The Parzupheim passed the fruit around the circle, each taking a bite. Outwardly, their movements were precise and cordial— each bowing respectfully as the fruit was passed to him—but Daniel felt he could see the truth within their hearts. They were like a horde of greedy cannibals, salivating to sample the divine flesh. Yet the rabid, starving light only burned from their eyes while the fruit filled their mouths.

By the time the mangled pomegranate returned to Enniel, purple juice stained the robes and faces of all participants. Daniel noticed that Sofia glared hungrily at the remains of the fruit as Enniel replaced it on the altar. She looked as if she might rise up, throw herself across the temple and gorge herself on the sticky fragments.

Daniel sensed that everyone, except perhaps for himself and Shemyaza, were suffused with a suppressed hysterical frenzy, which given the right stimuli might erupt into orgiastic madness. Even Enniel was behaving oddly. His normally bland expression held a hint of wildness. His hair appeared wantonly dishevelled, and all his actions were exaggerated. His colleagues were no different. Daniel would not have been surprised to notice erections pushing out the front of their robes, but as far as he could tell, they were not sexually aroused. Something had been conjured within them, yet despite this, the ritual itself seemed empty and mechanical. In some subtle way, it lacked the essential spark of spiritual feeling that should have united everyone present. Perhaps this was a symptom of what had been discussed at the meeting earlier; Grigori ritual had gone stale.

Now that the ceremonies of the haoma and the pomegranate were completed, the Parzupheim stood up, and changed positions again, moving in a clockwise direction around the pillars. Enniel stepped back to the altar and, with both hands, reverently lifted the gleaming peacock crown. He went to kneel before the throne, and held the crown up before Shemyaza's rigid body.

"Shemyaza, by what law dost thou reclaim the Crown of Melek Taus?"

Shem's voice sounded like a hollow echo. "Blood."

"Shemyaza, what dost thou deem to bestow upon thy subjects?"

"Knowledge."

"Shemyaza, what dost thou seek in thy destiny?"

"Truth."

Daniel was surprised to hear Shemyaza speak, and even more startled that he was aware of the correct responses. He was sure that Shemyaza had been mesmerised into complicity throughout the whole ritual. Shem, do you know what you are doing? he thought. Why are you playing their game? Daniel had wanted Shem to comply with the Parzupheim's wishes, simply to make sure he himself wasn't burdened with Shemyaza's responsibilities, but now that he was watching the coronation, he felt sick. It was a charade, a mockery.

Beside the throne, Enniel stood with his spine erect, holding the shining crown a few inches above Shemyaza's head. "According to the ancient laws, I crown thee in the name of Cyrus the Great. I exalt thee in the Highest, from Anu, Father of Heaven. And I bestow upon thee the sanctity which is thy blood." With these words, Enniel finally lowered the crown onto Shemyaza's head and the Parzupheim sank down to kneel upon one knee before him. They had their king now. They honoured him.

Daniel's heart contracted in his chest. Before his eyes, the image of Shemyaza seemed to expand and distort. His face and body were beginning to stretch and elongate. His eyes had become long and snake-like, glowing with a spectral yellow light. His gaze met Daniel's eyes across the temple and locked with him. Shem's lips, which were now bloodless and thin, peeled back from his teeth.

He expelled a long, low, sibilant hiss, and a ribbon of crimson tongue lashed out. Daniel was sure its burning end flicked against his cheek. He was horrified by what he saw, yet also strangely awed. What was happening? Was the coronation ceremony a means to transform Shemyaza into some hideous serpent king? He glanced around himself quickly, to see how the Parzupheim were reacting to the transformation, but no-one save himself seemed to have noticed it. Desperately, he hissed Sofia's name and she turned to look at him grudgingly, reluctant to tear her gaze away from the throne.

"What is it?" she whispered.

Daniel pointed at Shemyaza, unable to speak, but when he looked back at the throne, the frightening vision had vanished. Shem appeared as he had before; a beautiful angel in the robes and crown of a king. Daniel shook his head and signalled to Sofia that it was nothing. She shrugged and returned her attention to the proceedings before them.

Enniel stepped down, away from the throne and raised his arms to the Parzupheim. They all rose to their feet and turned towards the Master of Ceremonies. "Behold," Enniel cried. "The return of the Divine King! Shemyaza! Son of Anu, Father of Adam, Root of the Vine, from which all things proceed, to whom all things return. Pillar of Jacob, Bestower of Solomon's Wisdom, Foundation Stone, Builder of Life and Bringer of Salvation!"

The Parzupheim all threw up their arms, and cheered, shouting out the praises that would close the ritual. "Re harakti! Re harakti! Re harakti!"

"Son of the sun," whispered Daniel, frozen in his seat.

"Blood of the lamb," murmured Sofia beside him.

Chapter Twenty-Two
The Sea Maid

Tamara was sitting in her kitchen eating lunch when Barbelo walked in through her unlocked back door. The Grigori woman seemed nervous and excited. Tamara had not seen her for several days, and had begun to worry about it, frightened that Barbelo had changed her mind about including Tamara in her plans. But Barbelo sat down opposite her and said, "He is among us!"

Tamara's heart clenched in her chest, a desperate muscle. "You have seen him?"

Barbelo nodded, and removed her headscarf. "Oh yes! Soon, my dear, you will see him for yourself. Have you been empowering the site as I instructed you?"

"Yes. The thought-form is very clear now."

"And the boy, Delmar. Has he become more tractable?"

"Since I began feeding him that powder you gave me, yes."

Barbelo smiled. "Good. He has an important part to play, and I can't help feeling he is somewhat of a weak link. He is no Daniel Cranton, who's the Shining One's vizier, but I'm afraid he's going to have to assume some of that persona! You'll have to keep a tight curb on him, Tamara."

"I will, don't worry." Tamara wanted to ask what Shemyaza looked like, what he had said, but sensed that Barbelo would not want to answer. Over their relatively short acquaintance, Tamara had learned the Grigori woman liked to keep secrets, to maintain the balance of power between them.

"Tonight, you must enact the final rite," Barbelo said. "This afternoon, concentrate on the thought-form of Ishtahar, and send a call of desire to Shemyaza within High Crag. He must come to you tonight. Go the Mermaid's Cove at dusk, and conjure the power of the sea. Prepare Delmar as I have told you. Then project all the energy you possess into luring Shemyaza out to the cliff-top. I shall be aiding you from within the house. Once he emerges, it must proceed as we have discussed."

Tamara's heart was beating so fast, she was afraid she'd have a seizure. The time had come so quickly. She'd imagined she'd have days in which to prepare herself for this meeting. "What time will it happen?"

Barbelo shrugged. "I have no way of knowing precisely. Today, the elders of the Grigori families meet to discuss Shemyaza's future. It is most likely they will crown him as their Divine King before the day is out. All to the good." She paused. "Tamara, Shemyaza is a god, but he is also a man. Do not be foolish and allow his glamour to bewitch you. It is vital you remain in control. Love him as the Prince of Light, but despise the Adam in him. You, in some respects, are more powerful than he, for you are female. I am relying on you."

Tamara wondered why Barbelo wanted no part of this ritual herself. "Have no fear," she said. "I have waited for this too long to let it go awry."

After Barbelo had left, Tamara unplugged her telephone and closed all the curtains in the cottage. Delmar came to visit her every day after school now, so she had several hours in which to work before he arrived. Forcing herself not to hurry, she ritually prepared herself for the tasks ahead. Then, she went downstairs and pushed all the furniture in her parlour to the edges of the room, creating a space where she could meditate. Barbelo had given her special incense and over a dozen long, intricately-worked candles that were smeared with pungent oil. Tamara arranged these items in a circle, then lit the incense and the candles. Her parlour was transformed into a temple removed from the mundane world beyond her walls. She concentrated on the thought-form of Ishtahar, made her sing with longing and desire. Somewhere, she felt a presence become alert to her call. For a moment, her concentration wavered. It was him! A tide of desire threshed through her blood. Shemyaza! Rekindling her energy, she directed wave after wave of feeling towards him, until he would feel drunk and confused. Soon, she would touch his holy body.

After visiting Tamara as Barbelo, Sofia called on Salamiel before she went to High Crag. She found him almost hysterical with expectation. "Calm down, my dear," she breathed, gliding into his study.

"But what's happening?" Salamiel demanded. "Azazel has been at High Crag for two days, yet you still have not brought him here to me, where he belongs."

Sofia sat down, giving an impression of outward composure, though within she fought with the same maelstrom of emotion that showed plainly in Salamiel's face. "Be patient," she said. "All proceeds as it should."

Salamiel eyed her with suspicion. "You are sure the Parzupheim will not instruct Azazel to awake the Shamir for them?"

"Oh, quite sure." Sofia grinned. "You must stop worrying. Let Enniel's cronies anoint Azazel as their king. It serves only to augment his power, for us to use."

"Have you told him about me?"

Sofia shook her head, her brow creased. "No, not yet, but soon. Perhaps today, if I get the chance."

"Yes, today!" Salamiel got to his feet. "Bring him to me tonight."

Sofia turned down the corners of her mouth in a rueful smile. "It might not be tonight..."

"Then when?"

She sighed. "Your hysteria is beginning to get on my nerves. You've waited millennia, Sal. A few more days are hardly going to make much difference."

"A few more days! But what will happen to him in that time? The Parzupheim could contaminate his mind!"

Sofia laughed dryly. "You have no need to worry on that score."

Salamiel frowned. "How can you be so sure?"

She lifted her shoulders in a shrug.

"What are you planning?" The question was delivered in a low voice. "You *are* planning something, aren't you."

Sofia merely widened her smile into a predatory, reptile grin. "Fear not, my lovely. You are still a major part of my design. In the meantime, concentrate on Lily Winter. She should be the focus of your energies at this time."

At dusk, Tamara Trewlynn drove in her car to the lay-by near the cliff path to Mermaid's Cove. Delmar sat beside her, his expression blank. Before leaving her cottage, Tamara had taken the precaution of giving him a cup of strong, sweet tea, into which she'd stirred a liberal dose of

the herbal powder Barbelo had given her. She had guessed that the rest
of the Pelleth were now highly suspicious of her. It could be no coincidence that the Conclave had appeared to be inactive over the past few
days. Phone calls from Meggie had been non-existent. Most likely,
they were being *highly* active, but had chosen to exclude Tamara from
their work. They must be preparing their sacred sites by now for the
advent of Shemyaza. Tamara did not care what the Pelleth did. She felt
that she and Barbelo possessed far more power than they and must be a
greater lure for the Shining One. Meggie had probably also noticed, or
been informed, of a change in Delmar's behaviour. Now, he was entirely Tamara's creature. She had primed him with talk of Shemyaza,
and subdued his instinctive fears. "You will become the oracle of the
Sun Chief," she told him. "Do not be afraid."

Whether Delmar was impressed by this news was hard to
fathom, but at least he had kept his silence for her, and obeyed her
commands without question. His mother had been a bit of problem,
because she'd tried to prevent Delmar spending so much time away
from home. No doubt Meggie had told the Tremayne woman her
suspicions. Still, Delmar had been used to absolute freedom, and in
his passive, yet relentless way had managed to slip away from the
house whenever he wanted to.

The wind grabbed angrily at the land as Tamara led Delmar
down to the cove. By now, the lizard guardians were familiar with
her, and when she showed them the talisman, quickly stood aside to
let her pass. Even though the light was fast fading from the sky, the
cove was clearly visible, as if the waves themselves glowed with a
spectral light that illuminated the land. Tamara's awareness was
heightened because of the preparations she'd made earlier, and she
could see easily the slim form of a woman standing upon the wet
sand, her hair blowing around her head. Tamara addressed the image. "Ishtahar. It is I, your mistress."

The figure turned towards her, and fixed her with a sad, wide-
eyed stare. Tamara beckoned Delmar. "Go into the cave beneath
the cliff, Del. Lie down upon the rock and wait for my summons."

The boy obeyed without uttering a sound.

Words whispered inside Tamara's head. "You are a fool!
He is not Daniel, and you will never be me!"

Tamara dismissed the unwelcome presence from her mind.
"You're not *her* either, phantom!" The thought-form of Ishtahar
possessed more consciousness than she would have liked.

Turning her back on the forlorn image, Tamara walked towards the convulsing waves. It was true; the sea was glowing. There were shapes twisting in the breakers, lights moving beneath the churning surface. Tamara held out her arms to the elements. The wind lunged at her with hungry caresses, as if it would tear the clothes from her body. She could hear spirit-voices in its whistling thunder, voices from the sea that hailed from the lost temples of Lyonesse, long submerged beneath the waves. The spirits could smell Shemyaza's proximity. They were wild with desire for him, as she was. The restlessness and urgency of the ocean reached out to Tamara, filled her with a sense of power and command. Her clawed fingers clutched at the wild air. *I am the Sea Princess, Seference's daughter, more powerful than Ishtahar ever was!* The thought-form behind her was an empty shell, chained to this fierce shore, while she was strong and free, the channel of potential.

Tamara drew her spray-soaked robe over her head, and with an eerie cry ran naked into the waves.

Aninka and Emma sat together in their favourite drawing room. All was silent, but for the crackle of flames in the hearth and the slow tick of a grandfather clock in a corner of the room. Aninka sat on the sofa, her legs curled beneath her. She stared into the fire. Emma sat in an armchair to the side of the sofa, reading a popular novel and smoking a cigarette. The silence between the two women had been comfortable, but now Emma sensed that a tension had come sneaking into the room. Aninka had not spoken about the remark that Shemyaza had addressed to her over dinner, but Emma suspected it had upset her greatly. Gradually, Emma's eyes were drawn away from the page, to keep Aninka in the periphery of her vision. Aninka's relaxed, contemplative posture had stiffened. Now, she stared at the flames with wide, almost terrified eyes.

Emma put down her book. "Are you feeling OK, Ninka?"

Aninka shot her a furtive glance. "Yes...I'm fine."

Emma picked up her book again and pretended to read it. Presently, Aninka got up and went to the French windows. With a jerky movement, she cast aside the long drapes. Emma watched her peering out into the wet, stormy darkness. "You're not all right, are you. What's wrong?"

Aninka curled her arms about her breasts. "I...I'm not sure." She shivered and rubbed her arms. "I feel cold, sort of anxious."

Emma watched her warily as she began to pace up and down in front of the window. "Come back over here by the fire. You probably feel upset because of what's going on in the house today. Why not have a drink to calm your nerves."

Aninka shook her head. "No..." she suddenly stopped pacing. "What's that? Can you hear it?"

Emma listened. She could hear the clock, the flames, and a host of faint noises coming from various corners of the house, but nothing unusual. "What can you hear?"

Aninka pushed her hair behind her ears, lowered her head. "It's a wailing sound...very faint. You must be able to hear it! Come here!"

Emma stood up and went to Aninka's side, reached up to put an arm around the Grigori woman's shoulders. "I can't hear anything."

"It's like whale-song," Aninka said, and wriggled away from Emma's arm. She walked slowly back to the windows and Emma followed. Their reflections looked like ghosts hanging in the dark. "I feel...haunted," Aninka said in a low voice. "Someone just walked over my grave." She laughed nervously. Her hand snaked out and undid the lock on the window door. Before Emma could stop her, she'd opened it and stepped outside. Cold air rolled into the room, and filled it with a rank, salty stench. It was like the sea had entered the house. Emma ran to the window.

"Ninka, come in! You'll freeze out there! What the hell are you doing?"

Aninka said nothing, but Emma could see her tall, dark shape walking swiftly across the lawn in the direction of the cliff. Cursing, Emma ran after her and grabbed hold of her arm. "Stop this! Come back to the house!" Had Aninka gone mad?

Aninka brushed Emma off, easily disengaging herself from the woman's grasp. "The sea is ebbing and flowing within me," she said in a strange, cracked voice. "The tides pulls me."

"Ninka!" Emma was worried now. Her strength was no match for a Grigori woman. She knew she couldn't drag Aninka back inside on her own. What was out here? Emma glanced around herself fearfully, but could see nothing more threatening than the furiously tossed branches of the rhododendrons nearby.

Then, Aninka uttered a peculiar groan, and broke away from Emma. She ran down into the rhododendron grove, towards the cliff, her long legs devouring the distance effortlessly. Emma ran after her. As she emerged from the grove, she saw Aninka scrambling over the crumbled wall that provided the only barrier against the sheer drop to the cove beneath. "No!" Perhaps the panicked tone to her scream caused Aninka to waver. Emma leapt over the wall and with all the strength she possessed, enfolded Aninka in a tight embrace and threw both of them backward with the weight of her body. They fell heavily, landing upon broken rubble. Emma was afraid she'd broken bones in the fall, but when Aninka crawled away from her, found she was able to get up without pain. Aninka was on all fours before her, staring at the ground. Emma squatted down beside her. "What the hell did you think you were doing?"

Aninka looked up at her, her eyes glazed. "I...I don't know. Something called me." She shook her head. "I feel sick!"

"You could have killed yourself."

"I know." Aninka's body jerked and she retched.

Emma looked out at the place where Aninka had crawled through the broken wall. The sea looked very odd this evening, almost as if it was lit up from deep below. "It's a strange night," she said. "The sea looks like it's glowing."

Aninka got shakily to her feet, but seemed nervous of approaching the wall.

"Great Shem!" Emma's oath was uttered in a low, shocked voice. "Ninka, what's that?"

Reluctantly, Aninka came to stand beside her at the wall. They looked down upon the cove, where the sea sucked halfway up the sand. The sky was dark, the moon occluded by clouds, yet they could see through the spectral twilight as if every rock and grain of sand exuded its own sick light.

Something was crawling up the shore from the sea, crawling on its belly like the first primal fish that had struggled to its evolution on the land. Weed and foam plastered its flesh and its long, bedraggled hair. It was a woman, but no ordinary female. Emma felt as if they were looking upon some primordial Eve, a proto-woman clawing her way from the womb of the sea. Behind her in the flashing waves, the heads of seals bobbed and dove, and other more human-looking creatures rode the surf. They looked like mermen— half man, half fish—huge erections thrusting forth from the place where their barnacled tails began.

"They are oanes," Aninka murmured.

"Whats?" Emma swallowed thickly.

"Sea people."

Emma shuddered, filled with a sense of deja vu. She re-membered how she'd felt at the High Place in Little Moor as she'd watched Peverel Othman begin his invocations to the Ahriman. She felt the same way now. Something terrible was about to happen. She grabbed Aninka's arm. "Inside the house! Now!"

This time, Aninka did not fight her.

On the beach below, Tamara lay panting upon the sand. Her wild euphoria had ebbed. Now, she felt exhausted. She could hear the call of the seals and the oanes behind her, and sensed their frantic excitement. She herself was filled with the knowledge that soon Shemyaza would come to her. All around her, the shore vibrated with the energy of imminent transformation. Tamara rolled onto her back. She remembered being swallowed by the waves and the touch of slithering male hands upon her. She remembered riding the furi-ous surf with a slick, cold body clasped between her legs, its icy, inhuman phallus buried deep within her. Behind her, further up the shore, she sensed the thought-form of Ishtahar tugging at its psychic chains in panic. *Struggle on, feeble maiden.* Soon, the great earth serpent would awake. Tamara knew that when it did, she would be a goddess. She would ride its power. Laughing.

Chapter Twenty-Three
Fall, Sweet Sacrifice

Once the ritual of coronation ended, the Parzupheim seemed far more relaxed. They believed, Daniel realised, that Shemyaza was now wholly theirs; their Messiah, the saviour of their world. Enniel took Shem into an antechamber of the temple, presumably to divest him of his ceremonial garb. In the main room, lights bloomed dimly around the walls, and the Parzupheim filed out into another room. Daniel and Sofia were left alone. He sensed the woman was considering what she should say to him.

She thinks she has my measure, he thought, but she's still not wholly clear about it.

Sofia grinned at him, in a manner designed to be confidential and understanding. "Be kind to Shemyaza tonight," she said, laying a proprietorial hand on Daniel's shoulder. "If his behaviour is peculiar, indulge him."

Daniel nodded warily. "Of course."

Sofia rose from her seat and smoothed her skirt. "Well, there's no point in remaining here."

Daniel stood up. He wondered where Enniel would take Shem now. Would he be allowed to see him again tonight? He felt they should discuss what had happened today.

Sofia preceded him out to the corridor, where she turned to appraise him. "Well, Daniel, I expect we shall see each other tomorrow. I thought it best I stay here tonight."

Daniel couldn't prevent a frown. "Why? Are you expecting something to happen?" He had visions of the serpent stretching forth from sleep to burst up through the foundations of High Crag.

Sofia laughed faintly at the alarm in his voice. "My dear, it is just a precaution. I doubt if anything will happen instantaneously." She patted his shoulder. "Anyway, don't worry. Everything will work out fine. See you." She breezed away from him down the corridor.

Daniel watched her retreating form for a moment. There was something about the swagger in her walk that alerted him. What *was* Sofia's agenda?

Hoping to find Shemyaza, Daniel went to his suite on the first floor. It was empty, and smelled of old incense with a faint hint of wax. Daniel got into the bed, fully clothed, and sat resting against the headboard, watching the night outside through the open curtains. He sensed the flexing of the serpent beneath the earth, and his own belly churned in response. He sensed imminence, the approach of something vast and terrifying and wondrous.

Shem came into the room about half an hour later. Daniel said, "I need a drink. Can you get something?" He realised he wanted Shem to stay as he was, someone as involved with the trivia of everyday life as with the dark arcana of Grigori heritage. Would the Divine King be capable of fetching a bottle from a room downstairs?

Shem shrugged at him. He looked tired, but not that different from how he'd been before the ceremony. "OK." He picked up a phone extension next to the bed and called Austin's office; someone was on duty in there round the clock, like in a hotel. Shem asked for two bottles of wine to be sent up; one red, one white. Daniel was amused by this, but disappointed.

"You have slaves now," he said.

Shem lay down beside him on top of the bed and put his arms behind his head. "It's been a very strange day."

"It's a strange night, too."

"You're angry. What's wrong?"

Daniel sighed. "I feel...confused. Everything's happening so quickly. I feel like we have no control."

Shem turned onto his side, resting his head on one hand. "That's not the case. Don't let the Parzupheim's songs and dances upset you."

"It's not that! It's the rest of it. Sofia, this Salamiel. Shem, I'm suspicious of it."

"Really? I'm just curious."

Daniel sensed Shem's deliberate reticence. His interest, of course, involved rather more than curiosity.

A soft knock at the door signalled the arrival of the wine. Shem swung himself off the bed to answer it.

Daniel watched him as he poured two large glasses of dark red liquor. There was a tense atmosphere in the room, an omen that more was to be said. He accepted the glass from Shem and took a deep breath. Every doubt had to be aired. "Another thing I'm not happy with is the way you're trying to pass the buck onto me all the time."

Shem laughed and lay down on the bed again. "I'm not!"

"You are! You didn't just pass me a cloak of feathers to teach me how to fly. It was all about handing me your responsibilities. You want me to enter the underworld for you."

Shem took a drink of wine. "Well, I think you should. You're far more capable than I am."

Daniel could have hit him. "Are you mad? You know what the Parzupheim said to you. You're their Messiah. Enniel told us that you're the only one who can withstand the gaze of the serpent. Anyone else will probably just be...I don't know...burned alive! Is that what you want for me?"

"Daniel, whatever the Parzupheim think of me, I don't have the light of truth within me. I'm not their Messiah."

"Oh wake up, will you! They called you the son of the serpent, and I believe them. I know what's inside you, Shem."

"I can't do it."

"Then what was all that about today? Why did you go through with their little charade? And it was *little,* Shem."

Shem eyed him speculatively. "I thought that was what you wanted. What changed your mind?"

Daniel shook his head in confusion. "I don't know! Something felt wrong about it. You looked like an imbecile."

Shem laughed dryly. "Thanks."

Daniel reached out and touched his arm. "I'm not insulting you. They did something to you. Can't you remember? Did they drug you?"

"Probably. Anyway, it was just to satisfy them, silence their nagging. It doesn't mean I'm going to do what they ask of me."

"That's different. I still think you should. Not for the Parzupheim, but for yourself."

Shem glanced at the ceiling in exasperation. "No, Daniel. I really can't."

"You can. You must. Just overcome all the bitterness inside and take a leap of faith."

"How easy it is for you to say that!"

Daniel sensed Shem's withdrawal. This arguing would do no good, yet he felt unable to keep his thoughts to himself. "You're not just bitter, you're lazy! Shem, you're more than all the rest of the Grigori put together. Surely that's a privilege and a responsibility? Acting like a spoilt child is...well, it's ungrateful."

"Hah! So I'm supposed to be grateful for being tortured and abused am I? You ignorant little bastard! How can you say that? I never asked to have my soul imprisoned, along with all the memories of my original life, only to have it flung back at me now. My people did nothing for me. They ruined me. I only despise them now."

"This isn't just about *your* people, Shem, but the whole world."

"So fucking what!"

"I'm not condoning what happened to you in the past..."

"Shut up, you don't remember half of it."

"I do! In Little Moor I lived through your death. I saw it."

"Death? Is that all! Daniel go fuck someone and dream the rest of it will you? You've missed some salient details out."

"Oh Shem, stop being difficult for the sake of it."

"Right, OK, I'll go and do it for you, shall I? I'll just go down into this fucking underworld, wherever it is, and face their demons. That's what it's all about you know. Get real, Daniel, see it as it is. They don't want me to come out again, don't you understand? For me, afternoon tea with the serpent would be a one-way ticket. That's the bit you conveniently forget—my scapegoat aspect."

"You're afraid!"

"Yes!"

"But why? You have the power to survive, I know you do, even if the Parzupheim see you only as a sacrifice. Forget them. Think about us."

Shem narrowed his eyes at Daniel. "Oh? Why is this so important to you? Why should you care?" Daniel didn't answer, and Shem rolled his eyes in sarcasm. "Oh, *I see,* you care about the world. You green little queen!"

"Don't speak to me like that!"

"I don't want to speak to you at all. Shut the fuck up!"

Uttering an angry cry, Daniel threw his wine glass onto the floor and turned on his side. Silence descended like lint over a wound.

Shem finished his wine, drank another two glasses in quick succession, then got up from the bed and undressed himself. He turned off the lights and climbed in beside Daniel, who still lay with his back to him.

Daniel was taut with fury. Shem had never spoken to him like that before. He knew it was important their rift was healed, but was too angry to address it now. The reek of spilled wine was tart in the room, hanging there like an accusing symbol of the sourness between them. We can sort it out tomorrow, Daniel thought. Everything will be fine once we've talked it through. He hoped Shem would think about what they'd said.

Shem lay awake for hours and was aware of when Daniel's breathing changed, indicating he was asleep. Shem felt restless and frustrated. He hated the responsibility everyone was trying to project on him. It was as if they wanted him to marry a woman he found repulsive and who would eat him alive. The whole world annoyed him. The coronation had been embarrassing and pathetic, a travesty. All it represented to him was being bound by chains and authority, bureaucracy and tradition; stale, worn out and meaningless. None of what the Parzupheim had talked about that afternoon seemed real. He appreciated the existence of the serpent, and could sense its freezing breath burning the back of his neck, but felt the people around him were somehow missing the point of it all. They were trying to make it small and manageable, when in reality it was almost too huge and mystifying to comprehend. Daniel had a romantic view, believing that Shemyaza could ride into battle like a king, dressed in silver mail with a magic sword in his hand. He thought that the serpent was a physical creature and that Shem could simply approach it, tell it to wake, and save the world. But Shem feared the serpent was beyond their imaginations. The encounter could not be physical like that, but a psychic trauma. Now, Shem regretted what he'd said to Daniel, although not to the extent where he felt he should apologise. Why couldn't Daniel see sense? He'd fallen for the fairytales. Stop thinking about this, he told himself. Just sleep. Deal with it tomorrow.

Although he pushed all thoughts of the argument and its subject from his mind, Shem still couldn't sleep. Thoughts and fragmented memories churned through his brain. He found he was mixing up vague recollections of Aninka Prussoe with those

of Ishtahar, which were many thousands of years old. He saw
Ishtahar dressed in smart, modern clothes, standing in the middle
of a spreading corn-field, holding a mobile phone to her ear, staring up at the blood-soaked clouds of an eastern sunset. He saw
barbarian armies, mounted on shaggy ponies, charging down a
stretch of the M1, slashing at stalled, listing lorries with their swords.
He saw the sky in flames and the Garden in Eden crash down a
mountain slope into a deserted shopping mall. He saw bodies lying on steaming streets, where the waters of the flood had recently
receded. Bodies lying in mud and the stink of death everywhere.
These visions tortured him for hours.

Near dawn, Shemyaza woke up with a start. He sat up in
bed and glanced at the clock. Soon, it would be dawn. A new day
would start. Another day of questions, demands and embarrassment. His skin itched unbearably and his head beat with pain. He
needed the freshness of the wind upon his body. He needed to feel
the space of the sky above him, feel solid earth beneath his feet.
Quietly, he slipped from the bed and dressed himself. He went down
through the sleeping house and out into the garden. It was almost as
if a silky voice was calling to him through the chill air.

Shemyaza found himself standing at the place where the gardens
ended in a dizzying drop of cracked serpentine. The beach seemed
miles below. It was nearly high tide, and the waves were a milky
green colour, almost like liquid serpentine themselves. Images and
sounds pushed as the boundary of his perception, clamouring to
make contact with him. Wearily, Shem relaxed and opened himself
up to the environment. *Come on, then. Show me.* He could hear the
voices of sea spirits, joyful in the threshing foam, calling out to one
another. Their cries held a melancholic quality; it was the song of
the end of the world. When he closed his eyes, a great city rose
from the sea before him: Lyonesse, in all her splendour, reborn. Water
cascaded from her gleaming spires. It seemed she was made all of
glass or encrustations of ancient crystal. This was the city of his
ancestors, images of an ancient time, recaptured in the memories of
the tides. The sheer walls of the city were surrounded by tall, spreading trees, whose stretching upper branches failed to reach the marble
battlements. Music came from the hidden temples, borne on a skein
of incense smoke. He heard the keening song of the priestesses and
the slap of bare feet on marble. He heard the heart-song of the

drums, the artful chink of bells at wrists and ankles, and the whirl of gossamer fabric against satin flesh. He heard the priests calling out in voices that mimicked the lament of the sea folk and the cry of sea birds. The heat of the sun was on his skin, and the scents of lost summers in his nostrils.

Shemyaza opened his eyes.

It was dark mid-winter, and the grey sea heaved below him, shot with ghost-lights and the flash of iridescent foam. But still there remained in the sky, above the waves, a faint ghostly image of the lost city. The song of the priestesses still came whispering to his ears, the sounds plaiting and undulating in his mind, until it sounded as if it was a single woman who sang; a woman alone and melancholy, wearing the willow for a lost lover.

Shemyaza leaned against the crumbling wall, and his weight precipitated the looser stones to clatter down to the shore. Without thinking, he climbed over the rubble and stood on the narrow ledge at the very edge of the cliff. Eighteen inches of sandy, rock-strewn turf stretched between him and the yawning space beyond. The wind pushed and pulled at his body like spiteful hands, and snatched gleefully at his hair, blowing it forward across his face in star-spun waves. Shem held his flailing hair back from his eyes with both hands.

Show me, then. Show me why I'm here...

As if something had been awaiting his command, Shemyaza noticed movement in the cove below him: shadowy forms materialised spontaneously and began to slip across the sand towards the cliffs. They were primeval, amphibious shapes; indistinct, but emanating an aura of unthinkable antiquity. Slap of fin and flipper, glister of salt-polished hide. Humanoid, but far from human, far from Grigori too.

Are these mine to command? The shapes paused in their blundering progress, as if a noise had alerted them. Dark heads lifted and tasted the air. His scent would be carried to them; the salty, musky perfume of his masculinity, the smoky incense aroma of his thoughts.

A voice cut into his mind. *Where? Where?* Shemyaza was filled with anxiety and fear and a desperate need for haste. On the sand below, he saw the vague outline of a woman kneeling down. She patted the beach around her with urgent fingers, as if she were searching for something. Like the shadowy amphibians, she too appeared blind; her movements were undirected and random. She investigated the same area again and again, her hands skimming over the untested areas of sand. Shemyaza sensed that if he allowed it, he could recognise this woman. He forced his perception away from her and gazed out to sea.

Above the waves, the sky was greeny blue, bloated with clouds, which glowed with an eerie phosphorescence. Lithe, dark shapes frolicked in the hectic foam below, and Shemyaza could hear the deep, fluting bells of their voices. Their cries inspired him with a fierce excitement. He felt at once aroused and tranquil. As he gazed at the tumbling forms in the waves, he noticed that one of them had become still. It appeared to raise its head from the water, some yards out from shore. Something about its posture, the sense that this creature saw and recognised him, filled Shemyaza with anticipation. The beast looked as if it was swimming towards the beach, but as it approached, Shemyaza realised it was a human or humanoid figure that was walking out of the sea. It halted some feet from where the waves licked at the land, and held out its arms. Its perfect, slim body was androgynous. Although the smudge of male genitals could be discerned, its shape suggested femininity. Its hair was plastered to its chest, which was covered in weed and what appeared to be limpets. Its skin shone like nacre in the unnatural light and its eyes were dreaming holes in its long, hollow face. But for its lack of height, it would have looked like a drowned Watcher, disgorged by the sea. Something about the creature made Shemyaza think of Daniel; the boyish body, the aura of mystery. Was Daniel projecting an image to him, lying abandoned in uneasy slumber, suffering a nightmare? Then, Shemyaza saw the shape of Ishtahar shimmering within the occult figure below. The streaks upon its body were not swatches of damp weed, but curling tattoos. Shemyaza shuddered in apprehension. Ishtahar and Daniel in one body. It was his desire made flesh.

The androgynous figure let its mouth drop open and uttered a monotonous, wailing call. It sounded like the cry of birds, the symphonic bellow of whales. The song called to Shem: *My Lord of Light, you need a new guide to this old land. I am he. Come to me. Listen to my words, for I am the child of the serpent. I have waited here for your advent. Let me lead you to the secret caverns below the land. Let me walk before you. Give me your cloak of feathers. I will be your sacrifice.*

To Shemyaza, half drugged by the lure of the song, the offer seemed like an answer to a prayer. He wondered whether the figure below could be the spirit of one of the ancient Grigori, who had stepped ashore so long ago. Or perhaps it was one of their hybrid children, a secret guardian, whom the Parzupheim had not sniffed out. Perhaps the guardian had been waiting for Shem, and would only make itself known to him.

Come to me now. Step from the cliff, and come to me.

Shemyaza felt a wrenching in his mind and body. The urge to comply was tempered by fear or an instinct to survive. "I would come to you, but I cannot fly. I surrendered my wings."

Then call to the buzzard to lend you his wings. Call him and conjure him, then take this leap, the leap of faith...

Shemyaza gasped as if he'd been punched in the ribs. He flung back his head and his arms rose involuntarily towards the sky. He sucked in a lungful of the cold, wet air and tasted metal and ozone on his tongue. A sound was building up within his chest, swirling around inside him. He tried to disgorge it, vomit it out, but it seemed such a part of him, like a tumour. The sound expanded his lungs, growing in power, until with a concentration of effort he managed to expel it in a gust of breath. It flew out into the air, spreading its wings: an ear-splitting shriek. It was the weird, raw screech of a bird of prey. Now a flock of cries burst out of him. Shemyaza called to his bird-form, the shape he wore for astral flight. The wind flung his cries up into the air, scream upon scream, until the ground beneath his feet vibrated to the call. Soon, he heard the shush and clatter of wings approaching through the wind, and felt the bird-spirit buffet his head. Its claws tangled in his flying hair, and the carrion smell of it filled his head with the odour of rotten meat. Shemyaza called the spirit into him, until he was smothered in a mantle of fetid stench. He felt the cloak of feathers form around him, snug around his raised arms. He leaned forward into the wind, and felt its fierce, elemental fingers push up against the feathers.

Shemyaza had flown a thousand times in his mind, during trance. But never had he attempted the practice in reality. The smell of the wings surrounded him. He could feel the sharp ends of pinions digging into his flesh. This was no vision, but truth.

Now fly! Now come to me! The figure on the shore was glowing like the bilious clouds with a wan, greenish-yellow lustre.

Shemyaza flexed his wings and stepped from the cliff into a void.

The ground rushed up to meet him, each detail of the rocks below brought into sharp focus. Nano-seconds stretched into eternity. He knew he was falling fast, yet it seemed to take forever to reach the ground. *I was tricked! I am dying!* The scapegoat. Pushed from the cliff. Panic surged through his body, almost occluding consciousness. Then the ground disappeared, and he was falling into a black abyss. Down. Down. Through time. It could only be backwards.

Shemyaza fell from the sky, a burning angel. The sun was hot upon his wings and below him stretched a range of spiky mountains, which he knew were of the lost land of Eden. He thought he would fall straight to the ground and threshed his pinions in terror, but soon he remembered the technique of it, and soared upwards, riding the sizzling thermals. He flew over the mountains, until he saw the familiar landmarks of the Garden, Kharsag, a valley of fertility concealed by the punishing crags. This was the settlement of the Anannage, whom humanity called the Serpent People, the Feathered Serpents, the Angels. It was place of his birth, his torment and his death. In this place he'd held the office of Watcher, and humans knew him as a son of God, a son of the High Lord Anu. The Lord called all the Watchers his sons and claimed to love them.

Shemyaza circled the Garden several times. On the southern side, the mountains descended into the lush fertile lowlands, where the Anannage had conducted their education programmes with humans, whom they considered to be a primitive race. On the northern side, cliffs shielded the Garden from a barren wilderness where only savages lived. Instinctively, Shemyaza was drawn to this direction.

Half a day's walk north from the Garden, there was a place holy to the Anannage. They called it the Bowl of Giving and Receiving. Here, they offered sacrifices to the Elders, the source of their intelligence that existed beyond the universe. The Bowl was a large flat plateau on the mountainside, which hung out over a tortuous slope of scree that led down to the desert wilderness below. Shem recognised it immediately, and his wings faltered. He knew what he would see at this place, what he'd been brought here to remember.

A large amount of people had gathered on the Bowl, all dressed in ceremonial robes. A ritual was taking place there. Shemyaza flew lower, aware that no-one could sense his presence. He felt he should be reluctant to witness what he knew to be happening, but was empty of feeling. Then he saw himself down there.

The young Shemyaza: a foolish romantic, being led to the place of sacrifice by a phalanx of Serafim.

His older consciousness looked down in revulsion and despising. *Stupid idiot,* he thought. *You believed you were honoured and that your sacrifice was holy, but that was only a disguise for punishment. You fell for it, and then took the hardest fall.*

Ultimately, he had died because of his love for Ishtahar and the fruits of his bitterness, which had burgeoned from the punishment he'd suffered. But the events taking place below him now preceded the sentence of death by many years. This was the information that Daniel had not recalled and which had existed in Shem's memory only dimly. Now, it came gushing back with harsh clarity.

Long before the events that led to Shemyaza's execution, Anu's viziers had loosed their poison tongues in the Mountain House where Anu sat upon his throne. They had told the High Lord that Shemyaza and his colleagues had taken human lovers and were revealing Anannage secrets to the women. Anu had been astounded and angry, but his full wrath had not been invoked. He had been prepared to be lenient and had withheld the sentence of death. As Shemyaza was seen as the ringleader in this carnal cabal, Anu had held him responsible for his brothers' actions.

"You must be shrived of your sins, my son," he had said. "You shall be banished into the wilderness, and through your suffering shall expiate the transgressions of your brethren. Your sacrifice shall be that of comfort and warmth, and the love of your people. But when you have suffered enough and have learned true humility, you must return and instruct the Watchers in piety."

Ashamed at having been caught with his human lover, Shemyaza, young and devout, had thanked Anu for his mercy. He forced himself to view Ishtahar, his beloved, as a wicked seductress, who had tempted him with evil. He expelled from his mind all memory of their love and the happiness it gave them. She was a black and crawling thing, greedy and corrupt. Only the privations of exile could burn the contamination of her from his body and soul.

On the day of the sacrifice, Anu's serpent priests had stripped Shemyaza naked and rubbed his body with golden dust, so that he shone like the sun. They led him to the plateau that overlooked the savage lands and there a goat with gilded horns was sacrificed in his honour. They anointed the shining body of Shemyaza with the goat's blood, to give him the speed and agility of the animal as he roamed the wilderness. The blood also represented the sins of himself and his brothers, and those of the humans who had transgressed with them. Maidens sang and rattled bells as the blood was painted onto his skin. He had been drugged with the secret of the poppy, and smiled like an imbecile, his heart full of love and joy and the fierce desire to transcend his sin. The highest lords and ladies of the settlement came one by one to kiss his gilded lips, until Anu himself stepped forward. He took Shemyaza's chin in his hand and said, "Carry these sins out into the barren land, my most beautiful son. Purge yourself of them, and all who sinned shall be likewise purged. What has begun may be reversed."

"I will, Father."

Anu smiled gently and brushed his lips over Shemyaza's mouth. "Most beloved of my children," he said, and lifted Shemyaza in his arms. The Lord was taller than all other Anannage. In his hold, Shemyaza seemed no larger than a child.

There was no struggle. Anu carried his son to the edge of the plateau and then, as if releasing a captive bird, threw him into the air.

The gathering hurried to watch Shemyaza's fall. His drugged body bounced and jerked down the long slope of loose scree that led to the wilderness. Presently, all that could be seen was a smudge of gold and red, and the body lay still, its limbs sprawled out like a discarded puppet. Anu raised his arms, "Rejoice my people. Take meat and drink in my son's honour!" And the sacrificial goat was skinned and gutted, spitted and placed over a fire. Servants carried great barrels of wine out into the open. Soon, the plateau rang to the sounds of merriment and celebration.

Shemyaza, hanging onto life far below, heard these sounds. He had expected a beatific experience, something like astral flight, but now he lay broken and bleeding, discarded upon the rocks. He resented the sound of feasting above him. No-one knew whether he was dead or alive, and he realised it didn't matter. He had made the sacrifice. Now they could breathe more easily, sure that Anu's rage was appeased. *I will not die,* Shemyaza thought, energised by rage. *I will survive and return.*

He lay there, unmoving, until the sun sank behind the mountains. His mouth was dry and he was delirious with thirst. His skin had been blistered by the relentless heat. His brain and body throbbed with indescribable pain. His soul was withered with grief and stupefied amazement at what had been done to him. Only his will could keep him alive. As a cool tongue of breeze whispered over the desert, promising the sharper fangs of chilly night, Shemyaza crawled from the scree. Naked he went out into the wilderness, a bitter, desolate and lonely creature. He was beyond pain and his vision was stripped of its serpent scales. There could be no illusion. He had not been honoured, but scorned. Others feasted above him, as guilty as he of transgression, yet he had held out his arms to carry all of their sins. Without remorse, they had handed them over. *Take our shame, take it, that we may live and earn our father's pleasure once more.*

Like Cain, Shemyaza haunted the desert. For many days he staggered brokenly through day and night, burned by the sun, scalded by the ice of midnight. His wounds festered and raged upon his body. His cracked ribs screamed their fury. Each dawn, he licked scant moisture from the leaves of spindly plants and occasionally fell upon a small, desert creature and devoured it.

Eventually, he came upon a tribe of primitive people. These were not like the lowland folk, whom Anu's people had adopted and educated. They were violent, ignorant creatures, true savages. They were nomadic and fought brutal wars with other wandering tribes. Being close to animals, their instincts advised them not to kill the blistered, blackened figure that lurched out of the heat-haze towards their huddle of tents. He was abnormally tall, and an invisible fire burned all around him. The people knew the legends of the angels who lived in the High Place beyond the desert. When an angel fell from the clouds, the speed of his flight burned his skin and seared away his wings.

They circled Shemyaza cautiously as he staggered forward, and watched him, curious and patient.

For three days, he sat upon the parched ground just beyond their settlement, and refused to utter a word. The women brought him bowls of goat's milk, which he picked up with his withered

hands and gulped from greedily. His face was scored with the
wounds of the elements, but his eyes burned fierce and blue, like a
mad child's eyes. His hair was bleached white and hung to his waist
in coarse tangles. It was his only garment. In places, his blackened
skin shone gold, as if the pollen of his ruined wings still clung to
him. One of the young men was brave enough to approach him and
poke him cautiously with a wooden staff. Shemyaza bared his frightening white teeth in a snarl and the young man's staff burst aflame.
All those who saw this put their faces against the ground.

There was no doubt now that this man had come down from
the High Place where the angels lived. He had come to them.

On the third day, Shemyaza grabbed hold of one of the girls
who brought him food, threw her down upon the dusty ground and,
in full view of her astonished playmates, stormed the gates of her
body's temple. A group of tribesmen ran up and down like anxious
jackals some feet away from him, unsure whether to intervene or
not. The girl, who was already used to such treatment from her
brothers, lay quiescent beneath him. When he was replete, he tossed
the girl aside and stood up.

"I am naked!" he said in the human tongue. "Bring me
garments."

After this, the women brought him a dark robe and gave him
meat to eat. The whole community sensed his power and his energy. He told them to build him a dwelling, and gave them specific
instructions on its dimensions. It must be ten cubits high, thirty
cubits long and twelve cubits wide.

"I do not want to stoop and cower in my own tent," he told
them. "I want to stand up straight."

The dwelling was constructed of wooden frames, fitted together to form a rectangular structure. It was covered in swathes of
finely woven fabric, over which were stretched goatskins and the
hides of rams, which were dyed red. It was open at the eastern end,
but screened by a heavy curtain. Within, drapes of fine fabric created a private sanctuary for him, where his took his sleep. Around
the dwelling, was an open courtyard, surrounded by linen curtains
on a framework of bronze posts and silver rods.

While his new home was being constructed, Shemyaza lived
among the dry rocks, some distance from the settlement. He would
speak to no-one, but accepted food from the people. Once the dwelling
was built, Shemyaza moved into it. He washed away the grime and

dust of the desert and the crusts fell from his wounds. Beneath it, he was a man of bronze, whose hair was a halo of light. The tribes-people, being dark and swarthy, had never beheld such beauty. Shemyaza became obsessed with fastidious cleanliness. He required all those who attended him to wash themselves in ritual fashion, and gave specific instructions concerning the preparation of his food. Occasionally, when someone angered him with inattention to detail, he remembered how to summon a blaze of energy, and blasted the miscreant on the spot. The people believed that he called down fire from heaven. He became a hard, dark god, and the people revered him.

After a year, Shemyaza's hot madness cooled, and he decided to make his adopted people great. Anu had nurtured the lowland people; Shemyaza would evolve his own race of followers. Like the gentle lowlanders, they needed to be educated and brought on. First, he taught them about weapons and the arcana of forging metal. Then he instructed them in the strategies of battle. During this time, he took their women to his bed and spawned monstrous children with them. It became necessary to teach the wise women of the tribe how to cut open a woman's belly, so that a child too large for natural birth could be delivered. In his dwelling, he heard the screams of the women as the knives cut their flesh, or the screams of those who were too afraid of the knife and allowed the child to tear them apart as it fought its way into the world.

Shemyaza sent his armies out into the desert wilderness and beyond, and many cities fell before them. He taught them how to shatter the thickest walls with the sorcery of sounds. He taught them how to instil panic and fear in the hearts of their enemies. When his people angered him, he punished them with leprosy and pestilence, instilling the thoughts of disease into their gullible minds, so that they took root and blossomed in sores and sickness. But when his people pleased him, he gave them the gift of euphoria and victory in battle. He bestowed dark wisdom and made legends of their warriors. All the time, he kept his identity secret. The tribespeople guarded the mystery of their powerful god, held it close to their hearts, and although rumours of their sorcery abounded in adjacent lands, no-one uncovered the true source of their power.

After seven years, Shemyaza knew it was time to return to Kharsag. He told his people that, wherever they travelled, they should continue to erect his tent for him, but that henceforth only his spirit would dwell within it.

"I have made of you a great and powerful race," he told them. "Now, you must learn to rule yourselves."

He wrapped himself in a dark robe and covered his face with a black scarf. Carrying only a staff and a water leather, he walked back towards the mountains of his birth.

At first, Shemyaza was welcomed by his people like a Prodigal Son. Anu wept when Shemyaza came to him in his Hall of Meetings. They embraced as father and son, and Anu ordered that a great feast be prepared. But although Shemyaza smiled and kissed his brethren, who all seemed so joyous to see him alive, his heart was no longer the molten gold of love, but the hard rock of experience. He gazed about the Garden, which once had so delighted him, and saw it for what it was. The Anannage danced and feasted in delusion, ignoring the hard, bitter reality beyond the mountains. Famine, disease and war raged out there, but the Anannage chose to believe that all humanity were as the meek lowland folk, who humbly obeyed the commands of the serpent people. Their oasis of learning, with its bright water and viridian fields, was a hollow conceit.

Anu sensed a change in Shemyaza, but put it down to maturity. Physically, he was very different from the pale, attenuated creature who'd been hurled over the cliff. His skin was no longer soft and white, but seamed and weathered. His beauty was no longer puerile, but fierce. His mind was like an armoury now, and his tongue was the sharpest blade. Although he did not contradict Anu and his viziers outright, he earned a reputation for asking awkward questions. Subtly, he brought their attention to issues that the Lords of Kharsag would rather ignore. Anu was entertained by this, although others at the Mountain House were nervous of Shemyaza's bluntness. One day, Anu would take offence.

For another seven years, Shemyaza existed as a bright but challenging star of the Anannage. During this time, he took a vizier for himself, the boy Daniel, who had been groomed from infancy for his role. Daniel had been marked for the Mountain House, but Shemyaza asked Anu if he might take Daniel for himself. Anu agreed to this, perhaps thinking his dour son needed company, and that Daniel, being lovely, might bring perfume back to Shemyaza's barren bedchamber. Since his return, he had lain with neither male nor female, spending all of his time in trance or speaking with the Elders, who were beyond this world.

When Daniel was sixteen, and convinced his Lord would never touch him in love, Shemyaza initiated him into the ways of the flesh. His friends, privately, rejoiced. Perhaps soon some of Shemyaza's former carefree abandon might reappear. He never went down to the lowlands.

Then, one day, perhaps as a test, Anu sent Shemyaza down to the house of Hebob, the father of Ishtahar. Shemyaza did not appear concerned about this request, exhibiting neither eagerness nor reluctance. In his heart, he felt safe, for he did not expect to find his lost love still living in the house of her father. Fourteen years had passed. Now, she would be married, with a host of brats around her skirts, her beauty all used up and withered away. But as he stepped into the courtyard outside Hebob's dwelling, with Daniel at his side, he saw her come round the side of the building. She held a pannier under one arm, and her long black hair hung loose over her linen-swathed breasts. Although she wore her years on her face, her beauty had intensified. Shemyaza's heart stopped in his chest for the space of two beats. She saw him and equally started, her eyes widening, although her mouth became a grim line. Words passed between them without sound. She was a prisoner of her father's house, a slave to the temple because of her power as an oracle and channel. Her commerce with Shemyaza had brought her a strange reputation; she was both feared and shunned. No man would marry her, or wanted to plough the ground where Shemyaza had sown his seed.

Their thought contact was like the brush of feathers. She still loved him, though she thought he'd betrayed her. She'd known he'd returned to Kharsag, yet he'd sent her no word, not of comfort or friendship. In turn, he still partly blamed her for what had happened to him. She had seduced him in the corn, changed his life and his destiny, doomed him, but looking at her now, he realised he still loved her, and her beauty was an ache in his mind and heart. She was no longer a lissom maid, but a woman of grace and power. In that moment of brief contact, their contract was made. It was inevitable.

Their meetings were more clandestine than ever before. Shemyaza raged against this. He had known many women during his sojourn in the desert and resented having to creep down the mountains like a crafty lizard to take his pleasure. Ishtahar was frightened of the power of his feelings, his bitterness and frustration.

He seemed both more and less human to her now. The shining prince she had loved amid the corn had hardened into a relentless idol of bronze.

Covertly, he made contact once again with the tribespeople of the desert wilderness, who still worshipped him as a god. He incited them to war against the gentle lowland folk, crowning his monstrous sons with iron and blood. They were known and feared as the Nephilim, the hybrid sons of angels, ferocious and heartless warriors who destroyed the farms, the temples, the astronomical observatories and the sacred gardens. They raped women and devoured children. They bathed themselves in human blood.

Eventually, Anu's viziers realised who was behind the depredations and Shemyaza had to take sanctuary in a mountain fortress, which he charged his sons to build for him. Fearing for Ishtahar's safety, Shemyaza had the Nephilim enter her father's house at night, kill her brothers, and bring her to him. In his sanctuary, they would be safe. Djinn guarded the narrow, treacherous paths that led to fortress, and Nephilim hid among the rocks, ready to stone and impale any interlopers.

But Ishtahar was horrified by what Shemyaza had become and what he planned for their people. She knew that the Elders beyond the stars, with whom she had always communed, abhorred her involvement in Shemyaza's schemes. She could no longer reach them in her mind. For the space of a moon, she fought her conscience, then, beneath the cloak of a moonless night, managed to flee the fortress.

For many days, Ishtahar struggled across the cruel mountains. Swooning, she staggered into Kharsag, and there redeemed herself in the eyes of the Elders by betraying Shemyaza's whereabouts to Anu. Her heart was torn by love and bitter disappointment. The Seraphim took her back to the house of her father, and here she was shut into a room, from which all light was barred.

Alone, by the feeble flame of a tiny lamp, she wept for her beloved. How could their passion have become so warped, so blighted? Her family scorned her, and called her a murderess. It was no longer safe for her to leave the house.

As Ishtahar wept, so the sky rained tears. Her grief mirrored Anu's anger. He sought to purge the land of evil, and had the angels point the sonic instruments, which they used in their agriculture and to control the weather, towards the sky. The sun was hidden behind a shroud of rumbling clouds and the crops sickened in the fields. The rain fell and fell, until the land was flooded, and the Nephilim armies who foraged there were washed away.

The lowlands lay under water for the span of two moons. In his fury, Anu destroyed not only the lands below, but the settlement of his own people. The fabulous terraces of Kharsag were scourged by the torrents of a fierce deluge. The black domes of glass, the spreading fields of fecund crops, the glittering waterfalls, and shady arbours, were blanketed in mud. In the lowlands, many perished, but for the patriarch Noah and his family, whom Anu elected to spare. Through them, he planned to restart his experiments with cultivation, once the flood had passed.

Shemyaza and his monstrous generals were routed by Anu's warriors. The fallen renegade was taken alive and dragged, bound, to Kharsag, which lay in ruins. Ishtahar also survived the wars and the flood and was once again taken prisoner by the Anannage. Wary of her power, they interrogated her, and punished her by forcing her to watch Shemyaza's execution. After that, they incarcerated her in a temple, where she spent the rest of her life lamenting and uttering dire prophecies. Sometimes, when the moon was dark and caustic rain fell from the sky, bringing echoes of the flood, she would be let out upon the roof of the temple, where she would hold out her arms to the hidden stars, and the place where the soul of her lover hung for eternity; Orion, Shemyaza's celestial dungeon.

Shemyaza hung in the clouds, watching this final chapter of his tragic history. He saw Ishtahar, a gaunt, middle-aged woman, with streaks of grey in her flowing hair, hold out her arms to him, but she could not see him, nor hear him call her name. The rain soaked his wings until they were too heavy to hold him aloft and he fell, roaring, into a roiling torrent that carried him out to sea. For millennia he was tossed by crashing waves until he beheld ahead of him a wondrous sight. He saw a coastline, and its colours were red, gold and green. The slick cliff-face looked like a great serpent hugging the land. Here, Shemyaza shot out of the waves and flexed his wings. Reborn, he burst up into the sky like a comet and hung over the undulating cliffs. As he flew towards them, he saw the shape of a great lion looking out to sea, a natural simulacrum in the rock. Drawn to this, he landed between the lion's paws. The image of the sphinx was an ancient memory of his people, rooted in the time even before

Kharsag. His ancestors had originated in the place of the sphinx. As he gazed at the lion's face, its eyes glowed a dull red. Its voice boomed out. "Have you come to sing the lament for Serapis?" Between its paws, an enormous gateway materialised, causing the rock to crack and groan. Its pillars were scored with arcane carvings; hieroglyphs older than the most ancient of the pharaohs, a code of triangles, circles, curling lines and dots.

Shemyaza could not sing the lament. He was still too full of bitterness and anger, incapable of grief or passion.

The lion guardian uttered a low, rumbling growl that sounded as if the rocks of the earth were clashing together far underground. "I see into your soul, Shemyaza. Your heart is touched with the blackness of frost. You cannot enter the gate."

"Can I not?" Shemyaza did not care about the gateway, or the underworld he knew lay behind it, but he resented the critical tone of the guardian's words. He thought he would use the force of his anger to blast the gate apart. He would go down into the underworld, take the serpent by the throat, and throttle the life from it, awake or asleep. Leaning forward, he placed a hand upon one of the stone pillars.

The guardian roared in rage and its eyes spat bolts of crimson flame. Shemyaza was thrown backwards by the blast, back into the sea. He uttered a final cry of rage and hatred, before the waves closed over him.

"Wake, Shining One. Awake!"

Shemyaza opened his eyes. He was lying flat on his back on the cold, hard sand of Mermaid's Cove. His clothes were soaked through and covered in seaweed and fetid scum. Above him the sky was steely grey with a sullen dawn. Sea birds circled and screamed. A woman was leaning over him, swathed in a dark cloak with a hood. Her fair hair hung forward in ragged curls. She placed a soft hand upon his shoulder.

"Fear not, Holy One," she said. "For I am here."

Chapter Twenty-Four
The Covening

Daniel awoke and knew that Shem had gone. A corrupt sweetness lined the back of his throat, a taste of nightmare. In his dreams, he had flown above the world, his shoulder blades adorned with powerful wings. The freedom of flight had been exhilarating, but then someone had soared up behind him and cut off his wings with enormous shears. He'd fallen to earth, showered in his own blood. Now, he sat up abruptly in the bed and found himself alone. There was a space in his reality that Shemyaza had once filled, more than a simple absence from the room.

He got out of bed and dressed himself hurriedly. He would have to check the house and garden before raising an alarm, but in his heart he knew he would find nothing.

Daniel rebuked himself as he hastened along the silent corridors of High Crag. He should have taken Sofia's advice last night and been gentle with Shem, let him settle into his new role. Instead, he had carped and nagged and bullied. Shem had been angry and confused. He must have lain awake thinking about the argument. Now, he had walked out.

Could Shem have gone to Salamiel? Perhaps Sofia had been lying in wait, aware of the quarrel, pushing it along with her will and her desire.

He went to the drawing-room, where French windows led to the garden. The colour of the light outside looked unreal; greenish purple. Steeling himself, Daniel forced himself to open the windows and step beyond them. The dawn was attempting to fist its way through the dull, oppressive sky. The air felt strange against Daniel's skin, alive with unseen presences. He sensed that Shem had recently come this way. It was even possible he'd decided to go down to the beach. Had he chosen to fulfil his destiny after all? Perhaps, resolved, he had walked along the shore to the lion guardian of the underworld. And maybe the gate had opened to him, and he had been swallowed by the land. Daniel shivered. As Shem's vizier and psychic earthing rod, he should have been with him. As it was, a senseless quarrel might have propelled Shem alone, in a rage, into danger.

Daniel was drawn to approach the cliff edge and walked down the sloping lawn and through the rustling, glistening rhododendrons. As he emerged onto the mossy path beyond, he saw a tall figure limned against the metallic sky. It had to be Shem. Daniel paused, horrified. Shem was leaning forward, almost as if he was contemplating throwing himself over the edge. Daniel knew he must not cry out or dash forward. He must approach cautiously and, when he was within Shem's earshot, utter a few soothing words. The wind made eerie noises, like distant screams or the cry of birds. Overhead, the clouds boiled as if electrified by an exotic storm. Daniel saw Shem raise his arms to the sky. A piercing, hideous shriek echoed out. Daniel instinctively crouched down and put his hands over his ears. The air was full of invisible wings: beating, clattering, whispering. When Daniel dared to look up, it seemed as if Shem himself was winged, poised to take flight. Before Daniel could move or utter a sound, Shem let himself drop forward, arms still outflung, and fell from the edge of the cliff.

Panic stricken, Daniel ran towards the wall and clambered over its shifting stones. He threw himself down on his belly and peered down the side of the cliff, sure he would see Shem's smashed body lying on the beach below. But Shem had vanished. The sand below was sepulchrally white, and empty.

Daniel rested his cheek upon the sandy turf and expelled a groaning sigh. Shem had taken flight. And Daniel could not follow him.

At first, Daniel wasn't sure that Enniel believed him when he related what he'd seen in the garden. It was only when Sofia entered his study and seemed confident of Daniel's story that he started to look worried.

"We must send people down to the cove," he said. "There's a chance Shemyaza will turn up there."

Sofia shrugged. "It's out of our hands now, Enniel. Why worry? What's started is started. There's nothing we can do."

"And what exactly has started?" Enniel snapped.

"I think you know," Sofia replied. "He has chosen to enter the underworld."

"But that's ridiculous!" Enniel blustered. "He's had no preparation. He's not ready."

"He's as ready as he'll ever be, I'm sure," Sofia said.

"If he approaches the serpent now, he will most likely be destroyed."

Sofia laughed coldly. "Oh, Enniel, face reality. Shemyaza is no ordinary being. What would burn you or I might simply be the heat of a lover's body to him."

Daniel was unnerved by Sofia's apparent lack of concern. He had a nagging feeling she knew exactly where Shem was, and that it wasn't in the underworld. He wanted to speak to her alone. Sofia, perhaps sensing this, made it clear she had no desire for private conversation. When Daniel asked her outright if they could talk, she spoke of having things to do.

"Then I shall speak in front of Enniel," he said.

"Speak about what?" Enniel asked.

Sofia gave Daniel a hard look. "Yes, my dear. About what? Shem's safety, or even that of your friends?"

"Which friends?" Enniel demanded, but Daniel understood her meaning.

"Shemyaza is not where you think he is," Sofia said coldly. "Of that I can assure you in all sincerity."

"I'd like to know what you're talking about," Enniel said.

Sofia expelled another light, tinkling laugh. "Well, I suppose I'd have to tell you sooner or later." She fixed Daniel with an appraising stare. "The fact is, I have the Winter twins in safe keeping. Daniel obviously thinks I've spirited Shemyaza away to increase my collection. This is far from the case. It is my opinion that Shemyaza has taken matters into his own hands and has decided to act independently of any of us."

Daniel was confused by her frankness. She had not mentioned Salamiel but did not seem worried that Daniel might. What if he recounted to Enniel all that she had said to Shem and himself in the garden the day before? He couldn't understand the woman. She twisted and turned like an eel.

"I wish you'd told me about the twins before," Enniel said, a little lamely.

"Why?" Sofia shrugged. "To be honest, the Winters really are insignificant in the scheme of things." She sat down on the leather sofa. "They're very upset by all that's happened, so I thought it best to keep them away from the centre of operations. They're staying with a friend of mine nearby, quite safe."

Daniel hoped Enniel would not accept this glib explanation, and was gratified when he asked, "So when exactly did you *come across* the twins? The last we knew they'd been abandoned in London, at the mercy of some rather sinister characters."

Sofia was not ruffled by the question. "Well, they were of no use to the people who were looking for Shemyaza, and were, in effect, overlooked. All I did was, on a hunch, send a couple of my people up to London the following day to sniff around the Assembly Rooms. Lily and Owen were still there—terrified and confused—but unharmed. I must admit I felt sorry for them. I think Lily Winter has had more than enough of the shenanigans that follow Shemyaza around. She begged me for peace and quiet, and I was happy to help her."

Daniel knew that most of what Sofia said was untrue. He longed to relate, in a cool and cutting manner, all she had said to him concerning Salamiel and the twins. He wanted to expose her completely, and force her to answer probing questions from Enniel, but he was afraid. If she'd been cagey about Lily and Owen, he would have felt more confident. But it was as if she was daring him to initiate combat. Daniel had no doubt that, if he did, he'd only incur terrible retribution. So he kept quiet, and had to endure the sense of triumphant smugness that emanated from her mind. Still, he was fairly sure Shemyaza wasn't with Salamiel and the twins. In that case, Sofia's explanation seemed reasonable. He *had* gone off alone, either to fulfil his destiny or to escape it. Unless the woman had taken him somewhere else. Daniel couldn't see past her psychic armour to determine that. He realised he had to accept he could do nothing at the moment. As soon as was able, he'd attempt to make contact with Lily. Perhaps if he had an ally, he could find a way to penetrate Sofia's armour.

Enniel's staff spent the whole morning searching the coastline and surrounding countryside for Shemyaza. Most of the Parzupheim had stayed overnight at High Crag, and the two who hadn't lived relatively nearby and could be recalled immediately. At noon, Enniel convened another meeting, and Daniel was required to relate to the Parzupheim all that he had seen that morning. He elected not to mention the argument he and Shem had had the night before.

The Parzupheim seemed suspicious of Daniel, as if he was responsible for Shem's disappearance. "You assume too much of his mantle for yourself."

Daniel endured this accusation without comment, because he did not want the Parzupheim to know that Shemyaza had tried to pass responsibility to him.

Another spoke up. "Perhaps you drove him away."

As this tallied with Daniel's punishing thoughts about the quarrel, he was suffused with a sense of paranoia. His voice faltered. "It's not my fault! There was nothing I could do."

"As his vizier, it was your duty to be alert for him, to help him at all times."

"So, you were *asleep* at the time Shemyaza left the house?"

Daniel felt as if he was fighting for breath. "I thought he was sleeping too."

"Ah. I see. And, in the garden, he just *disappeared* before your eyes?"

"I *told* you," Daniel said miserably. "It looked like he jumped from the cliff, but when I ran to the edge, there was no sign of him. Anywhere!" As he listened to his own voice, Daniel came to the quiet conclusion that Shem wasn't anywhere in the vicinity in a physical sense. Regardless of his suspicions concerning Sofia and her true role in Shemyaza's development, he had seen, with his own eyes, Shem plunge into astral flight, and it appeared he had taken his earthly flesh with him. That could only mean he'd entered the dreamtime of the serpent...surely?

Sofia watched him through slitted eyes, although she deigned to make little contribution to the debate. Daniel heard himself become increasingly defensive, which inspired certain members of the Parzupheim to spice their attack with ever more causticity. A few, including Enniel, rallied to Daniel's defence and suggested that the Parzupheim's attitude to Shemyaza the previous day might have impelled him to act alone. This remark provoked a hot retort, and soon several seated around the table were blaming each other for Shem's disappearance.

Daniel, still under attack from another quarter, couldn't prevent himself from raising his voice. "None of you know what the hell's going on!" he yelled. "You with your stuffy rituals, legacies and histories! That's all you care about! It's all you have, and believe me, it doesn't mean anything! It doesn't relate to what's happening now!"

His words conjured a silence, until one voice broke it with sarcasm. "We are lucky to have such an expert among us."

"Shem's gone," Daniel said. "He's gone down to the underworld. *It's all started* and you don't even know it." Feeling these words were poignant enough, Daniel rose with dignity and left the room. His heart was pounding with fury and fear, but he managed to keep haste from his steps. He could feel Sofia's eyes boring into his back, and sensed her grudging approval.

Once free of the meeting room, he fled out into the garden, hid himself away in an arbour and surrendered himself to tears. He wept for Shem, he wept for himself. The past hour had only convinced him that what Sofia said was right. Shem had gone to face the serpent alone. Daniel was filled with a sense of hopelessness and impotency. "Shem, Shem, where *are* you?" he murmured into his hands. "How could you leave me here with them? Why aren't I with you?"

Lily felt as if she'd been staying at Pharos for weeks rather than just a few scant days. She'd already grown fond of the house, and the wild landscape around it. Salamiel had told her that soon she'd be reunited with her friends, but Lily no longer really cared. She enjoyed spending time in Salamiel's company and knew that, if she'd wanted to, she could seduce him. It was clear to her that he found her attractive, yet he did not push his attentions upon her. She sensed his reticence was due to simple respect. He liked to hear her stories about Shem, so she told him as much as she could remember of what had happened in Little Moor. Just to tease him, she even described, in graphic detail, the sex she'd had with Othman. Salamiel, however, listened with a scientific detachment.

In the afternoons, Salamiel often sought Lily's company. Usually, she was to be found in his library, not because of the books especially, but because of the smell of the room, and the way its dark walls played with the soft light that spilled through the window. Nina brought piles of garish magazines into the house, which Lily liked to browse through, but on the day that Shem disappeared, something impelled her to lay out her scrying stones on the baize-topped desk beneath the window. She wished she could read them properly. When she threw them down, significant patterns seemed to occur: Marmoset next to Zahtumuzgi, with Tarturophane nudging close. That must mean something surely, but what exactly? She could impose at least three interpretations on the result, but which, if any, were appropriate?

Salamiel came into the room, and stood behind her chair. He looked down at the stones with interest. "So what does the future hold?"

Lily shrugged, moved a few stones with her fingertips. "I don't know. I wish I did." She explained about how Johcasta used to read the stones. "I can remember all of their names, but I just can't understand their meanings."

Salamiel made a soft purring sound of interest and scooped up the stones in one long-fingered hand. Carelessly, he cast them onto the baize. "There. It is simple. A time of great change is indicated." His hand skimmed the stones. "And here, the frenzies of lust and greed." He grinned. "Perhaps that is Sofia. What do you think?"

Lily frowned up at him. "Have you done this before?"

He smiled at her. "No. I don't need to have done. You told me enough about them for me to scry." He gathered the stones up again in his hand. "The secret is to let them speak to you. They might not mean the same thing twice. You have to let their personalities come through."

Lily grinned. "Will you teach me?"

"Of course." He sat down on the edge of the desk.

Lily couldn't help being more interested in the fall of his red-gold hair and the way the wan winter light softened his features than in what he was trying to tell her about scrying.

He is very beautiful, she thought. *They are all beautiful. I would like to make love to every Grigori in the world.*

As if he'd caught her thought, Salamiel paused and looked into her eyes. It was a long moment. He reached out as if to touch her face or hair.

The door to the library crashed open. Lily jumped and looking up, saw Sofia framed in the doorway. She looked feral and dangerous. Salamiel's hand sped discreetly back to his lap. "Sofia! What is it?" From her entrance, it was clear something had occurred.

"A private word, my dear," she said in an icy voice. "Now." Before Salamiel had even risen from the desk, she had left the room.

Lily watched him follow Sofia into the hall. Hopefully, Shem was already beginning to run rings round them. She didn't want him to be taken in by Sofia. As this thought formed in her mind, she was suffused with the presence of Daniel. She shivered. It was as if he'd passed like a spirit through her body. The contact was brief, but it left a sweet feeling in its wake. Lily took a deep breath. *Daniel.* She closed her eyes and relaxed, hoping that he was trying to contact her, but all sense of him had vanished.

Salamiel was gone only about five minutes. When he returned, he was alone, and his face was creased with worry. "What happened?" Lily asked him.

He shook his head. "Azazel has already gone into the underworld."

"What?"

Salamiel walked to the window, stroking his chin with one hand. "That is what Sofia has told me. There is a furor at High Crag because Azazel was missing this morning." Lily intuited that whatever Sofia had told him, he didn't totally believe it. "I'm not happy about this. He should be with me. I should be by his side when he faces the serpent."

Lily had already questioned Salamiel about Shem's tasks, although she still wasn't entirely sure whether the serpent was a real beast that could be touched or a spiritual being. "Is he in danger?"

Salamiel sighed and took her hand. "The serpent has the potential to be used for good or evil. It represents the creative force or building blocks of the universe, which is dualistic. Come, sit with me on the couch and I'll try to explain."

Lily was happy to let him lead her away from the window.

"When Grigori work magic, we utilise god forms to empower our rituals," he said. "For example, Ahura Mazda, a god of light, and his dark counterpart, Ahriman. You know, of course, that Azazel, as Peverel Othman, worked with Ahriman."

Lily nodded, and shuddered. "Yes, I can remember him being dark."

"The truth and the lie. Well, when the serpent is awoken, the destiny of this land depends upon which frequency the Shamir adopts in its unleashing. If Azazel's heart is true, and he is a channel for light and truth, then that is what the Shamir will carry into the land. But if he is not, then the land is doomed."

Lily felt faintly sick. "Salamiel, Shem isn't ready. He really isn't." There was a note of panic in her voice. "He's not the light."

Salamiel stared at her steadily for a few moments. "Then we must send the light of our love out to him, wherever he roams, and trust it will find him, give him strength and clarity."

When Emma heard of Shem's disappearance, it affected her more than she'd have believed. Unable to stay in the house, she put on her coat and walked down to the nearest village. She had an idea that Shem might have gone there. Perhaps it reminded him of Little Moor. With her hands thrust into the deep pockets of her overcoat, she walked down the steep road that led to the heart of the village. There was a strange, tense atmosphere to the place, almost as if the inhabitants had some inkling of what was going on at High Crag. Needing cigarettes, Emma went into the local post office. It was very similar to the shop she'd once run in Little Moor: dingy and dusty. There was a vast array of goods on sale, many with packaging that was old and fading. Two other women were in the shop, one of whom was being served by the post mistress. The customers were typical of the kind that used to frequent the post office in Little Moor: elderly women, stout of girth, in drab heavy coats and knitted hats. Emma wandered over to a rack of pale pink and cream birthday cards and flicked through them dispiritedly. The customer and the post-mistress were gossiping in low voices. How familiar this scene! Only a few short months ago, Emma had been a raddled crone, squatting on a stool beside her daughter's counter, idly chatting with whoever came into the shop. It was hard for her to believe she'd ever lived like that now. She sensed a silence behind her and turned round. All three women were looking at her: an everyday reaction to strangers in a small community. Emma stepped forward. "Hello, twenty Silk Cut, please."

The post-mistress moved with insulting lethargy to comply with Emma's request. Emma felt very uncomfortable standing there, fixed by the unsmiling stares of the women. Perhaps a direct question wouldn't go amiss, although she doubted she'd get a satisfactory reply.

"I'm looking for a friend of mine. I don't expect you get many visitors at this time of year, so he'd stand out a lot. He's a tall young man with long fair hair, very striking in appearance. Have you seen him?"

If anything, the silence around her intensified. The post mistress put a packet of cigarettes down on the counter. "That'll be two pounds, fifty-three."

Emma delved into her purse, discovered she'd only got a fistful of change and spent several awkward moments sorting it out.

"You from High Crag?" one of the customers asked unexpectedly.

Emma glanced at her, noticed the grey wisps of hair escaping beneath the pale blue hat, the soft pink skin of the face. "I'm staying there with friends, yes. Why?"

The old woman said nothing. Her eyes were unnaturally bright. Shuddering, Emma handed over the money, picked up her purchase and fled.

Outside, she withdrew a cigarette from the packet and lit it with relief. Weird old biddies! Unthinkable to remember she had once been like that. She began to amble down the main street of the village, which was lined by gift shops and cafes, shut up for the winter. Pausing to browse in an antique shop window, she became aware that someone was following her. She took a nervous draw of the cigarette but did not turn round, keeping her eyes fixed on the window. She would see the reflection of her pursuer in it.

Don't be ridiculous, she told herself. This isn't like you, Emma Manden. You're a hard bitch, remember, frightened of nothing.

Why had those old women unnerved her so much? Perhaps whoever followed her wasn't human. She remembered the hideous attackers at the Assembly Rooms with dread, and just had to turn round and see who was there. It was the customer from the shop, who'd asked if she was staying at High Crag.

Stupid! Emma thought. She isn't following you. She just left the shop after you, that's all.

She waited for the woman to walk past, but when the crone drew level with her, she stopped walking. Emma couldn't help recoiling. The old woman pulled herself to her full height and stuck out her chin.

"Yes?" Emma asked, rather belligerently. She had the distinct impression the old biddy was about to spit at her.

"You're not one of *them,* are you." It was a statement rather than a question.

"I beg your pardon?"

"What's your name?"

Emma uttered a small, dry laugh. "Excuse me? What business is that of yours?" She made to walk away, but the old woman grabbed her arm.

"You're Emma Manden, aren't you."

Emma's voice came out in a hiss. "How the Hell do you know?"

The old woman's stern face broke into a slow smile. "Oh, I have my ways."

"So what if I am? What's it to you?" Emma pulled her arm away roughly from the woman's surprisingly strong grip.

"You're the Shining One's follower. We know that."

Emma glanced to left and right up the street. She didn't know whether to run away or find out what the woman wanted to say to her. "I don't know what you mean."

"Oh yes you do. You want to talk to me."

"Do I?"

The woman nodded. "Aye. I'm Meggie Penhaligon. We have interests in common. You're looking for him today? Well, we've been waiting for him a long time. Now, carry my shopping home for me, will you? You'll be coming with me." She held out an ancient tartan bag, bulging with tins.

Emma stared at this object in amazement. "I don't think..."

"Be sensible, girl! We must talk. I'll not harm you." She shook the bag. "Take it."

Emma paused for a moment, pursed her lips, then took the bag. "All right." Her curiosity was aroused. There was no way she could walk away from this woman now.

Meggie led Emma to the other side of the village. They walked in silence, as whenever Emma began to ask a question, Meggie said, "Quiet! Not here! Just wait on."

When they reached the cottage, Meggie opened the front door, which was unlocked, and preceded Emma into the dark, cramped hallway. Moth-eaten stuffed heads of foxes yawned down from the walls. Meggie took Emma into the kitchen, where she methodically unpacked her shopping. Then, she opened a can of chicken soup and transferred it to a saucepan, which she placed over the range. Emma sat down at the enormous table without asking and lit another cigarette. Without comment, Meggie placed an old saucer in front of her, which Emma presumed she was to use as an ashtray.

"This is a lovely house," Emma said as Meggie prepared a pot of tea. The cottage was much bigger within than it had appeared from the outside. Through the back window, Emma saw a large lawn, where several picnic tables stood.

"It's fine for our needs," Meggie said. "Been in our family a long time."

"I can tell," Emma replied, flicking ash into the saucer.

Meggie smiled wryly, but said nothing. Emma wondered what connection this strange old woman, who was very clearly human, had with Shemyaza. She presumed by "Shining One" Meggie had meant Shem. She'd assumed, from comments Aninka had made, that the local community had no interaction with the Grigori. She glanced around the spacious kitchen. Dried herbs hung on the walls and various ornaments on the dresser were of a certain occult appearance. It was easy to infer Meggie was an old witch.

Meggie placed a large cup and saucer beside Emma's makeshift ashtray. Into this she poured a stream of dark tea from an enormous china teapot. Then she busied herself with transferring her soup from the saucepan to a bowl. "You want some?" she offered.

Emma shook her head. "No thank you. I'd just like to know what it is you want to talk to me about."

Meggie set her soup bowl down on the table. "The Watcher Shemyaza." She sat down and began to pour herself a cup of tea. "There's no point beating about the bush."

Emma laughed. "I'm intrigued. What interest have you in such an—er—*eastern* concept?"

Meggie set the tea-pot down on the table, covered it carefully with a cosy. "The Grigori are very much a part of this land, as were their ancestors. You know this. We've been waiting for Shemyaza to return, and now he has. He will reawaken the power of the land." She took a spoonful of soup, holding her cutlery with a daintily cocked little finger.

"How many of you know about this?" Emma asked. "The Grigori have no idea people around here are aware of what's going on, never mind that you have an interest in it." She took a sip of tea.

Meggie shrugged. "We've kept ourselves to ourselves, as have they. But Shemyaza's light is for all, human and Grigori alike." She drank more soup.

Emma watched her in a daze. The juxtaposition of this bizarre conversation with the banality of consuming a tinned lunch seemed virtually unreal. "So where do I come in? As you obviously know, I am staying with the Prussoes at the moment. I don't think they'd approve of me talking to you."

Meggie smiled. "I can see you're not a woman to bother about that. Now, at the moment, I'm following my instincts and the advice of my goddess, and I have to trust you. It goes against my principles to reveal my business to an outsider, but this is a crucial time and the fact is, we have a problem."

Emma listened while Meggie gave her a sketchy picture of how Tamara had cut herself free from them, and also how she'd appropriated their oracle.

"We know the Grigori will balk at using a human seer, even if he is Shemyaza's vizier, but we have no such reservations. The reason I'm talking to you is this: we want Daniel Cranton to work with us. At this time, all factions are working to awaken the serpent, and there is room for Grigori and Pelleth involvement alike. But Daniel belongs with us. He is human."

"I don't think the Prussoes would agree with you."

"Then why should they find out?"

Emma frowned. "I don't know. I'd have to speak to Daniel. The truth is..." she paused. "I'm afraid Shemyaza has gone missing."

Meggie pulled a puzzled face. "Missing?"

Emma nodded. "Yes. When we all woke up this morning, he'd disappeared, left the house. Enniel's people have been looking for him since then, but there's no trace. Daniel thinks Shem might've gone off alone to begin awakening the serpent."

"Then we should speak to Daniel as soon as possible."

Emma tapped her lips with the fingers of one hand. "You don't suppose Shem's disappearance could have anything to do with this Tamara woman you told me about?"

Meggie considered. "No, she doesn't have that much power, I'm sure. She couldn't work alone so effectively." She paused. "Can you bring Daniel to me tonight, or tomorrow?"

Emma smiled. "Have I agreed to help you?"

"You must. It is vital."

"Oh, all right, I'll see what I can do." She pursed her lips. "But what incentives can I offer him? He's beside himself with worry for Shem. The Grigori are giving him a hard time. I can't make any promises to you on his behalf."

Meggie's face was stony. "Tell him he must fulfil his part of the great destiny. That's all. He must come because it's ordained he should. He must follow his master into the underworld, but he shouldn't attempt it without support. We, the Pelleth of Cornwall, have been waiting centuries for this time. We are the ones who must stand beside and behind the boy of our blood, who is the astral channel for the Fallen King." Her eyes took on a feverish light. "When the Shining One comes out of the earth, all shall be reborn!"

Emma took a last drag from her cigarette, studied the old face before her. Were the Pelleth hoping that Shemyaza would give them extended life? Were they his nuns, awaiting a second coming and the night of holy marriage? She glanced down at her arm, her own tanned, young skin. If the Pelleth got hold of Shem, they might well eat him alive.

Chapter Twenty-Five
The Watcher and the Maiden

He awoke with the perfume of the sea filling his head, but he was not exposed to the elements; his body was warm.

Shemyaza opened his eyes. He lay naked upon a window-seat, covered by several tartan car blankets, which scratched his sore flesh. The curtains beside his face were drawn, but he could see it was daylight outside. A fire, well built-up, roared in the hearth, and soft music was playing, something on flutes and hand-drums. The sea-smell, he realised, was a salty incense.

A woman glided into his line of sight. She was dressed in a long green caftan and her fair, curling hair was tossed up onto her head and confined with a stretchy velvet band. Talismans adorned her large breasts. Her face was round, her eyes rather staring, but despite the fact she was no conventional beauty, her body oozed a sense of sexuality and power. She carried a small, earthenware bowl in her outstretched hands, bearing it with a reverence that suggested it contained something holy.

Shemyaza raised his upper body a little and rested his weight on his forearms. His whole body ached. He could remember nothing of what had happened to him or how he had come to this place. His throat felt raw as if he'd gulped salt water, nearly drowned.

The woman knelt beside him, and placed the bowl in her lap. She regarded him with her watery, round eyes, which were the palest shade of sea green. "You are awake, my lord."

"So it appears." He looked at her in puzzlement. Was she a menial of his? He didn't recognise her. Where was this place? It had a northern feel. Even though the fire burned high, he could tell the air of the land was damp.

"Then I must anoint and soothe your flesh."

"Thank you, but I'd rather have something to drink."

The woman blinked slowly. "All your needs will be gratified, but first I must anoint you."

Shemyaza could tell she would have her way. He felt too weak and drained to argue. "Very well. If you must." He lay back down on the window seat.

Tamara, kneeling before him, was suffused with love and desire. It was hard to believe this *creature,* this perfect being, lay submissive before her. It had been difficult to get him back to the cottage unseen. After the ritual of the night, she and Delmar had fallen asleep in the cave at the bottom of the cliff. Neither of them had seen Shemyaza appear, but when they awoke and went out onto the beach, they had found him lying in a stupor at the tide's lip. Delmar, whom Tamara had been relying on for physical assistance, had appeared to be still in trance, caught up in the vision that he was a sea-born vizier for the Prince of Light. Dismissing the fey boy with a gesture of irritation, she had set about dragging Shemyaza back to her car. It had exhausted her hauling him back up the treacherous cliff face. The guardians had been thrown into euphoria by his proximity, and had wanted to hold him to themselves. Their strong grabbing limbs had only accentuated the dead weight of Shemyaza's body. By the time Tamara had managed to pull him onto the road at the cliff-top, she'd been near to tears and her whole body had been shaking with fatigue. Summoning the last of her strength, she bundled his tall frame into the back seat of her car and pushed the semi-catatonic Delmar into the front passenger seat. He'd been in such a state, she hadn't dared risk taking him home, and he now lay unconscious in her spare room. On the journey back from Mermaid's Cove, she'd been alert for signs of the Pelleth. They must not know she had Shemyaza. Perhaps it was a sign of the limit of their power that they had not sensed what had happened. Tamara was tortured by visions of finding Meggie Penhaligon crouched on her doorstep when she reached her cottage, but it seemed the Pelleth had no inkling of what she was doing. None of them had been in touch with her so far.

It had been a terrifying, wonderful night, and the exertion, both physical and spiritual, had nearly killed her. As she'd driven home, she'd been angry that Barbelo hadn't been there to help her. Yet now that she had Shemyaza helpless in her cottage, Tamara was glad her strange Grigori friend had kept her distance. Perhaps Barbelo had more understanding than she'd imagined. This hour belonged to Tamara alone.

She peeled back the tartan blankets and let her eyes linger on the perfect lines of his body. He was truly as lissom as a serpent, and his skin was so pale. Grigori flesh. His eyes were closed and the ferny fringes of his long, dark lashes rested against his cheeks. His tangled hair looked like unravelled swatches of raw silk, matted with slivers of driftwood and skeins of seaweed. She longed to comb it out. Her gaze travelled down his chest to the dark coins of his nipples, which seemed to call for a halo of lips to encircle them, for eager teeth to bite them. Further, her eyes drank in the beauty of the hollow of his belly that was plaited with muscle. Below, lay the ripe fruit of the tree of his body: his heavy genitals, lying in a nest of soft, curling hair. She longed to bury her face there, and her mouth filled with saliva, but she knew she must be patient. Just gazing upon him sharpened her breath.

Tamara placed the earthenware bowl of herbal unguent on the carpet before her knees. She scooped out a handful and kneaded it between her palms, so that it melted like butter. When the moment came to touch him, she paused, savouring the moment. Then she laid her hands upon him.

He made a small sound of pleasure as her warm slippery fingers began to massage the sacred ointment into his chest, and the scent of myrrh, camphor and cinnamon rose like incense around them. She rubbed the poppies of his nipples between her fingers, feeling herself grow loose and damp between the thighs. Steeling herself not to hurry, to enjoy each holy moment, she took another handful of unguent and rubbed it slowly, languorously into his belly. Then she moved to his feet and began the slow, sensual journey up to his groin. By the time she reached her goal, his pale, flaccid penis had become hard and dark. It rose from the mat of his pubic hair like the huge, phallic fungi she collected from the woods, emanating a scent of ozone and ripe corn. Gently, she rubbed her unguent into its shaft, feeling him shudder at the burn of the camphor. With her free hand she cupped his heavy balls, delighted to find she could not hold them in one hand. Her mouth was full of water; she swallowed twice to clear it. It seemed his taste was already on her tongue.

Leaning forward, she took the long, sloping mushroom head of his sex into her mouth, probed with her tongue into its secret recesses, sucked the salt liquor from him. He made an appreciative noise and put his hands on her head, pushing himself into her, so that the bitter tang of the unguent filled her mouth. His prick seemed to be growing inside her, pressing her tongue down, filling her throat. She tore herself away, gasping.

He did not raise his head, or even open his eyes, but he laughed softly. Tamara knelt there panting, her hands plunged between her knees. She could feel her cunt pulsing in time to her heartbeat. Still without speaking, Shemyaza reached out for her, found the hardness of a nipple poking through the taut fabric of her kaftan. His long fingers cupped her heavy breast, squeezed hard. Then he rose up like a serpent, and pushed her back onto the carpet. He towered over her where she lay with her knees raised, her kaftan riding up her thighs. He seemed utterly alien, yet the mere sight and smell of him made her feel as hot and demanding as a she-cat on heat. She tried to struggle from her garments, eager to be naked against him, but as she fought with the folds of cloth around her ears, she felt his head plunge in between her legs, felt his long tongue dive into her body. Instead of winning free of her clothes, she lay quiescent, with her arms flung over her head, blinded by fabric as he worked at her. He sucked dextrously at her clitoris as if it was a man he was pleasuring. She felt delirious with pleasure, almost beyond orgasm. But then the wave came furiously inside her and she felt a gush of liquids burst loose from her, which he drank from greedily. Without pausing, he turned her onto her belly and raised her hips. She could feel her muscles still contracting like a flower of flesh as his great organ slithered into her. As he punched in and out of her, she felt him grow, until it seemed she would have to burst and tear. His hands kneaded her buttocks and then reached around to massage her clitoris, until she heaved into a blinding, multiple orgasm. He stood up, holding her powerfully against him, her body dangling down, and she felt him spasm inside her. Then he unsheathed himself from her flesh and let her fall crumpled to the floor. She lay there, curled up, panting and shuddering, her genitals still convulsing in the last tides of climax.

When she was able to compose herself, she sat up. Her thighs were drenched in his seed and her own liquor. Sex had never been so raw for her before, so intense and immediate, so erotic in its simplicity. He was sitting in front of her on the window-seat, his head bowed, his hands dangling between his knees.

"Who are you?" he asked her.

She flicked her damp hair back off her breasts. "To you, I am Ishtahar," she said.

"Ishtahar?" As Tamara spoke the name, the shroud around his memory fell away. He remembered. Uttering a cry of pain and fear, his hands flew to his face.

Tamara watched in horror. Shemyaza screamed in agony. His sensuality she could cope with; his anguish was far greater to comprehend or control. She was also worried that someone outside might hear this gusting lament. The Pelleth might be lurking about by now.

"Hush!" She knelt before him, put her hands around his wrists and attempted to pull his arms down. After a moment, he relented and fell quiet. When she saw his eyes, they were dark and blank of emotion. She could feel the bones grinding in his wrists as he flexed his fingers. "It's all right," she said. "I am here to help you."

"You! You are human!"

She nodded. "Yes. As was she."

His eyes narrowed. "How did you find me?"

"I found you on the beach below High Crag. Do you remember what happened?"

He pulled away from her hold and rubbed his face. "Yes...The sea. The boy in the sea." He paused. "I flew into my own history. He made me do it."

Tamara laughed softly. "He is your true vizier."

Shemyaza frowned. "No, I have a vizier. Daniel. He has always been with me."

"And look what's happened to you! Did Daniel help you in the Garden? No. Delmar has more power, as do I. My lord, it is hard for me to say this, and will be hard for you to hear, but Ishtahar and Daniel are of the past, whereas I and Delmar are of the present. People have tried to keep you away from us, but we had faith. We knew we would triumph. And we have."

Shem still looked at her warily. "Do the Parzupheim know about you?"

Tamara did not know what the Parzupheim was, but answered quickly. "Everyone who knows about us wants to keep us apart from you. Your own people work against you! They want to contain you and control you."

Shemyaza rubbed his face again, looked to the side. "But Daniel..." He shook his head. "I don't know. I don't know about this."

"Trust me. I am here to help you fulfil your destiny. I am part of it: your priestess."

Shemyaza stared at her for a moment, then his lips peeled back from his teeth. He uttered a growl and pushed her away, rising up to tower over her. This was no moment of desire. She could see his power and it terrified her. He could crush her like a spring shoot, if he wanted to.

She steeled herself not to cower away from him. "My Lord, do not be angry! My only purpose is to serve you."

"You are just like them!" he cried. "I can't fulfil this destiny you all want for me so badly! I'm sick of hearing about it!"

Tamara saw the colours of anger and bitterness shining from his aura. Stupid Grigori, what had they done to him? He should have come to this shore in joy and strength. They had tortured him with their selfish demands. The Pelleth had always known of this, how Grigori greed would warp the Transformation when it came. Barbelo too must have known. She alone of the Grigori had the intelligence and honour to see the truth. "Shemyaza," she said, forcing her voice to remain steady. "You have been hurt, but it can be healed. You don't have to be bitter, angry, or sickened by what must be. There is another way to victory, and I can show you how. No-one knows this land as well as I. Its secrets are my secrets. I can bend its elements to my will. You don't have to go to the serpent alone."

Shemyaza expelled a short, snarling laugh. "Any who go with me die. Only I can withstand the gaze of the serpent, or so I've been told."

Tamara shook her head. "A lie! Delmar and I will be with you, I as your priestess and Delmar as your vizier. We are a sacred trinity, male, female and androgyne."

"Your Delmar is a boy! That's not remotely female."

"Physically, maybe, but he is also a melding of you and I, our essential spiritual components. He is stronger by far than Daniel." She saw him thinking about what she'd said. He wanted desperately to believe her, she could tell, for he was so tired and weary. Whatever he'd experienced when he'd leapt from the cliff had battered him like a hail of ironbound staffs.

Sighing, he sat down again. "I want a bath," he said, "and something to eat and drink."

The cold light had gone out of him. He seemed smaller, hardly more than a man. Tamara could see the fragility in him. She got to her feet. "I'll run a bath. There's plenty of hot water, and how about a cooked breakfast?"

He smiled up at her and nodded. "Yes...Thank you."

Tamara introduced Shemyaza to Delmar in the afternoon of their first day together. Delmar acted like a small child, shy and afraid. Shemyaza was clearly unimpressed. Barbelo had told Tamara that, in this life, Shemyaza had a predilection for working magically with the male principle, but he seemed to have no interest in Delmar. Personally, Tamara didn't blame him. Delmar was almost fishlike in his dank lack of passion, and his ocean eyes were empty of expression. He came alive only in his element, or in the throes of trance. "My vizier was warm," Shemyaza said, tilting Delmar's face in his hand. He turned to Tamara. "Is this boy a bit peculiar?"

Tamara, busy washing up, glanced over her shoulder. "He is sea-born. It'll be different once he's in his element, you'll see."

Shemyaza pulled a wry face and let Delmar go. He had a strong desire to wipe his hands after touching the boy. This was no Daniel. He looked back at Tamara. She, on the other hand, was vibrant and dynamic. If anyone could help him in the task everybody kept insisting was his destiny, he was prepared to believe she could. Sexually, she was voracious. She leapt upon him at every opportunity like a sacred whore. They had only been together for just over half a day, but had already had sex five times: before breakfast, after breakfast, mid-morning, before lunch, after lunch. No woman had aroused him as much since Ishtahar. Perhaps she was really telling the truth about herself. Now, he went up behind her and wrapped her in his long arms. She tilted back her head so that he could nuzzle her neck. His fingers crept down to between her thighs. He grew hard against her.

"I want you now," he said, nipping the skin below her ear. "I want you every hour."

"And you shall have me," she answered. She pushed her hips backwards against him, spreading her legs wide.

Delmar, sitting at the kitchen table, watched with cold eyes, as Shemyaza flipped up Tamara's skirts and started fucking her from behind.

It was little more than a week to the solstice night. Tamara knew the Pelleth had been priming their sacred sites, but she wanted to use this time to do a little priming of her own. She wanted to take Shemyaza to some of the sites and introduce him to them. It was strange that Barbelo didn't come to the cottage, but perhaps she was afraid of Shemyaza recognising her. She still called on the telephone every evening to see how Tamara was getting on, but insisted that Shemyaza not be told anything about her. Most nights she had instructions for Tamara, which were strictly obeyed. Tamara was a little frightened herself of Shemyaza and relied on Barbelo's verbal assistance on how to handle him. When he was being ordinary and almost human, she loved him and felt she had control, but when the shadow of his power, or his former existence, stole over his countenance, he became an alien, unpredictable creature, who might lash out and destroy anything within his reach. His mood changes were erratic. He could be almost carefree one moment, then either murderous or suicidal the next. Only sex seemed to calm him. Barbelo told her to exploit this, as it was her greatest tool of control. Happy to comply with this instruction, Tamara kept him well drugged with the elixir of her body.

On the day following his arrival at the cottage, Tamara took him out in her car to visit the first of the sites. She bundled him up in old clothes of her widowed father's that she stored in a trunk for the rare occasions when he came to stay with her; a heavy coat, stout wellington boots and an old hat, under which she concealed Shemyaza's shining hair. If any of the Pelleth spotted them, she hoped they would not penetrate his disguise.

As they drove along the narrow lanes in pelting rain, Shemyaza talked about his future. She saw this as an encouraging sign.

"I can't see the point of it all," he said. "What good can come of reawakening the power of the land? People will only abuse it, mine and yours alike."

"Well, people like you and I are here to prevent that happening. Have faith in yourself, my lord."

Shemyaza laughed. "I am Shem," he said. "At least that's what my friends call me. If I am lord, then you are my lady. We should be partners, not master and servant."

Tamara was pleased with his words, although she sensed they belonged to the ordinary aspect of his personality and would be quickly forgotten by the Fallen One when he was invoked. When he was existing normally, Shemyaza seemed almost oblivious of his darker side. She could tell he was attracted by the thought of believing and trusting her.

"So what will happen afterwards?" he asked her.

She glanced at him, changed gear to take a sharp bend. "Whatever you like. We'll be able to do anything. Stay here, leave here. I'd rather like to travel."

He nodded. "I could show you some wondrous things, places that no human has ever seen." He relaxed in his seat. "I could take you to the farthest mountains where ancient citadels lie empty to the air. You could touch the sacred paintings on the walls. You could drink from the pools of holy water that are colder than the void. I could take you to the barren deserts where cities lie beneath the sand. When the right ceremonies are performed, the portals of sealing will open and you can go down to walk the deserted streets. You could take the diadem of a princess from an open tomb and wear it for me."

Tamara wanted to believe all this was possible. She herself was unsure of what would happen once the serpent was awake. It was possible that the earthly aspect of Shemyaza, the Shem of him, would be burned away. "Here we are," she said and brought the car to a jolting halt.

They had to climb over a gate and walk across several fields to the site. On a bare hillside, a stone Celtic cross reared from the land. It stood upon a raised dais of three steps. Conveniently, the rain that day had kept all sightseers from the spot. As they trudged towards the cross, Tamara explained that it symbolised the grave of Constantine, an ancient Cornish king.

"What do you want me to do?" Shem asked. He seemed to be in good spirits, as if this was all a game.

"Touch the cross," she answered. They halted before it. "Tell me what you feel."

Shem grinned at her quizzically, then mounted the dais and extended a pale hand towards the stone. When his flesh made contact, Tamara felt a surge of power burst out from the monument. She staggered backwards under its force and her hat fell over her eyes. Gasping, she pushed it back and saw that two figures stood beside the cross. One was clearly Shem, but the other shimmered before her eyes. It was a man, clad in a long tabard of white and gold, his hair confined by a metal circlet. Tamara uttered a cry of surprise and concern.   Shemyaza had invoked the ghost of Constantine. She could sense the old king's overwhelming desire to acquire freedom and power. His hunger made him dangerous. Shemyaza seemed unconcerned, standing with his arms folded, staring curiously at the vision.

"Send him back!" Tamara yelled.

Shem turned his head to look at her. "Why? Isn't this what you wanted?"

Tamara shook her head frantically. "No!" She could feel her strength being sucked from her body by the thirsty spirit. "Shem, do it now! Lay him to rest! He'll kill us!"

Shem shrugged and placed his hand against the stone cross once more. The spirit uttered a despairing wail, before its substance disintegrated and was absorbed back into the stone like smoke.

Tamara exhaled a sigh of relief, and concentrated on calming her hysterical heart. "We must be careful, Shem. These ancient energies are desperate for release."

He came to her side and enfolded her in his arms. "It's nothing I can't handle. Remember, I'm capable of waking the serpent. Ghosts don't frighten me." He kissed her briefly on the lips. "We are partners. Share my power."

Just the feel of his arms around her woke Tamara's desire. She felt the familiar writhing demand in her womb. Tenderly, Shem lifted her in his arms and carried her to the dais. He sat her down upon the top step and opened her duffel coat. Then he lifted her thick fisherman's jumper and took her breasts in his hands. He leaned forward to suck the nipples. Tamara opened his trousers and freed his straining prick. She raised her skirts, which were drenched with rain. Beneath them, she wore no underwear. Then she wrapped her arms backward around the cross, raising her legs to grip Shem's body. He found his way into her instantly and they drenched the site with their own, special power.

The next night Tamara took Shemyaza down to the sea. Giggling like children, they invaded the holy cave of the Pelleth, knowing they courted danger and discovery. Shem sat upon the giant's throne, and she impaled herself on his lap, half wishing that Meggie and the others would appear at the mouth of cave, to witness her white, full body riding the staff of their god. He would leave his seed upon the sacred seat.

Afterwards, they walked hand in hand along the beach. The tide was low and they were able to stroll from cove to cove. At midnight, they reached St Michael's Mount, or Carreg Luz en Kuz as it was known in the ancient tongue. Here, Tamara wanted them to enter the water. They undressed in the chill air and left their clothes folded upon a rock. Then they joined hands and ran into the water like holidaymakers, or children. Shemyaza strode into the waves and began to swim. Tamara clung to his back, riding his powerful body. He dove beneath the surface and Tamara could see that the water was lit up with glowing globes of light that flashed around them. She saw that the spectral shapes of the oanes began to take on a more physical form. Their whale-song cries filled her head. Shem dove deeper, and it seemed neither he or Tamara needed air to breathe, for there was no discomfort in their lungs. The weedy spires of Lyonesse appeared before them through the gloom and Shem sped towards them, his body undulating like a fish. The water was filled with light, as if they swam beneath a Mediterranean sky. The wide streets of Lyonesse were empty, but glittering with the jewels of fishes and bubbles of air. Shem swam to the great temple, the omphalos of the city. Here, they found Delmar waiting for them. He sat upon the altar, where the holy drapes had been replaced by ribbons of weed. Shem spoke to Tamara through her mind. "Take him, my lady."

Tamara glanced at him in shock. "No! He is virgin. He must remain so. Until the night before his death."

Shem smiled and a stream of shining bubbles escaped his lips. "That is their way, not ours. Prepare him for me. The gift is mine, but I pass it to you."

Tamara swam to the altar. Delmar fixed her with his dark eyes. Here, beneath the sea, they were full of intelligence and understanding. He rose up from the altar to hang before her, a blade of shining flesh. His hair billowed around his head, strung with pearls and shells. Tamara floated down to lie upon the altar. She landed weightlessly like a single strand of weed meeting the ocean bed, and her limbs drifted lazily, like the tendrils of an anemone. "Come to me, Del," she thought.

The boy spread out his arms and kicked with his legs, until he hung over her, inches away from her body. His skin looked silvery green, and when he reached for her breasts with his hands, she could see the fingers were webbed. His prick, when he entered her, was freezing cold. "Who was your father, Del? Not Patrick Tremayne, that's for sure!" She closed her eyes, enjoying his slow, cautious movements inside her. A vision came to her of Ellen Tremayne walking down to the ocean on mid-summer night, to meet the cold, fishtailed lover who waited on the farthest rock for her. Delmar. Not meant for the world of light and air. Tamara wound her fingers in his floating hair. Then she heard him utter a seal cry in his mind. Opening her eyes, she saw Shemyaza over his shoulder. Soon the three of them were moving to a single, oceanic rhythm, Delmar caught between Shemyaza and Tamara as a symbol of both male and female. Pumping like a jellyfish, trailing fronds of limbs, they rose up through the water. Seals and oanes and fishes tumbled around them in a maelstrom of flashing hide and scales. Tamara felt slick skin brush against her outflung legs. She felt fishes nibbling her fingers. Their orgasm was one orgasm, melding them into a single creature.

Tamara felt the last of the air squeeze from her lungs. She was breathing water.

With a final push, they burst free of the surface, and Tamara gulped air. Delmar was still inside her. He gave her a final kiss, before pulling himself free of her body and diving back beneath the waves. Shemyaza took her in his arms. "Another site sanctified," he murmured.

They awoke on the beach before dawn, and Tamara wondered how much of what she'd experienced had been vision or dream. It was the middle of winter, yet her naked body did not feel cold. The light was breaking in the eastern sky, and the chapel on the mount was a dark sentinel looking down upon them. This was the test. The seat of Michael's power in this land, an old adversary of Shemyaza's.

They dressed themselves in silence and walked hand in hand towards the chapel. A tense atmosphere of expectation hung between them. "Are you ready for this?" Tamara asked.

Shem squeezed her fingers. "I am."

They went into the shadows of the building, where the dawn light had not yet reached. Tamara hung back by the door as Shem approached the altar. When he laid his hand upon it, the chapel filled with light. Outside the dawn sky had been shorn of clouds, and clear winter blue shone through. The sun came in through the stained glass windows and coloured Shemyaza crimson and gold.

Before him, in the air, the dawn light condensed into a glowing column. Tamara saw a shining figure form within it, haloed in fire, his armour made of gold. A sword hung from his slim hips. Michael, a manifestation of the sun god.

"Traitor! You dare to enter my citadel of the sun?" His voice was like a clash of falling bells.

"I dare," Shemyaza answered. "Go back whence you came. This is my kingdom now."

Tamara had shrunk back against the chapel door, terrified that this powerful entity would blast Shemyaza's fragile body of flesh and blood. But Shemyaza reached up and gripped the body of Michael round the waist. With apparently little effort he pushed the shining figure down through the stone of the altar. Michael writhed and screamed, but was unable to escape. His exhortations escaped his writhing lips in wisps of smoke. Finally, Shemyaza put his hand flat against the top of Michael's head and forced the last of him into the stone. A haze of sparkling motes was all that was left behind, which presently popped out of existence.

Shemyaza stood alone, limned in coloured light, gazing down upon the altar, his hands hanging slackly by his sides.

Tamara stood with her hands against her mouth. She could hardly believe what she'd seen. If Shemyaza could defeat Michael, he could defeat anything. She hurried towards him and took his arms in her hands.

"Now Shem. *Now* we can begin!"

Chapter Twenty-Six
Lament for Shemyaza

Emma had been surprised at how readily Daniel accepted the suggestion that he meet with the local witches. Perhaps it was because he
was so desperate about Shem. As a psychic, Daniel took it for granted
that information unavailable to others was easily accessible to him,
but he had lost all sense of Shemyaza, and could not contact him.

Daniel and Emma walked the few miles to Meggie's cottage
through fine, dreary rain in the late afternoon. "It makes sense that
these women should know about Shem," Daniel said. "What the old
woman said is right; Shem's power and light is not just for the Grigori.
It makes me feel better to know that humans are also working with
this frequency." He smiled. "And what better people than a coven
of genuine Cornish witches! They will be part of this land, Emma,
and therefore part of the serpent. If anyone can reach and help
Shem in this hour of uncertainty, I'm sure they can."

"But what about the Parzupheim?" Emma asked. "Surely,
they are more powerful?" Having known Peverel Othman so intimately, she was unconvinced any human was poky enough either to
help Shemyaza or augment his power.

Daniel made a scornful sound. "Those old farts? Huh! They
aren't anywhere near understanding what Shem is all about. They're
far too greedy and narrow-minded."

"I don't think you could call a conclave of angels "old farts',"
Emma said dryly. "However, let's just see what this Meggie has to offer.
Like you, I'm worried about Shem. He needs all the help he can get."

When they reached Meggie's cottage, and were sitting in the
kitchen with Meggie and her taciturn sister, Emma was alarmed at
how freely Daniel spilled his thoughts to them. There was an edge
of hysteria in his low voice. He kept brushing back his hair with a
jerky, frantic gesture.

Don't lose it, Emma thought. She wanted to take Daniel in
her arms, take him back to High Crag, but sensed he'd be far from
compliant.

"If Shem has gone to the serpent, I need to be with him," Daniel said. "But for some reason, I can't reach him. It's as if there's a dark wall around him, hiding him from my sight."

Meggie nodded slowly. "Hmm. It might be a good idea if you go into trance while sitting in the giant's chair. It is the seat of our oracle, and was placed in our sacred cave by the giants thousands of years ago. It was here that our oracle learned of your existence. If you call to Shemyaza from the chair, the Pelleth can combine their strength with yours to enhance your sight..."

"Yes!" Daniel interrupted. "With your help, I know I can reach him." He laughed shakily. "I can't believe how lucky I am to find you. Some greater power must be helping me at this time."

"It's the power of the serpent," Meggie answered, and smiled gently. "Of that you can be sure."

Privately, Emma considered how it was more a case of the Pelleth finding Daniel rather than the other way around, but she kept her thoughts silent, content to observe.

"I know how you must guard your secrets," Daniel said. "I can't thank you enough for allowing me into your circle."

Meggie shook her head. "Believe me, it is we who should be thanking you. This is a crucial time, and we have lost our oracle. We are debilitated without one. You are the Shining One's vizier. It is of great benefit to the Pelleth that you are prepared to work with us."

Emma, smoking a cigarette, watched Meggie through slitted eyes. She felt that the woman was leaving quite a lot unsaid. The Pelleth were too eager to have Daniel in their ranks, and although Meggie and Betsy cleverly disguised their fervour, Emma could sense it behind their words, boiling away like a kettle on the old black range. The heavy, ancient atmosphere of the cottage, with its sense of magic stretching back into the past, was clearly lulling Daniel into a sense of security. He was fixed on the grandmotherly aspects of the Pelleth women, blind to their aura of power, which Emma suspected could sometimes be cruel and passionless. Still, as long as she remained close to Daniel's side, she could make sure no harm came to him. Unlike the Parzupheim, in their arrogance and pride, the Pelleth had respect for Daniel's position and ability. Emma had to agree, grudgingly, that they might be able to help him, and as they so readily admitted, they'd long been preparing the land for Shemyaza's arrival.

That evening, the rest of the Pelleth Conclave arrived at Meggie's house. Jessie and Agatha, took Daniel away to a room upstairs and there prepared him for the ritual to come. Emma was asked to bathe, then dress herself in a simple green robe. It was the garment of a rank and file Pelleth. The rest of the women waited for her in the kitchen. When she returned to them, Meggie told her, "None but the Conclave have ever experienced the secrets of the sacred cave. I ask you to respect this privilege, that we allow your presence there tonight."

"Don't worry, I'm not going to say anything to anyone," Emma said.

Lissie was more friendly. She placed a hand on Emma's arm. "You will make up the numbers," she said. "Since we lost Tamara we've been incomplete, although you're really a bit young to take her place, even for a single night."

Emma laughed. "What? Don't you know what I am?"

There was a silence in the kitchen. "What do you mean?" Lissie asked.

"I'm a Grigori dependent, over a hundred and fifty years old," Emma answered, taking pleasure from the shock that sprang to the Pelleth's faces. "That's right. Believe it. The Grigori extended my life. If I'm lucky, I have many hundreds of years of life left to me."

"They can do that?" Rachel cried.

Emma smiled slowly. She knew that within each mind around her, the tantalising thought bloomed and shone: they could have this gift for themselves. Some of them banished the idea quickly, thinking it an abomination, but their denial was firmly rooted in horror at the sudden rush of desire and longing that had spired within them. "I thought that was what you'd want of Shem," Emma said lightly.

"We want no dark Grigori magic," Betsy Penhaligon boomed. "The Goddess gives us a life and it is her privilege to take it back when she desires. We will not cheat her."

Emma shrugged. "Oh well. It's your choice. But surely working with Shemyaza in any respect is 'dark Grigori magic'. Where do you draw the line?"

"Shemyaza is pure," Betsy said. "He is the Son of the Sun, born in an age before the Grigori fell to corruption."

"You clearly haven't met him," Emma said, enjoying herself immensely. "And believe me he is Grigori through and through. He's no pure-born angel."

"He could not choose the flesh his souls inhabits," Meggie said.

"True," Emma agreed, "and it is very fine flesh." She sensed her attitude offended Meggie and Betsy, although the two younger women found her intriguing, and would have liked to hear more about Shemyaza from someone who actually knew him, but before any questions could be asked, Jessie and Agatha brought Daniel back into the room. Emma uttered a sound of surprise and admiration. He was dressed only in a very short skirt of black and white feathers, and his head was crowned in coral. Clearly, the girls had already been working on inducing a trance state in his mind, for his dark eyes were dreamy, the pupils wide. His whole body seemed to shine from within. Emma realised then how beautiful Daniel had become. In Little Moor, she'd seen him as a gawky boy, but now, his svelte body was that of a very attractive young man. His hair, which had grown quickly since they'd left Little Moor, was scooped up and confined inside the crown. His neck was as long and swan-like as the neck of an Egyptian king, and his head was a perfect shape, the skull swelling backwards from the neck in a graceful curve. Emma shook her head, and her voice was full of wonder. "Daniel, you look like an angel."

He smiled at her. "I was Grigori once, Emma. Perhaps sometimes I can remember what that was like."

The Pelleth had fallen silent in awe at the sight of him. Emma went towards him and took his hands in her own. "He *must* love you, Daniel. You *will* reach him. Don't worry."

They walked in silence down to the cove below Meggie and Betsy's garden. Since seeing Daniel, Emma's mood had changed. She could feel the magic of the land throbbing all around her. She felt like weeping and laughing at the same time. When Lissie caught her eye and smiled in complicity, warmth ignited in Emma's heart. She felt as if she'd finally come home, to people that had always been *her* people. Women working magic together, a tradition as old as the earth Herself.

The sea lunged angrily at the shore as the women filed into the cave. Emma felt the hair on her skin prickle and rise. Power gusted all around them. While the Pelleth busied themselves with lighting candles and incense, Daniel went to stand before the chair. Emma stood beside him. "Are you all right, Dan?"

He shook his head, his eyes wide. When he spoke, his voice was a whisper, for Emma's ears alone. "Em, he's *been* here!"

"Are you sure?"

He looked at her, his brow creased into a frown. "No...I don't know. Perhaps he *will* come here. I can sense him in this place. He's connected to it in some way. Maybe because of the chair..."

"Will you tell the others this?"

"I don't know..." he shrugged. "Something doesn't feel right."

Emma squeezed his arm. "Stay cool, Danny. I'm with you."

He smiled at her uncertainly. "My guardian spirit."

She leaned over and kissed his cheek, reached out to smooth his hair. "Always that, my Daniel. Always that."

Once the preparations were complete, Daniel sat down cautiously upon the chair. Only Emma noticed that he winced slightly as he did so. Then the Pelleth began to circle him slowly, and intoned their ritual chant: "Om Sefer, Tu Sefer, Sefer, Sefer, Sahar!"

Lissie took Emma's hand and led her round the circle. Emma whispered the chant beneath her breath for a few circuits, then wanted and needed to speak it aloud. Lissie let go of her hand. She was with them now, enfolded by their magic. The chant became louder and faster. Their feet stamped the ground, as the circle became a wild, shamanic dance. They clapped their hands, slapped their thighs, spun around so that their hair flew out in whirling arcs. "Om Sefer! Tu Sefer! Sefer! Sefer! SAHAR!"

On the chair, Daniel's breathing became more rapid and more shallow. He groaned and gripped the stone arms beneath his fingers. His head jerked backwards, and he uttered a female-sounding cry. "Ma-ta-har! Rani!"

The women fell silent, and stopped dancing. Their panting breath steamed in the chill air. Their hair hung around their shoulders in damp rags.

"Ai! She comes!" Daniel cried. "She rises from the sea! So cold! Her winter hands enfold my heart!"

"Seference speaks through you, my son," Meggie said soothingly, stepping forward. "Let her come through."

Daniel was breathing quickly now, as if fighting for breath. His eyes had rolled back in their sockets. Then he spoke, and his voice was low and raw, a woman's voice. "He will go back to the old kingdom."

"Where?" Meggie asked.

Daniel's head rolled on his neck, then his chin sank onto his breast. His eyes stared out through a fringe of hair. They glowed with a greenish light. "Down to the sea. He will go down to the sea with her. They will drink the jewels of the old kingdom and make salt upon the ancient altars."

"Is Shemyaza in the underworld?" Meggie asked.

Daniel's head twisted painfully to the side. He regarded the women like a bird. His voice was a sibilant rasp. "In the darkness, he is, waiting for the serpent's breath. In the dark. She is there. She is with him."

"Who?"

"The Maiden. His love."

Meggie glanced at Emma.

"Ishtahar," Emma said. "It could be." She addressed Daniel. "Is it Ishtahar?"

"She has made herself so. Her cup is the grail for his loneliness."

"Daniel," Emma said in a slow, steady voice. "Speak to Shem. Call to him."

Daniel whined and threshed his head around. When he spoke, it was in his own voice. "No! No! She has covered him with her veil! He cannot hear me! Shem! Shem! It is I, your vizier. Turn to me!" He paused for a moment, and closed his eyes. Emma feared he had lost consciousness, then he spoke again in a voice that was barely more than a murmur. "Shem, I love you. I have worn your wings, held you inside me. Why do you turn away? Remember our contract." He shook his head. "Ah, she dances before you on the yawning beaches, and you can see nothing else. You are powerless and entranced. It is as it was before." His voice rose in bitterness. "Ishtahar, you deceived me! You want him only for yourself. You have seduced him and doomed him."

For several minutes, all was silence. The Pelleth instinctively joined hands, Emma among them, and projected a tide of strength towards the chair. Then, Daniel opened his eyes and raised his head. He looked directly at Emma. "It is no good." Slowly, he lowered his head again until it rested upon his raised palms. He wept.

Meggie nodded at Emma. "It is over."

Emma let go of Lissie and Rachel's hands and ran to the chair. She took Daniel in her arms. He leaned against her shoulder and rested there, shuddering. Against her hair, he whispered his pain. "Em, I could see him, but it didn't make sense. He couldn't hear me or sense me. He didn't even want to. Something's blocking me. A female influence. Ishtahar. But she's my guardian, my goddess. Why is she pushing me out?"

Emma held him close, kissed his hair. "Give it time, Danny. We've made a start. Try not to grieve."

"You don't understand," Daniel said. "He gave me everything. We are one, Emma. I can't bear this separation. If Ishtahar and Shem are together again, I should be part of it. Why is she doing this? I'm no threat to her. It hurts!"

"I know, I know." Emma made a sound of distress, wishing she could do something to help. Meggie came and touched her on the shoulder.

"Let's get him home," she said.

Emma looked up into the old woman's face and saw only love there. All her reservations about the Pelleth had fled. She nodded. "Yes."

"Do you think it would cause trouble if you stayed at my house tonight?"

Emma sighed and stood up, helping Daniel to his feet. "The Grigori probably won't even notice we're missing. Daniel means very little to them."

Meggie put one hand on Daniel's face. "You've done well," she said. "Now, take your rest. I'll give you the best night's sleep you've ever had. No nightmares. Not even a dream."

Daniel smiled at her, and wiped his eyes with the heel of one hand. "Thank you."

Meggie held out her arms and he went to her. The embrace was short, but poignant. Emma was surprised to find she didn't feel jealous or wary about it at all.

As the days slipped by towards the solstice, the temple at High Crag was in use continually. Rituals took place designed to help and guide Shemyaza through his lonely journey. After a couple of days, the Parzupheim became suspicious of Sofia's claims that Shemyaza had gone into the underworld. If he had, surely the serpent would be awake by now? Strange phenomena abounded in the land, but the earth energy was still dormant. Sofia, visiting the house every day, argued that in the underworld time passed in a different way. The Shamir would awake on the solstice and then Shemyaza would rise up from the serpent's lair. Reluctantly, the Parzupheim accepted her explanation.

Privately, Sofia rejoiced. How easy it was to manipulate everyone around her. The Parzupheim were stupid and short-sighted; Salamiel was a gullible fool; Daniel was nothing more than a love-lorn sycophant, while Tamara Trewlynn...Sofia smiled to herself. The silly witch was drunk on sex and highly suggestible. She believed every word spoken by her Grigori friend, Barbelo. Sofia had intuited by now that Emma and Daniel had joined the Pelleth, but as her opinion of the Cornish witches was so low, this did not concern her. Once the serpent was awake and Shemyaza was in her power, Daniel must be brought to Pharos, but until then, she was prepared to let him indulge himself with the Pelleth.

Sofia visualised shining strings emanating from each of her fingers and connected with the souls of her puppets. All she had to do to get them to perform was lift a finger and tweak a string. Simple. Occasionally, she longed to make herself known to Shemyaza, but knew it was best not to intrude on his dreamtime with Tamara. As Barbelo, she experienced Tamara's adventures second-hand. It was not enough, but there'd be time in the future for her own adventures with the Fallen King.

The land itself, sensing the change to come, shuddered in its sleep and dreamed strange dreams. The Grigori and Pelleth alike observed the weird phenomena with excitement and vigilance. The tides became unnaturally low, almost as if the sea was drawing back from the land to disgorge the lost cities hidden beneath its waves. A new pole star appeared in the sky. Freak weather occurred; the sun burning bright by day, while at night, freezing storms tore slates from the roofs and broke the backs of trees. There were minor earthquakes as the serpent turned over in its sleep. A child was swallowed by a fissure on the beach, which closed up again before the child's screaming parents could pull it free.

Emma announced to Aninka that she was now staying at a bed and breakfast in the village with Daniel, because Daniel had been upset by the way the Parzupheim had treated him. Aninka was furious about this, as she missed having her new friend around. She told Enniel what had happened, hoping he'd rectify the matter, but it seemed Daniel was no longer important to the Parzupheim. "He's just a plaything," Enniel said. "Get that straight, Aninka. He's worthless without Shemyaza, and Shemyaza could use anyone for Daniel's purpose, anyone at all."

Daniel carried on working with the Pelleth, attempting to reach Shemyaza in the underworld, and help and guide him. His efforts continued to be frustrated, but he trusted that the love and strength he directed at Shem would have a beneficial effect. Like the Parzupheim, the Pelleth believed that the serpent would finally awake on the solstice. On that night, they would enact a ritual on the cliff edge at the bottom of the Penhaligon garden.

Meggie had sensed that Daniel was a very special person. She suspected that, like Emma, he had been given extended life. His power was great, and she couldn't understand why he was failing to reach his master. Perhaps it was destiny that Shemyaza should travel alone to his fate. Meggie would have liked to keep Daniel as the Pelleth's oracle for years to come, but sensed that he might have to be sacrificed on the solstice night. She felt regret about this, but knew that the serpent might demand it, and if the Pelleth were to take control of the serpent power, they must satisfy its hungers. Still, if the sacrifice could be avoided, it would be an added bonus. Daniel was unlike any other oracle she'd known. He was no unformed youth, but a vibrant young man. If he survived the solstice, he might well survive for a long time to come. There was something feminine about him that suggested he could be trusted with women's secrets. Unlike Delmar, he was far from virgin, but she realised that this did not affect his abilities. If anything, his sexual experiences had enhanced his sight. She sensed that no woman had touched him and never would. Her beliefs balked at what this implied, for the worship of Seference revolved around the male-female polarity of nature. Anything else was regarded as impure and unnatural. A man who turned away from women could not, in Meggie's eyes, have magical power, yet Daniel clearly did. Times are changing, she thought. The new age brings new ways. She was wise enough to know that the death of one belief system and the birth of another sometimes entailed discomfort on a spiritual level.

At Pharos, Lily sensed the rising tension in Salamiel. One night, after dinner, she offered to massage his shoulders for him, to ease the tightness in his muscles. In the drawing room he sat on the floor

between her legs, while she sat on the sofa above him and dug her
fingers sensually into his flesh. His silky red hair fell over her hands.
He felt so young to her touch. She asked him to remove his shirt, for
she couldn't reach his shoulder-blades properly. Smiling, he obeyed
her, revealing a torso like furred marble. Lily asked him to lie on his
belly on the carpet. She knelt beside him, working her fingers up
his spine.

"Do you like women?" she asked him.

"Yes," he answered. "Why shouldn't I?"

She shrugged. "Well...I just wondered. Because of how
you feel about Shem."

Salamiel rolled over and fixed her with his dark gaze. "I
make no distinctions concerning gender, at least not when desire is
invoked."

Lily carefully put her hands on her knees. "And is it?"

He just raised his eyebrows, lying there with his arms behind his head.

Oh well, thought Lily, in for a penny...

She leaned over and took his face in her hands, lowered her
lips to his. He curled his arms around her and drew her to him.
After a while, he broke away from her and said, "Do you want to
make love with me?"

Lily couldn't suppress a laugh. "Well...I thought we were."

He sat up. "Not here. Come."

He took her to his bedroom and left her alone while he
went into his dressing room. Lily tore off her clothes and climbed
into the high bed. Where was he? What was he doing? After
some minutes, he returned, wearing a silk dressing gown decorated with embroidered peacocks. Lily had to smile. She felt like
a bride on her wedding night, being given a few minutes to prepare herself discreetly for her new husband. Salamiel sat on the
edge of the bed and removed his robe. Lily admired the long curve
of his spine, the shining fall of hair whose longest strands caressed
his waist, the sweet cleft where his buttocks began. He turned to
her and cast back the quilt. He laid one hand flat upon her belly.
"You are lovely," he said.

"So are you."

He smiled and lay down beside her, ran his hand down her
lean flank, let his fingers lightly tease the hair at her groin. She
opened her legs for him.

"The temple of the goddess," he said, and gently slid a finger inside her. She felt her belly convulse in a single stab of pleasurable pain. He seemed to touch something deep within her soul.

For a while, they played in the outer court of the temple, then Salamiel placed himself sinuously over Lily's body and slowly slid inside her. Buried to the hilt, he paused, resting his weight on straight arms and looked down into her eyes.

Lily reached up to his face. "I love sex," she said. "It's the best thing in the world."

"It is," he agreed, "and with the right person, it's true magic."

Lily sighed and closed her eyes, surrendered to the bliss conjured by his slow, deep movements. Even when she wanted him to thrust harder, he kept the rhythm lazy, until she stopped wriggling beneath him and matched her movements to his. Her orgasm came like a slow dawn breaking over the sea. He leaned down and kissed her tenderly, before allowing his own climax to occur. He uttered a single sound of wonderment, and lay down upon her body, his hair covering her face. She wrapped her arms around him and, perhaps a little belatedly, the earth shook beneath the house.

On the eve of the solstice, everyone in High Crag was so jittery that the atmosphere sparked almost visibly. The Parzupheim, who had been coming and going from the house all week, were all in residence again, and psyching themselves up for the ceremonies to come.

Emma came up to the house in the morning to have coffee with Aninka. The sun was unseasonably bright, hanging in an aching blue sky. They sat outside on the patio at the back of the house, on either side of an old, wooden table.

"It's like August," Emma said, lighting a cigarette. She was wearing sunglasses and a sleeveless dress. "You know, it was a bit like this in Little Moor. When Peverel Othman arrived the weather went freaky. It was very hot."

Aninka's stomach turned over as, nearby, the ground rumbled and slightly shook. I'm scared the house will fall off the cliff!" She poured coffee from a silver pot. "Anyway, I want to know why you haven't been here much this week. You've been really off with me. What have I done?"

Emma shrugged. "Nothing. I've just been with Daniel."

Aninka knew Emma was lying. She wished she could see her friend's eyes. "Do you blame me because the Parzupheim were nasty to Daniel?" She pushed a mug of coffee across the table top to Emma.

Emma shook her head, picked up the mug. "No. But you don't like him either, do you?"

Aninka leaned back in her seat. "I don't know, Emma. He was very cruel to Taziel, and I just feel a bit strange when he's around."

"He wasn't cruel to Taziel," Emma said. "Taziel got greedy, that's all." There was a harshness in her voice to which Aninka took exception.

Aninka made a sharp remark back, to which Emma responded hotly, and within seconds they were arguing heatedly about Daniel, about Emma's opinions of the Grigori, about Emma and Daniel's closeness to Shemyaza, and its undoubtedly contaminating effects.

Emma was aghast at the bitterness spilling from Aninka's mouth, but couldn't rein in enough to think about the reasons behind it. She leapt to her feet. "I'm not staying here to listen to this crap!" she cried. "We've made new friends in the village, Aninka. Neither Daniel nor I need you or the Grigori now."

This surprising revelation eclipsed Aninka's anger. "What new friends?"

Emma too sensed the winding down of emotion and realised she had spoken without thinking. Still, what harm could it do if the Grigori knew about the Pelleth? No doubt they'd simply scorn them. Briefly, she explained to Aninka how she had met Meggie Penhaligon and that Daniel was now working with the Pelleth.

Aninka took this information in with incredulity. Like most Grigori, she'd had no idea that humans in the area were aware of Shemyaza's existence.

"So that is where I'll be!" Emma concluded. "When, or if, you come to your senses and want to apologise for being so rude to me, you'll find me at Meggie's." With these words, Emma stalked away. In some ways, she'd rather like Aninka to turn up at the Penhaligon house, because Meggie and Betsy would be astounded. Emma did not agree with their view of the Grigori, and felt they really should make contact. But she doubted Aninka would lower herself to coming to the cottage. Did this mean her friendship with Aninka was over? Emma realised she didn't want that to happen.

After Emma left High Crag, Aninka went straight to Enniel and informed him of what Daniel was doing. To her intense gratification,

Enniel was furious. "That boy is a liability!" he raged. "What in Hell is he playing at? Tonight, Shemyaza will return, and his vizier is grubbing around with a coven of old hags! No doubt he's betraying Grigori secrets too. Wait till I get my hands on him!"

Aninka watched from the front porch as Enniel stormed from the house, jumped into his Range Rover and smoked off towards the village. She considered following, then decided against it. She had a feeling she'd be seeing Emma again soon.

Emma was still walking back to the village when Enniel's Range Rover careered past her. She recognised the vehicle and guessed immediately what had happened. "Damn!" she said aloud and began to run down the hill.

By the time Enniel reached Meggie's cottage, the whole village was aware that trouble was afoot. Not everyone who lived there knew what the owners of High Crag were, but those that did soon found out that Enniel Prussoe had come tearing through, in an obviously enraged emotional state, demanding where Meggie Penhaligon's house was. No-one, not even the ignorant, would have dared to respond to his questions with surly silence and dark looks. Enniel, in his fury, was a terrifying sight; an avenging angel who might have stepped from the frame of an apocalyptic painting.

"I don't think he's going to Meggie's to buy a corn dolly," remarked a woman to her friend as Enniel's Range Rover roared away from them.

Tom Penhaligon answered Enniel's wild hammering on the front door. Enniel appraised him coldly and demanded to speak with the "old woman".

Tom was unnerved by the tall stranger and felt he should get rid of him quickly. "There's no-one here," he said.

"Don't waste my time!" Enniel spat. "Fetch the old witch now or suffer the consequences."

Meggie, who was in the kitchen, heard raised voices and ventured into the hall. She recognised Enniel as Grigori immediately, and for a moment, leaned back in shock against the kitchen doorframe. Then, she mustered her courage and surged forward. "What is it, Tom?"

Tom glanced round at her with a mixture of relief and alarm. "Someone to see you, Mam," he said. "Someone with no manners."

Meggie came to the door, purpose emanating from her large frame, and Enniel took a step back. She was not going to let this creature step over her threshold. "What do you want?" she asked.

"I want the boy," Enniel said. "Don't bother denying you have him."

Meggie folded her arms, although she was not as calm as she appeared. "If you mean Daniel, he's happy enough here. Leave us be."

Enniel uttered a snort of contemptuous laughter. "Look, old woman. I don't know what you think you're doing, but you're dabbling in matters that are far beyond you. If you've any sense you'll back off."

"I don't like threats," said Meggie bluntly.

"You really have no idea, do you! You dare to speak to me like that? Don't you realise what I could do to you?" Enniel's lips peeled back into a sneer. "You're just a grubby beach witch! What is it you're after? Youth for your decaying body?"

Meggie, who was used to being treated with respect by all around her, objected strongly to Enniel's manner. Once her anger was roused, he became simply an obnoxious male, who must be put in his place. "Your kind will be destroyed!" she shouted, pointing an omenic finger at him. "You are filth and corruption! The Shining One is not for your greedy hands! Get from my garden! Crawl back to your stinking nest of dung-eating serpents!"

Enniel was clearly astounded by her belligerence, for he was silenced for a moment. Then he smiled. "So, you want to take me on, do you, hag? Very well. Step out here, match my power if you can."

How this confrontation would have ended, Meggie dared not imagine. She did not want to lock horns with a Grigori patriarch, but once challenged, she could not back down. Her heart was heavy in her breast as she took a step into the front garden. But before any more exchanges could follow, Daniel came running through the house and positioned himself between them. "What the hell's going on?" he demanded.

Meggie and Enniel began shouting at once. Daniel raised his arms, and yelled. "Enough!" Light sparked from his eyes. He looked like what he was, a part of Shemyaza.

Both Enniel and Meggie fell quiet.

Daniel turned from one to the other. "Look at the pair of you! You both want the same thing, yet you fight like selfish children!" He pointed at Enniel. "You! The serpent power is not just for Grigori, but for humans too." He turned on Meggie. "And you! You despise the Grigori, yet you should appreciate they are the descendants of Shemyaza." He shook his head in exasperation. "If anything, the Parzupheim and the Pelleth should be working together. You all want to control the serpent when it wakes, but none of you will. Don't you understand that only Shem will control it? Why are you screaming at one another? What good will that do? Shem is alone in the underworld, perhaps fighting for his soul and his life. We should be thinking of him now, not ourselves and our greeds! Have you no shame?"

Daniel's passion subdued both Enniel and Meggie. Enniel sighed and rubbed the back of his neck. "Daniel, I was concerned for you. I don't want you to be used."

Daniel uttered a choked laugh. "Don't say that to me. You were happy to use me yourself when you believed I had some use."

"That devil..." Meggie began, sensing victory, but Daniel interrupted her.

"Don't say anything, Megs. I know what you think of me, too. The Parzupheim believe I'm Shemyaza's toy, and your opinion hardly differs. You think I'm perverted."

"Daniel, that's not true!" Meggie said. "Your ways are different but..."

"I don't want to hear it," Daniel said. "All I want to hear is for you two to make your peace. You both have work to do tonight, and in my view, both methods are valid and necessary. The Grigori will do what they see fit, as will the Pelleth." He glanced at Enniel. "You can't stop humans being drawn to Shemyaza, or wanting to tap his power to work magic. It will always happen. He doesn't belong to you alone. So you might as well accept it. And the Pelleth must accept that the Grigori have a right to share in the serpent power."

"And who will you be working with?" Enniel asked coldly.

Daniel looked into his eyes. "Do you have a place for me in your temple?"

"If you want to..."

Daniel shook his head. "Oh no, don't even say it! You're not aware of what I am, are you?" He thumped his chest with a closed fist. "I served King Darius as his vizier at Taketi el Sulamain in Persia, the founder of Masonry and Grigori hierarchy. And before that, I served Shemyaza in Kharsag, and was murdered beside him. I was Grigori once, and I shall be so again. No-one is closer to Shemyaza than I am. I was with him in the beginning and I am with him now, which might be the end. Yet you scorn me and view me with contempt. Your people are no better than humanity, Enniel. It would do you good to live a human life and appreciate that. You're stuck in the past, all of you! To you, the blood spilled in Eden is still fresh." He sighed. "Oh, what's the point. You can't hear me, can you?"

Enniel's voice was soothing. "Come back to High Crag, Daniel. Let us make amends."

Daniel shook his head. "No, it's too late. I'm not wholly human, but my place tonight is with the people among whom I was born. None of us really know what's going to happen. We shall just have to live it."

Enniel looked at him steadily for a few moments, then said, "Very well. But we do need to talk at some stage. Come to High Crag tomorrow. By that time, we should know how the land lies."

Daniel nodded wearily. "I'll come."

Enniel turned to Meggie. "I'm afraid I can't apologise to you. Daniel might be wiser and more tolerant than I am, but it will take some time for me to accept what he suggests. Still, I realise he spoke the truth in some measure. I can't stop you performing your own rituals."

Meggie slowly shook her head. "No, you can't. But like you, I stand humbled by Daniel's words. Perhaps in the future, we may speak on this matter again."

Enniel nodded curtly, and marched back to his Range Rover. Daniel stood beside Meggie as they watched him drive away. Meggie put her arm around him. "Daniel, you shamed me."

"I didn't mean to, Megs, but I had to say what I felt."

"No, you were right to." She sighed. "Agh! It'll be hard living in the new world, and will take a lot of compromise. Hope I'm up to it!"

Daniel smiled at her, his faced slightly puzzled. "Of course you are."

They went back into the house.

Chapter Twenty-Seven
Solstice Night

In Tamara's cottage, Shemyaza, Tamara and Delmar prepared themselves for the night to come. The sun had been shining relentlessly all day, making a cauldron of the sea, a cinder of the land, but at dusk, thick clouds rolled across the sky, trapping the heat below. A warm wind chivvied the leafless trees, and the sound of distant thunder could be heard. Whether this deep elemental growling emanated from the sky or beneath the earth was difficult to discern.

The previous night, Tamara had hauled her sewing machine out of storage from beneath her bed, and had hastily fashioned three simple robes. Obeying instructions from Barbelo, Tamara would be dressed in red for the ceremony to come, Delmar in oceanic green, while Shemyaza would be swathed in white, girdled with rope of golden cord. Now the three of them stood naked in the parlour, with the robes spread out on the sofa. Before they dressed, Tamara anointed Delmar and Shemyaza with an herbal unguent, then applied it to her own skin. She was anxious about the work to come, and was still awaiting a phone call from Barbelo to give her final directions.

Once dressed, the three of them sat by candlelight in a circle and meditated in silence. Conversation had been stilted between them all day, and now the air vibrated with tension. When the phone rang, Tamara started so violently, she felt as if her bones jumped free of her body. Making sure the parlour door was closed firmly behind her, she hurried into the kitchen to answer the phone.

As Tamara had anticipated, the caller was Barbelo, although her voice sounded faint, as if she was calling from a long way away. "Listen to me, Tamara, for I will give you a song."

Tamara pressed the phone against her ear. "Yes?"

A shrill whistle shuddered down the line and pierced Tamara's ear. She uttered a short scream, and jerked her head away. For a moment, her head rang with the sound. Then it faded away. Gingerly, she replaced the phone to her ear. "What was that? It nearly deafened me."

"But it was your song, my darling!"

"Song? I didn't hear it!"

"You did, and you will remember it when the time comes. It is the lament for Serapis. This evening, you will sing it to the Lion Guardian." The phone clicked, then the dialling tone sounded. Tamara stared at the instrument in astonishment for a few moments. Was that all Barbelo was going to say? Had she been cut off? Puzzled, she went back into the parlour.

"Who was it?" Shemyaza asked. "Is your coven on to us?"

Tamara shook her head. "No. It was my father. I told him I was busy." She rubbed her hands together. "It is time now. We must leave. Put your coats on."

At the threshold to the cottage, Tamara took Shemyaza's hand in her own. "Are you afraid?" she asked him.

He shrugged. His expression was that of a beautiful, bewildered boy. "I don't know. I feel numb, as if this isn't real. Perhaps nothing will happen."

Tamara's heart turned over at the sight of him, but she suppressed her gentler emotions and shook her head. Her voice, when she spoke, was firm. "Remember what happened with Michael at the Mount yesterday! You really think nothing will happen?"

Shemyaza stared at her. "I'm still not sure I want to go through with this. The results..."

Tamara interrupted him. You must do this for me, my love."

Shemyaza smiled bleakly and walked past her towards the car.

Tamara knew that the Pelleth would be safely gathered at the Penhaligon house, and unlikely to be wandering about. She drove with confidence to the cliff top above the Lion's Head. Delmar had still been having trouble with his parents, and had to continue sneaking out of the house to be with Tamara. Ellen Tremayne was obviously aware her son had been working with Tamara, and was no doubt obeying the injunctions of the Pelleth in trying to prevent him doing so. However, Delmar was a law unto himself, and a slippery creature. It was virtually impossible to imprison him. Now he sat in the back of the car, his strange eyes shifting with mer-light. This was the night when the sea would come to the land, and in the advent of the serpent, the elements would fuse in primal hunger.

Tamara did not park in one of the coastal lay-bys, but turned up a narrow track, where she could secrete her vehicle beneath a grove of ancient oaks. Tamara watched Shemyaza ease himself gingerly out of the car as if his joints were aching. He looked slightly ridiculous with her father's old coat slung over his robe. She opened the back door for Delmar.

"We'll leave the coats here," she said. "It's only a short walk to the cliff-top, and it's not exactly cold tonight, is it."

Tamara led the way to the path that led down to the beach. Soon, she thought, the power of the serpent would be hers. Shemyaza, she felt she already owned. Let the Pelleth and the Grigori perform their feeble rituals. She knew, because Barbelo had told her, that everyone believed Shemyaza was already in the underworld. So much for their psychics and scrying pools.

They walked along the beach in silence. The light around them was green; neither day nor night. Above them, the edges of the clouds seemed tinged with phosphorescence. The sea was restless, churning with flickering lights and quick, dark shapes. Warm, damp breezes blew against their faces, a perfume spray of brine and earth.

Although Tamara had received no precise instructions for the ritual to come, she trusted that she'd know what to say and do at the right time. They rounded the cove and there was the majestic countenance of the guardian ahead of them, staring out to sea as it had done for millennia. Shemyaza seemed to be in a daze. He stumbled ahead of his companions and halted before the lion. Tamara watched in a kind of ghoulish fascination and anticipation. Shemyaza threw back his head, so that his hair poured down the back of his robe. He seemed to want to look the guardian in the eye, but at that moment the eyes were closed, just suggestions of shapes within the rock.

Tamara caught up with him, Delmar at her heels. "Speak to the guardian, Shem," she murmured through the wind.

"I don't know its name," he answered, his voice vague.

"It is Azumi," Delmar said.

Tamara glanced at the boy, knew immediately that the information was correct. "Azumi," she echoed and positioned herself behind Shemyaza, with Delmar at her left side.

Shemyaza sighed, then raised his arms. Although she could not see his face, Tamara guessed his eyes were closed. "Azumi! Hear me! It is I, Shemyaza. I seek entrance to the lair of the serpent."

For a moment, all was still, then came a small tumble of stones. Tamara felt the rock beneath her feet tremble slightly. Before them, the face of the lion became more distinct in the stone. The rock seemed to shift and seethe, until what appeared to be the perfect statue of a gigantic sphinx reared before them. Azumi. The guardian's eyes opened slowly, and twin fans of red light gouted out. Its jaw cracked ajar, with a sound like an avalanche of gravel. Its voice was the voice of the earth, a thunderous sound of rocks grinding together. Tamara fought an urge to put her hands over her ears, or press her fingers to her temples. The voice reverberated painfully inside her mind.

"Have you come to sing the Lament for Serapis?"

Shemyaza glanced round at Tamara. "Have I?" he asked.

Tamara collected herself, nodded and stepped up beside him, taking his hand in her own. "Say yes. Tell it your priestess will sing the Lament."

Shemyaza turned back to the lion. "The Lament will be sung. My priestess will sing it."

Tamara took a step back and withdrew the serpent talisman from a pocket in her robe. Holding it up before her face, she closed her eyes and focused her whole being upon the carved image and the power that Barbelo had instilled into it. In her mind, she saw a fine glowing haze begin to seep from the distended mouth of each snake, twin coils that twisted together into a single, writhing plume above the talisman. A newly born serpent of moist aether. Slowly, undulating on the air, it drifted like a questing viper towards her parted lips. Unconsciously, she gritted her teeth. When it touched her, the cold vapour prised her jaws apart, and began to probe the soft tissues of her mouth. creeping over her tongue and down her throat. Tamara had to fight the urge to retch, reminding herself this was merely a visualisation. The serpent breath filled her chest with a numbing cold; it felt as if a great reptile had curled itself around her lungs. And something moved there. A life of sorts.

Her jaw dropped open.

A tiny sound was building up within her throat, forcing its way upwards, out of her mouth. Gradually it rose in pitch, until the air around her seemed to vibrate. Then, the note changed key of its own volition; Tamara had no physical control over it. The keening flirted briefly with a lower tone, before soaring upward once more into an unbearable crescendo. The sound was beyond beauty, a formless language of raw music. Tamara sensed it did not originate from either Grigori or human tongues. Its message was a lament, like the cry hidden beneath the crashing of the waves, as the sea lunges in hungry desperation at the unyielding land. The caress of the Lament would eventually claim and reshape anything that it touched.

Before Tamara, Shemyaza stood motionless, allowing the song to wash through his entire body. All the glyphs carved upon the rearing stone stele before him were shining with a fierce light; it seemed they crept and crawled upon the surface of the portal. Instinctively, he reached out and placed his hands upon them. At the same moment, the resonance of the Lament reached an ear-splitting climax, and a deep vibration started up from somewhere behind the cliff, as if the song had woken a giant, sleeping heart. These sounds streamed painfully through every bone and muscle in Shemyaza's body, as if they would shake him apart. He knew he must somehow move beyond this stage of the ritual, otherwise it might destroy him. Steeling himself, he pushed the boundaries of his perception beyond the inflexible surface of the stone portal, threading his sight through the atoms of the rock. As he concentrated on this, the vibrations of the Lament seemed to die away. All he could hear was the steady, rhythmic thumping, emanating from deep within the earth. He perceived that a huge, pulsating ball of white light hovered beyond the portal, almost as if it were a spiritual guide that had been awaiting his arrival. Within it, Shemyaza could see moving spirals and gyrating lines of brighter light. He sensed a watchful intelligence within the radiant sphere; it seemed to be examining or assessing him.

"Do you know me?" he asked, within his mind. "Can you feel me?"

The sense of vigilance increased. Shemyaza was certain it heard him.

"I have come to the gate of your abyss," he told it, "led by a dark and impenetrable void inside me. Are you the light that should be within me? Are you what I am to become?"

The flickering brilliance made no response, merely spun upon the air in front of him.

"Take me unto you," Shemyaza said. "I need to pass through the portal, to look upon the source of your creation with living eyes."

The light began to retreat away into the darkness. Shemyaza felt a brief tug of grief within his heart. He could not follow it, and the rock still stood firm before him. As the light faded from his inner sight, he became aware once more of the eerie tones of the Lament around him. It no longer seemed to emanate from Tamara's throat, but from all around him, as if every living thing, every rock, every grain of sand, raised the voices of their essence in song.

Shemyaza opened his eyes. He gazed up at the face of Azumi and the eyes of the guardian changed from red to a deep, radiant gold. The Lament abruptly ceased, and the silence around him was absolute; no sound of wave or wind, not even a sea bird's cry. The waves themselves were stilled, as if holding their breath.

Shemyaza turned round to face Tamara, and became aware of the sound of her rasping breath. Her face looked sickly and pallid in the strange greenish light. Delmar was a starved, pale shape beside her. Shemyaza wanted to speak to them, tell them about the light beyond the cliff. The Lament had ended, it was used up, and the guardian within the cliff had assessed him, but they had failed, for the portal had not opened to him. Tamara's eyes stared back at him wildly. What could they say to one another now?

Shemyaza opened his mouth, but before he could utter any words, an immense cracking sound split the air around them. Tamara staggered into Delmar, and Shemyaza wheeled round to face the cliff. His vision seemed blurred, then he realised that the rock face before him was shaking. The cracking of stone bones resounded all around them, and slowly, so slowly, the stone portal between the sphinx's paws began to roll backwards. All that could be seen beyond it was a dense blackness.

Shemyaza glanced back at Tamara. Now was the time! There was no going back! Her image seemed smoky before him, somehow insubstantial, as if she was fading away out of existence. Then, as if a veil of dusky air was being drawn aside, her form solidified once more before him. Her body had become wreathed in a shifting smoke of diaphanous blue veils, but her face was visible. He uttered a low, agonised cry. It was not Tamara's face he saw, but that of his lost consort, Ishtahar. Her black eyes, full of the waters of life, stared directly at him. Her fine lips were drawn into a shy, sad smile. She projected an air of pleading and yearning, yet there was no hint of weakness about her. The spirit within her was strong and determined.

Shemyaza's felt as if a black crust that had encased his heart broke and fell away, to be absorbed by the tides of his blood. She had come to him at the final hour. She was here to guide and protect him! "Ishti," he murmured.

"Yes, I am she," the vision responded gently.

Shemyaza could not see that beneath the cloak of illusion, Tamara stood strong and still, gripping the serpent talisman in her hand. She was wreathed in the breath of the serpents, and it spun a deceitful image in Shemyaza's mind. "I am she, my beloved," Tamara crooned. "Behold, the way lies open to you."

Shemyaza turned back to the cliff. A lightless maw now lay between the paws of the sphinx. Steam purled out of it, accompanied by a long, sibilant hiss. As the vapour touched him, Shemyaza was engulfed in a fetid stink, the sulphur breath of the underworld. At first, the steam was cold, but as it coiled and twisted around his body, a snake of breath drawn from the deepest pit of land, it gradually became hotter, until he felt it would sear the skin from his bones. A deep thudding sound boomed through it, as if giant machinery churned beneath the earth.

"Enter!" cried Tamara.

Shemyaza hesitated, and looked back at her. "I can't!"

"You must!" she cried. "Shem, do it now. Do it for me, your love. Remember who I am. Unless you do this, the world will become barren. I will be barren. For the sake of our love, enter through the gate!"

Shemyaza stared at her for a moment. He was still unsure, having no idea what he would find beneath the earth, or even if he would be able to escape afterwards. Over the past week, he'd been lulled into accepting his fate by the succubus Tamara, but he knew that his heart was still poisoned by bitterness. Should he face the serpent feeling that way? Yet Ishtahar had come to him at last. How could he deny her? "Come with me!" he cried.

The image before him shook her head. "No. You know I cannot. You must go alone."

Shemyaza was afraid. If Ishtahar was not at his side to soothe his negative feelings, he felt he would be vulnerable in the underworld. He did not trust his own heart.

Then a cold hand touched his arm. Shemyaza saw that it was Delmar.

"My Lord, enter the gate. Go willingly. Do it for love, yes, but do it also for the liberty of this land, for I can see its light within you."

This was his vizier speaking, the one who advised him. How could he ignore the boy? How could he ignore the woman he loved?

"Wait for me," Shemyaza said, and stepped into the darkness.

At High Crag, the Parzupheim gathered in the temple. Enniel made ready to lead a ceremony designed to help Shemyaza accomplish his task in the underworld.

In the garden of the Penhaligon house, the Pelleth prepared for their cliff-top ritual. The women had smeared themselves with flying ointment. Now Meggie stood before them with her arms raised, and the warm, unnatural wind lifted her hair. "When the serpent comes, my sisters, we must fly with it! Fly!"

Emma moved closer to Daniel's side. "Will it happen? Can you sense anything?"

Daniel sighed in perplexity and shook his head. "It's so confused in my head. I can't tell." He uttered a furious sound. "Emma, I feel like I've been blinded!"

Emma squeezed his arm. "Have faith, my Daniel."

Lily felt on edge and jumpy. Salamiel had not been in the house all day, and she'd barely seen Nina. She knew that tonight, everyone expected something momentous to happen. Surely she wouldn't be left alone at that time? Restlessly, she roamed the house. Beyond the tall windows, the wind moaned in a horribly human voice. Shutters clattered, as if worried by spindly fingers seeking ingress. And below the harrying whine of the wind was a more terrible sound; the flexing of the muscles of the land as the serpent writhed at the threshold of wakefulness. Every few minutes, the ground shook, making the ancient artefacts that ornamented the shelves and nooks of the house rattle and wobble. Occasionally, a crash could be heard as something fell from its niche.

The library, normally the room Lily found the most welcoming, unnerved her. She thought of withered ghosts sitting in leather chairs, the creak of fleshless bones. In the cavernous hallway, the chandelier swung and chinked. Somewhere in the far reaches of the house, something uttered a cry, perhaps an animal. Lily hugged herself and spun around in the meagre sweeping spotlight of the chandelier. She felt as if the house was closing in on her. She emanated a psychic call to Daniel, but sensed only darkness. She called to Salamiel with her body and mind, but even though she had no idea where he was, she knew he was beyond hearing her. Even Nina's presence would be welcome now.

Lily mounted the stairs, resisting the urge to look back over her shoulder at the library door. Nina must be in her bedroom, probably painting her toenails ice-pink and listening to the radio. Despite the fact she was a Grigori dependent, she seemed an unimaginative, unshakeable person. But where was Nina's bedroom? A noise like a heavy chest dropping echoed through the house. It seemed to come from the cellars.

Lily ran up the stairs.

She paced up and down the main corridor on the first floor, pausing to listen at doors, hearing nothing but the restless shift of drapes at windows laced with drafts and the occasional rattle of objects on their shelves. Plucking up her courage, still fearful of ghosts, she opened a few of the doors, but found only desolate bed-chambers beyond them, lying under the thinnest patina of dust, illumined by the sick, green light from the sky outside.

Again, a heavy crash came from somewhere below the house. Lily ran to the stairs that led to the next floor. All lay in darkness above her, threatening and alive, yet she felt an intense compulsion to mount the stairs. Was it simply because she wanted to look for Nina or Salamiel? If she couldn't find them on the next floor, she'd go outside, try to use her psychic sense to locate the house where Daniel was staying. She couldn't bear to remain alone in this place. Why had Salamiel deserted her? Wasn't she to be part of Shem's destiny?

The second floor was silent and empty. Lily entered the bedroom she had slept in on her first night. She sensed a tension there, the phantom of her own anxiety, and shut the door on it quickly. Her feet led her down a narrow corridor and at the end was a door. Drawn to it, almost against her will, Lily turned the worn metal handle. Beyond the door, a narrow flight of stairs, illuminated by low-burning wall-lights, led up to the final floor.

The upper storey, where the long attics lay, was dark and cold. Lily put her hand on one of the ancient cast iron radiators and found it chilly to her touch. Here, the wallpaper was old and fading, and the overhead lights were eerily dim in their small glass shades, hanging from ancient fabric-coated wiring, strung with cobwebs. The air smelled musty and damp.

What am I doing here? she asked herself. Nina would not have a room up here; she was far too fond of warmth and light. Lily felt frightened, yet driven. As she crept along the thin carpet of a long corridor, a booming sound came from outside, and all the light fittings began to shake. Lily reached out for the wall. Her blood felt thick in her veins. She was close to screaming.

Try the doors, she told herself, but the thought of looking into the rooms terrified her. She was walking towards the end of a corridor, where a round window, with an arrangement of wedge-shaped panes, overlooked the garden. Some of the panes were cracked, and all were thick with grime. Lily expected to see a tall shape manifest before this mouth of leprous light, something hideous with arms outstretched, its hair waving around its head like a halo of vipers.

She found her hand upon the door to her left, even before she heard the sound.

It was a low murmuring, at once like a song and a litany of complaint.

The dull brass knob turned beneath her fingers and the door swung open. It neither creaked nor scraped upon the floor. Once the door was open, Lily's ears were assaulted by the wail of children, children in terrible pain, terrible fear, but there were no children in the tiny, black room, only the ghosts of their terror. She stood with frozen feet, gazing in horror and awe at the tableau before her.

The woman sat cross-legged in a shifting pool of dead snakes and serpent blood, as if she'd lately mutilated each reptile. Around her gory couch, black candles were stuck onto the floor, a flickering sea of light. Behind her, half cradled by the ripped snake flesh, lay a small, withered form. Lily dared not look too closely; it seemed too much like the corpse of an infant, sucked of life and juice. The woman wore a cloak of owl feathers, spiked with a cruel forest of severed beaks and claws. It was Sofia. She did not seem able to see Lily standing in the doorway, for her eyes were rolled upwards in their sockets. She seemed so far gone into some arcane trance that even her sharp senses were ignorant of the girl. A strange gibbering sound, which might have been torn words or the chittering of night creatures, came from her lips, which were stained with black saliva.

As she mumbled, she chewed. Lily could smell the scent of haoma, but it was almost eclipsed by the stench of rotten meat rising from the coiled carcasses. Sofia was naked beneath her grisly cloak, her body smeared with the black blood of the snakes. She was the most wretched and dark thing Lily had ever seen, or could ever imagine seeing. Even Peverel Othman in his worst guise had not been so close to abomination. She wanted to back from the room, deny what she'd seen, and uttered a sad sound of disgust.

Sofia's head snapped forward. Her eyes fixed on Lily. She held out her bloody arms, flexing the fingers like claws. "Ah, my pretty, pretty, here you are! Did you hear me call you? It is our time now."

Lily's stomach burned and an acid taste rose to her tongue. "No...Where is...No..." She felt sick, aware now that she had obeyed a silent summons. Some dark, hideous part of her had heard Sofia's call and followed it to its source.

Sofia uttered a chilling cackle. "Oh, come to me, my pretty one! Come sit upon my lap and I will take you to the secret places beneath the earth. Don't you understand your purpose? You are here because we hunt the Prince of Truth. Your husband, your lover, your despoiler." She extended a clawed hand. "Here, take my fingers in your own. Share my sight. He walks beneath the earth alone. He needs us now, my lovely one. You are to be his sacred bride."

"You are no part of Shem," Lily managed to say. She wanted to back from the room, but was incapable of moving. Sofia's eyes were locked with her own, and the strength of that pitiless stare would not let her leave.

"Oh, but I am part of him," Sofia said. "More so than the fools who sing his praises and litter his path with flowers. There are Grigori upon this planet, Lily, who are so old, you could not imagine them. They have waited for this hour, when their Dark Prince comes to lead them in the final battle. I am their Queen, their Priestess. When the Shamir wakes, its power shall be ours, and Azazel our king. With you, he will create a dynasty of kings that shall rule the earth for eternity. We shall take back all that was lost and the stargate will open unto us. Humanity will be cleansed from all the lands. Their love for war will climax in the war of all wars, and from the ashes Grigori will rise victorious, to reclaim their world."

"You are evil!" Lily cried. "Shem won't do what you want!"
She wished she could be sure of that.

"Oh, will he not?" Sofia laughed again. "Why fight it, Lily?
You know that you want and need him. He is confused now and we
must help him. The drivel and cant of the weak New Age must not
seduce him. Come now, join me, for we must extinguish his light,
lead him to the Lie. We must help him initiate the true renewal."

"No!"

Sofia shook her head slowly, her mouth stretched into a grin.
"Ah, you are a wilful girl! Still, that is all to the good. Azazel would
scorn a milk-thin maid." She pursed her mouth and nodded, as if
coming to a decision. "Lily, at this moment, Salamiel is calling to
his lord. He is our tool, and weak from love. You have bewitched
him, which I applaud. Come here to me, and we will augment
Salamiel's call. Azazel will hear you both. We must tell him to put
out the serpent's golden eyes. In its blind rage, it will energise this
land with the true power that is beyond all comprehension. Listen to
me, Lily. Feel your own power in your belly. Don't you know that
a child grows there? Your daughter will be a great priestess. Make
the way ready for her. Take what is yours by right!"

"I'm…I'm pregnant?" Lily felt she would be sick at any
moment. To hear this news in this terrible place, from the lips of a
she-demon, was too much to bear. Perhaps it wasn't true.

"Of course it's true," Sofia said softly, her eyes a mere slit.
"It is child of the black-skinned one, your sacrificial lover."

"Israel!" The word was uttered in a shocked whisper. All
the grief she had held in check, the revulsion, shame and horror,
erupted from some hidden corner of Lily's mind. The thought of
Israel's death and the fact she might be carrying his child gave her
the strength to act. It was perhaps the last thing Sofia had anticipated. Lily knew she could not fight Sofia, but now at least she had
the freedom to escape.

In one swift movement, Lily backed out of the room and
slammed the door. She heard Sofia's hideous laughter echoing out
and the cries of ghostly children shrieked louder, as if instruments of
torture had been tightened upon their flesh.

"Run, then, my darling! Run! You will be back! You have
nowhere to turn but to the one who rules your heart!"

With her stomach churning, Lily fled the upper storey. She
was in such haste, she felt she flew down the stairs without her feet

touching any of the treads. She had to get out! Was Salamiel part of Sofia's evil ritual? Had he lied to her?

Oh God, Owen! She couldn't leave him here. Skidding on the landing, Lily pelted down to Owen's room. She half expected to find Salamiel there, enacting some filthy rite upon her brother's body, but Owen sat upright in his bed as always, staring at the door, absurdly tranquil in the chaos of the night.

"O'! We have to go!" Lily ran to the bed. She had no time to dress him. Sofia might be slithering down from the attic room at this very moment. When she touched Owen's body, she felt him jerk.

"Owen! That's right. Help me! Please help me! Walk! We have to go! We're in danger! Please wake up!" She continued to exhort him as she half dragged him to the door. Owen's limbs moved spasmodically, like the limbs of a puppet, but at least he was making some contribution. Tearing a dressing gown from the back of the door as she left the room, Lily glanced to left and right up the corridor. All seemed quiet. She pushed Owen's arms into the robe. "Come on now. Help me. We must go." He was moving too slowly, too awkwardly.

They reached the top of the stairs that led down to the hall. Lily could see the front door. She prayed it was unlocked. "Come on, O'. That's right. Down here." She had her arms around him. He made a sound in his throat of consternation and distress. "Good, good. You're doing fine. We'll find Daniel, now. I promise. We'll get out of here."

They were almost at the bottom, when the door to the basements flew open. Lily's heart froze. Pale shapes were crawling out into the hall, stretching and writhing upon the stone floor. Emim!

"Oh, Great Shem!" Lily's curse was followed by a wail. The Emim reared up from their bellies like white cobras, sniffing the air. Their hair wafted around their heads like the tail feathers of white peacocks. Their eyes were filmed as if with a third eyelid. They yawned and flexed their limbs. Something had recently awoken them, Lily realised, and they were still sluggish. That was to her advantage.

Banishing all fear, Lily summoned her inner strength and lifted her brother in her arms. In her terror, Owen felt as light as a sick baby. Remembering her flight from the upper storey, she flew down the last few stairs, jumped over the reaching hands of the nearest Emim and hurled herself forward at the main door. Behind her, she heard the Emim hissing and chattering their teeth. She heard the slide of their pale bodies along the stone. Then the door was before her. With little effort, she slung Owen over one shoulder and turned the great handle. It opened immediately and the night rushed in around her, warm and damp and stinking of sulphur. Lily secured Owen's position with a shrug of her shoulder and ran out into the darkness. A furious wind grabbed at her hair. It seemed full of living creatures, which pawed and licked at her with tiny hands and tongues. She heard lascivious whispers in her ears.

Which way? Lily's head darted from the left to right. She could not afford to delay. Without making a conscious decision, she began to run down the gravel driveway towards the road. The pale stones shifted beneath her feet, impeding her progress. It was like the flight through a nightmare. Wind elementals formed in the air before her, grey, screaming shapes that whirled around in front of her face. She screamed and ducked, but the phantoms simply vanished, only to reappear when she tried to continue her escape. She felt spectral fingers, like the twigs of trees, snag in her hair and scrape her cheeks, but she had to fight on. What haunted the top storey of Pharos was worse than any ghost or elemental. Owen shuddered and groaned on her shoulder. Several times, she nearly dropped him. Her muscles shrieked with pain, but she dared not pause to move her brother's weight to her other shoulder.

Finally, the main gates were before her. She glanced backwards, but the Emim did not appear to have followed her. Quickly, Lily hurried through the gates and shut them behind her. For a moment, stillness. Would Sofia really let her escape so easily? Still, she hadn't seemed to care that Lily ran away, seeming confident she would be compelled to return.

Lily dropped Owen onto the road, and rubbed her neck and shoulders. She pressed her face against the wrought iron bars of the gate. Nothing. Pharos was in darkness, and there were no sounds other than the low whistle of the wind. Now where? She must not wait around here too long. The news that Sofia had given her hadn't yet sunk into her mind fully, but she realised there was another life at stake now, all that remained of Israel in the world.

She lifted Owen over her shoulder again. Which way? Where was Daniel?

Lily attempted to muster her thoughts for a moment. She must try to concentrate, pick up some sense of her friend. But there was only darkness and a dull buzzing in her head. Still, she could not stay here. "Which way, O'?" He made no sound, lying like a dead weight over her shoulder, his arms dangling down her back. She looked to the right, saw only a maelstrom of flickering grey shapes in the air, some feet from where she stood. The elementals were back, waiting to tease her. She realised they were no real physical threat, but balked at the idea of forcing her way through them. She looked to the left and saw a similar obstruction, dirty smoke full of the suggestion of grimacing faces and jostling limbs. It seemed there was little choice; both directions promised danger. Then the greyness seemed to part. Lily took a step in that direction. As the dirty fog drifted aside, she could see a blue light that wavered just above the surface of the road ahead. She heard a voice call to her.

"Come, my daughter. Come!" And the blue light became the figure of a woman, whose pale arm was raised in a gesture of beckoning.

"Ishtahar!" Lily began to jog towards the shimmering figure, hoping desperately this was no lie. The vision was clad in a floating cloud of peacock blue veils, but she appeared to have no face. Where her features should have been was only a blank whiteness.

No matter how fast Lily ran, the figure on the road retreated ahead of her, even though it did not appear to move. Lily knew she was being led, and part of her mind shrieked a warning, but she kept focused in her head the vision of Ishtahar she had seen at the High Place in Little Moor. Could the image of this benign goddess ever be used by dark forces? She had to trust that it would not.

She called out in her mind. "Lead me to Daniel! Help me!"

It seemed she ran for an eternity. Owen became heavier upon her shoulder. Her burst of unnatural strength had ebbed away. Her chest ached and her legs had become weak. Soon, she was merely staggering along the road, bowed down by the weight of her brother. Presently, she sank to her knees, the tears of frustration and fear spilling down her face. Behind her, she heard an unearthly howl, which was echoed many times around her. Emim! They were stalking her, smelling her warmth.

"Now, my Lily, have courage."

The voice came from nowhere, a soft and gentle chime of sound. A few feet away, she saw the image of the blue woman hovering at the side of the road. Behind her the ocean churned and roared. Lily pushed her hair furiously from her eyes. They had reached the coast. About half a mile away, an enormous house reared against the bilious sky, crowned with wisps of cloud. Lights blazed from its windows.

"This way, my child. Find your strength. I am with you."

Lily groaned and lurched to her feet. Was this the house where Daniel was? With her arms trembling from exertion, she hoisted Owen off the road. She could barely control his sprawling limbs. The house seemed so far away. The vision in blue hovered before her, hanging on the air.

"Down.... down...Here..."

The ghostly woman disappeared over the edge of the cliff. Lily could hear her faint call from below. "Come to me! Release me! Come, my daughter!"

Not to the house, then.

Lily staggered to the edge of the road, and saw a tortuous path leading downwards. She didn't think she'd be able to negotiate it with Owen in her arms, but knew she had to try. She took the first ginger step and felt loose stones slide beneath her feet. Within seconds, she had fallen onto her backside and was slithering downwards with Owen hanging in her lap, his weight dragging her onwards. Her skirt was ripped, pushed up around her waist, her knickers tore, leaving her vulnerable to the predations of the stones. As the landscape flashed by her, she had a nightmare vision of plummeting off the path and down to the beach below, but then, somehow, she managed to halt her descent. Her buttocks and the backs of her thighs smarted with grazes. Owen uttered a faint groan and pawed the air with limp hands. The side of his face was scraped and raw.

"Oh sweet goddess, help me!" Lily's prayer was a ragged cry. She slid up the rock wall to her left and began to drag Owen sideways down the path, keeping her spine pressed against the cliff. Stones showered her head from above, and she twisted her ankle painfully as she missed her footing. Then, a long, clawed hand curled around her face.

Lily screamed, and struggled, but strong arms held her against the cliff. A quick, lithe shape jumped over head and, turning in the air, landed on all fours in front of her. Its lizard face hissed at her, a crested ruff rising up around its head crowned with vicious spines. Just as Lily was sure she was about to die, she heard a low, fluting cry drift up from the beach. The lizard man cocked its head to listen, then lowered its spined ruff. The arms that gripped Lily pushed her away. She staggered forward and fell to her knees before the creature in front of her, her face inches from its own. She looked into its wise serpent eyes and could smell its reptile musk, but it made no move to attack her. Its mouth dropped open, revealing a dark maw. "Daughter..." The word was little more than a hiss.

Whimpering, Lily dragged Owen down the final stretch of the path to the beach. Here, she saw the image of Ishtahar standing upon the sand, her veils blowing around her. The sea was wild, the waves looked like screaming, foaming horses with dead, black eyes. As the waves crested and broke up on the shore, the sea beasts vanished, only for more to rear up behind them. Lily knelt upon the sand, shuddering and gulping air. She looked back at the cliff-face, and saw a host of stone faces staring out at her. They stretched their jaws wide, splintering stone, rolled their pebble eyes and uttered a lament of moans and piteous chanting. The cliff itself seemed to be disintegrating. Small land-slides of rock clattered down its face.

Lily squatted down and covered Owen with her body. He was shivering violently, his jaws clenched. She saw blood mixed with spittle on his lips. "Ishtahar," she breathed. "Ishtahar. Help us."

But the image of the blue woman kept her distance, a blade of pale light upon the sand.

In the temple of High Crag, the voices of the Parzupheim rang out, uttering incantations in lost tongues. In the drawing-room, Aninka stood with her face pressed against the panes of the French windows. The night called to her, but she was too afraid to face it.

On the cliff above Meggie's house, the Pelleth swayed to the wind, singing a shrieking, elemental song. Daniel stood straight, with his eyes squeezed shut, seeking an image of his master in the hectic night.

At Pharos, Sofia rolled in her bed of serpent blood, sending tendrils of her mind down to the lair of the serpent, tongues sugared with sweet lies. She beheld the image of Shemyaza feeling his way through the fire-shot darkness, and reached out to him. "Scapegoat, sacrifice! You are the Dying King, to die forever. Go to your death, boy-child. That is what they want. Feed their lies. Or will you turn to me, the dark serpent mother? Let me nurture your bitterness into an avenging blade. Be not the goat but the war-bird. Turn upon them! Be fierce! Be cruel! Unleash the serpent against them!" She felt her thoughts brush against the uncertainty in Shemyaza's mind. He was a foolish child, fretful and selfish. Part of his petulant, masculine soul heard her words and listened intently.

Salamiel lay like a five-pointed star upon the roof of his house, intoxicated by trance. His eyes stared blindly at the boiling sky. He meditated upon the light of truth. "Azazel, let your heart be true. Ahura Mazda, absolve him of his sins. Let the radiance of the true spiritual sun shine upon him in this hour of darkness. Azazel, look to the light of truth! Bring us hope through the love you once gave to the land. In Anu's name, amen..." his inner voice was nothing more than a small, silvery thread of sound that snaked in vain through the caverns of the underworld.

Chapter Twenty-Eight
Waking the Serpent

When Shemyaza entered the portal to the underworld, he found that the floor sloped down immediately. The cave within was lit by a dull orange radiance, which shone sickly through a viscous steam that clung to his legs, but there was no sign of the ball of light he'd perceived from outside. The incline before him was so sharp, Shemyaza was forced to scramble down it on his backside, using his hands and feet to steady his descent. It was a slow process, for slippery fragments of sharp slate cut into his fingers as they clawed for purchase, and he knew that if he tried to hurry, the shifting stone beneath him might give way entirely, send him plummeting downwards. Eventually, he reached the bottom of the slope, and here was able to walk upright. He found himself in a wide tunnel, lined on either side by recesses in the rock. Within each niche giant bones were resting, as if the labyrinth of tunnels was no more than an ancient catacomb, where the dead contemplated lightless eternity as they sifted away to dust. Then, beneath his feet, the rock vibrated, as if a coiled, living thing had flexed its scrolls of muscle far below. It reminded him that whatever this place might be, it was far more than a mausoleum for the dead.

Shemyaza walked along the winding tunnel for what seemed like many hours. Always the floor sloped downwards and, with each step he took, the air became hotter and more oppressive. To left and right, he saw the gaping mouths of side tunnels leading off into darkness, but kept his feet upon the straightest path. The bones of the giants lined the tunnel walls: silent, sentinel, prehistoric. They lay amid their rotted finery, the damp wink of jewels coruscating through their fibrous dust. It looked as if thousands had been entombed there.

As Shemyaza walked, he thought about how the parched bones around him had once thrilled with vitality: the empty, cracked craniums had bloomed with thoughts, desires, emotion. In the end, it had all fallen to powdery nothingness. This, in all truth, was his own inevitable destiny. But what punctuated the journey of his life could and *must* matter; he could effect changes. He could *be*. If he wanted it badly enough.

Now, there were faint voices hissing through the air around him. He heard snatches of conversation, whispered words. His name. "Shem! Shem!" Was that Daniel calling to him? No, Daniel was lost to him. He had chosen to abandon his vizier in favour of the sea-born boy. The spirits of guilt and unease rose up within him upon dark, tattered wings. He did not want to contemplate them, for he was afraid of the pain. Summoning his will, he dismissed all thoughts of Daniel from his mind.

Then, he heard a sibilant, feminine murmur, close to his ear. It was impossible to decipher the words exactly, but they seemed to coax him onwards to the serpent. Shem could sense their purpose; it was to inflame his outrage at the thought of others desiring him to be their scapegoat. Were these the ashen sentiments of some long-dead female giant, someone who understood about victimisation and who sympathised with his plight? He reached out with his inner voice, and asked the spirit to identify herself, speak to him plainly, but even as he did this, he sensed her withdrawal. The whispers faded from his mind, as if he'd passed through the substance of some resentful ghost.

Moments later, a low, desperate entreaty called to his pure heart, a prayer to the light of truth. Fleetingly, Shemyaza thought of his lost brethren, the other Watchers who'd shared his fate. *Salamiel? Is that you?* He tried to visualise Salamiel's face, but could not summon an image to his mind's eye. Even if Sofia had told the truth, and Salamiel was near, Shemyaza knew he could not venture into this territory.

These phantoms must all be in his own mind, and for that reason Shemyaza dismissed them from his consciousness. He must not listen to them. All that was real, all that mattered, was that he was making the journey at last, but not for the Parzupheim. He was making it for Tamara and Delmar, his faithful servants, who waited beyond the portal for him, patient and true. Tamara's face bloomed before his inner eye. Had she not guided and protected him? *But you are here, regardless,* a quiet voice murmured. *Despite your misgivings.*

Shemyaza shivered. He began to feel afraid, and his awareness seemed projected outside his body, looking into his brain, his heart. His fear was a swirling pit of dull yellow light, shot with ribbons of red. The colours of bitterness trailed through it, and the hues of shame and anger. He saw himself as a warped gestalt of fear, hatred and pain, surely an inappropriate manifestation to approach the serpent? Yet he could neither halt his progress nor turn back. A heavy weariness descended upon him. What must be must be. If he was to die, he could do nothing to prevent it. If he was to unleash dark forces upon the earth, it was the flower of his destiny. Others heaped him with responsibility, but ultimately he was just a catalyst, a tool.

The tunnel led through many lofty caverns, each deeper than the one before: yawning chambers rang with the echoes of ancient rites. Here, the dead giants were fixed upright to the uneven walls, their friable skeletons held together by fused armour. Rank upon rank, they disappeared into the shadows of above; a slumbering army of kings. As he passed them, Shemyaza imagined that a shred of awareness reached out to him from each desiccated corpse. *Have you come to wake us? Have you come to lead us to victory?*

He directed no answer towards them.

Eventually, the floor of the wide tunnel began to slope upwards once more. Soon, the path was too sheer to negotiate by feet alone, and he began to use his hands to help him climb. The light became ruddier, and the hot air was punctuated by inexplicable cold spots: columns of freezing, spiralling aether. Passing through them, Shemyaza heard terrible screams and could smell the meaty, metallic tang of blood. Above him, the steep path led to a ledge, over which poured clouds of billowing steam that smelled of ozone and salt. He pulled himself up onto the path.

Before him, stood a male figure, motionless and vigilant. The man was taller than Shemyaza himself, and clad in a long dark robe. He was undoubtedly Grigori. His head was entirely covered by a close fitting skull cap of silver metal, and he carried a staff crowned by the sigil of a Magian priest, the same double-serpent of Tamara's talisman. Shemyaza knew he was facing the guardian of this place, perhaps the first of many.

Shemyaza rested his hands on his knees, stooping forward to catch his breath. He sensed no direct threat from the figure before him, but perhaps a slight air of challenge. The stranger allowed him time to recompose himself and then stepped towards him. Shemyaza looked up into the long, ascetic face, the almond-shaped eyes of

deepest blue. Plaited locks of bone-white hair hung down from beneath the cap of silver, onto the priest's chest. His face seemed
incredibly ancient, yet also youthful. Humour shone from his eyes,
as well as wry wisdom. Shemyaza sensed he was looking upon the
face of a Grigori who had come to these shores long ago. The attenuated countenance before him reflected how the giants would
have appeared in those ancient times.

"You are a ghost, of course," he said, with some disdain. He
did not believe that one of the original giants could have survived
this long.

The figure inclined his head. "I am the guardian of the
serpent's realm, left here by those who laid the Shamir to rest. I
have waited a long time for you."

"Are you real?" Impulsively, Shemyaza reached out to touch
the guardian's robes, and the man did not flinch away. Shemyaza
felt rough cloth between his fingers, and a faint aroma of camphor
and myrrh wafted out from the dark folds.

The guardian's lips stretched into a crooked smile. "I have
slept and dreamed the serpent's dreams. Time has passed above and
below. I am aware of it, yet it seems like the blink of a child's eye,
all beheld in wonder."

"Tell me your name," Shemyaza said.

The priest bowed. "I am Ainzu, keeper of the gate to
every path."

"You know why I am here?"

Ainzu sighed theatrically, and glanced upwards in an exaggerated manner. "Do not ask questions to which you already know
the answers!" He turned round abruptly, in a swirl of cloth, and
began to stride quickly away along the precarious ledge. Loose
stones shifted and tumbled as his staff smashed against the ground
in time to his rapid steps.

"Wait!"

The priest ignored the call. Shemyaza was both confused
and annoyed by Ainzu's behaviour. Wasn't Ainzu's function, as guardian of the underworld, to help and guide him? Ainzu had already
disappeared around a corner of the path, although Shemyaza could
still hear the thump of his staff against the rock. He knew he had no
choice but to follow. Clinging to the right hand wall as best he
could, he hurried along the narrow ledge. Small, smooth stones
slipped from beneath his feet. He stumbled, fell to his knees, grazed

his palms on the rough rock as he groped for handholds. One glance over the ledge was enough for him to see that not even he could survive the fall into the abyss that lay below. How could Ainzu make him take this risk? The priest was obviously familiar with this domain. For Shemyaza, a stranger to its dangerous paths, the threat of death lay in haste.

He rounded a corner of the path and saw the dark, flapping robes of the priest up ahead, the silver flash of the sigil on his staff. "Wait!" Shemyaza called again, and this time, Ainzu slowed his pace a little. Encouraged, Shemyaza cried out, "Tell me what I have to do! That is your function, isn't it?"

Ainzu halted completely, and after a moment of what seemed to be consideration, turned back to face Shemyaza. His low chuckle resounded throughout the cavern. "Oh, no! That is *not* my function. You know already what you have to do. My purpose is one and the same as that of the rocks around you." He smashed his staff furiously against the rock, his eyes flashing with crimson fire. "I can tell you what is within your heart!"

Shemyaza felt his way forward, until he was only feet away from the priest. "Tell me what I must do now. My heart refuses to speak to me."

Ainzu narrowed his eyes and, after a few moments' consideration, spoke. "Very well. Go in unto the serpent. It rolls in its sleep and its skin is loose. Only when the serpent sheds its skin can you look upon its face, for at that time, it is blind. But remember, even in its blindness, it can sense and taste your heart. What it finds there, it will swallow and become. Are you brave enough to risk that? It can blink the scales from its eyes very quickly."

Shemyaza steadied himself against the rock. He felt weak, as if the fumes within the cavern had occluded his senses. "You said you could see what's in my heart, guardian. Tell me what you see."

Ainzu grinned and cocked his head to one side in appraisal. "Your heart is the fruit of the apple, and it hangs as a burning, blue star in your breast. Humanity has ached to bite into its shining flesh. Bite one side and you will taste liberty and salvation, yet bite the other and your mouth will fill with a bitter gall that will lead you straight to the high, narrow halls of Gehenna." He extended his hands and gripped Shemyaza's shoulders, stared steadily into his eyes.

Shemyaza found Ainzu's penetrating gaze hard to hold. There was no doubt he could peer right into Shemyaza's heart, even his soul. "Yes, Gehenna," Ainzu murmured. "Taste it, angel king. It is the domain of shame, where souls twist in frenzy between the despair of self-loathing, the injustice of martyrdom and the rage of abandonment." He shook his head sadly. "And which side of the fruit will the Shamir taste? What harvest will you reap for humanity this time? Shemyaza, Tree of Life, are you finally to be cut down now?"

Shemyaza knocked Ainzu's hands from his shoulders. "Stop this! Stop mocking me with words, priest! You might as well just laugh in my face!"

Ainzu again shook his head, still smiling, although his eyes were filled with sadness. "Ah, I have long forgotten how to express mirth so freely, my child king."

Shemyaza laughed uneasily. "Your words are magic, priest. They have filled me with despair. Is that what is to be?"

Ainzu said nothing.

"Then shrive me!" Shemyaza cried. "Cleanse from me the bitterness that sours my taste of life!"

Ainzu uttered a cold gust of laughter. "Oh, you think I am worthy of extinguishing the firebrand that is your shadow, and the shadow of humanity? That is flattering."

Shemyaza sighed, and pressed his fingers against his eyes for a moment. "Ainzu, listen to me. I am truly lost. I am here, yet unsure of what I must do, of what I want to do. What guided me here?"

"Faith guided you here," Ainzu remarked.

Shemyaza shrugged. "But faith in what?"

Ainzu was silent for a few moments, as if listening to an inner adviser, then he said, "Didn't you see the light at the portal?"

Shemyaza nodded. "Yes." He looked around himself. "But I don't see it now."

Ainzu shook his head. "Ah, Shemyaza, you are as blind as the Shamir! Couldn't you recognise your own light? It is now back within the eye of the great serpent, but it recognised you. You and the serpent are one, and that is what guided you here."

For a brief moment, Shemyaza heard once again the fading tones of the Lament for Serapis echoing around the cavern walls. A vision of Tamara's face, slack with desire, flashed before him. He shook his head wildly to dispel the image. He felt sick.

"See!" hissed the priest. "Guides, all guides, many of them. How you listen to them..."

Shemyaza put his hands against his eyes. "No! That was a lie!"

"Oh, you can see it now, then?" Ainzu's voice was amused.

Shemyaza nodded. "Yes. I was led here by the greed of an enchantress, beguiled into believing love was my guide."

"Ah," Ainzu sighed dramatically. "The boy king learns!" He touched Shemyaza's chest with his staff, placed a brief sensation of burning within his heart. "Oh, pay no heed to the manipulations of the woman. Whatever illusions she spun for you, there is no doubt that love led you here. Love and faith and knowledge. All one."

Shemyaza frowned. "But I have lost my love."

Ainzu made a dismissive gesture with one hand and turned away again, to disappear through a side tunnel in the rock. His voice echoed out from it. "What is lost can be found again. Come, it is near the time."

Shemyaza followed the priest into the darkness, unable to see him but guided by the click of Ainzu's staff against the stone floor.

Ainzu's voice came from up ahead. "Ah, what a black sun you are, angel king. The shadow of your rays has shone upon humanity for the last two thousand years. Will it shine for another millennium?"

Before Shemyaza could answer him, they turned a corner in the tunnel, and a blinding neon radiance spilled over them. Shemyaza had to shield his eyes; he could just make out the shadowy silhouette of the priest ahead.

"Come," Ainzu said. "Waste no more time." He led the way into a high, stone chamber, Shemyaza trailing him cautiously. An unnatural purple glow, which emanated from no visible source, illuminated the vault. The chamber's ceiling and walls were encrusted with points of quartz that sparkled with reflected light, while in its centre a single gigantic crystal grew up from the gem-littered floor. The whole chamber smelled of cold, clear water, yet there was no water to be seen.

Ainzu stalked into the chamber and stood, dwarfed, beneath the towering crystal. He held out his arms and cried, "Behold! The mirror, the gate and the heart." He beckoned for Shemyaza to approach.

Shemyaza took slow steps towards the priest. He sensed the immense power of the stone, the power of its memories, and feared what it might reveal to him.

"Look upon its surface, Shemyaza, look deep within it, for the pattern of your destiny is stored within this sacred stone. Look close, look backwards in time—what do you see?"

"I see nothing, transparent quartz."

"You are not looking!" Ainzu's staff thumped the ground, crushed fragile crystals to powder. "Look again, and look properly. This is the first part of your journey, the first steps on the path. You must take them."

Shemyaza flicked him a hard glance, then forced himself to stare into the stone. He was afraid of what he would see.

At first the details of the crystal remained clear before him— the imperfections in the quartz, the warped outline of the chamber wall beyond. Then, gradually, the centre of the crystal became milky, swirling like liquid. As Shemyaza stared into the depths of the crystal, a shape began to manifest within it, a stooped, shadowy shape.

"You see?" Ainzu whispered.

"Yes. It is myself. I did not expect otherwise." In the stone, Shemyaza saw himself as he'd appeared in the time before the Flood: a tall, dour warrior, commander of his Nefilim sons. He wore battered leather armour, scored with the cuts of many blades. His bare legs were splashed with blood, his sandals fastened with human gut. His hair was tied up on his head, wound around gory bones. In his face, Shemyaza saw the thirst for vengeance, the pain and bitterness that had filled his soul with rage. This was his dark shadow, the monster from whom Ishtahar had fled and had subsequently betrayed. Looking at his horrifying countenance, bereft of all compassion, Shemyaza understood why she had run. Uttering a cry of self-disgust, he turned away from the apparition. "Send it away, priest!"

Again, Ainzu uttered a soft laugh. "Oh, I can't do that, angel king. This warrior is yours to command, not mine. Perhaps you could send him in to the serpent for you, for he is undoubtedly without fear."

"Where is my other self?" Shemyaza demanded. "There has to be another side."

"Your other self flew from a cliff," Ainzu replied dryly, "and I suspect he still lies wounded beneath it."

"How can I reach him?"

Ainzu made an impatient sound. "Oh, use your will, Shemyaza. It is your greatest tool."

Shemyaza forced himself to turn back to the shimmering crystal and stare hard within it. He willed the violent image of himself to fade, and gradually, it did so.

Another shadow began to take form in the milky mist; a limping, halting shape, whose hands reached out for the walls of the crystal as if it was blind. Shemyaza uttered a single low moan. It was the image of his fall, which he still could not face without pain, or being engulfed by resentment. He did not want to look upon its ravaged face, its beaten, naked body, stained with gold paint and blood. Both aspects of himself were repugnant to him.

"Handsome, isn't he!" Ainzu remarked.

Shemyaza winced away from the image, but not before its grief and agony spilled over into his own heart. Tears filled his eyes, spilled down his face. He could feel the pain of wounds from that time, both within and upon his body. "Ainzu, are these archetypes all that I am, all that I have ever been?"

Ainzu's voice was calm. "Sometimes, the image of another can reflect to us what we truly are. Look, whose face is this appearing before us now, this most earthly angel?"

"No, I cannot look!"

"You can and must. Conquer your fear!"

Reluctantly, Shemyaza turned back to the crystal. His vision was blurred with tears, and he pressed the heels of his hands against his eyes to clear it. At first, it seemed that he was looking at another image of himself, lying sprawled out in the position of the five-pointed star, but the hair of this figure was golden-red, and its staring eyes burned deepest orange. Shemyaza took a step nearer the crystal. "Salamiel," he murmured. "My brother." He turned to Ainzu. "Where is he?"

"Closer to you than you have realised," Ainzu answered.

Shemyaza glanced once again at the motionless image. "I was told he was near." He screwed up his face. "But, like me, he fell. He is a despised creature, no bright angel."

Ainzu shook his head. "No. The fall from grace never touched his soul, for unlike you, he has lived with the consequences of his actions—and yours—with grace in his heart."

Shemyaza smiled wearily. "Yes, Salamiel was always full of grace..."

Ainzu gestured with his staff impatiently. "But he *is* you, Shemyaza, as you can be him. He is your brother. Even now, he aches to walk beside you."

Shemyaza extended a hand towards the crystal, but did not touch it. "I renounced my own kind, priest, to propagate a new race that was a dark shadow of my people."

Ainzu nodded. "Yes, and as your sons went forth, so evil was unleashed into the world."

"My brother is lost to me."

Ainzu uttered a harsh laugh. "More self-pity? Listen to me. You were always Azazel to Salamiel, just a scapegoat for all that happened. He has lived with the reminder of that evil and ignorance for many thousands of years, but it has not detracted from the true light of being for him. He had hope, Shemyaza, always hope. And as I said, what was lost can be found. Your brothers are not lost to you."

Shemyaza glanced at the priest. "I thought that I heard him, his voice in prayer, but I dared not believe."

Again, Ainzu nodded. "You heard him. Even though the dark shadow of another is cast upon him, he prays for your absolution."

Shemyaza narrowed his eyes. "The dark shadow of another?" He thought immediately of Sofia, and sensed a cold tongue of air reach out to touch his body, heard a faint sibilance as of whispered profanities.

"If you love him," Ainzu said, "then you can free him, as he prays to free you. But the time for that has yet to come."

Shemyaza sighed and smiled. "Love...oh to love again."

Ainzu snorted through his nose in scorn. "But you already do, angel king! Look now upon the crystal, and a love that you already have."

Shemyaza held the priest's eyes for a moment, then turned back to the stone. A perfect image of Daniel filled the centre of the crystal, his face composed and tranquil, his delicate lips drawn into a wise smile. The image was so lovely it punched shards of pain through Shemyaza's heart. He wanted to look away, but could not. How could he have forgotten this? "My beautiful one," he said. "Daniel. My eyes, my ears, my tongue, my heart."

"Indeed, he is beautiful," Ainzu agreed. "Look well, for you look upon your own spirit. That is what Daniel represents. Is he not a lamb to your lion? Have you not lain down together?"

As Shemyaza stared at the vision before him, he could see that Daniel was dressed as a shaman, a bird shaman of ancient times. He wore a headdress of feathers. It seemed as if the wind was on his face, blowing back the waving plumes and the tendrils of tawny hair. He appeared to be looking for someone, gazing straight ahead in trance. Now, his features were troubled by an expression of worry and confusion. Shemyaza wanted to call out to him, sure that Daniel was looking for him, but he sensed that he was beyond the boy's hearing. He tore his gaze away. "Ainzu, my spirit is not beautiful. Lions devour the sweetest of lambs, for that is their nature."

"Indeed, you are the beast," Ainzu said. "And is not the beast *of* the earth? And is the earth not beautiful?"

Shemyaza laughed coldly. "I have rarely seen its beauty, priest. I've only felt the all-consuming fire of its power. I do not have the heart to see beauty."

"Wrong, Shemyaza. Look now, and see the error of your words." Ainzu waved his staff in a slow yet complicated gesture. The image of Daniel faded in a flare of soft, white light, to be re-placed by an incandescent glare of blue radiance, which gradually grew in intensity, until it sharpened into the form of a woman.

Shemyaza uttered her name as a sigh. "Ishtahar!" She hung before him within the facets of the crystal, serene and vivid, her blue veils floating voluptuously around her.

"Yes," Ainzu said. "Your love. A woman of the earth. Haven't you ever wondered why you felt such all-consuming pas-sion for her?"

"I never understood why," Shemyaza answered, "and I never will."

"Ishtahar is the mother of humankind," Ainzu told him. "Your union with her was a union with the earth, the mother of all living things. Your love changed the evolution of life and initiated the great civilisations of humankind. That love can provide the way for you to return to your source." Ainzu paused for a moment. "The source of all things is perfection, and your buried love for it is un-paralleled. It is your purpose for being."

Shemyaza uttered a caustic laugh. "Is this me you're talking about? I think not!"

Ainzu frowned and made a dismissive gesture with his staff. "Listen to me. The ways of your people became barren in their attempts to achieve this spiritual goal. Your union with the earth crumbled their empire, and the time for human men and women, and their own ways, came about. It was a destiny that had been preordained since before the beginning of time. The return to the source is the way of the cosmos, and for this planet that journey is still in progress. A new age is dawning, and the return must be allowed to continue. Humans are bound by laws, which blind them to the journey. Shemyaza, you are about to go forth upon *your* destined journey to the source of creation, and you must take humanity with you."

There was silence for a moment, then Shemyaza said. "Why should I? I have no love for humanity."

Ainzu uttered an angry snort. "Your pain, anger and indifference, the stuff of your soul, is one and the same with humankind's."

Shemyaza glared at Ainzu in silence.

"The love you have for Ishtahar and the source is unconditional, and is the same as the love you *should have* for humanity and yourself. You are *their* source, Shemyaza. You are the pivot between humanity's heaven and the earth. Many humans have sought the secret of creation and the light of knowledge. In doing this, they were seeking for your light. For you are the gate to the Crown of Heaven and its limitless light. This is the secret of human divinity, which many have sought, and so few have found."

Shemyaza smiled scornfully. "So this is the secret that I created? So many pretty words, priest. Your kind are adept at conjuring them!"

Ainzu's face creased into a snarl. "Foolish child! Remember your sacrifice! *Self* sacrifice. That *was* and *is* the secret!" He raised both his arms. "Now go, Shemyaza. Go into the crystal and taste the breath of the source. Before you lies Ishtahar, the gate to creation. Before you lies the inferno of the earth, and the serpent awaits, to wake and move through it." Ainzu shook his staff in Shemyaza's face, and then turned in a whirl of ragged cloth, to stride off towards the cavern entrance. "The bonds of centuries will break this night!" he cried, the sound echoing around the chamber. "Orion will burn within the hearts of all those who seek the truth. Go, king angel, and *be* love, for love is the only truth!" For a while, the priest's staff could be heard thumping the ground as he walked away. Then, there was silence, and the sense of imminence that filled the world.

Shemyaza stood before the crystal and the perfect, unchanging image of Ishtahar. She was a dreaming woman, her eyes focused in upon herself. Shemyaza knew how much he shied away from her image and the memory of her, because it pained him too much. If he could not be with her, he would rather blot all trace of her from his heart and mind. Yet always she returned to him, a tantalising ghost, to torment his spirit. Perhaps he should surrender to her now.

He tried to focus his mind on all that the priest had said to him. At first the words seemed to reverberate around the cavities in his brain, fragmented nonsense, but gradually they settled within his heart, where, he realised they had always been. This moment reminded him of the first time he ever saw Ishtahar. He could almost hear her song, the song of her desire and her female power.

He moved closer to the crystal, reached out, and placed his hands flat against it where Ishtahar's image hung within the stone. His whole body felt pulled towards it, as if invisible hands gripped his arms and drew him to them. He leaned his face against the cold facets.

"Ishtahar, deliver me, draw me unto thyself and the source of thy power, the Shamir, the essence of our creator."

He drew away from the stone and looked up. Ishtahar's face seemed to ripple before him. Sparks of light danced before his eyes. Again, a strong sensation of being pulled overwhelmed him, and he realised it was no illusion. The crystal was sucking his body towards itself. As his face touched the cold stone, he felt his flesh begin to pass into it; a strange dissassembling of his being. He tried to withdraw, fight its pull, but could not. "Ishtahar! I am afraid!"

He heard her soft voice in his mind. "If you are afraid, my lord, then you are ready at last for this journey. Is not a babe afraid of its birth? Come my child, my lover, my father. Return to me in spirit so that I may return to you in flesh."

Shemyaza gasped for breath as the immense pressure of being drawn into the matrix of the crystal tortured his body. He felt squeezed, crushed. There was no pain exactly, but extreme discomfort. Then, abruptly, the uncomfortable sensations ceased, although he was aware of the weight of the stone around and within him. The silence was total. He could not even hear the sounds of his own breathing, his own heart. He realised he was hanging within the crystal, at one with the vision of Ishtahar. Her blue light surrounded him, invaded his body; she was a source of strength and comfort. His perception was completely overwhelmed by sparkling flecks of rainbow-coloured light. He wanted to laugh aloud, but could not. He had never experienced such a feeling of total wholeness. This was the gate.

Within it, Shemyaza began to become aware of the immaculate power of his being. He was the perfect sphere amongst all the spheres that comprised the Tree of Spiritual Life. He sensed the divinity symbolised by the archetype of the sacred, sacrificial king, an archetype that comprised all the hopes, aspirations and needs of a nation. He knew that, at the centre of all things, he could create or destroy, give or take, love or hate. He was the symbol of the creator on earth, of godhead incarnate. Pure joy spumed up within him. Now he could face the serpent.

Then, even before he could absorb this realisation fully, the surroundings shifted around him and the light within the crystal dimmed as if clouds had smothered the spiritual sun.

A voice came to him, seeped into his mind, like a caustic blade stabbing through the perfect serenity of the crystal environment. "So, you think you are the perfect sphere, great king?"

Shemyaza was engulfed in a suffocating chill that pierced his body with needles of ice. Low, cruel laughter swirled around his head.

"Ishtahar!" he cried, blind. "Is this you?"

The laughter rose in pitch until it became an hysterical cackle. "Oh, do you not know me, Azazel, my lord? I have been at your side throughout your descent into the underworld. Surely, your ears have bled with the touching lament I have sung for you?"

The voice was spined with sarcasm, but there was a fearless confidence about it that filled Shemyaza with angry terror. He felt helpless, hanging there within the crystal, enveloped by the lightless chill of the nameless presence. He tried to move, and his limbs convulsed with pain, held as they were in stasis. He wanted to scream, but no sound escaped his bound throat. His brain seemed to boil with frustration and rage.

"Ah," murmured the cruel voice. "That's it, my fair one! This is the god I know and love."

Shemyaza called out in his mind. "Ishtahar, where are you? Help me!"

The voice mocked him by mimicking the cry. "Ishtahar, where *are* you?" Callous laughter boomed around him. "She is where she belongs—a weak and feeble ideal within the dreams of men."

"Then who are you?"

Again, laughter. "I am *so* hurt you do not recognise me, my sweet beloved. Come, smell me, remember..."

A stench of carrion filled Shemyaza's head, and a thick reptilian scent that promised fatal poison. The taste of blood and the meat of rotting carcasses suffused his mouth and throat. The screams of terrified children hammered in his head. The bodiless voice spat through his mind. "Fool! Scapegoat! Victim! That's what you were and always will be. Don't your realise that your brothers and lovers care nothing for your fate? Indeed, they and the Parzupheim expect you to die here in the underworld so that, yet again, they can reap the benefits of your sacrifice. I am here to help you at last. You are no longer alone."

"I never have been," Shemyaza said. "Ishtahar, Daniel, Salamiel..."

"Pah! Weaklings! They have no power to help you. You will die without me."

"Then show yourself to me. Face me!"

"Very well. But you know me already."

The darkness within the crystal intensified, until Shemyaza was surrounded by a cloud of boiling blackness. From this void emerged a female shape, dark blue of skin, and sinuous, with snakes winding through her tangled hair. Her beauty was terrible. He knew her. He had seen her face before. The recognition made him want to laugh. "You," he said. "Sofia."

The woman hung before him and folded her inky arms. "Names are games. I have many names. Sofia is the one I choose to employ at present. In that form, I was venerated by the Gnostics as the mother of angels, who incited my holy sons to commit acts of carnality with human women. I became a whore in the sight of my worshippers, but they foolishly restored me to a position in their Heaven and honoured me as the greatest of angels." She shrugged insouciantly. "I have found an alternative heaven, ignorant king, which you now have no will to taste. How can you take on the mantle of the Solar Messiah when you refuse to rule *all* the spheres of the Tree? There is more to the universe than Heaven and Earth, and the darker spheres are as crucial to its pattern as any sphere of light." Her long arms reached out to him and her voice, when she spoke, had softened into a sensuous whisper. "Azazel, star and shining beast, come kiss me, and I will show you the true domain of a god."

Part of him wanted to resist. Part of his screaming mind tried to cling to the images of Ishtahar, Daniel and Salamiel, but Sofia's silky words kindled desire within him, a desire for power that had lain dormant for millennia. He allowed her to draw him to her, and when her cold lips touched his, freezing shockwaves thrilled his entire body. Her arms curled around him, until he felt as if he was bound in the embrace of writhing pythons. He could not move. Her voice was a black velvet cloak floating down upon his mind.

"Come, Azazel, rise up with me through the Tree of Life, the tree on which you hung in torment. Come with me to Da'ath, the abyss, the realm of all knowledge. It is the closest sphere to your precious source."

Shemyaza leaned against her, buried his face in her snaky hair. He experienced the sensation of flight, but could not tell in which direction they moved. He hung in her arms like a child; she was gigantic, all-powerful. Their speed increased and Shemyaza's head fell backwards. His hair streamed like ribbons of gold in the void. He saw garlands of stars flashing past him, cloudy nebulae, exploding suns. Sofia's freezing embrace filled him with a delicious terror. He was helpless in her arms. He could feel the tentacles of her greedy soul caressing the fibres of his heart, a sensation so intoxicating he felt sure he would die in the terror of this dark ecstasy.

Then, nothing. Stripped of all sensation, he found himself completely alone. There was no ground beneath his feet, no feeling of universe around him, no light, not even any dark, just utter emptiness. He willed his arms to lift, his fingers to move, but they encountered nothing before, behind or beside him. In desperation, he clung to consciousness and actuality, and reached for Sofia with the remnants of his panicking senses, but her dark presence had abandoned him. The only sound was the gasp of his frantic breath, and even that shuddered only within his mind. He spun around, helpless, and as he did so, he became aware of invisible presences gathering around him, discarnate entities reaching out to envelop him. All sense of identity was slipping away. Nothing seemed to be of consequence any more: he was nullity. The absolute darkness of the abyss seeped inside him, transformed him into a vacuum. All awareness of the mysteries of light he had attained melted into it, as if his knowledge had been only a tool to help him achieve this perfect hollow state.

Sofia's voice whispered through the void and touched his mind once more, and his consciousness expanded out into the abyss to meet her. "Ultimately, this is all that there is, Azazel. Do you not feel at peace now, at one with the essence of nothing, the source of our existence?"

Shemyaza fought with the compulsion to agree with her. Some shred of his will still remained. "No, this is an illusion of returning to the source, from within yourself. It is not the limitless light, but a reflection of its opposite. In the abyss, the source can be whatever you want it to be."

Her laughter was mocking, but strangely gentle. "The Tree of Life from whence you came is the illusion, Azazel. Let me show you the other Tree, the true Tree."

Gradually, balls of light began to appear around him, soft shadowy flares that grew in intensity, but not in brightness. Slowly, they spun and spiralled around him, using him as a pivot for their circular dance. Although he sensed they were growing larger in size, it was impossible to grasp the concept of size within the infinity of the abyss.

"Look within, mighty lord," Sofia murmured. "What do you see?"

Figures began to form within the circling spheres. They were vaguely humanoid in shape, but also hideously distorted; attenuated bodies and long faces, their mouths and eyes mere smoky holes that seeped noxious vapours. They were not solid beings, but projections of elemental emotions.

"Here are your brethren, angel king," Sofia said. "Here, where they have always been, within the abyss. Look into the blue light—see your brother, Penemue."

The blue sphere glowed dully before him, and as he looked into it, Shemyaza was hit by an intense feeling of pride. He had once owned the power to divide nations, to kill and conquer. All had bowed before him. Was any of this worthless? No. He had lived and experienced it.

Sofia uttered a soft sound of approval. "You see well, my lord. Now, look into the purple light. See your brother, Araqiel."

Proud and imperious, Shemyaza directed his attention to the next sphere that came to hover before his perception. A painful feeling shot through his heart. He thought of Daniel, safe in the world of humanity, ignorant of what his lord was experiencing. How Shemyaza envied Daniel. He wanted to be him. He thought of Enniel, with his riches, his vast house, his network of power. Surely, he should have Enniel's life? Enniel did not deserve its comforts, but he, Shemyaza, did. The sick purple light hovered and spun before him, its rays filling his being with the spikes of envy. Only Sofia's voice could break the spell it cast over him.

"Now, Azazel, look upon the red light, for this is your brother, Salamiel."

Reluctantly, Shemyaza turned his perception towards the bloody globe of light. He felt the aching sense of envy conjured by the purple sphere bleed out of him. In its place came a blinding sword of rage, fiery in its intensity. He wanted to hit out at all those who had oppressed him. He wanted to cut out their hearts, scatter their entrails over the fields of the land. He wanted blood, and the sweet euphony of agonised screams. In his wrath, he was all-powerful.

"Yes!" Sofia cried. "Now look, Azazel, upon the green light, for it is your brother, Pharmaros."

Empowered, Shemyaza had no difficulty in transferring his perception from the light of wrath. He turned towards the green light, and immediately, his entire body, from his loins to his heart, was convulsed by an overwhelming sexual desire. It was mindless, the need to sate his cravings, whatever the consequences. Pure lust. In comparison to its demands, all other considerations of life seemed worthless.

"How beautiful you are," Sofia purred. "Turn now. Look upon the silver light, and see your brother, Baraqijal."

Resentfully, Shemyaza tore his perception away from the green light and turned to the next sphere that came to dance before him. At once, all feelings of desire left him and he was engulfed by a paralysing sense of lethargy. What was the point of being here and experiencing this? It was all too tedious. It made him tired. He didn't care about it.

"You crave the light of sloth," Sofia said, "but turn and behold the orange light as it moves before you, for it is your brother, Gadreel."

Shemyaza could hardly summon the energy to obey her words, but painfully, slowly, moved his perception away from the dull, silvery light. Immediately, the numbing feelings of lethargy fled his senses, to be replaced by a cold realisation. He became aware of the falsehood of existence and the sense of self-justice in untruth. He understood the complexity of the reasoning behind all lies. There was no honesty in the universe.

"And lastly," Sofia said. "Look now upon the yellow sphere, for here is your brother, Kashday."

Of all the lights, this one hit Shemyaza the hardest with its assailing sensations. Its aspect struck at the fibres of his heart and soul with a ravenous feeling of greed. He knew that he had been hungry for the entirety of his existence, and it was a hunger that could never be satisfied, a thirst that could never be quenched. He craved power, adoration, riches, freedom, and no matter how much he managed to snatch from the world, it would never be enough.

"These are your attributes, your gates to power!" Sofia cried, and there she was before him, eclipsing with her dark light all the colours of the spheres. "Learn well, angel king, for these are the planets that spin around your pivot. You are the sun that propels their existence. Take all of their aspects and reflect them back. Shine for them, son of light, be the black sun that feeds the life substance of their nature. And be the perfect sphere. You shall not seek the source, Azazel, you shall *be* it."

Shemyaza raised his head to her, aware once more of corporeality, the flesh around his bones. "And what of you, Sofia? Are you to share this power?"

Sofia raised her arms above her head. The snakes in her hair lifted their gleaming coils and hissed her words in chorus. "I am the first and the last, the honoured and the despised, the whore and the holy one, wife and virgin, barren and fertile. And you will make me the queen of your heaven!"

Shemyaza bowed his head to her. "I thank you, Sofia, for showing and giving me this knowledge, for now I am equipped to be a king who rules all the spiritual realms."

Sofia threw back her head and laughed, the snakes twisting crazily around her in a feverish halo. "Indeed, my lord. Indeed! Now, fly back to the world of flesh, and take my strength with you!"

Shemyaza gazed beyond her gigantic form, out into the void. He gathered his will within him, and threw out his arms. Filled with a sense of power, he commanded the sphere of Da'ath to appear before him. It was there, an eclipsed sun, a ring of white fire around the ultimate dark.

He streaked towards it like an exploding star.

Shemyaza opened his eyes and found himself enveloped in a dim red light. He became aware of the crystal all around him, and the last fading echoes of a howling wind, the chill of the void. The crystal still held him in stasis, but he murmured within his mind. "Release me. I am ready."

The light dimmed to a red hue, and the weight of the stone seemed to lift from his body. A low, humming sound slyly invaded the silence of the crystal. Shemyaza tried to move his limbs and found that he could walk forward. It was like swimming through liquid glass. Something seemed to crack around him, and he was aware of cold air, and a slow, slithering sound, as of gigantic coils being dragged across wet stone. He looked back, and saw that he had passed completely through the crystal, which had returned to its original translucent state. He turned away. Now another tunnel lay before him, waiting for his feet to tread its worn floor. Red light spilled out from it, but it was not fire.

Shemyaza straightened his spine and walked forward, into the light. He felt empty of all feeling, and had become simply a purpose: to wake the serpent. Time no longer had any meaning. He could have walked for mere seconds or over an hour, but eventually he emerged into another cavern, that was far greater in size than the crystal chamber. A searing heat gusted around him, accompanied by a deep, roaring hiss. There could be no physical serpent here, surely? The Shamir was a symbol of the giants' power, nothing more. It would be a crystal, waiting to be energised, a blue flame to be rekindled. Its shrine would be decorated with ophidian symbols and talismans, and maybe a nest of vipers would curl around it, jealously guarding it from harm.

He was wrong.

The Shamir. Its head filled the cavern before him, the size of a fifteen storey building, while its body disappeared into the labyrinth of tunnels beyond. It was the colour of smouldering embers, and its eyes were filmed with a milky sheath. Around it lay drifts of discarded skin, which still hung down in rags from its gigantic yet elegant head. It emanated a musky, reptilian stench. Shemyaza halted before it, in wonder and terror. How could this creature be real? Its breath was like a hot, living hurricane against his skin.

Words burst up through Shemyaza's body, words that had perhaps been waiting for millennia to be spoken. "Father, I am here."

Only one eye was visible from where Shemyaza stood. At his words, it blinked open abruptly, and golden light flared out to bathe him in a blazing radiance. The eye was the size of a cathedral, emanating the light of sacred power. This was no blind snake. Shemyaza knew that it could see him, right into him, and that it was very much awake. Sluggish, maybe, but gathering power with every passing moment. Shemyaza felt hypnotised by its gaze. He was drawn towards the wondrous eye. Looking into it was like gazing into the sun, but it did not hurt at all.

His head was filled with the booming yet soundless words of the Shamir. "The sun of my eye sees the sun of thy soul. Our light together, my son, will be whole. Take thy true form, a serpent, as me, and come forth, for I have dreamed of thee."

Shemyaza felt then, the first stirrings of the inevitable transformation within his body. It wracked his entire being with feelings he could not describe, although they seemed weirdly familiar. Gradually, his flesh filled with a sensation of ecstasy. Golden light streamed from his eyes and from the pores of his skin. Every fibre, every cell, shifted and advanced onto a higher genetic level—an evolution that should take millions of years to achieve. And yet, despite being aware of this, Shemyaza also knew that the form he was transforming into was a return to a primal state that transcended the boundaries of earth history. He could feel his body stretching, his neck elongating, his face and limbs becoming longer. The desperate ache of yearning, which had yoked him for twelve thousand years lifted from his soul. A sense of limitless freedom filled his body, heart and mind as if he had drunk deeply from a holy grail. All the knowledge ever guarded by his ancestors flooded into his brain, and his perception was dominated by a vision of the constellation of Orion, the heavenly lights of the prison from which Daniel had released him. Beyond Orion, he beheld the stars of immeasurable galaxies. His new form possessed the power to cross vast distances and dimensions, to ride the stars. It had the instinctual ability to fold space and time to its will. Now, he was a keeper of the universe and a bestower of evolution. He was pure life force in its most potent form, sent forth from the source to propagate the schemes and cycles of whole universes. He was a god.

Shemyaza, serpent man, stood before the immense, gaping mouth of the Shamir. "Father, I come unto thee, for the black sun is rising and the time of reckoning is now."

The Shamir exhaled a hurricane of breath. "Your shape is as me, the seed of life, from the creator be, to fertilise this world, the earth through she, a timeless voyage across morphic sea."

Shemyaza rose up on his golden coils and slid like a shaft of light into the waiting mouth of the Shamir. His destiny was sealed.

Chapter Twenty-Nine
Flight of the Serpent

On the beach below the Lion's Head, Tamara waited at the entrance to the underworld, standing on stiff, splayed legs, her arms held out above her head. She was the sacred whore, waiting to ride the seven-headed serpent. She would ride its power, take it, direct it. Already she could sense its consciousness waking up below her. The land-scape around her was unnaturally still and silent. No birds sang, even though dawn was fast approaching. The sea looked turbid, restless, but there were hardly any waves. Then, the ground began to shake. It was as if an army of horsemen was galloping up through the earth from a deep cavern; the sound of thunder. Delmar whim-pered in consternation, and Tamara was hard-pressed to keep her stance upon the rock. "Go down to the beach," she said.

Delmar scampered down the stony incline and crouched behind a large rock, gazing up at her. Tamara began to utter a mo-notonous chant, calling the serpent to her. The sound of the earth-thunder became louder, drowning out her words. Tamara shrieked her invocation, and then the face of the Lion exploded outwards. Tamara's shouted words became a shriek of horror. For a moment, she saw the gigantic head of the serpent looking out at her, then its jaws dropped open and it lunged forward, swallowing her as a horse might swallow a mayfly.

Below, Delmar cringed back against the rock. He saw the great body of the Shamir coil out of the cliff-face and shoot towards the sea. Over the troubled ocean, it became a streak of red-golden light that crashed against the chapel on St Michael's Mount. The Mount glowed as if it was on fire, its chapel had become a ball of radiance, emanating blistering spears of white light. It was happen-ing! The serpent power was coming alive! But something was wrong. Where was Tamara? She was not riding its power as she'd promised. And where was Shemyaza? Even as Delmar stared out to sea, the sky became black; the stars, the moon, were all eclipsed. And then the sun reared above the horizon, but it was not the dawn that Delmar knew. This was a black sun, ringed with crimson fire. The sea heaved and shuddered beneath its hellish glow, and the water began to recede from the beach, faster than Delmar had ever seen it. The sea was leaving the land. His element! He would die! Delmar shrank back against the rock as hard as he could and covered his head with his hands. It had happened all wrong.

Aninka, still with her face pressed against the panes of the French windows at High Crag, saw the sky go black. She felt sick, dizzy, yet also full of energy. She had to smell the air. What would it smell like? She opened the windows and stepped out into the garden, which was dark, yet lit with a spectral glow. Aninka was drawn to the cliff edge, as if in a dream. Part of her was afraid that she'd be unable to resist throwing herself over, as Shemyaza had done. Yet she could not fight the impulse to go there.

As she put her hands upon the crumbling rock wall, the black sun lifted above the horizon. Aninka stared at it in amazement. She should not be able to see, because there was no light, yet everything around her stood out in stark relief, as if releasing light from within. She heard a sound, and looked down to the beach. A girl was down there, scrabbling around in the sand, and a male figure with pale hair lay stretched out beside her. Aninka's first thought was that the male was Shemyaza. She ran along the wall and presently found the steep wooden stairway that led down to the beach. It was very difficult to move quickly, for the thick air was almost impossible to breathe, yet she knew she had to reach the girl and her companion quickly.

In her stockinged feet, Aninka ran across the damp sand. She glanced at the sea, and saw that it had retreated beyond the horizon. What was happening? Fear drummed at her courage. Hurry. Hurry. She felt both excitement and dread.

The girl looked up at her in terror as she approached. Aninka could only gasp out, "The house! The house! Come quickly!"

"No," the girl answered. "I must find the shell!"

"What shell? Don't be stupid! You must leave this place!"

The girl pursed her lips and pushed her hair back behind her ears. "Here, it's here...somewhere...I must find it." She began to dig like a frantic puppy. Then she uttered a startled yelp.

Aninka watched in fascinated horror as the girl's hands plunged deeply into the wet sand, as if it had no more substance than air. It seemed as if the beach itself were sucking the girl down-wards. Quicksand? Aninka leapt forward and grabbed the girl by the shoulders, ignoring the shriek of protest. It felt as if a hundred strong hands were holding onto the girl's slender wrists. Aninka could not pull her free. A blue vapour began to stream up from the sand, curling around their struggling bodies like incense smoke. Should I leave her here? Aninka thought. Should I save myself? She glimpsed the girl's terrified face within the veil of her thresh-ing wet hair. No. Aninka could not simply leave her. With this realisation, the ground abruptly released its hold on its captive and both she and Aninka fell backwards. Aninka quickly scrambled to her feet. The girl knelt before her on hands and knees, her body shuddering to silent sobs. In her hands, like an icon, she held a perfect cowry shell.

"Now!" Aninka cried. "Hurry!" She dashed past the kneel-ing girl and lifted the male figure in her arms, seeing at once that it was not Shemyaza. Was it still that important to carry him to safety? The girl had now leapt to her feet and was attempting to drag the young man from Aninka's arms.

"No, let him go! Let him go!"

"Don't be stupid!" Aninka gasped. "You're in danger! Come with me now!"

"I don't know you..." the girl began, but Aninka inter-rupted her.

"For Shem's sake, look at the sea! Look!"

The girl turned her head and froze. The tide was returning, but in height and power. A wall of water was gathering on the hori-zon, beyond the empty reaches of sand. Its crest glittered red be-neath the black sun. "Oh my god!"

"Run!" Aninka screamed. "Run!"

Both women fled towards the cliff stair, Aninka carrying the boy over her shoulder. They seemed to possess preternatural strength in their fear, and all but flew up the rickety stairs. At the garden wall, Aninka glanced back and felt her heart contract in awe and horror. The wave was surging towards the land, rearing higher into the sky with each moment. Surely High Crag could not resist such an el-emental onslaught, but where else could they seek shelter?

"Quickly!" she cried and led the way back to the house. She could see the French windows hanging open and uttered a groan of despair. What barrier could fragile glass provide against tons of

water? Would they be safer in the attics or the cellars? As they drew
nearer, Enniel appeared at the window, gesturing for her to hurry.
"Where have you been? Get in here!" His face was drawn and
tense. Aninka virtually threw herself against him, gabbling a string
of nonsensical words.

"Be calm, Ninka. We must work together." He pulled the
girl into the house behind her.

"The house will be destroyed! We'll drown!"

Enniel ignored her words and closed the windows. Aninka
was barely aware of the weight of the boy on her shoulder. The girl
stood beside her, wide-eyed in silent terror, the cowry shell still held
in both hands.

"Come, upstairs," Enniel ordered.

Aninka followed him. Her legs felt weak. She was aware of
the power and weight of the wave gathering behind her. How could
they hope to survive it?

As they moved through the tense air of the house, Aninka
saw that all her relatives, all the ancients who hid or dreamed
within the catacomb of rooms had emerged from their sanctuar-
ies. They thronged the corridors in silent lines, humming softly
beneath their breath.

"Station yourselves at every point of entry," Enniel said
to them.

He led Aninka and her companions to the top storey of
the house, where gabled windows looked out from the wide, empty
attics. Here, the Parzupheim had already gathered. Aninka
dropped her burden on the floor, and the girl hurried over to lift
the boy's body in her arms. Aninka ran to one of the small windows and looked out. Her mouth filled with saliva at what she
saw; she wanted to vomit.

The sea, a citadel of crushing water, was moving slowly, so
slowly, towards the land. She tried to estimate how far over the cliff-
top it would tower, but it was impossible to guess. It seemed the sky
was blotted out by the rearing wave. Aninka thought of drowned
Lyonesse, subject of so many childhood tales. Was Cornwall doomed
to follow its sister kingdom into the sea? She wiped her numb lips
convulsively, and then felt Enniel's calm hand upon her shoulder.

"Enniel, it's hopeless. What are we doing here? We should
be driving away from this place as fast as we can. We'd have more
chance."

"Have faith, Ninka," Enniel said softly, and kissed her hair. "We will create our own barrier of protection."

Aninka gestured weakly at the sight beyond the window. "Against that? Are you serious? Oh, Great Shem, we shouldn't be up here. We should be in the cellars, or would that be worse?"

"Aninka, you must calm down," Enniel said sharply. "Allow yourself to trust me."

Aninka uttered a sad bitter laugh.

"Look around you," Enniel continued. "The strongest Grigori of all the kingdoms of Albion are here to safeguard you. Don't be afraid. This is just a memory of the Great Deluge replaying in the mind of the earth."

Aninka could not believe what the evidence of her eyes contested. The water was real and solid, no dream. "I just hope it's quick," she said. Her eyes were drawn back to the window, in morbid fascination. The sight was incredible, beautiful and terrible. The weight of the water, she thought. The weight of the water. Her knees gave way. Staggering, she backed into the centre of the room. The Parzupheim had formed a circle, and Aninka went to crouch with the girl she had found on the beach, who still held the boy in her lap.

"I'm afraid," the girl whispered.

Aninka put her hand on the girl's shoulder. "So am I."

"Are you Grigori?" the girl asked her.

Aninka nodded. "Yes."

"Do you know Shem?"

Aninka was surprised. "Yes. Do you?"

"Of course. I know him very well." Her face crumpled. "Is he dead? Oh God, what's happening?"

"Are you Lily?" Aninka asked her. "Lily Winter?"

The girl's face was creased up in fear. The question seemed to annoy her. "Yes. Yes. Oh, what does it matter? We've no chance! None!"

"Don't worry," Aninka said. "These men here are the most powerful of Grigori. They'll protect us." She wished she could believe it herself.

The wave was at the cliff now, towering up what looked like a hundred feet above it. From outside, High Crag would look dwarfed beneath it, a feeble match-stick construction that could be crushed and washed away by only a gallon of water. The Parzupheim were chanting steadily, constructing a cone of power around the building.

It won't be enough, Aninka thought. It won't be enough.

"Let it happen quickly," Lily Winter said suddenly. "I can't bear it." She buried her head against Aninka's side. The attic was filled with a dark green light. Slowly, Aninka turned her head and forced herself to look out of the window. All she could see was water, water that seemed to defy gravity, flowing upwards. It must only be feet away from the house. She screamed, unable to help herself, for the power of the wave was the naked face of death, inexorable. Then, she saw a flash of white and, with an explosion of sound, the wave crashed down upon them.

On the cliff-top at the bottom of the Penhaligon garden, the Pelleth witnessed the Shamir explode out of the cliff and shoot towards the Mount. Their dancing and chanting became wild, ecstatic, but was short-lived. As soon as Meggie saw the black sun rise, and the tide retreat, she knew what would follow. The sea would exact a price from the land. She looked quickly at Daniel. Could she sacrifice him now? Would the offering of Shemyaza's vizier be enough to satisfy the Serpent Mother, so that she would curb the wild horses of the foam, and not throw them against the land?

Daniel seemed to sense her thoughts and glanced at her sharply. He was standing tense and still, as if removed from the wild proceedings around him. "You want me to be your scapegoat," he said.

Meggie said nothing.

"That was not a question," Daniel continued. "Shall I leap from the cliff for you?"

"Would you do that willingly?" Meggie couldn't help asking.

Daniel shrugged. "My purpose for living has gone. Yes, I will do that, if you think it will do any good."

Meggie stepped up to him and put her hands on his arms. She could feel the life thrumming through his body. "No, it would not be right," she said. She glanced over her shoulder at the horizon. "Daniel, you still have purpose. Take my people to safety. I trust they will find sanctuary with you."

Daniel looked down into her eyes. "If that's what you want." He seemed to have no will of his own.

Meggie shook him. "It is. It is." Around them, the Pelleth continued to jump up and down, clapping at the sky. It had yet to dawn upon them what the withdrawal of the sea must signify. "In the distant past," Meggie said in a low voice, "when the Great Flood drowned the earth, people survived upon the mountaintops. Go to the hill fort of Enoch's Tower. It is not far from here, but you'll have to hurry. Take my sight with you, Daniel, let it guide you. I think you'll be safe there."

"Very well." Daniel paused. "Why can't you lead them there yourself?"

Meggie sighed and shook her head, pursing her lips together. "It is time," she said. "And I'm too old to run. That's all. Now go, quickly." She shouted out to her sisters to silence them. "Go with the boy! Go now. The Serpent Mother does not want your lives!"

The women all stared at her with wide eyes, frozen in position, some with their hands still held to the sky.

"Go now!" Meggie urged. She sensed the rising power of the sea behind her. Emma realised what was happening and began to chivvy the women towards the house. Agatha ran to Meggie's side. "I'm not leaving you, Gran!"

"You must!" Meggie said in a hard voice. "Daniel, take her!"

Daniel picked up the child in his arms. She wailed and fought against him, but he held on to her tightly and ran up the garden. For a moment, he paused and looked back. He saw Meggie and her sister standing straight at the edge of the cliff, and behind them the sky rippled and surged.

"Gran!" Agatha cried.

Daniel remembered his responsibility, and fled towards the house. As he ran, he felt as if wings fanned out from his shoulders. He could fly now if he wanted to. His feet skimmed the ground, and the women scurried along behind him, their robes fluttering around them. They were like a wild hunt flying over the land, following the Sacred King who led them.

They skirted the house and spilled out into the lane, spinning around, uttering eerie screams. Daniel had no idea where he was supposed to be taking them, but let his feet lead him, trusting that Meggie's clear sight guided his body. Behind him, beyond the cliff, the sky was a wall of water.

Meggie and Betsy held hands at the edge of the cliff. The element of the Serpent Mother was coming to claim them. They were so tiny before her power, like two shells waiting to be taken by the tide. Just before the wave fell over them, Meggie saw a host of sea-faces peering out, and extended arms that were waiting to embrace them. Then the water crashed down and a great slice of cliff broke away beneath the impact. The Serpent Mother claimed her sacrifice.

When Delmar saw the wave approaching, he was filled with relief. He stood up from where he shuddered on the shore and walked out to meet his element. He crossed through the wall of water as if passing through a veil. For him, the time of living on the land was over. He was never seen again.

And as the wave crashed down upon the land, the serpent power flared out from the chapel on St Michael's Mount, empowering the first site on its journey across the landscape. Everywhere, people attuned to the mysteries were drawn out to the ancient sites. They saw the strange sky, and the black sun rise. It seemed as if the end of the world had come. But then the power came, surging along the ancient corridor, filling each shrine, holy hill, stone circle, church and cathedral with exploding light, which rained down upon the people who had come to bear witness.

Of all those who had gathered, throughout the country at the old, sacred sites, some had been drawn by an unrecognised sense, others by knowledge, a recognition of what was happening in the land. Occult fraternities of all creeds performed secret and traditional rituals, to herald a new order. Christians bathed in the light of heaven that flooded their churches, and waited for the coming of the Lamb of God. Pagans danced at stone circles, celebrating the return of the old gods in the wake of the revenge of Mother Earth. People of all faiths and religions came to experience the reawakening, and through their own beliefs, recognised the spirit of change. Every spirit, ghost, god-form and guardian of the old places of power awoke and rose to the serpent's breath. Albion's sacred heritage was alive. Past and present came together in their quest for the future. And the meaning inherent within the history of the ancient past touched the hearts of all the people. Like ripples gyring out from a stone cast into a pool, the whole of the land became brilliant with the sacred radiance that flamed in the wake of the serpent's journey. A shining new age had dawned at last, and through the hallowed blood of the serpent, humanity's soul would be nourished, its spirit evolve. Britain, the land of the setting sun, the land in the west, had *become.*

Chapter Thirty
The Dawn

In the aftermath of the wave and the surge of the serpent power, people were drawn out to the cliff top all along the Lizard. The water had caused surprisingly little damage. Gardens were drowned and sheds washed away, but the village and its surrounding area was mainly intact. It seemed the greatest concentration of the wave had centred on two areas alone: Mermaid's Cove and the beach below the house of Meggie and Betsy Penhaligon.

Daniel and Emma led the bedraggled Pelleth down from the hill fort. The dazed inhabitants of High Crag ventured out into the morning. Some were drawn to a single point; the shattered rock where once the great lion had stared out to sea. Daniel and Emma were there first, soon followed by Lily and Aninka, and the Parzupheim.

Daniel did not know why he'd felt compelled to come to this place. He was overwhelmed by grief. Shem had become one with the serpent and Daniel felt sure he would never see him physically again. But for what? Had it worked? A black sun had risen, and the power had surged throughout the arteries of the land that had been waiting to be filled, but what had energised the serpent, hatred or love? The destiny of the land was sealed, but as yet there was no way of knowing what direction that would take.

Sofia awoke in her bed of serpent flesh, her mouth filled with a sour taste, her nostrils with the stench of rotting meat. Around her, Pharos lay in silence. Candles guttered on the floor and from the window no light came. This was the dawn of darkness.

Stretching languorously, Sofia rose up, and cast off the rags that covered her body. Naked, she padded out into the dim corridor, beyond her room of enchantment, and from there down through the house. Beyond the windows, she saw the wan light of the true dawn break above the horizon. She had experienced the force of the wave in her mind, and had sensed the Shamir's explosion from the cliff-face. She felt drunk, ecstatic. Her power had fed the prince of light, and she had taught him her darkest secrets. He had faced the Shamir filled with the knowledge of the lightless spheres. There could be no flimsy New Age now, but a raw millennium of change and cleansing. Soon, the world would belong to the Grigori once more, and with this power they could gain access to the sealed chambers hidden among desert sands, where the vestiges of their ancestors' knowledge lay hidden. The stargate would be opened once again, and the route to the source be made available to them. Azazel would be their king, she their queen. This was the destiny of the world, and these islands were but a small part of it.

Sofia took a shower in one of Salamiel's guest-rooms, and dressed herself in the black dress she had left there the previous night. Of Salamiel himself there was no sign. Sofia was not concerned about it. He could be recalled when the moment was right. For now, she had to concentrate on bringing Azazel back to the house, to give him rest and succour. When he was strong enough, the half-breed girl, Lily, would be made his dark concubine and produce for him new giant sons. Salamiel would submit to the king's lust to seal their contract. But all this was in the future.

Sofia drove down the coast road in good spirits. She left her car on a lay-by and strolled jauntily down to the cliff path. Below, the beach was a litter of shattered rock and marine debris. Strange rotting carcasses, that looked like seals but were not, lolled brokenly from rock-pools. Swatches of red and green weed that might have been the shorn hair of giant mermaids shawled the sands. Sea birds wheeled and screamed hysterically, disturbed by the recent occult phenomena. Sofia surveyed all this with a serene eye. She picked her way carefully down the cliff path to the beach, and from there to the gaping hole in the rock that was all that remained of Azumi. Fetid gases curled out from the cave at ground level, but otherwise there was no sign of activity. Sofia positioned herself before the cave mouth and called out, "Azazel, come forth!" There was no response, no sound of movement from within. Had Azazel been killed by all he'd experienced? She realised, ultimately, that it did not matter. He had fulfilled one function at least, had acted as the required catalyst for all that would come, and if he was not to be part of the Grigori's future, there would be other Watchers left in the world she might find and use for her purposes.

"Azazel, I command you!"

Sofia heard the tumble of stones from within the cave, and presently saw a pale shape moving in the shadows. Her heartbeat increased. She realised she would be disappointed if the angel king had died.

"Azazel!"

A figure came out into the daylight, but Sofia saw at once it was not Azazel. "Salamiel," she said. "What have you seen?"

Salamiel stumbled out onto the shore. He looked stricken, bewildered. "Nothing," he answered, "but for a thousand bones."

Impatiently, Sofia marched past him under the shadow of the rock. For a few moments, she stood with her hands on her hips, gazing into the darkness. She felt reluctant to search the cave system herself, perhaps because the guardian, Ainzu, might still be around, although it seemed most likely he would have perished once the reason for his existence had been curtailed. Sofia was not afraid of Ainzu, but was wisely wary of him. He was almost unthinkably ancient, and she was unsure of the extent of his power. She did not want to be bothered with involving herself in any minor skirmishes. All she cared about was Azazel. Yet, if he still lived, surely he would have emerged by now? Sofia turned back to Salamiel. "How far did you search for him in this place? Did you venture into every chamber?"

Salamiel nodded. "As far as I was able. Did you kill him, Sofia?"

"Shut up," Sofia answered dully, then returned her attention to the darkness ahead. "Well, there seems little point in remaining here..."

She began to pick her way back over the rock, while Salamiel remained staring into the cave. She would leave him here to mourn for a while. Eventually, he would return to Pharos and then she could decide what his next purpose would be.

Sofia stumbled into a rock pool, and put out one hand to steady herself against a shattered boulder. At that moment, a white shape reared up before her from behind the rock and hissed malevolently in her face. She recoiled in surprise. Emim! Salamiel had brought his creatures with him. She did not fear them, but was offended that the Emim did not appear to fear her. She turned round to address Salamiel sharply.

The beach behind her was filled with the crouching shapes of naked Emim. Salamiel stood behind them, his back pressed against the serpentine rocks. Sofia laughed. Did he think to threaten her with these creatures? The Emim watched her with unblinking eyes. She could wither them if she chose. Was Salamiel mad?

Then her eyes were drawn to the cave mouth. Another figure stood there, taller than Salamiel, more pale than the watchful Emim. Sofia nearly fell to her knees, but mustered her senses, and ran forward, pushing the Emim from her path. "Azazel! My lord!"

He stood there, dusty and bloody, his hair in disarray over the grey rags that covered his chest. Sofia knew he appeared at that moment as he had at the time his father, Anu, had sacrificed him as the scapegoat. But here was no bewildered victim. His face was serene, his eyes staring at her in complete tranquillity. Did the dark fire burn within him now? She had bestowed the greatest of gifts, turned the path of his destiny. He was a god, the incarnation of divine power and beauty.

When she was a few feet away from him, Sofia halted. "My lord, have you come to claim your kingdom?"

He smiled. "Of course. It is you who helped me understand it."

"I merely guided your feet to the required path." Sofia felt slightly unnerved by the directness of his stare. She should expect that he'd possess far greater power now, but hoped it was not beyond her control. "Look, here is your brother, Salamiel, waiting for you. Let us return to his house together."

He turned his gaze to Salamiel, and beckoned him to approach. Sofia watched in satisfaction as they embraced, Salamiel dwarfed in the arms of his king. This was as it should be.

"Did you hear me in the underworld?" Salamiel asked.

The angel king took his brother's head between his hands. "I heard you." He released Salamiel and took a few steps towards Sofia. "Would you like to see what I've become?"

She felt wary. "I can see that already."

The angel king shook his head slowly. "Oh, I don't think so. You took me from the crystal, the first gate to the source, and dragged me into the abyss. You sought to eclipse all knowledge of light from my soul, so that I would become your dark god. But Sofia..." and here he paused with a smile. "Don't you understand that by showing me the dark of the Tree, you made me into the perfect avatar of the Shamir? The true king must have knowledge of both light and dark. You gave me this."

Sofia narrowed her eyes at him. "Of course I sought only to aid you."

He laughed softly. "Did you now? Look upon me. I am the serpent."

A blaze of golden light burst out of his eyes. Sofia saw him stretch his arms up above his head, saw his neck grow longer, his body transform into rings of shining coils. He became a radiant serpent from the chest down, while his upper body returned to an earlier Grigori form, with a long face and neck and slanting eyes. His hair was alive around him, seething upon the air. The light of him burned her skin. She saw Salamiel cringe away, fall to his knees before this vision of ophidian power.

The angel king uttered an angry hiss. "You deceived me, enchantress, demon mother. You delivered me into the hands of deceivers, the witch and her boy. You used the face of my love to twist my destiny." Rays of light spun upon his brow like a dazzling crown. Sofia fought the urge to duck away from them.

"I did what was necessary," she snapped. "My only purpose was to aid you. Didn't I find and keep your brother for you? He is yours. As well as your pretty twin playthings and the boy you deign to call your vizier. I am *the* Sofia, Azazel. Your mate, your confederate."

"Never," he said. "You will never be that."

Sofia grinned and shook her head. "Times change, people change. Wake up, Azazel. I can give you everything you want or need. It was my strength that sustained you in the underworld, my power that helped you wake the Shamir."

The angel king opened his eyes wider, and bolts of golden light flashed from them. "Too late," he hissed. He leaned towards her on his shining coils, his arms reaching out with clawed hands.

"Azazel," Sofia said in desperation. "You must come with me. Return to your mortal shape and we shall talk. I will explain our purpose, our destiny."

The angel king shook his head. "I am not Azazel, demoness. You were waiting for someone else. Now I will crush the darkness from you."

Sofia's lips peeled back from her long teeth. As the angel king's arms snaked out to embrace her she leapt backwards with a raw squawk. Did he truly think he could beat her? Sofia tossed her head wildly, shook her body until it seemed she moved so fast she was made only of black vapour. The angel king before her clearly sensed she was transforming and lunged forward. Too late. Sofia screamed out her fury and her form burst up into the sky. She became Leviathan, the primal sea-dragon, a hideous creature of black spines and tattered wings. The angel king reared up to envelop her, and she reached for him with her clawed feet. Together, in a screaming embrace, they rose, spiralling up towards the sun. She clawed and bit at his substance, he seared her with light. Below, Salamiel's Emim clustered together about their master, whimpering in fear. Salamiel covered his head with his hands and the scent of hallowed blood rained down upon him.

On the cliff top, Daniel and his companions stood in complete silence and stillness, as if in mourning. A single sea bird uttered a sad cry overhead.

Shem, we should have been together, Daniel thought. Now I have lost you forever. A brief image of himself and Lily and Owen flashed through his mind. They would live out the rest of their lives now; shattered and damaged. As an old woman, perhaps hundreds of years in the future, Lily would still be feeding Owen, cleaning him, and Daniel would be an empty husk of a man, given extended life, only to suffer it in loneliness. He could not bear to contemplate this bleak prospect. He wanted to turn to Emma or Lily for comfort, but was unable to move, knowing that comfort could not be found, because any arms that held him now could never be the ones he craved.

The sky should still be black, Daniel thought bitterly, because the King is dead. A week ago, the women were lamenting. Why are they silent now?

Then the silence of the morning was broken by a roaring scream, a cry so loud that everyone covered their ears in pain. The ground beneath them shook. People fell to their knees, their faces. Daniel sank down to crouch upon the edge of the cliff. He saw the monstrous shapes rise up into the sky, saw the gouts of black blood, of golden light, spray out of them.

Lily crawled to Daniel's side. "Dan, what's happening? What's that noise?" She was looking around herself in panic, and Daniel realised she could not see the creatures grappling in the sky. He put his arms around her.

"I don't know." He closed his eyes, tried to concentrate on picking up information. Behind him, the Parzupheim had begun to chant, presumably because they understood what was happening.

"Shem," Daniel sighed, and opened his eyes. Was that golden beast all that was left of his beloved king, all that he had become? He stared in horror and wonder at the sight. A dark female power had him in its grip. Not Ishtahar, something full of hate. He picked up vestiges of Sofia, saw her grinning face.

I must help him, Daniel thought, but how?

"Think of the High Place," Daniel said to Lily. "Remember it."

"Why?" Her face was buried against his shoulder.

"The goddess. Ishtahar. Summon her, Lily. Be a channel for her."

Lily lifted her head and blinked at the sky. "There are shadows against the clouds," she said.

"It's Shem," Daniel told her. "Shem and Sofia. They are battling for his soul."

Lily swallowed with a shudder and pushed herself away from Daniel. Slowly, she got to her feet and for a few moments stood swaying before him. Then, she put her hand into the pocket of her dress and took out the cowry shell. She glanced at Daniel. "This is our tool." He blinked at her slowly to signify his confidence in her, his trust.

Lily turned away from him and raised her arms to the sky, the shell held aloft in both hands. Her voice was unsteady to begin with, but gradually strengthened into a resonant, pure sound. "Ishtahar! Ishtar! Asharah! Astoroth! Enanna! Ereshkigal!"

Daniel looked up at her, and saw that the cowry shell had begun to vibrate with a deep, blue light. As he stared at it, it turned into what looked like an unblinking eye, which gradually enlarged, its light eclipsing Lily from his sight. Now the eye hung in the air before him, a beautiful dark eye full of the mysteries of female allure, growing in size with every moment. It wept a shining vapour of peacock-blue mist, which swirled up and around it. Slowly, the mist began to take on form; a belly, a torso, breasts swathed in flowing fabric. The goddess formed herself against the sky, a goddess whose belly was adorned with the sacred eye. Ishtahar.

For a brief moment, she smiled down upon Daniel and Lily and then slowly turned towards the creatures fighting behind her. They were dwarfed by her immense size. The elegant pillars of her legs carried her towards them. Her dark hair, strung with stars, streamed out behind her. Her voice was the clamour of bells. "Lilith, my sister whore! Hear me! Know me! See me!"

The dragon-beast tore its head away from the golden serpent, shining flesh hanging from its red jaws. Its mouth dropped open and an evil hiss cataracted out. "Never! You are powerless, feeble goddess!"

Ishtahar smiled and shook her head. With one gargantuan hand, she reached out and plucked the golden serpent from the dragon's hold. This she curled around her left wrist, where it clung like a bracelet. Thoughtfully, she put this hand behind her back, as if to protect her precious jewellery.

The Leviathan screamed its rage and with each horrific bellow increased in size. "Fight me! See if your power matches mine!"

Again Ishtahar laughed. "Ah, but your power has already played its part, dark mother. Be gone! You have no purpose here now."

The voice of the Sofia-beast boomed out in rage. "Played its part? I have only just begun to play. Do not shelter the Shemyaza serpent from me. Release him to finish what is started!"

Ishtahar shook her head. "It is already finished, demoness. You attempt to play out the eternal struggle here today, a struggle as old as time, but you can never win. The source created divine goodness within the Sun King, Shemyaza, and also created all that is evil. Our source is perfect, and to be perfect is to be free, to own the ability to choose between good and evil. Humankind has always had the choice of pursuing the path of light or darkness, for if they did not own this choice, they would be slaves, and the source does not traffic in slaves." Her voice lowered. "Shemyaza's struggle to understand this has made him what he is. He can never be yours."

Such was the quiet confidence in Ishtahar's voice, that the vast, twisted Leviathan seemed to shrink before her, its wrath diminish. Its voice was a hoarse croak. "You cannot banish me, Ishtahar, for I am part of you. Your dark sister. I am the evil you are too weak to be!"

"Indeed, but I have many parts, many sisters and many faces. Listen, do you not hear the siren song of the sea?" Ishtahar raised her hand and gestured gracefully at the waves, her arm undulating on the air, her long fingers curling and uncurling. Her movement seemed to act as a summons. A high and haunting note, like that uttered by a pure, female voice, lapped off the foaming water, lifted up like mist to drift across the cliff top. The vision of Ishtahar turned and gestured at Lily and Emma. "Come, my daughters, call with me to our sister, Seference, who dwells within the light of the sea-foam."

As if in a trance, Lily and Emma were drawn to the very edge of the cliff, followed by the Pelleth. Led by Emma, they lifted their voices in a rhythmic chant, "Om Sefer, Tu Sefer, Sefer, Sefer, Sahar!"

Beneath them, the sea began to roil and glow with a vibrant, blue-green radiance. It seemed as if a hundred other female voices rose up from the waves and joined in the chant. The weaving sounds created a harmony that both lulled and excited the senses of everyone assembled on the cliff top. The dragon beat its wings frantically, caught in an unexpected updraught of air. Below it, a wall of iridescent green water slowly rose up into the sky.

Crouching down behind Lily and Emma, Daniel stared in horror at the smooth mountain of water, fearing that another tidal wave had come to engulf them. But then, within the sheer glassy surface, he saw the dripping and weed-swathed form of an immense woman shimmer into existence. Seference. Her eyes shone green with the dark light of the ocean depths. Her hair was a swirling purl of salty foam. Her body was draped with a shining cloak of black weed, threaded with the spars of long-sunk, forgotten ships. For a brief moment, Daniel thought that within the writhing fibres of Seference's robe, he could see the faces of Meggie and Betsy Penhaligon peering out, along with a multitude of other female faces he did not recognise. Emotion choked him. He bowed his head.

Seference's voice, when she spoke, was the crashing of waves against the jagged coast. "Unholy sister, return to the lowest depths of the earth, where you chose to dwell after you cast yourself out from the High Place."

The dragon hissed down at her malevolently, its jaws dribbling strings of clotted blood. Its wings clawed against the air, but it was drawn down relentlessly before the wall of water.

Seference turned her head towards Ishtahar. "Sister. Together." She extended her arms from the water wall.

Ishtahar stretched out her own arms and waded towards the waiting embrace of her ocean-born sister. As their palms touched, they corralled the Leviathan between them. It uttered a howl of frustrated fury and lashed its spiny tail. It wings battered the air frantically in an attempt to fly away.

Ishtahar uttered a command. "Look, unholy sister, into the eye of my belly, the cauldron of my power! You cannot escape us, for you look upon yourself. My eye is a mirror for all female power. You cannot escape yourself."

The dragon screamed in terror as the two shining goddesses drew nearer to each other.

The voice of Seference boomed out. "Now we shall send you back to the depths, where you will not rule, nor scheme nor rage, but sleep in humility. Your time will come again, dark queen, but come, let us embrace as sisters at last."

Ishtahar stepped forward into the luminous wall of water, and as all three goddesses merged into one, a dazzling flare of turquoise light blazed out. Sofia's last struggles were engulfed. For a second, the water spurted upwards, and then collapsed with a crash back into the ocean. Slowly seething, the sea gradually sank back to calm. Ishtahar was gone, and the golden serpent, Shemyaza, had gone with her, clasped to her sacred wrist.

Lily lowered her arms and put the shell back into her pocket. She glanced round at Daniel, and beyond him to the unreadable faces of the Grigori who still stood in a line behind them. Emma stood rigid, as if in shock, her hands against her mouth, the Pelleth behind her, their faces pale. How much had they all seen? Daniel groaned and huddled against the ground, hugging himself. He felt sick, elated, immeasurably sad.

Now it was over. The power of hate had been vanquished, but love had vanished with it.

Then, below the cliff, the rocks shifted loosely. Lily gasped and took a step backwards, afraid that more of the land was going to subside. Others were inspired to follow her move.

Emma leaned down and put her hand on Daniel's arm. "Come, Danny," she murmured. "There's no point staying here."

"No!" he hissed at her. "You go if you want to. I have to stay."

More rocks clattered against one another below them. Daniel froze. Emma tried to pull him away, but he shook her off roughly. He staggered to his feet and took a step towards the jagged edge of the cliff, where the piled, shattered rocks sloped down towards the shore.

"Daniel, no!" Emma cried.

He did not hear her. He heard instead more rocks moving, then more and more. His heart began to beat wildly. For a moment, all was held in stasis, and then a pale, feebly-moving thing groped its way over the cliff top. Daniel plunged forward and grabbed hold of it. Long, agile fingers curled around his own. Deaf to the cries of concern behind him, he pulled with all his strength. He hauled a dusty, bloody body from the rubble, and then Shemyaza was in his arms, alive.

Daniel could do nothing but shower Shemyaza's face and hair with kisses, repeating a mantra of relief. "Forgive me, I lost faith. Forgive me."

Shem raised a weak hand and touched his face. "No, my Daniel, it was I who lost the faith. Forgive me."

Daniel uttered an anguished sound and pulled Shemyaza closer against him, prompting a groan of pain. Shemyaza felt so vulnerable in his arms, so human. "Where is Ishtahar?" Daniel asked. "I know you were with her."

Shemyaza shook his head. "Gone. For now." He pulled away from Daniel a little. "Help me up. I will tell you everything later."

Enniel had kept everyone else at a distance while Daniel spoke with Shemyaza. Now, as Shemyaza rose uncertainly to his feet, Enniel stepped forward. He wanted to utter some ritual greeting, welcome the Sacred King as saviour and deliverer. All he could do was take Shemyaza in his arms, murmur, "Thank Shem, thank Shem." There were no other words he could think of.

Shemyaza returned the embrace, then drew away from Enniel. He called Daniel, Lily and Emma to him and pulled them against his body. Then, he released them and turned to Aninka, who stood at Enniel's side.

"I wronged you," he said.

She nodded. "Yes, and I allowed it. Don't ask for my forgiveness, Pev, because I can't give it."

He smiled sadly. "It would help if you could believe I am no longer Peverel Othman."

"It's too late. I could never forget that."

Shemyaza looked into her eyes, and Aninka saw that he understood she could never forgive him, simply because he was unable to love her in the way she desired. Even now, she wished this knowledge could change his feelings, but she knew it was impossible. He would waste no more words on pleading.

Salamiel had climbed the rubble from the beach, and now came to stand beside the angel king. Shemyaza turned from Aninka and held out his arms to Salamiel. "You are the first," Shemyaza said. "There must be others."

Salamiel curled into his embrace. "Together we shall find them."

Enniel raised his arms. "This is a day of great joy! We shall celebrate at High Crag!" He turned to Daniel. "Bring your friends from the village, boy. This feast is to be shared by human and Grigori alike."

"There is something first that needs to be done," Shemyaza said. He addressed Lily. "Where is your brother, my daughter?"

"At the house," Lily said. "Shem, can you..." she dared not ask the question.

He reached out and touched her hair. "Long overdue," he replied. "Bring him down to Mermaid's Cove."

The procession wound its way along the cliff-top to the grounds of High Crag, which were draped in swathes of deep-sea weeds, so that it looked like some drowned garden that had risen from the ocean. Daniel and Emma walked at Shemyaza's side, holding onto his arms. Both sensed Shem's overwhelming exhaustion, which he was trying hard to keep at bay. His body was battered and cut, his mind wearied.

Later he would tell them of how he'd awoken on the beach, at the mouth of the rubble-filled cave that had been hidden behind the lion's head. At the time he'd believed his encounter with Ainzu and the Shamir, his battle with Sofia, had been physical, but now he wondered whether only his spirit had travelled through the labyrinth of underground tunnels and risen into the sky to fight a dragon. His soul had fused with the serpent power, helped initiate the energising of the ancient sites, but perhaps his body had lain unconscious on the rocky floor beyond Azumi's portal. He would never know for sure.

Everyone gathered on the beach at Mermaid's Cove, where the sea licked innocuously at the land with tiny wavelets. Lily and Aninka went to fetch Owen from the house.

Shemyaza stood upon the beach, gazing down at the spot where he sensed Tamara had buried the cowry shell that had chained a fragment of Ishtahar's soul. He instructed the women to strip Owen of his clothes and carry him to the water's edge. Lily still carried the shell, and Shemyaza instructed her to fill it with sea water from the tide's lip.

Owen lay in the shallow water, his empty eyes fixed on the sky. Aninka and Emma supported his body in their arms. Lily filled the cowry as instructed, then held it up to Shem, who took it from her and held it close to his side, near his belly, where a wound dripped blood into the delicate shell.

"Shem!" Lily cried. "You're hurt! We didn't notice!"

"It is an old wound that would not heal," Shem said.

Lily knew then that the water within the shell was no longer simply brine.

Shem knelt before Owen, the rags of his tattered robes swirling around him in the water. He placed the lip of the shell against Owen's mouth. "Reawaken, my child, through this vessel, the womb of our mother, Ishtahar. Reawaken in light, for your blood and mine are one."

Owen's throat worked convulsively as the liquid poured down it. He coughed and flailed his arms. Then he lay blinking and panting in the water, his expression that of astonishment. Lily splashed through the water to reach him. "O'! It's me! O'! Are you with us? Are you?"

Painfully, Owen sat up, using Aninka and Emma as support. "Lily," he said weakly. She wrapped him in her arms.

Daniel, watching this reunion, wanted to turn away. He was dreading Owen's eyes finding his own. Part of him, he realised, did not want Owen to reawaken. Shem came to his side.

"Before you say anything, I'd rather not hear it," Daniel said, sensing a sanctimonious reprimand was imminent. He knew Shem could see right into his heart and folded his arms defensively.

"I wasn't going to say anything," Shem replied. "I haven't turned into a pious bore, Daniel."

"Good."

"Take me to High Crag," Shem said. "I need your attentions and a long sleep."

Daniel smiled and put his arm round Shem's waist. They began to walk towards the wooden stairway that led to the garden.

Enniel caught up with them. "Of course you must be exhausted," he said, "but perhaps you could rest and show your face later. I think it would be appreciated. Many people have been with you in spirit, Shemyaza, and I want them all to partake of the celebratory feast."

Shem shrugged. "Whatever."

Enniel opened his mouth to speak, then hesitated. Finally, he said, "So what do you intend to do now?"

Shemyaza glanced behind him to where Salamiel was following at a polite distance. Later, they would talk. Then he looked down at the empty cowry shell, which he still held in his hand. "I'm going home," he said.

Storm Constantine Biography

Storm Constantine decided somewhere about fifteen years ago that life should be more exciting than a backroom 9 to 5 for a local charity, and decided to do something about it. With one of the luckiest breaks into publishing (a tale still rare enough in SF to be dined out on) she started her career as a writer with the *Wraeththu* trilogy, published by MacDonald Orbit, about a post-human race of androgyne hermaphrodites coming to terms with themselves and their new world. Ten years later she is currently in the middle of her second trilogy, the *Grigori* series, for Penguin. In a way, everything in between, over some eleven novels and numerous short stories can be seen as leading almost inevitably to this point: Storm's long fascination with angels, mythology, the recurrent themes of magic and sexuality, secret knowledge, dark and charismatic figures on the edge of society and outside convention. But this is not merely coming full circle. Each book in its way, from the SF cyber-paganism of *Hermetech*, the threatened elohim of *Burying the Shadow*, the structural nested story games in *Calenture*, and the enigmatic revolutionary messiah of *Sign for the Sacred*, illuminate different facets of a body of work that is unmistakably 'Storm Constantine'.

Who is Storm Constantine? She lives in the Midlands with as many cats as she has published books, in a house that looks entirely conventional until you step inside, and houses a library of Pre-Raphaelite art and esoteric reference books that you would cheerfully kill (or at least lightly maim) for.

A sense of style, in appearance as much as on the page, that would drop jaws at Storm's early appearances at SF conventions. Black clad, in a million silver bangles, with spiky hair and exotic makeup, the Constantine entourage would turn heads in astonishment, and not a little envy amongst the regulars of SF fandom.

Here was Showtime.

The appearance is a little less flamboyant now (though she still takes *ages* to get ready to go anywhere) but can still evoke a spontaneous hug for a stunned waitress in a US bar who recently asked for her ID. She is a born, almost compulsive storyteller. She has numerous short stories in anthologies, magazines and fanzines and small press publications. And you don't get rich by doing the last two; at most you might get a couple of complimentary copies. So why? Because Storm is a fan too. She found SF fandom at the same time she started writing, and never left (you never really do). Which is why her current project, *Visionary Tongue*, is a writers' workshop fanzine that grew out of her involvement in teaching creative writing classes. And its third issue boasts some seriously fine writing, and almost a dozen SF and fantasy authors on a volunteer editorial board that any professional publication would be jealous of. Because you can always give something back, and you can never run out of stories.

The Complete Constantine
A Storm Constantine Bibliography

Novels, Novellas, Full Length Non-Fiction and Short Story Collections

The Enchantments of Flesh and Spirit
(1987 Macdonald h/b. 1988 Futura p/b. 1990 TOR p/b USA 1996 Heyne p/b Germany as Der Zauber von Fleisch und Geist)

The Bewitchments of Love and Hate
(1988 Macdonald h/b. 1988 Futura p/b. 1990 TOR p/b USA 1996 Heyne p/b Germany as Im Bann von Liebe und Hass)

The Fulfilments of Fate and Desire
(1989 Drunken Dragon Press h/b. 1989 Orbit p/b. 1991 TOR p/b USA 1996 Heyne p/b Germany as Die Erfullung von Schicksal und Begehren)

The Monstrous Regiment
(1990 Orbit t/p/b. 1991 Orbit p/b)

Hermetech
(1991 Headline h/b, t/p/b. 1991 Headline p/b. 1993 Heyne p/b Germany)

Aleph
(1991 Orbit t/p/b)

Burying the Shadow
(1992 Headline h/b, t/p/b; 1992 Headline p/b; 1995 Heyne p/b Germany as 'Schattengraber')

Sign for the Sacred
(1993 Headline h/b, t/p/b. 1993 Headline p/b)

Wraeththu
(Omnibus: The Enchantments of Flesh and Spirit, Bewitchments of Love and Hate, Fulfilments of Fate and Desire)
(1993 TOR t/p/b)

Calenture
(1994 Headline h/b. 1994 Headline p/b)

Stalking Tender Prey
(1995 p/b Creed/Signet; 1998 p/b Meisha Merlin, USA)

Scenting Hallowed Blood
(1996 p/b Signet; 1999 p/b (1999 Meisha Merlin, USA)

Three Heralds of the Storm
'Such a Nice Girl', 'How Enlightenment..' & 'Last Come Assimilation
(1997 p/b Meisha-Merlin, US, 1997)

Stealing Sacred Fire
(1997 p/b Signet; forthcoming 2000 Meisha Merlin, USA)

The Inward Revolution
(with Deborah Benstead)
Non-fiction esoteric psychology, (1998 Warner, UK)

Thin Air
(1999 Warner p/b)

The Thorn Boy
(1999 novella, p/b, Eidolon Press, Australia)

The Oracle Lips
(1999 short story collection: The Vitreous Suzerain; Of a Cat, But Her Skin; Sweet Bruising Skin; Heir to a Tendency; Remedy of the Bane; The Time She Became; Curse of the Snake; Panquilia in the Ruins; Candle Magic; Blue Flame of a Candle; By the River of If Only…; Immaculate; The Rust Islands; Fire Born; Nocturne; As It Flows to the Sea; The Oracle Lips; The Deliveress; God Be With You; Angel of the Hate Wind; The Feet, They Dance; Return to Gehenna; A Change of Season; The Seduction of Angels (poem), Stark Press, USA, h/b)

Sea Dragon Heir (book one of the Magravandias Chronicles)
(1999, h/b Gollancz UK; (forthcoming 1999, TOR, USA)

Bast and Sekhmet: Eyes of Ra
With Eloise Coquio
(1999 (forthcoming) non-fiction book on the feline deities of Ancient Egypt; Robert Hale, h/b)

The Crown of Silence (book two of the Magravandias Chronicles)
(2000, forthcoming, Gollancz h/b UK; TOR, p/b USA)

Short Stories (Published)

By the River of If Only...	1988 Paragenesis/1991 Fear, January (Wraeththu story) UK
So What's Forever?	1989 GM Magazine, Vol 1 #7 Mar. UK
God Be With You	1989 GM Magazine, Vol 2 #4 Dec. UK
They Hunt....	1989 Drabble Project #1 UK
The Pleasure Giver Taken	1989 Zenith 1 (anthology), Sphere, UK
As it Flows to the Sea	1990 Tarot Tales (anthology), Legend, UK

Last Come Assimilation	1990 Digital Dreams (anthology), NEL, UK
The Time She Became	1990 Zenith 2 (anthology), Sphere, UK
Did You Ever See Oysters Walking Down the Stairs?	1990 More Tales from the Forbidden Planet (anth), UK
The Heart of Fairen D'eath	1990 Weird Tales, USA
Lacrymata	1990 Deathwing, Warhammer anthology, Games Workshop, UK
The Vitreous Suzerain	1991 The Gate Magazine (#2), UK
The College Spirit	1991 Temps (anthology), Penguin/Roc, UK
Immaculate	1991 New Worlds (anthology) Gollancz (Nominated for BSFA award 1992) UK
The Deliveress	1992 Villains (anthology), Penguin/Roc, UK
Poisoning the Sea	1992 Dedalus Book of Femme Fatales, UK
A Change of Season	1992 The Weerde (anthology), Penguin/Roc (Inspiration for novel **Stalking Tender Prey**) UK
How Enlightenment Came to the Tower	1992 Scheherazade magazine (#2), UK
Priest of Hands	1992 Interzone magazine (#58) (Used in novel **Calenture**), UK
The Law of Being	1992 Eurotemps (anthology), Penguin/Roc, UK
The Preservation	1992 REM magazine (#2), UK
An Elemental Tale	1992 Inception (limited edition chapbook), UK
Built on Blood	1992 Interzone magazine (#64), UK

The Green Calling	1993 Interzone magazine (#73), UK
Sweet Bruising Skin	1994 Black Thorn, White Rose (anth) AvoNova Morrow USA
Candle Magic	1994 Blue Motel: Narrow Houses III (anthology), Little Brown UK
Blue Flame of a Candle	1995 Tombs: Tales Beyond the Crypt (anth) White Wolf USA
Return to Gehenna	1996 Dante's Disciples, (anth) White Wolf USA
An Old Passion	1996 Festival of the Imagination programme, Aust.
Remedy of the Bane	1996 Realms of Fantasy mag., USA (August)
Dancer for the World's Death	1996 Inception chapbook, UK
Kiss Booties Night Night	1996 Cybersex, (anthology) ed. Richard G Jones, Robinson UK
Fire Born	1996 Science Fiction Age magazine, USA (October)
Of a Cat, but her Skin...	1996 Twists of the Tale, (anthology), ed. Ellen Datlow, Dell, USA
Angel of the Hate Wind	1997 Destination Unknown (anth), ed P Crowther White Wolf, USA
The Rust Islands	1997 Interzone magazine, UK
Such a Nice Girl	1997 'Three Heralds of the Storm' chapbook, Meisha-Merlin, USA
The Oracle Lips	1998 Fortune Tellers (anth) ed. L Schimel, USA
Prelude	1998 Mage: The Sorcerer's Crusade, White Wolf USA
My Lady of the Hearth	1998 Sirens and other daemon lovers (anth.) ed E Datlow andT Windling, Harper Prism, USA

Paragenesis	1998 Crow anthology, ed. E Kramer & J O'Barr, USA
Night's Damozel	1998 (with Eloise Coquio), Interzone, UK
Curse of the Snake	1999 The Oracle Lips collection, Stark House, USA
Nocturne: The Twilight Community	1999 The Oracle Lips collection, Stark House, USA
Panquilia in the Ruins	1999 The Oracle Lips collection, Stark House, USA
Heir to a Tendency	1999 The Oracle Lips collection, Stark House, USA
The Feet, They Dance	1999 The Oracle Lips collection, Stark House, USA

Short Stories & Novellas (Unpublished)

True Destiny of the Heir of Emiraldra, The	1987
Spinning for Gold	1987
Germ of Life, The	1988
Time Beginning at Break of Day	1988
The Face of Sekt	1999

Short Story Reprints

Last Come Assimilation	1991 Digital Dreams (Hebrew translation) Opus Ltd, Israel
Immaculate	1994 Cyberpunk, (Italian trans.) Editrice Nord, Italy
Poisoning the Sea	1994 Das Grosse Lesebuch der Femme Fatale (German trans), Goldmann (Germany) as 'Gift-ins Meer giessen'

Immaculate	1995 The End of Century SF Masterpieces (Japanese trans.) Kinokuniya Co Ltd, Japan
Immaculate	1995 Women of Wonder: The Contemporary years (anthology)Harcourt, Brace & Co (USA)
Immaculate	1995 Tahtivaeltaja magazine, (Finnish translation) Finland
Sweet Bruising Skin	1996 Black Thorn, White Rose (anthology) Signet (UK)
Candle Magic	1996 Blue Motel: Narrow Houses 3 anth, White Wolf, USA
As it Flows to the Sea	1996 Tarot Tales (anthology) Ace Books, USA
How Enlightenment Came to the Tower	1997 'Three Heralds of the Storm', Meisha-Merlin, US
Last Come Assimilation	1997 'Three Heralds of the Storm', Meisha-Merlin, US
Such a Nice Girl	1997 Dark Terrors 3, ed. S Jones & D Sutton,Gollancz, UK
Of a Cat, But Her Skin	1997 Best New Horror 8, Robinson, UK & Bantam USA
Of a Cat, But Her Skin	(forthcoming) Czechoslovakian ed. of Twists of the Tale
The Vitreous Suzerain	1999 The Oracle Lips collection, Stark House, USA
Of a Cat, But Her Skin	1999 The Oracle Lips collection, Stark House, USA
Sweet Bruising Skin	1999 The Oracle Lips collection, Stark House, USA
Remedy of the Bane	1999 The Oracle Lips collection, Stark House, USA
The Time She Became	1999 The Oracle Lips collection, Stark House, USA

Candle Magic	1999 The Oracle Lips collection, Stark House, USA
Blue Flame of a Candle	1999 The Oracle Lips collection, Stark House, USA
By the River of If Only...	1999 The Oracle Lips collection, Stark House, USA
Immaculate	1999 The Oracle Lips collection, Stark House, USA
The Rust Islands	1999 The Oracle Lips collection, Stark House, USA
Fire Born	1999 The Oracle Lips collection, Stark House, USA
As It Flows to the Sea	1999 The Oracle Lips collection, Stark House, USA
The Oracle Lips	1999 The Oracle Lips collection, Stark House, USA
The Deliveress	1999 The Oracle Lips collection, Stark House, USA
God Be With You	1999 The Oracle Lips collection, Stark House, USA
Angel of the Hate Wind	1999 The Oracle Lips collection, Stark House, USA
Return to Gehenna	1999 The Oracle Lips collection, Stark House, USA
A Change of Season	1999 The Oracle Lips collection, Stark House, USA

Articles & Features

Sex and Chaos	1991 Fear magazine (neo-paganism)
A Man's Gotta Do...	1992 Siren magazine (Interview with Carl McCoy)
Ghostriders	1992 Siren magazine (Interview with ENDG)

Poems

In the Dark	1991 Now We Are Sick (h/bk collection) DreamHaven Books, (USA) (1994 Pbk ed)
Colurastes	1995 Collection, Inception
Ishtahar's Confession	1995 Visionary Tongue 1 zine (as Eden Crane) U
The Gift of Flight	1995 Visionary Tongue 1 zine (as Eden Crane) UK
The Seduction of Angels	1999 The Oracle Lips collection, Stark House, USA

Rick Berry Biography

Rick Berry is an award winning oil painter, draftsman, and a pioneer in new media; in 1984 he created the world's first digital cover illustration for a work of fiction, William Gibson's *Neuromancer*.

He left school at age 17 to begin a career in underground comics. After hitching east to Boston from Colorado, he shifted his artistic focus to books, film, and fine art. He has produced hundreds of illustrations for books, magazines, games, and comics. In 1991 *Communications Arts* showcased four of Berry's seven oil paintings in Peter Straub's *Mrs. God*.

This year's distinctions include: *Gold Award*, editorial, Spectrum Art Annual; *Best Book Cover*, 9th Annual *Publish* Design Contest; *Artist Guest of Honor* at The 1997 World Horror Convention in Niagara Falls. Selected works are included in this year's Computer Art & Design Annual, From *Print Magazine*, in Society of Illustrators' traveling exhibition—*Illustration: Past, Present, and Future* and *The Digital Show*, Museum of Illustration, NYC, in *The History of Science Fiction Art* by Vincent DiFate, Penquin Art Books; and he is the featured artist in OMNI Magazine's *Dark Echo* world wide web literary site.

Berry has an abiding interest in collaborative work, and, in 1993 , joined with Phil Hale to produce *Double Memory*, an 110 page art book. William Gibson wrote of their book, "...Nervy, pervy, and utterly assured, their work haunts with the disturbing intensity of half-remembered dreams."

Berry and Gibson worked together again in 1995 when Braid Media Arts (Berry, Darrel Anderson, and Gene Bodio) designed and executed the CGI cyberspace climax of Tristar Productions' film (now on video) *Johnny Mnemonic*. The sequence was featured in SIGGRAPH's animation review, 1996.

Barry's early experience in the print production trenches of comics has evolved into specialty editions design work and sent him to some interesting places. (He was flown to Hong Kong in 1993 to supervise presses and advise the Chinese on current electronic press capabilities...*in english*.)

His fine art work can be seen in galleries internationally and on the world wide web, (http://www.braid.com)

Barry teaches *Digital Art: A Collaborative Approach* at Tufts University, as well as conduction lectures and workshops at colleges and corporations nationally on the nature of creativity.

Rick Berry

Come check out our web site for details on these Meisha Merlin authors!

Kevin J. Anderson
Storm Constantine
Sylvia Engdahl
Jim Grimsley
Keith Hartman
Beth Hilgartner
Tanya Huff
Janet Kagan
Caitlin R. Kiernan
Lee Killough
Lee Martindale
Sharon Lee & Steve Miller
Jim Moore
Adam Niswander
Selina Rosen
Kristine Kathryn Rusch
S. P. Somtow
Allen Steele
Michael Scott

http://www.angelfire.com/biz/MeishaMerlin

If you would like a free copy of
Meisha Merlin Publishing, Inc.'s new cataloge, please
send a self addressed stamped envelope to:

Meisha Merlin Publishing, Inc.
P. O. Box 7
Decatur, GA 30031